25/3/17 .
30/1/18

ITEM

Please renew or return items by the date shown on your receipt

www.hertsdirect.org/libraries

Renewals and enquiries: 0300 123 4049

Textphone for hearing or 0300 123 4041
speech impaired users:

L32

Claire McGowan grew up in a small village in Northern Ireland. After completing a degree in English and French from Oxford University, she moved to London and worked in the charity sector. She is currently the Director of the Crime Writers' Association. After spells in exciting places like France, Oxford, China, and Kentish Town, she now lives in Tunbridge Wells, where she tries to pretend she's not middle-class by laughing at the middle-class things she overhears and putting them on Twitter.

You can discover more about the author at www.clairemcgowan.net
And on Twitter @inkstainsclaire

THE DEAD GROUND

A stolen baby. A murdered woman. A decades-old atrocity. Something connects them all . . . A month before Christmas, and Ballyterrin on the Irish border lies under a thick pall of snow. When a newborn baby goes missing from hospital, it's all too close to home for forensic psychologist Paula Maguire, who's wrestling with the hardest decision of her life. Then a woman is found in a stone circle with her stomach cut open, and it's clear a brutal killer is on the loose. As another child is taken and a pregnant woman goes missing, Paula is caught up in the hunt for a killer no one can trace, and who will stop at nothing to get what they want.

Books by Claire McGowan
Published by Ulverscroft:

THE LOST

CLAIRE McGOWAN

THE DEAD GROUND

Complete and Unabridged

CHARNWOOD
Leicester

First published in Great Britain in 2014 by
Headline
An Hachette Livre UK Company
London

First Charnwood Edition
published 2015
by arrangement with
Headline Publishing Group
An Hachette Livre UK Company
London

A catalogue record for this book is available
from the British Library.

ISBN 978–1–4448–2457–5

Published by
F. A. Thorpe (Publishing)
Anstey, Leicestershire

Set by Words & Graphics Ltd.
Anstey, Leicestershire
Printed and bound in Great Britain by
T. J. International Ltd., Padstow, Cornwall

This book is printed on acid-free paper

For Stav Sherez, *il miglior fabbro*

Prologue

Ballyterrin, Northern Ireland
1993

It starts with the smallest thing: the beat of your heart. When everything around you is horror, you focus on that. The pulse. The life. You focus and get on with it.

It shouldn't be like this. The phone call fills you with dread and you don't know why. You've been a police officer since 1972, all the way through the hardest years of the Troubles. You've seen things beyond your worst dreams. A child blown up in a chip shop, the money for tea still clasped in their severed hand on the floor. A shooting in a pub, all broken glass and brain matter and country music still playing on the jukebox. A woman burned in a firebomb, her skin hanging off her like a shawl. Yes, you've seen plenty, more than you thought you could ever live with. You did live, though. It's either that or die. But now this one, this one is filling you with sick fear.

The call comes in the early hours of the morning, as the worst ones always do. After so many years you're awake at once, silencing it even before you realise, trying not to wake Margaret. But then she never stirs. Her back is an immovable wall beside you. Then you're up and stumbling into your trousers in a dawn as dark as pitch. You pause for a moment outside

1

your daughter's door, her teenage breathing thick and deep. Please God, she'll sleep right through this and never hear a word. So as not to wake your women, you put on your boots at the bottom of the stairs, dry toast clamped in your mouth. You swallow your tea too fast and burn your mouth; all day you'll be tonguing at that one raw spot on your lip.

Movement at the top of the stairs. Margaret, her face pale in the cloud of her red hair. Her voice is tired. 'What is it this time?'

You can't tell her. God help you. Can't say there's a man just been found in a bog in Louth, small-time crook, back of his head shot out, and you have to go now to some farm and tell this news to his wife. You can't tell her. It's Margaret's worst nightmare, the same happening to you, never coming home again. She's been on at you for years to give the job up, do something else. But what else is there? What else is there to do? 'Early start,' you mumble. 'See you later, love.'

She stands for a moment, as if she might say something, and then she turns her face away. It is the last thing you see, floating over the railings like a white oval. Later, when all the rest of her has faded entirely, you will try and catch at it, her face in the morning gloom that day, her voice cracked and dry, and how she turns away, once and for good, into the dark.

★   ★   ★

You drive through empty streets, a winter mist already rising off the roads, your breath like

2

steam. It's October, dark now until eight a.m. The road down to the farm is black, rising red in the east. *Red sky in the morning, Shepherd's warning*. That's what your daughter will say when she wakes up for school in an hour. Even the animals seem asleep, faint movement somewhere in dark fields soaked with dew. Parked on the front drive, Bob Hamilton's already there, a nervous new constable in tow.

There's Bob, out of the car, stamping feet and billowing breath in the cold. Sergeant Bob he is now, and never let you forget it. Of course he's been promoted. Of course the loyal Orangeman Bob has been promoted over you, awkward Catholic that you are. There's never been any doubt. There's no reason you should mind at all.

Across the yard, leaning on a battered Ford, is Mick Quinn, the Guard who woke you this morning with the news. He's parked far away, as if there's an invisible battle line, and is cupping a fag in the icy morning air. The Guard works over the border in the South, where the husband's body has washed up, but your territory merges, it bleeds into each other, and these early-morning calls are more common than either of you would like to think.

Mick is a tall fair fella with an easy smile, but this morning he's pale as milk. 'PJ.'

'Mick. You going in?'

'Not our turf, son. You tear away.'

You are technically in the North here, so it's your ball game, but you wish all the same the Irishman could be at your back, instead of

3

bloody Sideshow Bob, red-faced and dour, not to mention the wet-behind-the-ears constable, who looks ready to boke into his cap. You trudge back over to them.

'Did you knock?'

Bob shakes his head. 'No answer.'

'Is she not home?'

'No, it's . . .' Bob hesitates. 'Her sister's been ringing her. She rang us too, apparently, to say the phone wasn't being answered. Wanted us to come out here.'

Christ. 'When?'

Reluctant. 'Three days back.'

'She's been here three days on her own? What did they do to her?' You know the husband has been taken by the IRA. It has all the hallmarks. He'll have been informing, or invading their turf on drugs or guns, or maybe nothing at all, maybe he just crossed the wrong person. Happens all the time. But the woman. They must have done something very bad, for her not to answer the phone in three days.

Your heart starts to pound. Focus, focus. 'We have to go in.'

'There's something else.'

'What?' Christ, spit it out, Bob. There's a woman behind those dark windows and whatever's been done to her it means she can't so much as pick up a phone to her sister. And they've known for three days, three whole days before the husband's body surfaced in the wet bog, and no one has done a thing.

'She's pregnant. Seven months, the sister said.'

Focus.

4

A few swift kicks and the weak door splinters. 'Jesus!'

Bob flinches at your blasphemy but then turns pale himself. The constable is retching in a flower bed. You clamp your nose shut. The smell is what you'd imagine after three days. Blood, and piss, and something worse, a terrible meaty smell that seems to reach out and envelop you.

'Mrs Rourke?' You step into the carpeted hallway, lined with pictures of a family. Wedding shots. Happy smiles. 'Hello?' You move into the living room, see how it's disordered, chairs thrown round the place, a boot kicked through the TV. The kitchen is small, off the living room, behind a bubbled glass door. You can see something on the other side of it, a dark shape. The smell is coming from there.

You stop, the three of you, Bob and you and the poor wee constable who's all of twenty. Kevin, that's his name. First month on the job. You stop and then you realise it's going to be you who opens that door and sees what is on the other side. You start to walk.

★ ★ ★

At first it looks like a mangled mess of flesh. Your feet catch in the tacky slick of blood which has stretched over the lino. The room feels like it has no oxygen at all, so cold you can see your breath on the foetid air. You bend down to the body, or what is left of it. 'Mrs Rourke?'

5

She's dead. She must be, all that blood — her face has been beaten to meat, red and pulpy, her clothes soaked black with it. And her stomach, is that — no, Jesus, it's even worse. The tangle of skin and blood on her stomach, that's her baby.

The baby is purple, its tiny eyes shut. It's still attached to her by the blue umbilical cord. It lies on her ruined stomach as if exhausted. On one of the woman's hands the nails are encrusted with blood, and you see she's been trying to claw through her own skin. The other hand is stretched above her head, handcuffed to the handle of a drawer. You see what has happened. She's been beaten, then locked in this kitchen for three days. In that time her baby has come, and there was no one, no one at all to help. A knife lies beside her, bloodied, and you see what she has done, trying to free the child from the prison of her own body. A little girl. You want to put the poor wee thing under your jacket.

'Kevin!' You're shouting for the constable. 'Don't come in here, son, don't look! Get Mick — call an ambulance. There's a dead female and an infant, stillborn . . . '

You hear a noise and turn back. A bubble of spit forms in the woman's cracked lips. 'Mrs Rourke? Christ, I think she's — '

'No . . . No . . . ' The free hand reaches towards the baby. 'No dead, no . . . '

'I'm sorry. She's gone, love. She's gone.'

The woman tenses for a second, then slumps back in the pool of her own mess. The limp hand slips from her child's blood-slick head, and you scrabble on her damp neck for a pulse. Nothing.

6

Nothing. In your own chest your heart goes pounding on, reminding you you're still alive, and that this bloodied kitchen with the melamine cupboards will be with you till the day you lie down and die yourself.

★ ★ ★

You were sure the woman would die. How could she not? She'd been in that freezing kitchen for days, bleeding out across the patterned lino; the dehydration alone should have killed her. Then she'd be joining the poor scrap she'd given birth to. But you've been waiting in the hospital for hours now and no one has come with the death forms for you to sign. You wonder if Margaret's right, if something in you has hardened and died too.

Bob's gone to the station to start the investigation. Much good it'll do them. They'll not be able to pin it on any particular group of thugs. No one will have seen anything, and in the houses you go to they'll hear your Catholic name and look at you as if to say: traitor. Scab. Legitimate target. They were lucky to even find the husband's body, and God knows things are bad when you feel lucky to have a half-headless corpse on your hands instead of another name to add to the lost. You know exactly how it was for Brian Rourke. His pregnant wife beaten, house wrecked, blindfold over his head and out to the car. The sound of his own breath. Drive to some lonely spot. A march in the dark, kneeling in the dirt, then a shot to the back of the head. And she was likely dead too now, the whole family gone in one night.

But as you sit twisting your hat, watching the clock inch round, a doctor comes out. Everyone in the waiting room looks up with dull hope, but she comes to you. A woman in blue scrubs, tired and creased. There are bloody handprints on her white coat — her own, or someone else's?

'DC Maguire.' She rubs her eyes behind her glasses. 'I'm afraid the child is dead, as you thought. I think she was stillborn — they beat the mother, and that must have brought the labour on.' You nod, expecting to hear, 'And we did everything for the mother, but . . .'

'She won't be able to answer questions for a while, but when she wakes up you can try an ID. She must have seen them, even if they wore balaclavas.'

'She's *alive?*'

The doctor nods wearily. 'I don't know how, but yes. We think the child was born yesterday. She must have realised it was in trouble, from the beating, and tried to — well, she tried to give herself a Caesarean, it seems. It might have worked, too, if you'd got there sooner. I think she has medical training. It was crude, but in the right place.'

You're thinking of your own child, safe at home, please God safe at home, born red and wriggling as a new pup. 'Can she have any more?'

'I'm afraid not.' The doctor — Dr Alison Bates, her badge says, not a local name, and the accent not local either, she must be English — says, 'There was too much bleeding, so I had

8

to perform a hysterectomy. But she'll live.'

'Does she know?'

The doctor hesitates. 'I've told her, though she's very woozy. She — well, we had to restrain her. She was very distressed. We gave her sedation.'

For a moment the doctor flops down in the seat beside you. A small woman, dark-haired. She seems to have given way.

'She's alive.' You can't take it in, and for a moment you wonder if it would be better the other way, an end to it, be with the child and the husband again, if you believe in that kind of thing, and these days you just aren't sure if you do.

'Yes.' The doctor rubs her face, her nails short and dirtied with blood. 'Yes.'

But it doesn't feel like success, to you who have both fought to save her. Then the doctor's beeper begins to sound, and she springs up, muttering a curse, and dashes off down the corridor, where a flurry of activity has begun. On the tiled floor, her feet make a rapid rhythmic pattering, and she is gone.

Not knowing what else to do, you head home, every inch of you tired and stiff, sticky with the woman's blood and the barnyard smell of the kitchen. You keep picturing the baby, its mottled purple skin, something not fit for the eyes of the world, like a bird fallen from a nest. *Untimely ripped* — the quote comes to you, something you've seen on your daughter's homework. She's doing *Macbeth* for her English, that's it. Untimely ripped.

You park your Volvo in the street and see with surprise the curtains in the house aren't drawn. It's six p.m., long dark, winter-dark, and Margaret hates to have them open, worried about people 'looking in on you'. You open the door with your key. Your daughter sits at the table in her maroon school uniform, chewing on a pen in that absent teenage way, homework spread around. Her red hair is untidy and you notice she hasn't put on the radio or TV, not like her. 'Where's your mum?'

The kitchen is cold, no dinner cooking in the oven. 'Paula?'

Your daughter raises her eyes to yours, and for the second time that day you feel your stomach fail. 'She wasn't here,' Paula says, her voice slipping into the panic she's obviously been holding back since she came home. 'I thought you'd know. I thought you'd know where she was.'

Your heart, you think irrationally. Focus on the heart. It's thumping in your chest like the feet of the doctor running down the corridor. One two one two. Running for a life.

1

'Jesus Christ!'

'Sorry! God, I'm sorry.' Paula put her head down on the conference-room table, under which she had just vomited all over the feet of her superior officers. Bob Hamilton, the senior sergeant, and Guy Brooking, the Detective Inspector, had leapt up in alarm as she leaned forward, convulsing, right in the middle of a case presentation.

'It's OK, Paula,' said Guy awkwardly, moving his expensive brogues away from the stain on the threadbare grey carpet. 'Are you all right?'

She could feel beads of sweat along her forehead. 'Uh — I don't know. I must have eaten something bad.'

'Why don't you go and clean up — we need to leave in five minutes, anyway.'

'OK.' She dragged herself out of the conference room, stomach roiling, and behind her she heard Bob Hamilton's plaintive tones: 'She's after boking on my shoes, so she is.'

She fled to the Ladies, hanging over the sink for a while until it stopped, then running cool water over her face and rinsing the sour taste from her mouth, shaking. She'd thrown up every morning now for the past month, but this was the first time it had happened at work, and the

11

first time anyone else had seen. She was fairly sure her father, who she lived with, had noticed — the ex-policeman missed very little — but so far he was choosing not to say anything.

Paula raised the edge of her thick grey jumper and examined her stomach in the mirror of the Ladies. Still flat. But not for much longer, unless she made a decision and bloody soon. She started counting backwards in her head. If only she could be sure which time. Or which man, for that matter.

The door opened and she smoothed the jumper down quickly.

'Paula, are you OK?' Avril Wright, the intelligence analyst, was the only other woman on their small team at the MPRU, or Missing Persons Response Unit, an obscure team set up in the Northern Irish town to consult on cases north and south of the border. They were supposed to look at old cases with a view to reopening any with new evidence, and also make sure the investigation was properly coordinated when a new person went missing. Which sadly was what had happened today. 'The boss sent me to check on you.'

Avril as usual looked fresh out of the box, in a crisp blue blouse and pencil skirt. Paula felt oozy and rumpled. 'I'm OK.'

'You don't want to go home?'

'No, no, not when there's a big case like this.'

Avril's pretty face grew sombre. 'I don't know who would do such a thing. A wee baby!'

Paula looked at her own pallid face in the mirror. She did know. That was the worst part of her job as a forensic psychologist, working out exactly who would do the most horrific crimes, and why. Entering into their minds, understanding. People said that understanding everything meant forgiving everything. She'd never known if that was true. 'Come on.' She pushed back lank strands of her hair. 'We're not going to find him like this, are we?'

Coming out, she saw Guy through the glass of the conference room, down on his hands and knees in his good grey suit. He was dabbing at the patch of bile with a wad of kitchen roll, his fair hair falling over his forehead with the effort. Formerly a big deal in the London Met, he'd come over to Northern Ireland several months before to run the unit and made more of a noise than anyone had expected, even recruiting Paula from her own London job back to her dreaded home town. She'd been supposed to stay for one case only, but that had reached its traumatic conclusion weeks before, and now it was a month to Christmas and she was still here. Her hand once more crept to her stomach. She had to tell him. Shit, she couldn't. Not today. Not when a case this big had just come in.

'You coming to the hospital?' Gerard Monaghan, one of the detectives from the local PSNI station who was seconded to the unit, was holding her coat. 'This bloody snow's made the traffic murder. Fiacra's digging the cars out.' Fiacra Quinn was the final member of their team, a young Detective Garda from Dundalk, who'd been brought in to act as liaison to the South.

Focus, for God's sake, Maguire. 'Coming.'

13

Paula had long believed that nothing good ever happened in Ballyterrin General Hospital. It was where they'd taken the two bodies they'd found in the nineties, women who for a while they'd thought could have been her missing mother. One washed up on a beach in Wexford, one unearthed in a drain during building works. Twice Paula had made the journey up from school in her maroon uniform, to meet her father at the morgue. It hadn't been worth it either time, the trip in some teacher's car, hands clasped between trembling knees. No trace of Margaret Maguire had ever surfaced and she was stilled in Paula's memory forever as she'd been on the last day, tidying the kitchen in her wool dressing gown as Paula had slunk out to school, bleary-eyed, crunching cereal. She'd been thirteen, just. She'd barely even said goodbye to her mother — why would she, when every day in life Margaret had been there in the same spot when she came home, a pot of tea on the stove?

The hospital was also the place Paula had been taken, aged eighteen, when she'd swallowed the contents of the medicine cabinet and had her stomach pumped. And that was Aidan's fault too, wasn't it? No. *No, Maguire*. However angry she got at him she knew she couldn't blame that on anyone but herself.

'Where are we going?' They'd parked the car in the icy, grit-scattered car park, and she was now trying to keep up with Guy as he barged through the double doors and onto a second-floor ward of the hospital. Too late she realised where it was — Christ, how stupid was she. Maternity. Of all the places to be today.

The entire area had been cordoned off, and uniformed PSNI officers stood about. An early December snowfall had hit the town that morning, and had been causing chaos even before all this. Trails of greyish snow melted up and down the packed corridors, full of confused women in nightclothes, angry men, flustered nurses. Tinsel decorations hung from the walls but there was no sense of festive cheer. Weak and queasy, Paula trotted after Guy in her black suede boots, already stained with damp sludge. When he got like this, there was no keeping up with him. He approached the cordon flashing his badge. 'Detective Inspector Guy Brooking, MPRU. Let us past, please.'

No, nothing good ever happened in Ballyterrin General Hospital, and the fact that it was from here the baby had been stolen, well, that didn't surprise Paula at all.

★ ★ ★

In front of the private maternity room, a woman in a grey trouser-suit and red heels was talking to Gerard Monaghan. It was no surprise he'd got there first, as Guy scrupulously obeyed the town speed limits, and Gerard, like all locals, looked on them as a good wee joke. He looked up uneasily as Guy arrived. This woman was his other boss, DCI Helen Corry, head of Serious

15

Crime for the area. Gerard's work as liaison to the Unit left him uncomfortably torn between the two and their constantly simmering feud.

Guy said, 'What have we got?'

Helen Corry saw them but carried on and finished her sentence. ' . . . And get the CCTV quick as you can. We need to see if the child's still in the building. Threaten them if you have to.' Only then did she turn to the new arrivals. 'Inspector Brooking, Dr Maguire. We have nothing. *I* have an abducted newborn, by the looks of it.'

Guy was pressing his lips together, a sure sign of contained fury. 'Why weren't we called in sooner?'

Helen Corry smoothed back a blond hair. Her nails were painted the same red as her shoes. 'They called the police, quite naturally, so we came.'

'We're first point of contact on all missing per — '

'You're here now, Inspector, aren't you? And as we'll be supplying all the manpower, or personpower, for this case, I'm guessing you want to keep us on board.'

Paula, no stranger to professional pissing contests herself, raised her eyebrows at Gerard, who shook his head helplessly. Between the two, he was on balance probably more scared of Corry.

The woman herself was now saying, 'As I understand it, your role is to coordinate and ensure a swift response to new missing persons cases. So what actions would your coordination create in this instance?'

'Well, I'd seal the area — '

'Done, as you saw — though you seem to have breached it.'

' — I'd prevent all staff and patients from leaving — '

'Also done, though we can't hold them forever. So it might be good if you let me get on and interview them.'

Guy spoke in a rush. ' — interview any eyewitnesses, get CCTV and artist's impressions, and ask my psychology consult to assess the MO.'

Finally Helen Corry gave Paula one of her trademark unreadable expressions. 'Good job you brought her, then. I'm fine with Dr Maguire being involved.'

'I didn't ask if you were,' Guy muttered, but only after Corry had moved out of earshot to berate the uniformed officers at the cordon.

Gerard sighed, his wide shoulders sagging. 'It's true what she said, sir. She's ordered it all already, what you'd have done. She's even got them checking the databases in case it's happened before anywhere. Not much for us to do.'

Guy turned to Paula. 'We've got one thing she hasn't. Ready to talk to the parents?'

★ ★ ★

Damian and Kasia Pachek had loved Ireland, he explained during the interview. They loved the green mountains, the pubs, the wisecracking stoicism of the people. So much so that when Kasia became pregnant, they'd decided to have their baby in Ballyterrin, instead of going home to Krakow as their families had wanted. The hospital room had cards on the nightstand, a big bunch of flowers still in crinkly plastic, a blue teddy inside the cot which until two hours before had held their newborn son, Alek.

Now Kasia lay on the bed, dressed in short pink pyjamas, a drip in her pale hand. She kept up a steady and monotonous weeping, the kind of sound you quickly stopped noticing. Her husband sat in an uncomfortable plastic chair, staring in front of him, mashing a paper coffee cup between his fingers. They were a young couple, Paula guessed. Mid-twenties, no more. Damian worked as a technician in a commercial lab outside town, and Kasia was a yoga instructor. Guy had already established as much from Gerard.

'I lost him,' said Damian Pachek again. His wife said something in Polish, swallowed in tears, and he lowered his head into his hands, eyes screwed up.

Guy looked to Paula, who stepped in. 'Mr Pachek. I know this is hard, but there's every chance we will find Alek, and soon. Now I'm sorry we have to do this so soon, when you're in shock, but time is really important in a case like this, before you forget any of it. I'll take you through a special interview to help you remember all the details you can.'

The man nodded, eyes still fixed on something invisible in the middle distance. His whole body

18

was shaking. Paula took a deep breath and sat down in another plastic chair, Guy still leaning against the wall. The weight of it all settled round her, the responsibility to find and bring home this child whose first toy lay abandoned in his crib.

'Damian.' She said his name quietly, and he focussed on her. 'I'm very sorry this has happened, but it isn't your fault. It could have been anyone.'

On the bed, Kasia moaned and choked out a few words of Polish. Damian passed a hand over his face. 'She says I should have watched — I should not have taken my eyes from him.'

Paula glanced at the woman, who was burying her face in the pillow, shoulders quietly heaving. 'It's not your fault,' she said again. 'Whoever came and took Alek, it's their fault, you understand? They're the one responsible. So I need you to tell me everything, every detail you remember, to help us find them.'

Tears were now pooling on his face. 'Kasy was sleeping. She was so tired — I'm tired too but I was awake, I was excited.'

Paula nodded.

'I was looking at him, at — at Alek, and I was happy, I was thinking I had to make a phone call, tell my mother she is *babcia* now.' His voice caught. 'Then a nurse came and she said she has to take Alek for tests. Kasia was sleeping, so I — I went — ' Words seemed to fail him and he gestured with one hand down the corridor. 'I go out to phone, so I do not wake her, Kasia . . . '

'The nurse,' Paula prompted. 'It was a woman, you said?'

'Yes. She had the outfit, sort of blue colour.' He waved a hand near his torso. 'Like they wear.' His English, perfect at the start, seemed to be breaking down under stress.

'Damian. I need you to remember. Slow down and just let it come — every detail.'

The young man had his head in his hands. 'She came in the door. Her feet are so quiet — I nearly don't hear her until she was there. She said — I forget — 'Time for baby's tests now.' And she started wheeling the, the cot. I didn't have time to think, OK, this is strange, you know.'

'Her voice,' Paula asked, 'did she have an accent?'

He shook his head. 'From here, I think. Like you. Not like him.' He pointed to Guy, who was pure Home Counties English. 'She was tall, I think. Black hair, blue outfit like a nurse.'

She had an idea. 'Was it an actual nurse's uniform, or maybe someone trying to look like a nurse?'

He thought about it. 'Maybe. I don't look. I — I don't know.'

Paula understood. Overwhelmed with new parenthood and lack of sleep, you didn't question the authority of a medical professional. Even if they weren't a real one. 'So when you went to phone, what happened then?'

'I went, but something made me look back, and I see the thing, this — ' He pointed helplessly.

20

'The cot?'

'Yes — I saw it in the corridor, kind of spinning. She wasn't there, and Alek, she lifted him out — oh God.' He started to shake hard. 'I could have run after her, but I didn't know, I think it's OK.'

'What happened next, Damian?'

'I — I called, and everyone at home is so happy, crying happy, saying when will we bring him there.' He shuddered, somewhere between laughter and tears. 'Then I came back, he's gone but I didn't worry. I waited maybe half an hour, then I went to the nurse station and they said — that's all. I can't remember. I'm sorry.'

'It's OK.' She went to touch his arm, earning a watchful look from Guy, and pulled back.

He took over. 'Mr Pachek. We'll do our best to find your son. Every member of staff here will be questioned, and we'll be going through the CCTV as soon as we can.'

'Who would do this?' Fingers stretched over his face like a mask, he looked to them for answers. 'Who would take someone's baby like this?' They had none.

'We'll send an officer over to be with you the whole time, keep you updated.' With those crumbs of comfort, they rose to go.

Guy walked quickly down the corridor, buttoning his suit jacket. 'First thoughts?'

Paula tried to keep pace. 'I've read about this kind of case. Usually it's a woman, as he said. Someone who's recently lost a baby or desperately wants one. They most likely won't want to harm Alek, but the danger with a newborn is that the abductor can't feed it, or look after it properly. There may not be much time.'

He rounded a sharp corner to the nurses' station. 'We need the CCTV. We can't hold people here indefinitely. Unless it shows something, we'll have to let everyone go.'

'We'll interview the staff?'

'If Corry lets us.' He turned to her suddenly and the force of his grey eyes hit her like a punch. Paula skidded to a halt, boots slipping on the polished hospital floor.

'What?'

'You should go home.'

'Why?' She bristled.

'Because you threw up on my shoes earlier.'

'Oh.'

'You're as white as a ghost, Paula. There's nothing you can do here.'

'But — ' She looked back to the room where the couple sat, stunned by the loss of what was so recently acquired.

'We'll do everything we can, I promise. Why don't you make a start on an offender profile? Corry's going to want one asap.'

'OK.' She stopped suddenly. If she was white as a ghost, there was one coming right towards her. A ghost that refused to stay laid.

Guy followed her gaze and gave a grunt of indignation. 'For God's sake, I told everyone not a word to the media.'

'He always knows,' said Paula wearily. 'I don't know how. He sniffs it out like a dog.'

Aidan was several yards down the cordoned-off corridor, which was crowded with police and patients. He was talking animatedly to the officers at the barrier, and hadn't seen her yet. She knew right then she couldn't face him, not with Guy there too, both of them and the secret ticking away inside her like a bomb. She looked at Guy helplessly. 'Can I get out of here? I can't — '

He seemed to understand. 'There's some stairs round the corner. Show your ID card and say I sent you. I'll handle O'Hara. He has no right to be here.' He hesitated. 'Listen, when you feel better, Paula, I think we should talk. About — everything. About what happened with us last month.'

She froze for a second. He couldn't know, could he? No, she hadn't told anyone and the only person who'd guessed was in London. She forced a smile. 'Sure. Soon.'

Paula ducked around the corner, just in time to see Aidan O'Hara, editor of the local paper and also her ex-boyfriend, stride up to Guy waving his press card. He'd shaved since she saw him last, a month before, bleeding on a stretcher, shot through the arm by a desperate man. Halloween night, the air full of smoke and danger, and Paula and Aidan almost getting themselves killed trying to find out what had happened to a local girl pulled dead from the canal.

He looked different now. He looked sober, healthy, full of energy. Her hands crept over her stomach. Damn you, Aidan O'Hara. Damn and blast you to hell. Then she turned and almost ran before he saw her.

2

Paula took the stairs at a gallop all the way down to the ground floor, which was also swarming with officers, everywhere people asking questions about what had happened and when they could leave. Flashing her police ID, she pushed through the springy doors to A & E. There was only one person she could think of who'd help her now.

She was no longer sure how to think of Dr Saoirse McLoughlin. Best friend once, yes, for the whole of primary and secondary school. But then Paula had turned eighteen and left Ballyterrin, determined never to go back. It would take a while for Saoirse to forgive those years of absence, but they were at least back in a sort of strained contact.

Paula spied her friend coming out of a cubicle, drawing back the blue plastic curtains. She saw Paula through the crowd and came towards Reception, hands in the pocket of her white lab coat. Its sleeves were turned up to leave free Saoirse's small hands.

'I'm taking a break, Ricky,' Saoirse told the young man behind the counter, whose nose ring was glinting under the strip lighting.

'Any word of when people can go?' He indicated the waiting room, where every seat was occupied, some people with clean white bandages on, others bloodied and bashed-up, children chasing between the seats. The din was terrible. The unexpected snow had brought its usual quota of twisted ankles, tobogganing accidents, car skids. Coupled with the fact police were sealing every exit, the place was heaving.

'I'll get onto them. It's unacceptable to impede our work like this.' Saoirse glanced at Paula, who as one of 'them' looked awkwardly about her. Saoirse inclined her head. 'Come on, I've got five minutes, if no one's allowed in or out.'

In her small office, she shut the door and sat at her desk. 'Bit of a disaster, this. Management are going mad.'

'Mm.' Paula leaned against a filing cabinet, heart still hammering from the run downstairs. 'At least in cases like these the baby usually isn't harmed. Not on purpose, anyway. Do you have anything I can add to my profile? What do we need to look out for?'

Saoirse's face changed. 'He'll be cold, and hungry. They go downhill very fast if they're not kept warm and fed. Do you really think they're still here?'

'No, they'll be long gone. I'm sure we'll lift the restrictions soon. They're just checking the CCTV, I think.'

'You think it was staff? A nurse took him, I heard.' News travelled fast round the hospital.

'I don't know. It's easy enough to steal a uniform, or just wear something that looks like one. I'd say it was someone who felt at home here, though. They knew the procedures, and how to get out quickly, and that they'd not be

25

stopped.' And it was most likely someone who desperately wanted a child, but she didn't say this. Paula didn't need to ask how Saoirse's own pregnancy quest was going. She could see the answer in her friend's drawn, set face.

'I can't believe it happened here.' Saoirse was shaking her head. 'It's so busy today — how could they have got out with him?'

'I don't know. We think they just walked straight out. I mean — Oh.' Paula stopped.

'You OK?' Saoirse was up, doctor face on. 'You've gone green.'

'Yeah, I just — ' Oh God, it was happening again. She gestured blindly. 'Have you a bin, quick?'

Saoirse snatched her small metal bin, and Paula threw up in it, a neat gob of bile landing on top of a tissue. No food in her left to come up.

Saoirse was watching her strangely. 'Are you sick?'

'I'm OK.' Paula wiped her mouth with shaking hands.

'Has this happened before?'

'A few times.'

'Since everything?'

Saoirse knew Paula had been having trouble getting over that night the previous month. She'd called in several times while Paula was recovering from the shock and bruises she'd sustained. Bringing chocolates, cheer, kindness. Saoirse did all these things properly, in her quiet way. Her mammy had reared her right.

Saoirse was still watching, and Paula could

feel it spurting up in her. Not vomit this time, but the urge to tell. 'I saw Aidan,' she said. 'Upstairs. Just there now. I ran away.'

'Not *again*. What's with you two now?'

'Nothing! We just — we had words.' In fact the lack of words was the problem. 'We've not really spoken since — you know, everything.' Everything meaning that night in the lonely farmhouse, fireworks outside, gunshots inside. She pushed the memories away.

'Why not? I thought he was helping you with that case.'

'He was. But something happened with us just before, and we never really talked about it.'

'You slept together?'

Paula was embarrassed; how stupid. They were thirty, not twelve. 'Little bit.'

Saoirse sat down on her desk, hands in her pockets. 'So?'

'So, I've been boking my ring up ever since.'

The shift in her friend's expression was very subtle. You'd have to know her very well to notice the tightening round her mouth. 'I see. Well, that's great news.'

'Is it?'

'Is it not?' Saoirse frowned. 'I know you and Aidan have your differences, but there must be something there, if you keep going back. You were eighteen when all this started and it's still going on.'

'You're right. There is *something*. I just don't know what. Thing is — I'm not actually sure he's the father. There was someone else. Round the same time. Ah — ' she indicated a vague

27

upwards direction. 'The, ah, the Inspector.'

'Brooking! Jesus, but he's *old!*'

'He's forty!'

'He's married!'

'Separated!' Though actually she wasn't even sure if that was true now. They'd been getting a divorce, she'd thought, at the time, but since then she'd had a run-in with Guy's wife Tess, who was very definitely not happy about the fact Paula had slept with him.

'Right.' Saoirse tapped her small foot on the floor. 'You know, you *can* actually buy condoms in Ireland these days.'

'I know! Christ, sometimes they break, OK?' Not that she'd even used one with Aidan, carried away with lust and fear and sadness. God, she was an eejit.

'So what are you going to do?'

'I don't know. What can I do?'

'Keep it. Don't keep it. Choices are pretty limited.'

Paula recoiled slightly, but then leaned into the blow. What had she expected, coming to her Catholic friend, who'd been trying for five years to have what Paula had stumbled upon after a few stupid nights? 'If I didn't want to . . . what can I do? I'm sorry. I don't know who else to ask.'

Saoirse sighed and opened her desk drawer. 'This is the best place to go.' She passed over a green-coloured leaflet. 'They'll be able to tell you what the options are.'

Ballyterrin Women's Centre, Paula read. *Choices for women. Dr Alison Bates, owner/*

operator. A picture of a severe-looking woman, grey hair pulled back, white coat on. 'But — it's illegal here.'

'Duh. She doesn't do them here, obviously, but she'll refer you to England. She's English herself, actually. Been over here for years. Drives both sides mad, you can imagine. The hard-line Taigs and Presbyterians — you see them both on the pavement most days outside the clinic, blocking the way.'

Paula could feel the shiny paper between her fingers. 'I don't know if I — I don't know what I want.' *Abortion*. She couldn't even say the word.

Saoirse moved her mouse to bring her computer to life. She seemed to feel the need to do things, offer solutions, be a doctor and not Paula's friend. 'I can make you an appointment. Do you want me to make you an antenatal appointment too? That way you'll have options.'

Options. Choices. That was what everyone said. So why did she feel she'd no choice at all, like walking down a corridor with only one locked door?

'Um, no. Not yet.'

'But you need to — '

'I can't, Seersh. Not yet.' She put the paper carefully into the pocket of her wool coat. She felt unbearably ashamed. 'I appreciate it, though. I mean, especially with — '

Saoirse stood up abruptly. 'How far along are you? I mean, at a guess.'

'About two months, I think.' In fact she knew exactly. It was either eight weeks or it was six, depending on the man.

29

'Hmm. Decide soon, will you? Either way it's only going to get worse.'

*　　*　　*

When Paula got back from the hospital she felt exhausted, bone-tired and cold. The CCTV had apparently been viewed, and revealed that the abductor had left the building immediately after the incident, so when the exits were opened she thought she might as well go home and actually follow Guy's instructions for once. Her father was in the kitchen, putting the kettle on, a Tupperware container of iced biscuits open on the counter.

'Pat make those?' Paula's depleted stomach growled.

'Aye,' said PJ Maguire, hobbling on his crutches. An old injury had left his leg stiff, and he'd broken it badly again some months before, the plaster just off. 'You never went out in suede boots in that snow, did you?'

Paula rolled her eyes. 'Yeah. So?'

'You'll catch your death. You were down at the hospital, I take it.'

Paula dropped her coat on the stairs and lifted two biscuits. She'd long since accepted that her father, who'd been in the RUC for thirty years, knew everything that went on in the town. 'It was on the news, was it?'

He swallowed his tea. 'Aye, God love them. It's a terrible thing.'

'This kind of case, you've seen it before in Ireland?' She accepted the thick brown mug of

30

tea he offered and dipped a biscuit into it.

'Once or twice.' He stumped over to the table. 'If it's like this, a wee baby gone, it's usually a woman. They only want to love the wee one, but sad thing is, sometimes it dies since they've no idea what they're doing. You need to find him soon.'

'They want a profile already,' Paula sighed, pushing back her red hair, where snowflakes had settled in the short journey from the car to the door. It was going to lie overnight, she thought. 'It's all very well they ask for one, but then if it's in any way out they eat you for breakfast.'

'Profiles,' PJ scoffed. 'Common sense is what it is.'

Paula didn't say this meant a lot of her job would be pointless. She crunched a biscuit. 'These are nice. Thanks to Pat I've put on about a stone since I've been here.' Immediately she wished she hadn't drawn attention to it. If anything she'd lost weight, with all the fun puking she'd been doing.

'She was asking after you today. You should call in with her.'

'Hmm.' Paula loved Pat O'Hara dearly — her mother's best friend, she'd known the woman all her life. But Pat was also Aidan's mother, and that was something Paula just couldn't cope with right now.

'I — ' She was going to say something else about the case, ask her dad's opinion, when she felt the biscuits make an unwelcome reappearance. Christ, not again. 'I — just — hang on.' Hands over her mouth, she bolted up the stairs

31

and retched on her knees before the toilet. When the nausea released its grip, she leaned her head against the porcelain of the nasty lime-green bath.

'You OK, pet?' PJ was calling up the stairs, worried.

'Yes.' Her voice sounded weak and weedy. 'I just — I had something bad for lunch.' How many people was she going to say this to today?

She felt his silence all the way up the stairs. PJ wasn't a man you could easily lie to. 'Well, come down and I'll make you a hot water bottle.'

Paula closed her eyes, thinking of Guy Brooking, so tall and straight-backed in his grey suit, striding down corridors, handing out orders. Of Aidan O'Hara, in his ripped jeans and Springsteen T-shirt, pen behind his ear, chasing stories. Wishing she'd never set eyes on the pair of them.

3

'Morning, everyone. Briefing packs.'

As the staff of the MPRU trooped into the office early the next day, kicking dirty snow off their shoes and unwinding scarves from cold necks, it was no surprise to see Guy there already, shirtsleeves up, briefing sheets printed out and neatly stapled in a pile on the conference room table. Since his lapse at the end of October, when his own teenage daughter had run away from home and been thought kidnapped, Guy had seemed keen to reassert his authority and race through the backlog of missing persons' cases the team had been tasked with clearing. It had been a month of long days, going through files, chasing up old leads, interviewing slightly stunned families of the long-missing, jumping on any new case that came up, even though they were mostly schoolkids who'd fought with their parents and were back after a night. Nothing high-profile until the missing baby, and sometimes Paula wondered were they doing more harm than good. If they couldn't find these people, why stir up the past, like poking a stick into a murky pond?

Sitting down, she noticed a dark stain on the carpet, and tried not to meet anyone's eyes. Please God she'd manage to hold onto the contents of her stomach today. The others were settling into their seats, Avril ready with her laptop, Fiacra fiddling with his iPod, Gerard drumming his fingers on the table in impatience, while Bob Hamilton blew his nose on a cotton hankie. Their small team had been in place only a few months, but faced a daily barrage of funding issues, local hostility, and competition from the regular police force, the PSNI, a sort of slick reanimation of the old RUC.

Guy had put up a picture of the lost person on the projector, as was his habit. It focussed the team on what really mattered. 'This is the only photo so far taken of Alek Pachek,' he said briskly. 'The father took it on his mobile minutes after the child was born.' In the blurry shot, the baby's eyes were shut, mouth open in a wail. He was clasped in someone's arms — his mother's, probably. Paula recognised the pink fabric of her pyjamas. 'Can you give us an update on the PSNI's actions, Sergeant Hamilton?'

It always took Bob Hamilton just a moment too long to have the facts to hand. An old-school officer of the former RUC, he was supposed to take over the unit as a putting-out-to-pasture role when Guy eventually went back to London. Whenever that might be. 'Eh . . . right. After the incident, the hospital was sealed and searched, so it was. The child and his abductor had clearly left the vicinity, so it was subsequently reopened. The cameras in the lobby showed the attacker exiting the area into the car park. So far nothing has been reported from traffic cameras and no one on the ward saw anything happen. Miss Wright has the footage, I believe.' You'd never know from his dry delivery that Avril was in fact his niece. She caught Paula's eye and smiled fleetingly. Typical Bob.

Guy waited; that was it from Bob, apparently, so he took charge again. 'Now it seems Serious Crime have jumped the gun on this one already, but I want our full resources put to use anyway — Avril, let's look in the files for any similar cases. Chances are they might have done this sort of thing before.' Avril nodded her blond head, typing fast at her laptop.

'Look for attempted abductions too,' Paula put in. 'Often they need to work up to something like this. Practice, almost.'

Guy switched off the projector. 'I'm afraid it looks as if we'll be playing catch-up on this case to up the hill, but let's do what we can.' 'Up the hill' was their shorthand for the PSNI station across town, Corry's domain. Paula understood Guy's annoyance. The unit's funding was never secure, and they had to prove there was a need for an all-Ireland body to coordinate cases, someone to move quickly to search, to seek, and hopefully to find. If Helen Corry was bogarting all the new cases, that wouldn't happen.

Avril Wright raised a timid hand. 'Do you want to see the CCTV, sir? I got it from the hospital.' She spun her laptop. They were looking at black-and-white footage of the Maternity corridor. 'That's the Pacheks' room.' On screen, a tall woman in a nurse's uniform approached the room confidently. For a moment she paused at the door, then opened it and went in. A minute later she exited, wheeling the baby in a

35

cot. The father had held the door open for his son's kidnapper. Then the woman vanished down the corridor. Her face was turned away from the camera the whole time.

'Now this.' Avril clicked again. 'This was a shot of the waiting area on the second floor. That's just outside the ward. Look in the corner there.'

At first it was difficult to see, but the same figure was now rooting behind a chair. Then she quickly slipped the baby out of his cot and into what looked like a black shoulder bag. Like a caught fish. No one seemed to notice. In a corner, a man argued with the receptionist.

'She put him in a *bag*?' Paula stared at the screen.

'Yeah. Now look here.' The front doors of the hospital sliding back. The woman hurrying out, bag held close to her body. Avril froze the screen. 'We lose her after that. Basically she was out in about two minutes. She went down the stairs, not the lift. She didn't park in the car park or anything. She took him and was gone before anyone knew it.'

'She'd have had a car though,' said Fiacra thoughtfully. 'Babies are heavy enough to carry, like. And there's snow on the ground.'

Gerard shook his head. 'We got nothing off the traffic cams so far. We'd need a vehicle description or a licence plate or something. Also, Corry said there were no prints on the cot or anything like that. It'd been wiped off, looked like, or she wore gloves. She knew what she was doing.'

Guy frowned. 'And no one saw a thing. As you said, it's hard to believe, isn't it? There must have been hundreds of people on the ward that day.'

They all fell silent, marvelling at how few leads there could be in a case where someone had walked into a busy place and brazenly taken a baby that wasn't theirs.

Paula cleared her throat. 'She looks very calm doing that, doesn't she?'

'Yes?' Guy leapt on this comment. 'You think that's significant?'

'Well, you'd be nervous, wouldn't you, if you were going to walk in and take a child from under his parents' noses. Unless maybe you felt you had a right to.'

'Meaning?'

She spoke carefully. 'If I had to guess . . . '

'Do.'

'I'd say maybe she does work at the hospital. Or used to. Can we question all the staff on that floor? Someone will have seen her, but if she works there they might not have realised she was the abductor. Hiding in plain sight, you know.'

Guy said, 'It's the snow that's the issue here. Half the staff didn't even make it in that day, and apparently they were phoning round to get people in from leave and so on. So we can't be sure who was even there. Corry's brought in a police artist to work with the husband, try to get a face. We can get this footage enhanced too. Send it over to Tech, Avril.'

'It's been done,' said Gerard gloomily. 'Corry.'

Guy looked annoyed. 'Paula? What's your progress with a profile?'

'As we've seen, it's almost certainly a woman, and I would say someone with a connection to the hospital. It's also someone who wants a child and doesn't have one for some reason. I'd look at present and recent staff, in particular anyone who may have lost a child. Maternity leave records should show if anyone recently had a baby.'

'Unless it was a miscarriage,' Avril offered. 'There'd be no record then.'

Paula nodded. That was good thinking. 'All staff should be asked if they know who might recently have been pregnant or lost a baby.'

'We can do that.' Guy was hungry, clearly desperate to hang onto the case. 'What else?'

Paula looked at her notes, made while awake till three a.m. the night before. 'We've discussed that they may have done it before. We should put out an appeal — see if any families with young children noticed someone hanging about, taking an unusual interest in their babies. Also see if anyone knows someone who's suddenly come home with a newborn.'

'So anyone with a baby could be a suspect.' Gerard was picking at his cuticles.

'Essentially, yes.' Paula waited for him to contradict her, which he duly did, turning to Guy.

'Boss — you don't think maybe it's to do with them being Polish?'

Guy looked puzzled at Gerard's change of topic. 'Explain?'

Gerard rested his elbows on the table. 'The Polish who come here, they're all Catholics, yeah? And the local UVF fellas, they know that. Last year we had a family burned out of their house.'

'You're saying this is a sectarian incident, DC Monaghan?'

'I'm just saying, before we go into all these theories — ' he waved a dismissive hand at Paula — 'maybe it's something more likely. The usual story round here. The family is clearly Catholic, and they come over here and get jobs, and someone doesn't like it.'

Paula scowled. 'It seems a really weird way to get that point across. What about the old staples? Petrol bombs, graffiti? Why kidnap a baby, for God's sake?'

'That's your department.' Gerard sat back, linking his hands behind his head.

Paula decided to ignore him. 'I would highly doubt if there were a sectarian motive in this case. I've outlined the areas where I feel we should start looking. We should also think about what she did with the bracelet.'

Guy frowned again. 'Bracelet?'

'You know, the little name tag.' She encircled her wrist with her fingers, remembering her own — *Baby Girl Maguire*. A small thing saved and treasured by her mother. Used as evidence over the years on the side of — *no, she'd never have left. She loved me, she kept this.*

Guy was looking at her. She tried to pay attention. 'I mean, the child will have had ID on him, if we can find it. It's hospital procedure, isn't it?'

He nodded. 'All right. Interesting theories,

39

everyone. Our main resource will be our access to all databases — and of course Paula's ability to give us a rough profile of the offender.'

That was alarming. 'I can only give an educated guess, you know.'

'Better than nothing.'

'You want me on something, boss?' asked Fiacra Quinn. He'd taken out his white headphones for the meeting, but they dangled over the collar of his shirt.

'Yes,' said Guy. 'You can check databases in the South for anything similar. We may also need you to do home interviews — some of the hospital's staff live over the border, I gather, so there may be jurisdiction issues. Sergeant Hamilton will be assisting with those too. We're talking hundreds of people.'

He was saying 'we', but Paula felt they all knew DCI Corry would be running the show. 'Will there be a TV appeal?'

Guy rested his eyes on her. 'Yes, but Corry wants to do it. Something about speaking woman to woman . . . ' He grimaced. 'She'll need your profile asap for that, by the way. That's all, everyone. I can't stress how little time we have here — a newborn can die within hours if not properly looked after.' He dismissed them neatly, squaring off his briefing papers.

Paula's first instinct was to rush out, but he started to speak, and then so did she, and their words clashed. He smiled thinly. 'I wondered if you felt any better.'

'Yeah,' she lied. 'Must have been a twenty-four-hour thing.' Twenty-four years, more like. A worm of panic twisted in her chest.

'Have you got ten minutes today to talk? I know things are incredibly busy.'

She started to say yes, then remembered today was the bloody appointment Saoirse had booked for her at the clinic. For a moment she thought about not going. But the idea of leaving it was even more frightening. 'I have to go out for a bit. Is it important?'

He seemed to hesitate. 'It can wait. But where are you going? You know Corry needs the profile.'

'Yes — um. It's a lead I'm following.' He looked at her hard and she squirmed, remembering the trouble she'd got into on the last case for working on her own. 'Honest, it is.'

'All right. Just keep me in the loop.' He turned his attention back to the briefing sheets, scouring them for some fact they might have missed, and she crept out, feeling her secret clasped tight in her pocket.

4

The address on the leaflet Saoirse had given Paula turned out to be above a video shop on a dilapidated street behind the market. The whole area spoke of the shady and seedy, but the office itself had a sturdy, recently refurbished door, and a very complicated buzzer entryphone. The windows on the first floor were tinted glass. Paula had scanned the street carefully, looking for a sign of the protestors Saoirse mentioned, but it was deserted. A placard tied to the lamppost opposite declared that the clinic murdered babies. Paula averted her eyes from the pictures. She checked the display on her phone — she really didn't have time for this today — then leaned on the buzzer, looking furtively round her.

There was an answer on the intercom. A girl's voice came over it, harassed. 'Yes?'

'Um . . . I've got an appointment.' It was silly, but she didn't want to say her name aloud in the street.

'Who did you make it through?'

'Dr McLoughlin, up at the hospital?' Paula was getting irritated — she needed this appointment, difficult as it was, to be as quick and soothing as possible. She needed to get back to her life and help find Alek Pachek and bring him home.

Over the intercom, the girl sighed. 'You better

come up.' The door buzzed open and Paula went up a flight of polished stairs. It was the same at the top, a clinical but comfortable space.

At the reception desk, a dark-haired girl was speaking into the phone in annoyed tones. 'Well I know, miss, but I can't do anything about it. We can reschedule, maybe. Don't shout at me, miss. I'm only doing my job.' She sat the receiver down with a clatter. 'Sorry about the buzzer,' she said, unapologetically, to Paula. 'Security, like. There's been threats.'

'I can imagine. Er . . . what's happening?'

The girl threw up her hands in exasperation. 'Listen, she can't see you today.'

'Oh.' Paula held on tight to the strap of her bag. 'Why?'

Another sigh. The girl wore a pair of cheap grey trousers, and had long shiny black hair and red nails. 'She didn't turn up.'

'Who?'

'The doctor, of course. Dr Bates.'

'Is she sick?'

'I don't know. She never thought I might need to be told. I've been getting dog's abuse all morning for it.'

Paula was trying to adjust. 'OK — so she just didn't turn up this morning?'

'That's what I said. I've rung her mobile and it's not on, even though if she can't get hold of me within five minutes she's losing the head.'

'Is there anyone at home you could try?'

The girl's sneer deepened. 'I'm not allowed her home number, am I? 'Security'.'

'I'm sorry — what's your name?'

43

A pause. 'Erin.'

'Well, Erin, is this the kind of thing she'd do?' Without thinking she'd slipped into work mode, the questions you always asked. Being the one who looked, who sought. That was better than lying on a couch in a doctor's office with your legs wide open, having to make some kind of decision about the rest of your life.

'No way,' Erin was saying. 'She'd go mental if I took a sick day. I have to ring her by seven to let her know. And she's mad on data protection. All the appointment details are protected, the client names and that. I can't even get into them without her.'

Paula looked round at the waiting room, the racks of pastel leaflets on contraception and choices — that word again. 'When did it open?'

'This summer. She said it was a disgrace we're in the UK but the women here have to go to England for abortions. Some people come to her for coils and that, but mostly it's for termination referrals.' She looked at Paula as if suddenly remembering that was probably why she'd come too. 'Anyway, there was lots of trouble — bricks in the window of her house and even death threats. She had to go ex-directory and all that. She gave me one of those alarms, you know the ones, you can set them off if you get raped or something.'

'But you like working here, even so?'

Erin twisted her mouth, considering. 'I suppose. She's a massive cow, like, but it's only 'cos she cares. This place is like her life.'

'You're pro-choice, I take it?'

44

'Yes.' Said defiantly. 'I don't see why some girl in London can get help if she needs it, but 'cos I live in Ballyterrin I'd have to go all the way there. Anyway, we put them on the Friday night plane and they stay in a hostel in London.' She suddenly stopped, as if she'd shared too much. 'Why're you asking anyway?'

'Oh.' Paula had forgotten where she was. 'Listen, I work with the police — you know, the unit for missing people.'

'The one that's always in the paper?'

'Yeah.' Bloody Aidan and his so-called exposés. He'd do whatever he could to stick the boot into the unit — he thought it was a waste of money that should have gone to prosecuting former terrorists. 'If Dr Bates can't be located by the end of today, you should call this number.' She managed to find a dog-eared card in her bag, under a litter of pens, sweet wrappers, and tampons. Wouldn't be needing those, not unless she did something fast. 'The police won't usually act before twenty-four hours are up, but if as you say there've been death threats, we need to be fast. If you come straight to us we can get moving on it right away; you don't have to go through the PSNI switchboard.' It wasn't strictly speaking proto-col, but Paula thought Corry could stand to lose a case or two.

The girl looked uncertain as she took the card. 'You think something's happened to her?'

'Chances are she's fine, but it doesn't hurt to check.'

Erin clutched the card, clearly realigning her

45

world view. 'Eh — do you want to reschedule your appointment?'

'Let's see what happens for now. Is there any way you could find out if she's at home?'

'Her partner — she works in the hospital, in accounts. I could ring her. She's nice to me.'

'Good idea.' The hospital again. And Paula had noted the 'she' — if the doctor was a lesbian who advocated abortion, chances were she wasn't too popular in Ballyterrin. She hoped Alison Bates was just sick at home, but if not, they wouldn't have to look too far to find someone who would wish her ill.

*　*　*

Ignoring a certain feeling of relief at the cancelled appointment, Paula dashed back to the office to immerse herself in work. As she went in Guy was on the phone, and gestured to her through the plate glass. He put the receiver down and came to the door. A thin crease of annoyance had taken up permanent residence between his eyebrows. 'She's only bloody called a press conference for this afternoon.'

'Who, Corry?'

'Who else? We'll have to shift it to get our initial report done. She's insisting we have the conference up there. I tried to argue, but — oh, you know what she's like.'

Paula was shrugging her coat off. Helen Corry was one of the few people she'd met who actually cowed her into silence. Guy looked pointedly at his watch. 'Get your thing done?'

'Yes thanks.' Bloody cheek of him, interrogating her, when it was most likely his fault she was in this mess. She thought about mentioning the missing doctor, but decided it was too soon, and in any case it would be too hard to explain what she'd been doing there.

'OK. Well, Corry wants your profile now, basically.'

'I'll do my best. She does realise I don't actually know who did it?'

'Knowing her, she thinks it's our fault we can't personally see through time and space and have an arrest already. Just do your best.'

5

'Inspector Guy Brooking. Yes, Brooking, as in Sir Trevor — oh, never mind. You know me. I've been up here pretty much every other day for a year. Can you let us in now?' Paula could hear the irritation in Guy's voice as they waited in the reception of the PSNI station. Someone had hung a 'HAPPY HOLIDAYS' banner over the desk, which must have seemed a rather grim irony to the criminals and victims who passed by it every day. Lacking security passes for the main station, the staff of the unit always had to wait like any punter off the street, and the desk sergeants seemed remarkably lacking in the most basic facial recognition skills. Finally the security doors were opened and the team trooped into the main part of the station. Avril was carrying her laptop still, as if she needed it by her side at all times. Paula felt tired and empty, her stomach a hollow pit after another quick puking session. She thought she'd managed to cover this one up by running the hand drier as she retched.

The large conference room of the station was lined in fold-up chairs, and at the front a banner bearing the logo of the PSNI hung on the wall above a long table with three microphones on it. The room was filling up with reporters and police staff. A uniformed officer directed them to sit at the back. The chairs were so tight together Guy had to draw his knees right up to his chest.

Gerard was at the front, in the crowd of PSNI staff. The mood was controlled and slick, a plasma screen set up beside the table.

'Smoke and mirrors,' Paula heard Guy snipe, just before the side door opened and Helen Corry came out in a black suit with a knee-length skirt, flanked by two uniformed officers, a man and a woman.

'Who're the uniforms?' Paula asked Guy under her breath.

He indicated first left, then right. 'Area Superintendent. Assistant Chief Constable. Big guns.'

Despite the presence of these illustrious names, it was clearly Helen Corry's show to run. Her face was composed, and when she folded her hands on the table, it showed off her French manicure. 'Ladies and gentlemen, thank you for coming today. As you know, we're in the middle of a major investigation. Yesterday at approximately oh nine hundred hours, an infant was taken from his parents at Ballyterrin General Hospital. Alek Pachek is now one day old. We believe he was taken by a woman posing as a nurse, who then placed him inside a bag and left the premises. He will be weak, and needing his mother's milk, and he must be kept as warm as possible, especially in this weather.' She faced the cameras, her face beautifully photogenic. 'Alek's mother is Kasia. She is too distraught to be with us today, so I am speaking to you for her, as a police officer and also as a mother myself.'

Beside her, Paula heard Guy mutter something inaudible.

'Kasia and her husband are desperate to know Alek is safe. They only had a few hours to hold him before he was taken. Alek has a family who love and need him. If you have seen anything, if you know anyone who suddenly seems to have a young baby or is acting suspiciously, please contact us at once. And if that is you on the CCTV film, if you have him — please let us help you. We know you don't want to hurt him, or cause his family any more grief. Please — bring Alek home.' She was good, bloody good. Paula could hardly look at Guy, who had his arms folded.

Corry had opened the floor to questions. Someone asked about an offender profile. She said, 'We are making the best use of all our resources, and our profile suggests a woman who has recently lost a child, or been unable to have her own for some reason. Her partner may not be aware of the loss — she may even have been faking a pregnancy for several months.' Paula's own words, coming out of another's mouth. She wasn't sure if it was annoying or gratifying.

Another reporter had asked about the possible racism angle, also Gerard's theory. Corry was in her element answering these, you could tell. 'It's sad to say that members of the Polish community here do from time to time experience hate crime and intimidation from a very small minority of the population. At this time we are not treating this as a racial or sectarian incident.'

A fat man stood up, in a check sport jacket. 'Will the MPRU be involved?'

50

Beside Paula, Guy tensed. This was a reporter with one of the Belfast papers, which had a strong Republican slant and had printed an article a few months back slating the unit for the 'sectarian bias' of the cases they'd recommended for review.

Helen Corry did not even look at the back of the room where the unit staff sat. 'We're very grateful to have the advice and resources of the unit, but this is a Serious Crime inquiry, and will be dealt with from this station.' Her eyes scanned the room. 'One more question — yes, Mr O'Hara.'

Paula flinched. Bloody hell, she hadn't seen Aidan come in, but there he was, up near the front, unusually smart in a white shirt, collar open. 'DCI Corry.' His voice was clear. 'Is there any truth in the rumour you've called in a psychic to help find Alek?'

Guy turned to Paula, eyes wide with surprise. But if the question was also a shock to Corry, she didn't let on. 'As I said, we'll be using every resource we can access. The family have requested we consult a renowned faith healer, well known in the town — Mrs Magdalena Croft. She has previously worked with other forces and brought some considerable insight to the investigations. Thank you for your question, Mr O'Hara.'

Aidan couldn't be silenced so easily. From the back Paula could see he'd recently had his black hair cut, and was twisting a pen in one hand, something he did when he wanted a cigarette. 'You can really justify spending money on that?

51

Aren't there very strict protocols on UK police forces using psychic intervention?'

At this, Corry smiled. 'I believe that word is yours, not ours, Mr O'Hara. Not so long ago psychological profiling was also seen as close to voodoo. We'll take whatever support we can get to bring little Alek home. And you can rest easy about costs — the lady has volunteered her help.' Aidan sat back, and Paula caught the small smile on his lips. He knew when he was beaten.

The conference wrapped up with an appeal for information and a hotline phone number being given out. Corry pushed back her chair to leave.

Guy stood up as the room cleared. 'Wait for me. I'm not having this.'

★ ★ ★

'Wow! Listen to him shout,' whispered Avril to Paula. They were waiting for Guy on a line of bolted-down chairs outside Helen Corry's office, like schoolchildren expecting a telling-off. The noticeboard opposite had health and safety posters, ads for flat shares and car boot sales, reminders to turn off the lights and save energy.

Paula watched the closed door. 'If it came to a fight, I'd put my money on her.'

'She always looks beautiful, doesn't she? I love her clothes.'

'Mmm. Like a cobra in Louise Kennedy.' Paula tried to make out the rumble of Guy's voice.

' . . . You're supposed to take our advice and guidance on missing persons cases, so why do I

52

only hear about this faith healer rubbish along with the media? It's an unacceptable breach of protocol and I'll be going to the Chief Constable.'

Corry's voice was calmer, harder to hear. She was saying something about it being a PSNI prerogative to bring in outside help.

'You're the one who's always protesting scarcity of resources, but you're willing to spend time working with some charlatan?'

There was the sound of a chair being scraped back. Helen Corry spoke loudly. 'Inspector. This isn't London. This is a country town. We're a mile from the border with Ireland, where divorce was only legalised in 1996. Religion is part of daily life.'

'You think I don't understand religion? Chief Inspector, I policed Hackney for five years.'

'So you should know it matters. In gaining trust. Showing respect.'

'I don't respect frauds who prey on the vulnerable.'

'Have a look at that.' Silence. Paula leaned close to the door, frustrated.

She heard Guy say, 'That doesn't prove anything. She made a lucky guess, is all.'

'The Guards were convinced that child had been abducted by his father, taken back to Bahrain. They'd never be able to find him again, they thought. Then Magdalena Croft said, no, he's not with his father, he's in this country, and you'll find him near water. And there's his remains on a beach in Galway, exactly as she said. He was two years old and he'd wandered

53

four miles from his home. They'd never have found him without her. He'd be just another stat for your pile.'

Guy said nothing for a while. Then, 'You can't believe she really has these visions. The Virgin Mary comes and tells her where to look? I mean, come on.'

'You're one hundred per cent sure she doesn't?'

'I'm not one hundred per cent sure of anything. Empiricists aren't.'

'Well. I don't know what it is she does or how she sees things, but if she can find me a missing baby I'm certainly going to let her try. And has it not occurred to you that if a woman's so desperate for a child she steals one, she might have consulted with a faith healer first? Magdalena Croft has supposedly helped more people get pregnant than an IVF specialist.'

More silence. Paula realised she was leaning over so far her ear was almost pressed to the door. She sat back just in time as Guy burst out. 'Come on, everyone. Let's go.'

Behind the door, Paula glimpsed the DCI at her desk, just as neat and calm as before. 'Dr Maguire,' Corry called. 'Thank you for your profile. It was very helpful.'

'That's OK,' Paula said, abashed. Guy's back was receding down the corridor. 'I have to go.'

'If you ever get bored, I can always use you here.' Corry's nails flashed like little blades. Paula fled.

★ ★ ★

54

Down at the unit, all was deserted. Guy, who'd driven back in irritated silence, was further annoyed. 'Someone should be here at all times. Where the hell's Fiacra?'

'Here, boss.' Fiacra barged through the glass doors, a tray of paper cups in each hand and tinny music emanating from his headphones. 'Avril texted me about the conference. Thought yous might need coffee — we might be pulling a late one.'

'Why, did something come in?' Paula could see Guy debating whether or not to tell him off for going out. He was very fond of coffee and the stuff at the station was vile.

'Yeah.' Fiacra licked at the frothy milk cascading from his own cup. 'This might cheer you up, boss. It's a potential big case, and they came right to us. So, we have jurisdiction.'

Mollified, Guy lifted the lid from a cup and blew on it. 'What is it?'

'A doctor. Never turned up for work and nobody's seen hide nor hair of her since this morning. I know that's not long but she was flagged by the system 'cos she'd had death threats. The name's — '

'Alison Bates?' Paula took a sip of her drink — she assumed the only tea was for her — and for a moment enjoyed the look of surprise on her colleagues' faces. Then she realised — bugger, how could she explain why she'd been visiting the town's local abortionist?

6

'You're sure I can't get you anything else?' Veronica Cole couldn't sit still, hopping up and down into the kitchen or to show more photos of herself and Dr Alison Bates in various parts of the world. The small bungalow was crammed with wooden bowls, batik cushions, incense holders. A smell of sandalwood hung in the air. Paula followed the source to a joss stick burning in front of a framed picture of Alison, decades younger but still unsmiling, holding a diploma. Her hair had been darker then, but the eyes behind the glasses were as steely as those in her clinic leaflet photo.

Veronica saw Paula looking at the incense. 'It's silly, I know, but I picked up the habit in Indonesia. I'm praying for her.'

'No different to lighting a candle in church,' said Paula, trying to be soothing.

The woman was clearly half-mad with anxiety. Tall and bowed, Veronica Cole had long grey hair that she wore loose, dangling silver earrings, and a green tunic top. 'It's just not like Ali at all. She'd never worry herself, but she knows I would. Those horrible letters. I know she'd have rung if she could.'

Paula spoke gently. 'Ms Cole — '

'It's Veronica, please.'

'Veronica, would you like to sit down? We'll drink the tea and you can tell us what happened.'

They'd said no to tea, but she'd brought some anyway, green leaves in little glass cups. Distracted, she'd also added milk, so bits of leaf floated in it unappetisingly. Guy, who didn't like tea at the best of times, was prodding at his with a little gold spoon.

Veronica Cole did finally sit, but her eyes kept flitting to the door. 'I keep thinking she's going to walk in and say Ronni, you daft article, you forgot I had that conference or something . . . but after the letters, you see — '

'You did the right thing,' Guy said, setting his cup down with a tinkle. 'We take this kind of incident very seriously. Can you tell us about the letters?'

Paula glanced at him. 'Or maybe — tell us first how you met Dr Bates?' Calm her, ease her in. Guy nodded, almost imperceptibly. They had their routine all worked out.

'Well — we met at Queens. You know, the university in Belfast.' She seemed to be explaining this for the Englishman's benefit. 'I was doing Accounting and she was a medical student. We were in the same women's rights group. The seventies, you know — we were all so right on.' A sad smile. 'Ali and I agreed that women's rights were just as important as religious issues. We were good friends.' She heard the unasked question. 'Just friends then. I was — my parents were very devout. I didn't even know what it meant, myself.'

Paula asked, 'You're from Ballyterrin, I take it? And Dr Bates?'

'Ali was born in Norfolk, but she said she

57

couldn't wait to leave. She came to university here because I think she wanted to be part of something. Civil Rights. Then after college, she stayed on for medical training. I moved back here to mind Mammy and Daddy. They were getting on a bit, you know how it is. We lost touch for a while, just life really.'

Veronica was babbling, perhaps reluctant to think about what was actually wrong. They saw this quite a lot. Paula shifted; the embroidered cushions were digging into her back. She totally failed to understand the point of cushions — all they did was get in the way. 'When did you meet again?'

'It was at the airport, if you can believe. I used to go on wee trips over to Soho. You know, after I — realised. She'd been at a conference, and there she was, and I just saw her right away in the airport queue. We didn't have to say anything. You know how it's like that sometimes — you see someone and you know right away, that's the one for me? There's something special between you, and things are never the same after that?'

Guy and Paula avoided each other's gaze. 'Mmm,' she said, drinking her tea. 'Could you tell us about the clinic, Ms Cole?'

Veronica wrung her thin hands, eyes darting to the door again. 'It was her pet project. She thinks it's a disgrace that there's no abortion here, more than thirty years since we campaigned on it at college. She thinks it's a medical procedure, like having your tonsils out, and that it shouldn't be political.'

'I see.' Guy wrote this down. 'And there were threats?'

'The letters started after there was a sermon against her. A Presbyterian preacher, out in the country. Then one time, it was a brick.' She looked at the front window. 'The police said go ex-directory, vary your route home, that sort of thing.'

'Must have been frightening,' said Paula.

'Very. But she wouldn't give up. That's Ali. It's who she is.' Her eyes went to the door again. 'Do you think something's happened to her?'

Guy said the words they always used, designed to give hope, but not too much. 'In most cases a missing person is found again quite quickly, safe and well. Alison hasn't been gone very long. You saw her this morning?'

'Not really. She gets up early. She tries not to wake me, but I heard the car start. They told us we should check under, you know, for bombs. So I always wake up when it goes. Then Erin — that's Ali's assistant — she rang to say Ali never turned up.'

'And that wasn't like her?'

'Not like her at all.' She leaned forward confidentially. 'The women who go there — the girls — Ali always said they were under enough pressure. It was her job to be on time, to be unemotional, give them all the facts.'

Paula tried to keep her face blank, thinking it was possible she'd have made a decision by now if the doctor had been there.

'I've tried all our friends,' Veronica went on. 'Ali has a sister, but they're not in contact. No

59

one knows anything. Her car — I suppose if we could find that — '

'The PSNI are looking for it now,' Guy reassured her. 'They'll find it soon, I'm sure.'

'Erin said the clinic was still locked when she arrived. Normally Ali would open it — she didn't even like Erin having a key, she's so security conscious.'

And something of a control freak, it seemed. Not the type to up and run away, unless something in her had finally snapped. 'Does she have a home computer?' Paula asked. 'Often we can get useful information from those.'

'Yes, a laptop. She doesn't let me use it! She'd have it with her, normally; she keeps everything on there. Even all her clinic stuff, the patient records. She doesn't want anyone else to have access, you know, in case some of these extremist people get hold of it.'

That was enough to make Paula shiver, seeing as her own records were in there.

'Ms Cole,' Guy was saying. 'Is there anyone else Alison might have gone to see, anyone at all we could check with — a distant friend, a relative?'

Veronica paused. 'I was trying to think. I suppose there's a chance she went to see Heather. They'd had that falling-out, of course, but it's possible Ali wanted to make it up with her.'

'And who's Heather?' asked Guy, making notes.

'Ali's daughter.' She saw their expressions. 'You didn't know she was married?'

'I'll drop you back,' Guy said, ushering Paula out to his BMW. 'You're very pale still. Are you sure you're OK to be working?'

She put on her seat belt, wearier than she wanted him to know. At least the puking had subsided. 'I can't be off now, can I?'

'No,' he admitted. 'We're running out of time with the baby, and if Dr Bates doesn't turn up soon — '

'You think it looks bad?'

'I do. I don't like the sound of those death threats.'

'It's an inflammatory issue here, abortion. And her living with a woman too — some would see that as deliberate provocation.'

Guy did what she'd come to think of as his Ballyterrin look, a sort of 'I can't believe how backward these people are' shake of the head. It made Paula bristle in defence of her home town, then realise sadly that some things were indefensible. 'What were you doing there anyway?' he asked. She froze. He retracted. 'Sorry. It's just you said you had a lead. I take it that's why you knew her name.'

She stared out the window and spoke carefully. 'I had an idea that she might know about women who'd lost babies in the town — you know, if they'd had abortions. Then when I got there, she was missing.'

As she'd hoped, he either bought it or didn't want to ask further. 'I suppose it was worth looking at. You should have told me, though.'

61

They were pulling into her street now, snow suspended in the air beneath the street lights, a pinkish hue over all. 'I know.'

'It's just — you remember what happened last time you went it alone — '

'Do I remember having a gun held to my head? Yes. I do.' An awkward silence fell. She could see her breath in front of her. 'Sorry. Have they worked out who was on the ward that day?'

'Not entirely, with the snow causing problems. They checked the Maternity leave records — that was a good idea of yours, thank you — but everyone's child is accounted for. Do you have any ideas?'

'There's a technique called cognitive reconstruction. We might be able to take them back and recall who they saw. Our brains can't consciously process everything we see, especially somewhere busy like a hospital, but it might be in there anyway.'

'Good idea. Otherwise we have to hope there's a response to the TV appeal.'

'And Dr Bates?' she said. 'Will we start with the daughter?'

'If we proceed. Maybe she'll turn up tomorrow.'

'Mmm. Maybe not.'

'Let's dig out those letters she received. They'll be on the system, if they were reported. Can you knock up a quick victim assessment?'

'I can try. She doesn't sound the type to wander off. If it's an extremist, they'll let us know they have her, and soon. Otherwise there's no point.'

'Right. Oh — I nearly forgot.' He made a face. 'Listen, Corry wants you to see this faith healer tomorrow, if you can bear it. She thinks you can work out if the woman's for real, or something. You can refuse if you want. It's hugely disrespectful. I can't believe she had the gall to compare you to some money-grubbing fraudster.'

Paula didn't mind. 'The way I see it, if this woman knows things, if she's getting so much right that she couldn't know otherwise, she's finding out somehow. And I'd like to know how that is.'

He was smiling, very slightly. 'I knew I could count on you.'

She had the door open and small flurries of snow were landing on her coat. 'It's really coming down out there.'

'Be careful on the ice.'

She paused. 'Was there something you wanted to tell me, earlier?'

He opened his mouth, then seemed to change his mind. 'You look tired. Tomorrow, if we get a chance.'

'OK. Night.'

As she crunched over the new-fallen snow in her boots, she knew with a certainty deep in her spine he was watching her, making sure she got to the door safe, but when she turned, his car was nothing but a ghostly set of lights receding into the pink-tinged dark.

★   ★   ★

'Dad?' She took off her coat and wiped her boots on the mat. 'I'm home.'

PJ was at the table, surrounded by official-looking papers, and seemed to jump slightly as she came into the kitchen. 'You're back late.'

'We had another case come in. What's up?'

'What's 'up'? This isn't America, Paula. Nothing is 'up'. I'm going through some papers is all.' Paula recognised the several small black notebooks PJ was now stuffing out of sight. He'd been looking through his old police notes. She knew he'd been doing this since he retired, going over past cases. Why, she hadn't asked. She wasn't sure she wanted to know.

'Why?' She rummaged in the bread bin and slotted some white sliced pan into the toaster. She'd been running all day on tea and office HobNobs.

'I might redo my will, I was thinking.'

'Why, see who gets custody of me?' She nibbled a corner of bread.

He looked irritated. 'Don't be putting crumbs all over the clean counter.'

Paula ignored him. She was thirty and pregnant by one of two possible men. Surely she had the right to make crumbs wherever she chose.

PJ was clearing away the papers and Paula caught a flash of green — her birth certificate. Paula Mary Maguire. Father, Patrick Joseph Maguire; mother, Margaret Catherine Maguire. Somewhere in there would be her parents' marriage certificate, back when her mother had still been Margaret Sheeran. No death certificate, of course — there'd never been a body to bury.

PJ stumped off towards the living room, the documents back in a taped-together manila envelope under his arm. 'That snow's lying. You may wear better shoes tomorrow, or you'll be sliding all over the show.'

She rolled her eyes, so hungry she took the toast upstairs, picking at it with her fingers instead of buttering it. In the cold little room where she'd spent all her teenage years, she turned on her laptop and called up the website of Magdalena Croft — psychic, visionary, and faith healer. The site contained a lot of interest about Mrs Croft, but nothing that made Paula feel better about the upcoming interview. The woman had been in Ballyterrin for a long time, it seemed, at least fifteen years, though she wasn't a native — her accent on the site videos was not Northern. As well as having visions, during which she claimed the Virgin Mary appeared to her, she also held faith rallies in the barn behind her house, where, in front of hundreds of people, she healed the sick, helped 'barren' women conceive, and could even 'drive out the demons that cause homosexual urges'. Paula couldn't believe the size of the crowds pictured on the site — a video showed the scale of it, Magdalena Croft too far away to even see her face, laying hands on a child in a wheelchair.

What interested Paula was the fact she seemed to have collected a lot of money from her followers to build a proper church behind her house, but five years on there was still no sign of it. There was also information on how to stay at the house for a 'healing' experience — for a lot of money — and a number you could call for phone or private psychic consultations. Paula was going to have to bite her tongue so hard it'd be hinged in the middle. Because there was no denying Croft was doing something. There were hundreds of testimonials on the site from happy customers.

Realising how late it was, she turned off the computer with a sigh and lay down, hoping that her mind and stomach would stop churning and let her sleep.

7

'It was very good of you to come in, Mrs Campbell. We didn't realise about your condition.'

Guy had Heather Campbell, Alison Bates's daughter, installed in the interview room, in the most comfortable chair the unit could muster — still not great. Heather had her mother's cool, unmoving face, and her hair, held up by a jewelled clip, was the same dark black the doctor's might have been before it turned iron. She was also heavily pregnant, and wearing a crucifix around her neck. Her expression was sour and unhappy, and the huge bulk of her stomach meant she couldn't get near enough to the table where her cup of tea rested. There'd been a moment of consternation when she'd asked for herbal tea — the unit tended to live off dark stewed Barry's — but Avril had come to the rescue with some sachets from her desk drawer.

Heather frowned. 'I'd rather come here than have you tramping all round my house.' After giving Paula a first, suspicious once-over, from her shoes to her untidy hair, she had refused to look either of them in the face.

'You live just outside Ballyterrin? How's the snow been?'

'Bad. Can we get on with this?'

'I'm sorry if we've kept you from work or anything.' Guy was trying his hardest with her,

67

but it wasn't being reciprocated.

'I'm on maternity leave.'

'I see. You're due soon, then?'

'After Christmas. I took some time off.' She looked at him. 'Look, it's snowing out there, and I'd like to get home to my husband. You better ask me those questions.'

'Of course. As I explained on the phone, your mother is currently missing — though we haven't yet put out an official report. Ms Cole thought you might have seen her.'

Heather scowled at Veronica's name. 'I don't know why she'd say that. I haven't spoken to my mother in months.'

'She knows about the baby?'

Heather was rubbing her stomach in slow, firm circles. The bulge of it under the maternity smock and layers of scarves and coats had Paula transfixed, as she sat quietly beside Guy. 'I went to see her when we found out. I told her I didn't want to see her any more. I mean, I don't talk to her much — the odd time maybe. But not after this.' She looked Guy straight in the eyes. 'She helps kill babies. She did it herself when she lived in London and she'd do it here if they let her. So why would she care that I actually want mine? It didn't mean a thing to her.'

'Was she upset when you told her?' asked Guy.

'How would I know? She never shows any emotion. She just said, 'Well, Heather, you're an adult; you can make your own choices.' *Choice.* It's all she ever talks about. I was upset — but Jim — that's my husband — and Daddy, they convinced me it was for the best. I don't need her.'

'How old were you when your parents divorced?' Paula asked, speaking for the first time.

'Fifteen.' Heather twisted her own wedding ring, which dug into her swollen finger. 'Daddy' was Roy Bates, one of Belfast's top cardiologists, Paula knew. A typical marriage of doctors, career equals — except it hadn't lasted.

'And was it acrimonious?' Guy took over again. 'Is it worth contacting your father?'

'Only if you've time to waste — they haven't talked since. Daddy hates me being in touch with her. He says she walked out on us. I mean — I understand, it happens, you fall in love — but how could she marry Daddy and then go off with a woman?'

'You don't get on with Ms Cole?'

'I've never met her. But it must have been her fault. They say they can't help what they are, the gays, but my mother, she loved Daddy before. She could have helped it. She's always on about choice — well the way I see it she made hers, and it was that kind of life over Daddy and me. Maybe she was making some kind of feminist point, I don't know. All I know is she left me.'

Guy let that one subside for a moment. 'So, Mrs Campbell, can you give us any idea where your mother might be, or who she'd go to?'

'No. She had no friends, just that woman.'

'You have an aunt, I think?' he persevered.

'On her side, you mean? Yes, Auntie Angela. She didn't talk to Mum, either, but we're in

69

touch a bit. Facebook, you know. I'll have to tell her Mum's missing. She lives in Norwich.'

'Heather,' said Guy gently. 'You realise that if your mother hasn't gone to a friend or relation, that could mean something has happened to her?'

It seemed to register. 'What kind of thing?'

'Well, perhaps she's been taken ill, or hurt somewhere, or — ' he stopped.

Heather was biting her lip. 'Those letters. She didn't tell me, but that — Veronica wrote to me about it. She was scared.'

'Did you write back?'

'No.' Heather grasped at the crucifix she wore around her neck, gold cutting white against red chapped skin. Suddenly she looked up. 'You know what she did to me, my mother? When I went to see her that day, where she works, she'd put me in the system as an appointment. Just like anyone who goes to her. Like I didn't even want my baby. Like I hadn't been trying for three years, and . . . Have you any idea how hurtful that was? Her own grandchild and she just sees it as . . . well. I couldn't believe she would do that. But that's her. That's the kind of person she is.'

Guy broke the awkward silence. 'Well, we're already looking for her, so just be on the alert, and do let us know if you hear anything at all.'

'Can I go?' Heather was pushing against the table with all her might. 'I want to go home to Jim.'

'Of course. Are you OK to drive, because — '

'Just let me go.' She pushed out, walking tired

70

and heavy, her shoulders softly heaving. Guy met Paula's eyes and subtly shook his head; they'd get nothing from her.

'I'll see you out, Mrs Campbell.' He followed her to the corridor and Paula began gathering her things.

'Tough one?' She jumped as Gerard opened the door into the room, eating a bag of bacon-flavoured crisps. 'Not sure we should be hauling in pregnant women for questioning. She looks about ready to pop.'

'She wanted to come in. Didn't fancy having your size twelves on her good carpet.'

Gerard harrumphed. But having spent an entire winter with police ripping through her own home, searching for any clues about her mother's fate, Paula understood Heather's impulse. 'Got something?' She'd seen the piece of paper in Gerard's greasy hand.

'I'm telling him first,' said Gerard stubbornly. 'Boss?'

'Yes?' Guy reappeared in the doorway, back from seeing Heather out.

'We've just found Dr Bates's car. Other side of the market near the clinic — so she most likely did head to work that day.'

Guy thought about this. 'But the clinic hadn't been opened when the receptionist arrived — so something happened to her in between parking and arriving there.'

'What does that mean?' Paula asked.

'We're going to have to officially declare her missing, I think.'

8

'Not a bad place she's got,' Gerard observed as
he powered the police Land Rover down the
country lane. It wasn't strictly necessary to drive
an armoured Jeep in these days of peace, but he
seemed to like it. He also liked playing Bon Jovi
at high volume in the car. It was disconcerting to
go to crime scenes with 'Shot Through the
Heart' ringing in your ears.

It was snowing again, and Paula watched
uneasily as the first soft flakes began to settle.
'She's loaded, by the sounds of it. Her
supporters give her all their dosh — usual story.'
Paula wasn't at all surprised at the large house
they were drawing up beside. Set outside
Ballyterrin in the countryside, it was the kind of
pillared and posted, overly large mansion that
proliferated in the borderlands. The smell of
money all about. The countryside around was
barren and beautiful, white as bone under the
fallen snow, green and wet where it had melted
over the day.

Gerard was shaking his head as he manoeuvred the car over a cattle grid towards a paved
courtyard at the back of the house, where several
other cars were parked. 'Can't believe the boss is
making us do this. Interview some mad old
biddy when we should be finding the doctor?'

'He's just trying to keep pace with your other
boss.' Paula undid her seat belt.

At the mention of Helen Corry, Gerard looked wary. 'You'd be wise not to try and take her on. She's a tough one.'

'What's her story, Corry?'

'Divorced. Some kids, I think. The guys moan about her — say it's no wonder her fella left when she's such a ball-breaker. But she's good. Expects a lot, but then she gives you a lot back. She's put me up for the DS exams next year, even though I'm only twenty-eight.'

'She's good all right. It's quite crafty, sending us here, when Croft sees a lot of women who want to get preg — ' Paula stopped. 'Oh no,' she groaned, seeing a battered red Clio parked in the courtyard. On the bonnet was perched a dark-haired man in ripped jeans and a grey AC/DC T-shirt. 'Oh for fuck's sake. Not him.'

Gerard wound down the window and growled at the man. 'What are you doing here, O'Hara?'

Aidan smiled widely. 'So you *are* meeting with the faith healer. Now there's a story.'

Paula got out, slammed her door shut. 'Let me guess — taxpayers' money wasted, unemployment levels high, why don't we close down all public services and make you Pope. I could write these stories for you, Aidan.'

His dark eyes were amused. 'I'd not be the best Pope, Maguire, as you would know.'

Bloody Aidan. She looked at her feet. Gerard glowered out the window of the car. 'You shouldn't be here. You nearly derailed our last investigation with your rag of a paper.'

'I'm hurt, DC Monaghan. The *Ballyterrin*

73

Gazette is the best paper in town. Well, it's the only paper, but still.'

Grunting in irritation, Gerard put up the window and turned off the engine. Aidan seemed unmoved by their attitude. 'What's up with your man — was he off sick the day of the 'good cop' training module or something?'

'Leave him be. He's right, you've no business being here.'

'Maybe I wanted to see you. Seems I caught a flash of red hair at the hospital the other day — avoiding me, are you?'

'If you wanted to talk I'm sure you knew where to find me for the past month, when you've not been in touch.'

He frowned; she'd got him. 'I was busy reopening the paper. You know it's got new investors — I was busy. And you weren't well anyway.'

'Neither were you.' She felt the ache in her temple where the gun had been pressed, the night she and Aidan had come face to face with a desperate man. They'd got through that ordeal alive — not everyone had — but it had left scars. 'Tell me this. How's the arm?'

Wrong-footed, Aidan blinked down at his shoulder, where the bullet wound was barely healed. Snow was settling in his eyelashes. 'It's all right. I'm supposed to do physio on it, but it'll be grand.'

She turned to approach the house. 'Then I suggest you get in your crappy car and fuck off out of here, or I'll have Gerard arrest you.'

'Maguire! You're so tough these days. What,

did you watch too much *Law and Order* when you were off sick?'

'I mean it. You need to leave right now.'

As she walked off she could hear Aidan's laughter in her ears. She forced herself not to look.

* * *

The door of the large white mansion was opened by a priest. That was a surprise. Paula's mind went blank.

Gerard stepped forward. 'Morning, Father. Is Mrs Croft in, please? We're from the MPRU.' He flashed his ID. Paula remembered and righted herself — this was the psychic's 'spiritual adviser', Father Brendan, a Catholic priest she'd convinced of her visions.

The priest was middle-aged, his head pink and bald as a baby's, small glasses slipping down his nose. 'Could you give your feet a wee wipe there,' he said, fussily moving the doormat. 'All that snow's so dirty when it melts.'

The house was expensively furnished — mahogany chairs, large ceramic vases — but with no sign of being lived in. There was an echoing feel, and a smell of new plaster. Rooms stretched off on either side of the corridor they walked down, and Paula had the impression of a large building around her. She knew people came to stay sometimes, trying to get cured of terminal illnesses, and often conveniently leaving all their money to Mrs Croft when it didn't work.

'She's praying,' the priest whispered, as he

opened the door to the sitting room. 'Don't disturb her.'

'You'd think she'd have been able to predict we were coming,' Paula muttered, once he was out of earshot. The woman in question was sitting forward on a blue-and-cream striped sofa, hands on her knees, lips muttering. She wasn't what Paula had expected at all. She couldn't have said what she *had* expected, but not a woman in her early fifties with grey hair plaited round her head, glasses on a jewelled string, and dressed in an acrylic jumper and slacks. She looked like somebody's auntie.

The door creaked as Gerard and Paula went in, and Magdalena Croft's eyes opened. She gave a little yawn, as if waking from a refreshing nap. 'The police?'

'The MPRU.' Gerard dipped his head respectfully. 'Ma'am.'

She put the glasses on and peered at them. 'You're very young, both of you.'

What to say to that? Sorry? Thanks? Paula sat down, struggling to get any purchase on the slippery cushions of the sofa. 'DCI Corry sent us to have a word with you, Mrs Croft, to see if you can help us find Alek Pachek.'

'Do you believe I can?' A direct stare.

'Erm — I don't know.' Gerard shot Paula a look when she confessed this, but the psychic looked pleased.

'An honest girl. It's Dr Maguire, is it? Over from England?'

'Yes. Paula. I grew up in Ballyterrin, though.'

'And what's your name, son?' She smiled at

76

Gerard, who seemed suddenly shy.

'DC Monaghan.' He paused. 'I mean, it's Gerard. Ma'am.'

'Well, Gerard, maybe you would pop out there to Father Brendan and ask for tea. I'd like a wee word with your colleague alone. It's the energy,' she explained. 'The Holy Virgin sometimes won't come to me if there's men around.'

Gerard took his large frame out, casting curious backwards glances. Paula and the psychic regarded each other. She'd expected to approach this interview as if assessing someone deluded, hallucinating, but now she had the distinct feeling she was being assessed herself. 'Um — I understand you're acquainted with Alek's family, and they asked for you to be brought in.'

'Poor young people. They came to me when she had trouble falling pregnant.' She indicated a small end table, which held a box of tissues, a crossword book, and a blue teddy. Paula knew where she'd seen that teddy before — in Alek's empty crib. The psychic's hand stroked the toy's soft ears. 'It helps if I have something they touched — not much choice for Alek, poor wean.' Her accent was hard to pin down, veering on different words between Irish and English and possibly American.

'And can you see anything?'

The psychic seemed amused. 'Not yet, Dr Maguire. I'm praying. I don't just ring the Holy Virgin up on the telephone, you know.'

'What do you do?' She met the woman's eyes, framed by the large glasses.

'I'm often asked this question. I say it's like standing with your back turned, and when you aren't expecting it someone comes up behind you and takes you in their arms. When I was a child I heard the Holy Mother speak — she said carry your cross, Magdalena, and go on the roads of Ireland. Bring my grace to everyone you see, and I will give you the gift of healing. And she did. You can talk to any number of people I've made well again.'

'I see.' Paula tried to keep her face neutral. 'Do you understand how it works — your gift?'

'It's a miracle. I'm not required to understand and neither are you.'

'Yeah. Mrs Croft — do you keep records of the women you see who want a baby?'

'Records?'

'Yes. You see, we think Alek was taken by someone who can't have their own child, and we wondered if they'd come to you.'

Magdalena smiled; it was strangely chilling. 'Dr Maguire. If you came to me for help in your darkest hour, would you like to think I'd pass your name on to the police?'

'No, but we are the police, and — '

Suddenly the woman got up and came over to Paula. She was wearing slippers over her tights. She sat down beside her and laid a cool, firm hand on Paula's forehead and another on her stomach, over the baggy jumper. Her hands felt very heavy. Paula froze against the sofa. Magdalena's eyes were closed. 'Yes. You have a very deep heart. Your mother — she's no longer with you?'

Paula was paralysed under the hand. 'That's one way of putting it.' She tried to hide the quiver in her voice. The whole town knew about Margaret Maguire's disappearance. It hardly required a psychic gift to recognise who Paula was. The hair was distinctive enough.

'You know, I could see her, maybe, if I had something of hers, something she touched — '

Paula jerked away. 'Please. *Stop it.*'

Mrs Croft withdrew. 'Enough. I can see right into you.'

'Good for you.' She was quaking.

'I don't think you really want to lose this baby, do you, Paula?'

'Alek? Of course not, that's why we're here. That's why I'm asking you these questions, so if you could help us and — '

'Not Alek.' The woman stood up. 'I mean the one in your belly.'

A rattle. The door opened, Gerard and the priest coming in with tea on a tray, slopping over on the floral pattern. Magdalena straightened up. 'We'll not need the tea after all, Brendan. Our guests won't be staying. I can't see anything for wee Alek, not yet. Let's pray the Virgin comes to me soon.'

Gerard gave a quizzical look at Paula, who was still shaking, dragging herself to her feet. He said, 'OK. Thanks for your time, Mrs Croft.'

Paula stopped at the door. Her voice was trembling as much as her hands. 'Alison Bates. Does that name mean anything to you?'

The woman's face was blank as water. 'I think everyone knows who Dr Bates is. Everyone who

79

follows God's way, that is.'

'What does that mean?'

'It means she's evil. That woman kills children. The people of Ballyterrin don't want her living among them, spreading her sin.'

'Have you ever met her? Have you seen her recently?'

'How would I ever meet a person like that?' Magdalena Croft stood there, her face placid and unreadable.

Gerard caught Paula's arm. 'Come on, Maguire, let's go. Thanks again, ma'am.'

★ ★ ★

'You OK?' Gerard looked at her curiously as he started the Jeep, wipers clearing a new fall of snow from the windscreen. A new car had arrived in the car park, inside it a young couple who seemed to be having a tearful row. More supplicants to Magdalena?

'Yeah. Just cold.'

Gerard fiddled with the heater, letting stale hot air spew in, and drove out to the road. 'You reckon there's anything to it, what she does?'

'Of course not. It's tricks is all — the same as what fortune tellers do.' That's all it was. It was easy to see a pregnancy, wasn't it, if you knew what to look for? Tess Brooking, Guy's wife, had guessed it nearly a month ago, with her midwifery expertise.

'I'd an aunt went to Croft once,' Gerard was saying. 'Auntie Louise. She was desperate for a wean — ten years married and nothing. This

Magdalena gave her some kind of powder to put on her tongue. From the Virgin Mary, she said. Load of crap.'

'And did she get pregnant?'

'Oh. Well, she did, actually. But you hear that a lot, don't you, when people believe it can happen.'

'Yeah. It's bollocks. She's just a fraudster, like Guy — Inspector Brooking says.'

Gerard glanced at her again. 'Why'd you ask that about Dr Bates? I thought we hadn't put out yet that she'd gone missing.'

'No. I know. But I remembered Croft mentioned her once, at one of her rallies or whatever they are. It was on YouTube. She basically denounced the doctor, said she was going to Hell.'

'So did a lot of people, though. She was hardly flavour of the month in town.'

'I know. Let's just go, OK?' Whether it was the cold or what had happened, Paula didn't stop shaking all the way back to Ballyterrin.

* * *

When they arrived at the unit, it was clear something was different — that familiar tang in the air, activity and fear.

She still had her coat on when Guy came out of the office. He wore a black sweater over his shirt and tie. 'Well?'

He was holding his phone.

'That was Corry. We're going to the town centre.'

'Why?'

'After you left, Magdalena Croft went into a trance. She's told them exactly where to find Alek.'

'And was she right?'

'That's what we're going to see.'

9

Ballyterrin was full of churches. Catholic, Methodist, Presbyterian — there was one on nearly every street, and the largest was the cathedral, a gloomy Gothic structure in the heart of town, among the charity shops and discount stores that passed for a retail hub in these post-recession times. By the time they reached it, it was snowing so hard the building was nothing but a shadowy bulk.

'You stay here,' said Guy, pulling on his coat.

'But — '

'I mean it, Paula. Tactical Support are still in. It could be dangerous. I'll send for you.' And he was gone, wrenching the door open in the gale, so the breath of snow blew her hair round her face.

Inside Guy's BMW was calm and warm, compared to the flurry of activity she could see up and down the steps of the building. Yellow coats flashed in the dark, obscured by a new veil of snow, falling like ashes in a nuclear winter and whirled against the car windows by a slicing wind. Tensed like a bow, Paula scrubbed at the patch of window to try to keep track of things. There was the cold blue light and thin wail of an ambulance illuminating the snow, and a rush of bodies. What was going on?

This was intolerable. Unable to stand the wait, she flung open the door, shielding her face against the onslaught of snow. The wind seemed to tear layers off her skin. At the door of the church, a bundled paramedic emerged with something pressed to their chest, and then sirens kicked up a howl as they raced to the ambulance. Was that Alek? Paula staggered up the steps of the cathedral, past several uniformed officers in huge jackets, unrecognisable beneath their layers. She shouted her name over the wind and hauled back the heavy door into the dark exterior. The sound dropped away.

In the dark, incense-scented aisle she stopped, suddenly afraid. What would she find? She'd been in all kinds of crime scenes, faced down sociopaths, even been taken hostage. But this. Babies. The soft warm place where the bones didn't meet. No way to protect yourself.

She made herself walk towards the altar, where they were rigging up huge lights that made her blink, black spots swimming. The pews and naves were busy with techs and police officers, surely the oddest congregation the place had ever seen. High-vis jackets struck an incongruous note against the old stone. There was Helen Corry, already directing everything with her own brand of ruthless authority. She wore a grey coat with a black fur collar, like Julie Christie in *Dr Zhivago*. 'Dr Maguire. We're hoping you can shed some light on this.' She looked up at the spot lamps. 'No joke intended.'

'Where was he?' She was scanning the altar — tabernacle, candles, advent wreath with one candle lit for the first Sunday in December. Over to the side, a nativity scene with waist-high

84

wooden figures of Mary and Joseph, plus assorted animal companions. It was charming in a primary-school way, and made Paula yearn for something she couldn't quite name. No baby.

'There.' Corry pointed. 'The blankets.'

'In the crib?'

In the manger, where the Jesus figurine would be placed come Christmas Day, was a pile of white cot blankets, soft waffle knit. The kind with silky edges. The kind you wrap babies up in.

'Taking the place of Our Lord himself,' said Corry drily. 'Apparently he's fine. A wee bit cold but basically OK. He wasn't here long, they say. The priest only left an hour back.'

'He was exactly where she said,' Guy said, his hands in the pockets of his long black coat. The snow in his hair made him look older, distinguished.

'Um — ' Paula tried to focus. 'So putting him in the manger, that could be one of two things. Either thumbing the nose at the police — a mockery sort of thing. Or some kind of delusion. And if he was well treated — '

'Yes,' said Corry. 'The paramedics said the baby clothes were fresh, and he'd been given a bath. Nappy new on — also, he didn't have those blankets when he was taken. Someone's been looking after him.'

'So that doesn't really fit.' Paula circled the altar, trying to get a sense of it. It was very cold inside the church, icy. breezes catching you at odd angles, the spire vanishing up into gloom. The faces of the statues shrouded in darkness, the rack of devotional candles guttering in the draught, casting shadows that moved and wavered. She hugged her arms to herself over her coat. 'Giving the baby back is very unusual. What you'd expect in this kind of case is you'd either hear nothing again — the child would grow up in a new family, or perhaps die, since this kind of abductor often doesn't know how to care for them. Or else they'd be found through police work. But to voluntarily return him — ' She shook her head. 'They don't do that.'

'I'm glad we bother making all those appeals asking them to then,' said Corry. 'Anything else?'

She was thinking. 'Why a church? I mean, they needed somewhere safe and anonymous — back at the hospital would be the most obvious. It's cold in here and there's not much chance he'd be found by casual visitors.'

'Is it left open all the time?' Guy had a Londoner's instinct for security.

'Churches are supposed to be open at all times, Inspector. To offer a place for prayer.' From Corry's delivery, it was impossible to tell if she believed this herself.

'Sanctuary,' Paula murmured, thinking aloud. 'Maybe it's somewhere she feels safe. The abductor.'

'*She*.'' Guy stressed. 'You're sure?'

'Fairly. We had the CCTV too.'

'It's a woman,' said Corry confidently.

'How do you know?' demanded Guy.

'The nappy. How many men would have known to do that?'

Paula couldn't help it. She let out a short, startled laugh and covered her mouth. Guy's

86

frown deepened. 'Some of us have changed plenty of them, Chief Inspector. Anyway, what can the unit help with?'

Corry said, 'We're still doing interviews with hospital staff — so far no one remembers a thing. We had a sketch artist in with Damian Pachek, but same story there. It was so busy, anyone could have been through the place that day.'

Guy said, 'Dr Maguire had some thoughts on interview techniques.'

'Good.' Corry nodded. 'Have you anything to add to the offender profile, Doctor?'

Paula said, 'I'd like to go over the literature further. There's a lot of research on infant abduction and it might give us some idea where to focus inquiries.'

'That's what I like to hear.'

Paula had a terrible urge to please Helen Corry, like a strict schoolteacher. 'I think — ' she hesitated. 'The thing is, and we need to be aware of this — this person, they will have wanted a child. Unless possibly it was done for revenge, to hurt the family, but that seems so unlikely.'

'They had no enemies, the father said, and I don't buy this sectarian motive that's been floated.'

'So this person desperately wants a baby, enough to walk in and take one — but now, for whatever reason, they don't have him any more. You see what I mean?'

'I see.' Corry's mouth twisted. 'It's going to happen again.'

10

'Saoirse?' After another late night tying up ends on the Pachek case, Paula was back working at her desk the next morning. She was looking for other cases of abducted babies when the phone rang, her friend's voice on the end. 'What's up?'

Saoirse said, 'Don't be cross. I've made you an appointment for today. They had a slot.'

She genuinely didn't get it for a moment. 'An appointment for what?'

Saoirse sighed. '*Paula*. Antenatal, of course.'

Paula felt as if the front half of her body was trying to run away from the back. 'Oh, I can't. We're really swamped here, we just found Alek Pachek, and — '

Corry's face hadn't been off the news since Alek had been found safe and well the night before — she was taking all the credit, and as Guy hadn't even wanted to call in the psychic in the first place, the unit hadn't come off well. Paula was up to her eyes in research on child abduction and the phone was ringing off the hook with worried parents, wondering if the baby-snatcher might strike again, and journalists looking for a quote from a 'child abduction expert'. She was not keen on that label. It sounded as if she gave lessons.

'You're going.' Saoirse was stern. 'No arguments.'

'But I'm not ready. I don't know what to do

88

yet.' Paula could hear the panic in her own voice. 'There isn't time!'

Saoirse spoke patiently, as if to a small child. 'There isn't time not to. It's not going away. Either way, you have to see someone. So just go, and tell them the situation. If you're going to have this baby you need taking care of.'

'And what if I'm not?'

'Then at least you'll have all the information.' Saoirse was always such a know-it-all. 'I can't . . . Will you come with me?'

A small pause. Was it too much to ask? 'Call in and see me first. You'll be grand.'

★ ★ ★

'Seersh?' Paula rapped on the door of the office and after a short delay, it was opened, not by her friend, but by Dave, Saoirse's husband of five years. Six foot three and almost as wide. She stumbled over the words. 'Oh, hiya. I didn't — I was looking for Saoirse.'

'She's here. I'm just going, myself. Come in, Paula.'

She went in but stayed leaning against the door. With no experience of anything approximating a long-term relationship, she didn't know how much Saoirse would have told Dave about her 'situation'. 'Erm — I'm just after a wee word with Saoirse. About a case.' She caught her friend's eye and Saoirse's infinitesimal head-shake told her Dave didn't know. She was relieved. One less person then.

Dave was putting on his coat, a navy one with

reflective shoulder patches. 'OK so. Nice to see you. If you're talking to Aidan, tell him I'm up for that jar, any night but Thursday.'

'We're . . . not really talking.'

Dave looked embarrassed. He obviously hadn't yet learned, as Saoirse had, to steer well away from the deep channels that ran between Paula and Aidan. 'He's busy, I'd say, with the paper and all that.'

'Sure.'

Dave turned back to his wife, cupping her face in two big hands. 'You're OK, love?'

'I will be.'

Paula looked away as they kissed, feeling like an intruder. When he went out Saoirse spun round in her chair. 'So, no luck with the Pachek case?'

'Nope. I mean it's great we found him, but we still need to catch the person. The staff interviews have thrown up nothing, and we've no prints or traffic data, nothing useful at all. Looks like no one saw anything. And this doctor's missing as well.' Dr Bates had been officially announced as missing that morning, once the good news about Alek Pachek's recovery had everyone busy. Corry always had an eye for the press and whether or not they'd show her department up as incompetent.

Saoirse took off her glasses and rubbed her eyes. 'That's bad. I mean, she wasn't much liked in town, but the idea someone would actually hurt her — it scares me, when people start going after doctors.'

'We might find her safe. You never know.'

90

'Hmm. Did you go to see that psychic?'

'Croft? Yeah, I did. She's . . . I can't describe it. But I'm not surprised she can persuade people that her healing works.'

'Are you so sure it doesn't?' Saoirse turned to her computer.

'You don't believe in it, surely?'

Saoirse shrugged. 'Mammy went to a fortune teller before she met Daddy. The woman told her Daddy's name, his job, and that he'd be the oldest child of six — all true.'

'You think it's possible to be psychic then?'

'I don't think we understand how everything works yet.'

Paula tried to hide her frustration. 'But you've got medical training — how do you explain these so-called miracles she does?'

'The body and mind are linked. Like I say, I don't think we understand it all. A few centuries ago you'd have said most science was magic too.'

'But what if people refuse medical care and just rely on her tricks? They'd die, wouldn't they? I looked her up, Seersh. She's taken a lot of money off dying people, convinced them to stop their treatments. Did you know she went to America a few years back, collecting donations to build her own church? It's still hardly even been started. So where's the money? And all these people wanting babies, going to her, paying good money. It's just . . . I hate to think of people being ripped off by her.'

But Saoirse was unmoved by this. A stubborn, secretive look came over her face; Paula recognised it well from school when her

91

friend was in a mood about an unjust teacher or who sat with whom at lunchtime. 'Sometimes there's nothing we can do for people anyway. I don't think it's up to us to tell people how to feel.'

Paula sighed. 'All right. Listen. I have to go anyway.' As she moved to the door her friend was hunched over the computer, and Paula wondered how it could be that someone you'd once known inside out could become a total stranger. She could feel it between them, the knowledge that her friend had been trying for five years to get pregnant, and the tests they were having clearly weren't going well. 'Listen, Seersh, I know it's not — thank you for helping me with all this. I . . . '

'Ah, go on, you'll be late.' Saoirse turned back to her computer, mouth lifting slightly at the old nickname.

★   ★   ★

Babies. They were everywhere. Missing babies, found babies, and in the waiting room of Ballyterrin General Hospital Obs and Gynae unit, so many babies you were practically falling over them. Toddlers running round, newborns howling, and at each turn the swollen bellies of expectant mothers. Paula kept patting her own surreptitiously under her jumper, to see if it had done the same. It felt tight and hard, but still flat enough. She tried to read the report she'd brought with her, on an infant abduction from an English hospital, but it seemed so inappropriate in this place that she could barely concentrate.

'Paula?'

At first she thought they were calling her, and hurriedly dropped her jumper, but then she was confused at the sight of Fiacra Quinn's smiling, cherubic face. 'You're here?' she said, startled. He was off duty, she saw now, in jeans and a Gaelic football jersey; he looked like a teenager.

'I'm bringing my sister.' He indicated a young woman behind him, equally fair and angelic. She was also visibly pregnant. 'Aisling, this is Paula out of my work.'

Aisling plonked herself beside Paula, who quickly hid her reading material. 'How are you, Paula? He never shuts up about that unit. Loves it, so he does.'

'I never said — '

'Fiacra, go and get me a jukebox, will you?'

He went, the easy obedience of a boy with four sisters.

Aisling made herself comfortable. 'What brings you in, Paula?'

'Um — just a check-up.' It was a gynaecology unit too, so she hoped that would cover it. Was it not a bit rude to ask someone what they were in for, in a hospital? People in this town couldn't seem to keep their noses in their own business.

'Right so. Tell me this now. Our Fiacra does be awful secretive about his love life. Who's this Avril he's always on about?'

'Avril? She's our intelligence analyst. They're just friends, aren't they? I think she has a boyfriend.' As far as Paula knew, Avril was

93

romantically involved in some way with the pastor of her church, a whey-faced youth called Alan whose picture adorned her desk at the unit.

Aisling was agog. 'Oh really? That can't be it then. He must have a girl, Mammy says. We do be drowning in the smell of his Lynx every morning.' She gave Paula a speculative look, as if preparing to transfer her suspicions to the only other woman in the unit.

'I don't know.' Paula cast about for a change of subject. 'How far along are you?'

'Seven months. I'm scared to death,' she said frankly. 'Do you ever watch that show, that *One Born Every Minute?* The noises they make on it. Jaysus!'

'Oh. Well, it's nice of Fiacra to bring you.'

'I'm staying with him.' She rubbed her bump. 'The peelers gave him a flat in town, so if I stay with him I can come here instead of the hospitals down south — it's much better in the north, between you and me. He's been good to me, since this one's da fecked off.' She indicated her stomach.

'Oh?'

'Aye, he went back to Nigeria before they kicked him out. We could have got married, I said, for his visa, but he'd a roving eye. Mammy said so and she's always right.' Aisling Quinn said all this with the same cheerful expression on her pink and white face, gold curls rippling down her back. She was clearly one of those people who'd never been taught how your secrets could be used against you.

Paula wasn't sure what to say to all that, but

luckily at that point the nurse with the clipboard called her name, in a bored way. She gathered her papers. 'That's me, anyway. Nice to meet you, Aisling.'

Soon she was left spread-eagled on the edge of a medical couch, awaiting the midwife. She'd been instructed by the nurse to remove her boots, jeans, and pants, and lie back with the blue tissue paper over her. It was about the most vulnerable position she could imagine, so she already felt far from her best when the curtains swished open and Guy's wife stood there.

Paula sat upright, holding the pathetically thin tissue paper round herself. 'Oh my God!'

Tess Brooking was staring at her with the dark suspicious eyes that had seen right through Paula on their first meeting, a month before. Dressed in blue scrubs, her curly hair was tucked up in a bun. She looked from Paula to the clipboard she was carrying, and blinked slowly. 'P. Maguire. I should have realised.' Tess's reaction was odd. She began to laugh softly. 'So I was right. You are pregnant after all.'

Paula's heart was pounding. 'Looks that way.'

'And you're going ahead with it?'

'I — I don't know. What are you — why are you in Ballyterrin?' Last time she'd seen Tess it was in West London, where as far as Paula knew she'd gone back to live, without Guy.

Tess folded her arms, leaning against the desk as if trying to protect herself from Paula's mere presence. 'I had a job offer here, and Katie needed to go back to school. It seemed like the right thing to do. I take it he didn't tell you.'

Katie was her daughter — Guy's daughter — who'd run away from home the previous month.

Paula hugged her knees. 'No. No, he didn't.' He'd chickened out, clearly. Guy, whose bravery she'd always so admired.

'Well.' Tess tapped her pen on the clipboard. 'This is a problem, isn't it?'

Paula wasn't sure what she meant. Whatever way you looked at it, it was a problem.

'I can't be your midwife. You know that, don't you? You wouldn't want me anyway.'

She didn't even know if she'd need a midwife, but events seemed to be thundering on ahead while she stood in the wake, waving weakly. 'I just — I can't believe he didn't tell me.'

Tess laughed again, short and sharp. 'You haven't told him yet either, have you?' She indicated Paula's supine position.

'I'm not sure what I'm doing yet. And I told you, there was someone else at the same time.' Aidan bloody O'Hara. If only she could be sure which man it was.

Tess clasped her arms tight over the clipboard. 'Look, Paula. I know you didn't mean to get yourself in this situation, but you are in it. And as for Guy — we've had our ups and downs, but I won't let you hurt him.' That was a bit rich coming from the woman who'd tried to divorce him in the middle of their grief for their dead son, but whatever. As if reading her mind, Tess said, 'What happened with Jamie, it really broke him. And here you are, maybe carrying his child — have you any idea what that would do to him?'

Paula just sat, horrified to feel tears prick at her eyes at the thought of Guy's son, who'd been killed in London earlier that year, accidentally shot by gang members intending to frighten his policeman father. 'I just don't know how it happened.' Her voice hitched. 'I don't know how I ended up like this.'

'I'll draw you a diagram if you like,' said Tess frostily. But then something softened in her face and she sighed. 'Look, I can see you need help. Let me get someone else to talk to you.'

She picked up a phone on the desk. 'Is Bernice back off leave? Right, can you send her to consulting room three?'

It was only a minute or two until the door opened, but the tension between her and Tess seemed to snap and bite like stretched elastic bands. Tess fiddled with some papers on the desk; Paula read a poster about the stages of pregnancy, the baby swelling in the hollow inside, the pulsing blues and reds of the veins. She opened her mouth to say something — maybe try to explain she'd only slept with Guy because she thought he was getting divorced, because of the terrible pressure they'd been under, having just pulled a girl's body from the canal — but then the door handle turned and another midwife came in, tall and smiling, black hair greying at the temples.

'Bernice.' The relief in Tess's voice was palpable. 'This is Ms Maguire. We just realised we know each other, so if you could take her on instead, that would be great.'

'Of course, of course. Now isn't that a coincidence, you knowing each other?'

'We met in London,' Paula said, clearing her throat. It was, strictly speaking, the truth.

'Thanks, Bernice.' Tess made for the door, throwing a backwards glance at Paula. It very clearly said: *watch your step*.

The new midwife was doing things with a machine and lots of cables. 'Now, let's get you sorted.' She produced a white plastic probe. 'Lift the wee sheet up for me, pet.' The gel on Paula's stomach was cold and the pressure firmer than she'd expected. She tried to breathe. Bernice turned the probe, staring at the screen. 'You want to see the baby?'

'Er . . . ' Once again she was paralysed. From her vulnerable position, Paula found herself nodding at the ceiling. Even though she knew this was some irrevocable moment, some Rubicon being crossed.

It looked like nothing. A black and white scribble on an abstract painting. 'Oh, I see. Thanks.' She saw nothing. The machine hummed gently.

'There you go. It all looks good, Paula. Good size and heartbeat. You're about seven weeks along, I'd say.'

Seven. Not six or eight. Her mind tried to do the maths and collapsed in on itself. She thought of what the faith healer had said. 'Can you — is it possible to see the gender?' Why was she asking?

'It's a wee bit early for that. A few weeks on and we might know.'

'OK.'

'Congratulations, Paula. Is Daddy not here today?'

'The thing is . . . ' Paula rearranged the paper covering her in a pathetic attempt to gain some dignity. 'I'm not sure who the father is.'

'Oh?' The woman was clearly trying to keep her face neutral, but Paula had seen the look that flashed over it. She decided it was best to press on.

'And also — I don't know what I'm doing yet. If I'm keeping it. I'm sorry. I just didn't know where to come. I don't know what to do.'

There was a very short pause. 'All right. We can't do anything for you here, of course. It's illegal, as I'm sure you're aware. But it's your choice.'

'But I just don't know!' She thought she might start crying again. 'I can't think.' This was what she'd been afraid of, why she hadn't wanted to come to hospital. If there was one thing which united Catholic and Protestant in Ireland, it was a firm hatred of abortion. 'I didn't mean this to happen. It was an accident. I — I'm sorry.'

'Come on now.' The midwife was helping her sit up, handing her a tissue with gloved hands. 'You're not the first, Paula, and you won't be the last. You're a smart girl, aren't you? And I bet you've a good job?'

She nodded, sniffing.

'Have you family in the town?'

'Yeah.' PJ. Pat, she was practically family. And by extension, Aidan? Her fists clenched at the thought of him.

99

'Well, then, you'll be fine either way. Have you talked to the daddy, I mean, to whoever it might be?'

'It's one of two people.' It was a relief to finally talk about it, in the anonymous clean of the room. She imagined this happening in London, how no one would bat an eyelid, probably book you in for an abortion that same day. But here — the idea of having to fly to England, stay in a hotel somewhere, sore and bleeding — she shrank from it. 'You see, there were two people right next to each other, and I used, ah, contraception, but I just don't know how . . . I don't know.'

Bernice patted her shoulder. 'Listen now. Here's what we'll do. We'll make a follow-up appointment, and I'll also give you the details of the counsellor. She'll be able to help you think through the decision.'

'Thank you.' Up close, the midwife's face was tired and paunchy, her skin stretched oddly over the bones of her face. But Paula could have hugged her, it was such a relief to unburden herself. The ties of family, home, community — they bound you tight and kept you safe, but they were almost impossible to sever. And she, having done it once and walked away without a backward glance, had let herself almost effortlessly get tied up again.

11

She made it back to the unit as the afternoon briefing was starting. Guy gave her a very quick glance and then a flick of his eyes to the clock. She had to sit on her anger to stop it spilling out.

He launched right into it. 'As you know, Alek Pachek was found safe and well yesterday evening. A great result; however, we can't stop there. Serious Crime will be trying to find the abductor, and fast. Paula thinks there's a strong chance they will do it again.' When he said her name, she gritted her teeth. 'We'll provide assistance as needed. However, our main case is now Dr Alison Bates.' He clicked the pointer and the wall lit up, Dr Bates appearing cold and austere in her lab coat. 'She's been missing for two days only, but I'm very worried about this one, as she's been receiving death threats for several months.' This was Guy in business mood, not the broken man who'd laid his head in Paula's lap the night they'd slept together, when all this mess had started. 'Avril, if you could pull any old threats to family planning providers. That should lead us to some likely groups. Oh, and as we're still looking for Alek's abductor, Corry would like us to put a rush on digging out those cases of child abduction or attempted child abduction.'

Avril was typing. 'I started this, but there's a

lot. Can we add age limits?'

Guy looked at her. 'Paula? That's more your area.'

'Five or under, I'd say. Most likely under two, but you never know for sure.' She risked a look back at Guy. 'What am I doing?'

'Corry wants a fuller profile of the abductor. I think she's imagining you can tell what music they listen to and if they like cabbage or not. I'd also like a risk assessment on Alison Bates, if she went off of her own accord, what could have triggered this, that sort of thing. Where would she go? One angle of interest is her missing laptop with all the patient records. It's entirely possible someone made a fictitious appointment to see her, and then attacked her outside her office.'

Paula made notes on her pad, trying not to betray her worry that they'd find out exactly why she'd been there herself that day.

'And I also want us checking out this faith healer further. Officially she's a police consultant, but she gave us the exact place we'd find Alek. I for one find that suspicious.'

Gerard said, 'It was maybe a lucky guess, boss. Somewhere quiet, indoors . . . you know.'

'Mm. I go for Occam's Razor, myself. If she knew for certain, she must be involved somehow.'

Gerard raised his eyebrows at Paula over the table. Questioning Corry's expert? This was a new development. 'We can't take her in, boss, surely.'

'Not yet. Let's look into her — we should get

102

Fiacra on that, she's mostly been in the South, I gather. Where is he?'

'He'd something to do with his family,' said Avril, in a tone that implied chummy secrets.

'You make a start then. Find out everything you can about her — was she really married? If so, what was her maiden name? What did she do before the healing work?'

Paula asked, 'Is there no forensic evidence from the Pachek scene — either scene?'

Guy shook his head. 'No prints were lifted, no fibres, no foot impressions. This person leaves no trace. And the blankets were generic, available in five different outlets in the town.'

'So nothing.'

'Nothing. But let's be clear that the Bates case is ours to coordinate — we can direct and call upon the resources of the local station, but we're in charge. That's it, everyone. Off you go.'

Gerard muttered, 'Musta got stung on that baby case.' A stand-off between Corry and Guy would leave him in an awkward situation, as technically he was employed by the station and not the unit.

Everyone was getting up, shuffling their papers. Bob shrugged into his suit jacket. 'I'll give you a lift up to the station, DC Monaghan.'

Gerard hesitated. Bob had a Skoda and drove it as if leading a funeral cortège. 'Thank you. I'll get my bag, sir.'

Guy was tidying up his papers. He looked up inquiringly at Paula as the others left. 'You OK? You've had a few appointments and things recently, I see.'

103

She took a deep breath. 'Why didn't you tell me Tess was back?'

He continued to tidy, movements gradually slowing down. 'I was going to. You saw her, then.'

'We bumped into each other.' Paula could hear how bitter she sounded, suddenly full of rage that they'd both been stupid and drunk, but it was her who had to encounter his wife with only a piece of tissue paper covering her bits.

'I'm sorry. I meant to tell you before that happened.'

'What does it mean, Guy?'

'Well, Tess felt Katie needed both parents with her at the moment. She's here for now, but she and I — I don't know what will happen. It's . . . ' He was struggling. 'It's difficult. She just arrived back.'

'I see.' She didn't.

'We never did get to talk properly, did we? After everything. I thought there'd be some down time, but then there was the Pachek case, and now this doctor is missing too, everything was just so busy. And you were recovering — I didn't want to burden you with my problems.'

'You should have told me.'

'Yes. I tried. There wasn't a good time.'

She said nothing for a moment. 'There'll never be a good time, will there?' She was asking something more than this and they both knew it.

He ran his hands through his hair. 'I don't know. It's just — the timing. Everything that's happened . . . '

'And you and me?'

His face twisted. 'I don't know. She came

104

back. What can I do?'

'Right.' She got up. Her legs were suddenly wobbly. 'I hope — I really hope things work out for you. For Katie's sake, as well.' She was moving to the door when Gerard burst through it, his coat on.

'Boss — there's been another one. Corry wants you two out now.'

Guy didn't get it. 'Another what?'

'Another baby's gone missing.'

12

Both Caroline Williams and her husband were wearing his 'n' her Ugg boots in their detached three-bedroom new-build house. The husband, Shane Williams, had his planted on the floor, elbows on his knees as he sobbed. 'We only had her a few months! How could someone just take her?' The noises he made were loud and spluttering.

By contrast, Caroline could not sit down or stop moving. Grey tracksuit bottoms pushed into her own Uggs, she paced up and down, tearing at her nails, which had been bitten to the quick. 'You took ages to get here! What's the point of ringing if you can't even help us?'

'We came as soon as we could, Mrs Williams. Now, what can you tell us about Darcy, please?' Guy spoke calmly, but Paula knew him well enough to realise he was not feeling it. 'It's important we start looking as soon as possible.'

'I saw on the news some woman was taking babies. I think she came and took our Darcy too. Darcy's gone.' Shock seemed to bloom in her voice. She began to shake, wrapping her arms round herself. 'She's gone.'

Shane Williams choked. 'God, you have to find her, please, sir, miss, please! Ma'am, I mean. *Please.*'

Paula was oddly touched by the ma'am. 'We're going to try, but you need to tell us everything that happened. As quickly as you can, please. Were you here, sir?'

He said, 'I went into work — I mean, I'd like to be here more with Car and — and Darcy, but you know how it is. I have to work.'

'What's your job?'

'Insurance.' Caroline answered for him, tearing at her ragged cuticles. 'He's in insurance. Two days, they gave him off, when she was born. Two bloody days.'

'She's three months old?' Paula was very carefully using the present tense, as they always did until they knew differently.

'Three months, ten days, four hours,' said Caroline, resuming her pacing.

Paula transferred her attention to the wife. Bleached hair, polished nails. One of them had snapped and it was this she was worrying at with her teeth. 'Can you tell us what happened to Darcy then, Mrs Williams?'

Muttered. 'Don't you say her name.'

'I'm sorry?' Paula glanced at Guy.

'What right have you to say her name, when you never even met her? No one met her. No one will now.' Her voice was dry and savage.

Paula kept hers equable. 'I'm sorry. If you just tell me what happened, then.'

'I was putting the washing out.' Caroline indicated the neat lawn beyond the French windows of their semi. In the early-evening gloom they could see shrubs in boxes, B&Q decking, a barbecue with a coating of snow. Further back in the narrow lane, Corry's officers had rigged up lights to search the bushes; dark

107

shapes moving. Paula craned her neck but could see no sign of washing on the line. Caroline was saying, 'I had her in her pram, and the phone went, so I just — I went in to get it and when I came back she'd gone.'

Shane convulsed in tears again. Paula spoke carefully. 'I just need to picture it, if I can, Caroline. You put the washing out in the snow?'

'I needed to air it! I was going to take it in. There's bloody — look, there's no space.' She waved her hands. True enough, every radiator in the room was draped in drying baby clothes, the air close and damp.

'OK. And someone came into the garden?'

'Well, they must have, yeah? She can hardly hold her head up, never mind get out and walk! For God's sake.'

'OK . . . so you think someone came over the fence?'

'There's a gate out to the back lane.'

'And where does that lead?'

'Out to the main road. I told him!' She turned on her husband. 'I told him it wasn't safe, me and her on our own all day. Anyone could come in and get us. But he was too busy to put on the gate lock. He's always too busy.'

Shane Williams just shook his head, face buried in his hands. Paula saw his wedding ring turned to her. 'Was the gate open then, when you went back out again, Caroline? Had the person left it open?'

'I don't know. Yeah. Probably.'

'And were there footprints?'

'What?' Caroline stared at her.

108

'In the snow. The snow's still lying out there, isn't it?'

Caroline said nothing for a moment, eyes blazing at Paula. 'You think I noticed wee things like that? *My baby was taken.* Some madwoman's stealing babies, and she's got my Darcy. I want to know what you're gonna do about it.' Her finger stabbed the air. 'That baby in the hospital, you looked everywhere for him. All over the news it's been. Some Polish family, coming over here and taking our jobs. Well, we're just local people, born and bred, so will you do the same for us?'

Paula passed the floor to Guy with an undetectable shrug. He got it. 'Of course we will, Mrs Williams. Dr Maguire is right, though. If there are any footprints we can take imprints, do gait analysis.'

'The gate?' Shane was confused.

'Er . . . the way the person walked, I mean. Have you touched anything in the garden since?'

Shane shook his head. 'We called yous right away. Car rang me in a state and I came home, then we phoned you. I mean, we walked on it ourselves — we looked everywhere for her. Was that not right?'

Guy said, 'It's OK. Now here's what will happen. Search teams are going to seal off the lane and comb it for clues at first light tomorrow. I'm afraid the roads are still quite bad, and it may snow again later, so that slows us up. We'll also interview all your neighbours and put out appeals for anyone who could have been driving on the main road earlier today.'

Caroline looked up. 'Will you do one of those reconstruction things, like on telly?'

'Possibly. I need you to tell us what Darcy was wearing, please, and if you have a picture of her, we'd like that too.'

'There's loads of photos,' Caroline said, sucking her nail. 'He's never stopped snapping that phone at her since she was born.'

'So what did she have on?'

Afterwards, Paula thought that Caroline hesitated for a second. Shane jumped in. 'She'd her wee pink tights on in the morning. Her grey dress with the kittens. Did you put her coat on, love, when — '

'Of course I put her coat on. It's freezing, isn't it? She'd her purple dress on, her woolly yellow tights, and stripy mittens. And blue buckle shoes. OK? I had to change her when you went to work. She boked up her lunch. She always bokes.'

'She has this condition, they said,' Shane tried to explain. 'Reflux or something. They said she might need an operation — Caroline couldn't breastfeed her, see — '

'I don't think they want to hear that, Shane. Anyway, she had on yellow tights and a purple dress. And her coat and hat and that. OK?'

Guy was writing. 'Thank you. We'll get an appeal out as soon as we can. And perhaps if we need to, in a few days, you would consider doing a press conference, both of you? They can be quite effective — Alek Pachek was returned after we held one.'

'You wouldn't make Car do that, would you?'

110

said Shane anxiously. 'She's not fit.'

'I am too fit,' she said agitatedly. 'I'd do anything to bring Darcy back. Anything.'

Paula wouldn't leave it. 'So you didn't see anyone in the lane, or out the window, when you went to answer the phone — where's it kept?'

Caroline pointed. A cordless phone on its cradle, it was beside the fridge, which had a clear view of the garden and back fence. 'It was in the living room,' Caroline said, catching Paula's look. 'He never puts it back on the hook. I had to go into the living room to get it.'

The living room, attractively decorated in purple wallpaper and scatter cushions, looked out on the road, the wrong direction for the back garden. Caroline glared at Paula. 'I know what you're thinking — why did I leave her? But it was only a minute. Less than a minute, and no one was there, and we were waiting on the bank ringing, we need to talk to them, and I just went in. It only takes two seconds, when there's mad people about.'

'Of course,' Guy said. 'No one is suggesting anything, Mrs Williams. Now, I'm afraid we may need to get in here, search the house.'

Caroline jerked. 'What? She went from the *garden*. You're not even listening to me.'

'We are, Mrs Williams. It's just standard procedure. Forensics.' Guy made a 'stupid me' gesture. 'Who knows what they get up to?'

'I don't want people walking snow through the house.'

'We'll be very careful.'

'But — '

'It's OK, Car.' Her husband fumbled for her hand. 'We'll go to Mam's. You won't have to watch. They won't wreck her things.'

Caroline's hand lay dead in his. 'I got her nursery all nice.'

'That's right. You have it lovely. Darcy loves it, doesn't she?' He chafed her hand in his, tears glinting. 'We'll get her back, love. They'll find her. They found the other baby, they'll find her too.'

Caroline would not be comforted. 'You didn't catch the person who did it.'

'No,' admitted Guy. 'But, Mrs Williams, there's no proof yet that this is even the same person, you know.'

'It must be!' she snapped. 'Who else could it be?'

'One last thing,' Paula asked. 'You didn't notice anyone trying to befriend you, maybe, while you were pregnant, or at the hospital? Or did you go to any childcare groups?'

'The Little Monkeys group.' Shane grasped at it. 'You didn't like it there, did you?'

'No.' Caroline went back to chewing her ruined nails.

'Was that why you never went back, was someone funny to you, or — '

'No! For Christ's sake. I just didn't have time. I've got a wee baby to mind and the house to run and I'm working nights in the nursing home. I don't know how all these mums get the time to run about to baby groups.'

'Little Monkeys, you said?' Guy made a note.

112

'Where was that based?'

'In the family centre, wasn't it, love?' Shane again. 'You think maybe that's it, someone from there, or — '

'We don't know, but we'll look into every angle, as we said.' Guy shut his notebook. 'Thank you very much. We'll be leaving a liaison officer with you to keep you updated on everything we do.'

Caroline pointed at them, shaky. 'You two. Have you any children?'

They exchanged a quick glance. Paula's stomach turned over. Guy said, 'I do, yes. A daughter.'

She knew what it cost him to say he had only one child. Caroline looked at Paula and she did a blank shake of the head. 'Well, you can't imagine it,' Caroline was saying. 'You can't imagine what I'm feeling right now.' *I*, she said, not *we*.

'I'm very sorry,' said Guy. 'Would we be able to have a quick look round the house, please?'

Caroline looked as if she might say no, but Shane was already on his feet. Everything in the house was new, stylish, the kitchen painfully clean but with red-marked bills pinned to the fridge with magnets in the shape of fruit — bananas, apples. The bathroom, conversely, was sticky with soap and grime, a child's plastic bath floating in several inches of dirty water, yellow ducks with innocent smiling beaks. This was where Darcy should have been, or safe in her nursery, which was upholstered in various shades of pink. Over her empty crib hung a mobile of floating fairies. It was too sad to look at it and

113

Paula went back to the kitchen as soon as she could.

After saying goodbye and giving assurances that everything possible would be done, Guy and Paula went out into the car and shut the door against the cold. There was no sign of Corry, but the front lawn was already churned up by officers and techs, blinding lights shining out from the police vans that blocked the small cul-de-sac. Paula imagined Caroline Williams staring at them through the mullioned windows.

'Christ. What a thing to cope with,' Guy said, clearing the windscreen with a chamois leather sponge. A fresh light coating of snow had started to drift down. 'She was in such a state.'

'I'd say she had a touch of post-natal depression, the mother. Trauma, even.'

'Are you sure it's not just fear? Her baby's gone.'

Paula shook her head. 'Something wasn't right before. I saw her nails, and the bills — the way she talked to him, even. They've spent a lot of money on that place, but I'd say they maybe can't afford it any more.'

'So?' Guy waited for her point.

'So if somebody reached out to her, she might have opened up to them. Maybe said she was struggling. This abductor may have a misplaced sense that they're helping the families. She can care for the child and they can't, that sort of thing.'

Guy wasn't convinced. 'But the Pacheks? They were desperate for that baby. They even went to Croft for help, you said. And it wasn't as if Kasia

114

even got the time to be with her child, let alone struggle with caring for it.'

This was true. 'Oh, I don't know. Nothing about this seems to fit. Every time I put it in a box something plops back out.'

'I know. I'll send Gerard round to this baby group. Those things can be mini-fiefdoms. I remember from when Tess was — ' He broke off and she sighed.

'You can say her name, you know.'

He started the car as if she hadn't spoken. 'Anyway, it's as good a lead as we've got.'

'That's just it, though.' Paula chewed on her own fingernail, as if aping the gesture from the woman in the house. 'We've got nothing but leads. More leads than a bloody overstocked pet shop, and not a single suspect.'

He didn't respond. Paula resumed her gnawing. As they moved past the police vans to the end of the cul-de-sac, Guy said, 'At least we can pinpoint the time of disappearance quite accurately, if we check the phone records for the Williams's house. That will help with alibis.'

'We don't have anyone to get an alibi from.'

'No.' They thought for a while more in tense silence. As the uniformed officers at the end of the road waved them out, a small band of journalists were already waiting, clamouring for answers. Another child missing. She could only imagine the media interest. She wondered was Aidan there among them, as the lights of the car swept over the crowd. The thought occurred: *he would know what to do*. If only she were speaking to him.

'I — Paula.' Guy stopped. 'About earlier. I never meant for things to happen this way, you know.'

She looked out the window at the icy night. 'No. I don't think anyone ever does.'

13

'There you are, Maguire.'

Gerard was passing, arms swinging with purpose, as he liked to be. The unit was already busy when Paula pushed open its doors on Monday morning. She was slightly late after another boking incident, but she doubted Guy would say anything after the bollocking she'd given him on Friday. The unit had worked all weekend, investigating all possible leads on the Williams and Bates cases. Paula had spent it reading everything she could about infant abduction, but was still no nearer to any answers as to who might have taken either child.

Aidan's paper, the *Ballyterrin Gazette*, came out on a Monday, and she'd tried her best not to read it over breakfast, but failed. Rather than praise the unit and PSNI for finding Alek Pachek, it was plastered with pictures of Darcy Williams, her sobbing parents, her pink-and-white face and huge blue eyes. FIND MY BABY was the headline. Since Alek had gone, the mood in town was fearful. There were reports of crèches closing down, parents taking holiday from work to avoid leaving their babies alone. The PSNI hotline was overwhelmed with sightings of anyone remotely shifty seen in a ten-metre radius of a newborn. There was also a full-page investigation of Magdalena Croft, hinting that she'd extorted money from her clients. Having just recovered after one libel claim nearly bankrupted the paper, Aidan was sailing close to the wind again. Bloody eejit. She hoped Guy hadn't seen it, or he'd be in a tetchy mood all day.

'What's going on?' She saw Gerard had his coat on, as if about to go out. 'Is it Darcy?' Maybe they'd found her safe.

'No. You didn't hear? Someone found a body, up by the Knockcree pass. By the standing stones.'

'A baby?' She stopped short.

'Nah, a woman.'

She started taking her coat off, then put it back on in case they had to go out. 'Is it Dr Bates?'

'We don't know. Just a woman, they said.'

'Who found her, a dog walker?'

'Yeah.'

'Maybe they should criminalise that, make our lives easier. They seem to find everyone.' She was babbling. She was nervous, she realised.

Gerard gave her an exasperated look. 'Are you coming out — did the boss say you could?'

'I'm sure he will,' she said firmly. 'If I can see the body it helps me understand what happened.'

Gerard frowned. 'It'll be Corry's call, will it not? It's Serious Crime now, if it's a murder.'

She hadn't thought of that. But then Guy came out, winding a grey scarf round his neck. 'Right, Gerard, we're going to the scene. She's asked for you too, Paula, if you're ready. You heard there's a body in the snow?'

118

'Yeah. Corry asked for me?'

'Yes. Any idea why?'

'No. I am ready though, definitely.'

*　*　*

A fresh snow had fallen overnight, overlaying the sludge with a crisp white icing. 'That'll screw up the analysis,' Gerard complained. He'd commandeered the front seat of Guy's car, his footballer's thighs spread out, so that Paula had to cram into the back like a kid.

Paula leaned forward, trying to chip in. 'Do we know how long she's been there?'

Gerard knew. 'The guy says he takes the dog out every day — some hill farmer, doesn't mind the snow. He didn't see anything until this morning.'

'I'm sure they'll tell us,' said Guy firmly. He disliked speculation in advance of the facts. He also disliked music in the car on the way to crime scenes, whereas Fiacra would play gangsta rap and Gerard usually had something by the kind of group that still wore bandanas. So they drove in silence out of town, up to the hills round Ballyterrin. An old mill town, it huddled grey and brown in the scoop of wet, green hills, currently frosted white with snow. The ground was dead and cold after so many weeks frozen.

The crime scene could only be reached by a narrow dirt track, now treacherously icy. They saw a police van trying to make it up, wheels spinning in the snow. Guy slowed his car beside it. 'Can we go closer?'

'If you can make it,' shouted the bald driver over the noise of tyres. 'A few of the lads just walked it. It's bad all right.'

Guy's BMW made it halfway up before starting to slip, wheels spinning. 'Wow!' Paula braced herself and then had the alarming realisation that in that split second of panic, her hands had flown straight to her stomach. The car came to rest, one tyre off the track, and Guy killed the engine. 'We better just walk the rest.' His eyes found hers in the mirror. 'OK?'

'Fine.' She'd put on stout boots that morning, with gripping soles. Thinking about the ice, about what would happen if she slipped. Even PJ had expressed his approval.

'Come on, then.' The rest of the way was about fifty metres up, but hazardous and slow-going due to holes ankle-deep, patches of melt-water under other footprints frozen into ice. Guy disappeared up to the knee of his expensive suit and withdrew it, cursing. At the top was Knockcree stone circle. The kind of priceless Neolithic site the Irish were always tripping over and trying to build great big bungalows on top of. Several of the stones in the ring were graffitied, and a litter of beer cans stained the snow around them.

'It's a genuine stone circle?' Guy was shaking sludge off his shoes.

Paula and Gerard looked at each other blankly. Knockcree had always just been there. She shrugged. 'We did it at school. Some kind of early religious site? Like Newgrange, I think.'

120

'It's amazing to find it here, in the middle of nowhere.' He peered round at the shapes of stones in the dull light, then his gaze stopped. In the middle of the stones and the ring of police tape, a white-suited CSI was bent over something splayed and stiff. The body. Subtly the three of them shifted, shoulders braced, jaws squaring. This was it — the moment before you saw the puzzle you'd been set, when you asked yourself if you'd be able to look at it without losing your composure or the contents of your stomach.

'Inspector.' Helen Corry materialised before them. No one was quite sure of the protocol here — when a missing person became a murder victim, there was supposed to be a sort of handover between the teams. But she was there, clearly in charge again, this time in a cream wool coat that despite its obvious impracticality — you'd never be done dry-cleaning it — struck a glamorous note against the fallen snow.

'Chief Inspector,' said Guy back, equally cool. 'Is it her?'

Corry flicked snow from her blond hair. 'It seems to be. She looks like her picture — the face is untouched. Firstly, Inspector, we have to keep the press out of this. Her background, this place — ' She gestured to the lichened stones, weathered but immovable, older than millennia. 'Can you imagine it? A body found at an old druid site?'

'Absolutely.' No one wanted to even think the word 'satanic'. Once you did you'd be drowning in cult theories and ritual sacrifice, and the truth would vanish down the rabbit hole, whisking its little white tail.

'So we'll say a body was found in the Ballyterrin hills. No specifics, though it'll leak out anyway, I'm sure.'

'Where are we with the scene?' Once again Guy was trying, and failing, to gain control.

'FMO's on their way, if they can make it up.'

Paula wondered would it be Saoirse, who was on the rota of doctors who attended and certified deaths. Without Saoirse she'd never have been at the clinic that day, never realised Dr Bates was missing so soon.

Corry was still talking. 'One CSI's in now — he walked up the hill with his kit, God love him. They've got tyre trails in the snow over that way.' She pointed to the opposite side of the circle, where two officers were unfurling crime scene tape. 'They'll be doing a fingertip search once we get more people up, so don't walk over there unless you've a suit and slippers on.' It was hard to imagine Corry in the ignominy of the white paper onesies the CSIs used.

Guy was impatient; they knew all this, as Corry was very well aware. 'If it's her, we need to arrange for next of kin to come in.'

'Of course. There's a daughter, I hear. Dr Maguire?'

Paula jumped slightly; she'd been thinking about pregnant Heather Campbell. 'You wanted me?'

'I'd like your thoughts on this setting, if you have some.'

'She died here?'

'Kemal says so. There's blood all over the scene.'

'Weapon?' asked Guy.

'The blade's in her hand, so we can't rule out suicide.'

'Oh?' Guy hadn't been expecting that. 'How?'

'That's what I want Dr Maguire's opinion on. She's had her stomach slashed, right across.' Helen Corry made a cutting motion against her coat, below where the navel would be. 'Hardly the obvious way to do it, or the quickest. And how would she get up here in all this snow, when her car's down by the market where we found it?'

'So maybe not suicide.' Guy looked perplexed and wrong-footed — not his favourite things to be, Paula knew. 'What kind of blade was it?'

'That's the other strange thing. It seems to be a surgical scalpel. Not everyone could even get hold of one of those.'

Paula realised her teeth were chattering. 'Can I take a quick look at the scene?'

Guy looked at her. 'God, you're freezing! Do you need to go back to the car?'

'N-no. I'd like to see it, please.' She appreciated their trust in letting her come to the site and didn't want special treatment, but it was so cold, a damp chill that seemed to roll off those old stones like a malevolent breath. Even the light was eerie, blue-tinged like the lips of someone dying. They crunched over a few steps to the crime scene tape, where a tall, slim man was removing plastic gloves. He pulled down his white hood to reveal huge dark

123

eyes, rimmed as if with kohl.

'Dr Maguire, Inspector Brooking, this is Kemal, our crime scene genius.' Corry doing the introducing once again.

'Pleased to meet you.' His hand was frozen when Paula removed her own purple wool glove to shake it, and he was shivering under the white suit. 'I'm afraid I can't tell you very much until we get the van up, but she died here, I would say. There is a lot of blood.'

'When?' Guy was trying to see past him into the circle. The silence of snow was all about.

'I would guess last night. A large slashing wound to her stomach, as you've no doubt heard.' His accent was carefully stripped, modulated. Paula thought he was maybe Egyptian. 'It isn't a fast way to go.'

'And was she eviscerated?' Guy asked. They hid their horror behind neat clinical phrases, a snick of surgical scissors.

'Not exactly. It was lower, with no sign of disembowelment. More like a Caesarean section. She will most likely have died of hypothermia before the blood loss took effect.'

'I see.' Guy glanced at Paula. 'Can we look?'

'Of course. I haven't moved her.'

Paula had to plant her boots firmly on the snow to prepare for what she was about to see. Just a broken body. Nobody there any more. Nothing to hurt, or be hurt by.

The body which was almost certainly Dr Alison Bates lay in the middle of the stone circle, the snow further out white and pristine except for a single track of churned footprints cordoned

124

off by the police for access. Flakes had also fallen on her overnight, a drift like flowers over her hair and legs, obscuring the worst of the damage. Around her the snow was rust-coloured, red-brown, and her arms were clasped over her stomach, which seemed an odd shape — almost caved in. The snow was darker there, and Paula saw something gleaming beside her in the odd low light. The scalpel, presumably. Her legs were bent out, as if she'd been kneeling when the knife took her. 'Any thoughts on whether it was suicide?' Paula wiped snow from her eyes and looked at the CSI.

'Well. From the angle, it's indeed possible she did it herself. But there are marks around her wrists, I think.'

'Ligatures?'

'Perhaps. The pathologist will tell you more.'

Paula took a deep breath, and Guy noticed. 'Enough?'

'Yes. Can I go to the car?'

'Of course. I'll send Gerard to walk you down while I finish with Corry.' He signalled to Gerard, who'd been chatting to a uniformed officer near the brow of the hill. 'Take Paula down, will you? She's freezing.'

'I'm fine!' she protested, though she wasn't. The last thing she needed was Guy treating her differently. 'I've seen enough, that's all.'

'Bet we'll get taken off it now,' Gerard was grumbling, as they slipped and skidded down to the car. 'It's a swizz. As soon as the cases get interesting we lose them to Serious Crime. Wish I wasn't seconded sometimes. She even has her claws in you now.'

'I'm sure she doesn't.' Paula focussed on putting one step in front of the other, ignoring the image of that pale dead face, eyes filled up unseeing with fresh snow. There was no real expression in death, but the doctor had looked terrified all the same. What a place to meet your end, desolate and silent but for the softness of falling snow.

'She does, she wants you to ring her and all. Arrange a meeting. I reckon she's after poaching you.'

'Don't be daft, Gerard. The other day she compared what I do to faith healing.'

'Aye, but she's a canny one. She'd get you in for the PR alone.'

'I wish you'd stop — shit!' A patch of ground turned suddenly treacherous, and she grabbed Gerard's arm as she fell. Luckily it was there, solid as the boom of a sailing boat under his blue ski jacket.

'You OK? Here, you look like you're about to boke. Thought you'd seen a load of bodies?'

'I have!' Despite the cold, sweat prickled under her wool hat. 'I just slipped.'

She righted herself as Guy came sliding down, prancing nimbly in his Gucci shoes.

'Maguire can't handle the gory bits,' said Gerard in an I'm-telling-teacher voice.

'Well, I didn't see you going up to look,' she fired back.

Guy ignored their spat. 'Can you handle it, Paula? You looked rather faint. I don't want you coming out if it's too much.'

126

'I'm fine! It's just *cold*.'

'I hope it is fine. Because DCI Corry's taking over this case now, but she wants you on it too.'

* * *

There were always mixed emotions at the start of an inquiry. A certain pulse of energy as you pieced the clues together. It was sad, but it was also your job, and you wanted to be good at it. So sometimes a feeling of near excitement could kick in. But this was always tempered when it came to telling the family.

Around three p.m., pushing past the band of journalists who'd gathered outside already, shivering in the snow — no sign of Aidan — Gerard arrived in the PSNI Reception with a pale and waddling Heather Campbell. She would fill in some forms and then be taken to the mortuary to identify her mother's body. Heather was apparently listed as official next of kin.

'Is that wise?' Paula said to Guy, watching the woman through the glass walls. 'Could the partner not have done it?'

'Ms Cole can't face it, it seems. And Heather insisted. I think she wants to punish herself, you know.'

'Mm.' Paula did know. If it happened now, if they found something that could possibly be her own mother's remains, she would go, no matter how awful it was. To be there. To bear witness, in a way, with her own eyes.

'Don't worry, she'll only have to see the face.'

127

And that had been unscathed. The same features, just stiff and waxy, as she'd imagined herself so many times. Except that's not how it would be, would it? Paula's mother had likely died seventeen years ago, if she was indeed dead at all. She'd be nothing like herself. It was pointless to keep imagining those well-loved features, frozen in time. She had to stop.

14

Later, in the storm's eye between phone records and press calls and door-to-doors and tyre-track analysis and the body being moved to Belfast for a post-mortem, Paula tried to put what she'd seen and heard into some kind of pattern. Often, she felt her job was like turning over a piece of embroidery, feeling along the stitches of the thing that had been left. The dumping in the stone circle, that had a certain flair to it, a dark theatricality. From what the CSI said, Dr Bates had probably been marched there, bound at the wrists, then forced to kneel in the snow, and — what? You wouldn't get someone to kneel if you were going to slash their stomach. The height, the angle, it was all wrong. It was a classic paramilitary execution pose — walked to some lonely place, then the shot to the head. But she hadn't been shot. Had she been made to do the slashing herself? It was a horribly fitting end for an abortionist, who many in Ballyterrin would consider to be a cold-blooded murderer of innocents, and one who'd had the gall to charge for her crimes. The more Paula thought about it, the more the staging reminded her of another tableau recently left for them. Baby Alek, waving his hands and legs in the wooden manger.

★ ★ ★

'I want us to consider the possibility the cases are linked,' she announced. 'The baby abductions and Dr Bates, I mean.'

Around the conference room table came the silence she'd expected from the team, the faint tut from Gerard, who didn't approve of wild theories. Helen Corry, who'd reluctantly agreed to have the meeting at the cramped MPRU offices, put her chin in one hand. 'Why?'

'I don't know yet, really. But she was slashed low down, you said. Not the stomach, but where the uterus would be. It's very odd, and not an efficient way to kill someone. Plus, she was maybe forced to do it herself.'

'Ritual suicide?' Fiacra perked up. 'That there Japanese thing — hara-kiri?'

'There could be something in that — I don't know. I know it's a tenuous link, but the odds on two random abductions in this town are very low.' Paula struggled to marshal her thoughts. 'I just think it's all connected somehow — babies, abortions . . . you know. They gave Alek back, then took Darcy. What if the doctor was involved too?'

The DCI gave Paula an appraising look that made her heart sink. 'You don't think it's much more likely she's been targeted by extremists? You're maybe not aware of it, Dr Maguire, but over the past few years the pro-life movement in Ireland has become very radicalised. They fire-bombed a pregnancy advisory service in Dublin last year. Go into town any Saturday and you'll find them on the streets, with their flyers and their stalls. That's why I leaned towards the idea it was someone posing as a patient, if we could find her laptop with the records. The woman offered abortion referrals. It's hard to explain how angry that makes people here.'

'I know that.' Of course she knew; she might have been away twelve years but she did grow up in the province. 'I can't explain what I think, really. It's just that the mode of death is very unusual.'

Guy looked to be thinking hard. 'As a theory it just about holds up, I suppose, and I agree the odds of two abductors are very slim, but what link could there be? Does it give us any fresh leads we can pursue?'

'No.' That was the frustrating thing. 'But I would continue the lines of inquiry we have open — the hospital staff, and the death threats to the doctor. Cross-referencing might throw up something that gives a breakthrough.'

'It wouldn't hurt to look for any links, I suppose.' Helen Corry was watching her. She hadn't taken any notes throughout the briefing. 'You still think it's a woman? Dr Bates was strong and healthy. Not easy to overpower her.'

'It's always women in these types of abduction cases — unless they have a man as an accomplice, to help them get a baby away.'

'What a world,' muttered Bob, who'd been in the RUC for forty years, but still considered Ballyterrin the last bastion against a rising global tide of sin.

'So we could be looking at a couple?' Fiacra's question made everyone groan. Conspiracies were deadly to solve, even harder to prove.

Paula shook her head. 'Like I say, I really don't know. It's just an idea.'

Corry was looking sceptical. 'I'm far from convinced by random hunches, Dr Maguire, but I'm open to trying this approach, since we have basically nothing else.'

Paula subsided, chewing her lip. She desperately wanted to bring something to Corry and Guy, impress them, but all her insights had deserted her, like looking at a crossword upside down. 'Did we find out anything about the Williams family?'

Gerard answered briefly. 'They'd money troubles. The phone call from the bank checks out — apparently they're this close to losing the house.' He rubbed his fingers together. 'So she probably did leave the wean alone to answer it.'

This had been Paula's theory, but something still didn't feel right. 'OK. So if someone approached Caroline, seemed friendly, she might have admitted she couldn't cope.'

Guy placed his hands on the table. 'Where have we got to on the death threats to Dr Bates? DCI Corry, you'll want to get your team on this, but we did some preliminary inquiries into who might have wanted to harm her.'

'And?'

'Easier to say who didn't,' piped up Fiacra, and then coloured. 'Ma'am.'

'Go on,' Guy encouraged him.

'Avril and me went over the threats the doctor received — well, there's a load of them. She'd been denounced by everyone from the Catholic

132

Archbishop to the Presbyterian Chief Moderator.'

'Also by Magdalena Croft,' Guy added. 'Your expert, DCI Corry. She spoke against Dr Bates at one of her rallies.'

Corry didn't react. Fiacra glanced at Avril, who took over seamlessly.

'But most of the threatening phone calls came from the one number, which I've managed to trace. It's registered to a Mrs Melissa Dunne, who lives near the border. She runs a pro-life group called Life4All. The 'for' is like the number four, though.'

'Is she North or South?' asked Corry. The question you always asked on a border. The border itself was nothing — only a line on a map, no longer anything physical to show for it. All the same, you could stand as close to it as you liked, but you were still on one side or the other.

'South. That's why Fiacra was helping. We also have her prints on file — she got arrested a few times at demos, so she did. We could run them against the letters to Dr Bates, see if we can get any prints off them.'

'Why wasn't this done at the time?' Guy was frowning. Everyone looked down.

Helen Corry answered. 'Unfortunately the death threat is something of a staple of Northern Ireland life, Inspector. Ask any of our local councillors. If she'd been sent bullets in the post, or got followed home, we'd have been more worried. It happens.'

'Well, can we run the prints like Avril suggests?

133

We should get this Dunne in for questioning, I think.'

'Of course.' Corry still wasn't even making notes. Paula wondered what it would take to really rattle her. 'What about the Pachek and Williams cases — you said you were looking into the files?'

Avril answered again. 'We ran all the child abduction cases for the past ten years, north and south of the border. There weren't many and they've all been resolved.'

'We could go back further,' Gerard suggested. 'She's, what, in her late forties by the look of the tape. Could have been younger when she first did it.'

Avril's fingers were poised over her laptop. 'So, what, twenty years?'

Paula was thinking about it. 'Typically this kind of behaviour is triggered by a woman losing their own child, or not being able to conceive. There are some cases of younger women doing it but usually not. I'd say twenty years back would do it. Check all unsolved abductions — even if the child was returned safe, like Alek — and anything involving women.' Once again she felt Helen Corry appraising her, nodding as if pleased. 'I can't add much to my profile of the abductor, I'm afraid. There is some professional literature on it, which suggests they are often overweight, for some reason, or otherwise lack control over some area of their appearance. Sometimes they actually believe they are pregnant — this is a condition called pseudocyesis. False pregnancy, it means. They can even have all the symptoms — weight gain, no periods. But then when there's no baby at the end of it, they find one somewhere else.'

Corry was listening intently. 'So it's a control thing?'

'Often, yes. They want a baby and can't have one, so they take it instead. There's one more thing. The vast majority of these women had made contact with the family first. So it's worth asking the Pacheks and Williams again if they remember anyone being over-friendly, perhaps at antenatal clinics or just out and about. The women often pretend to be pregnant, even if they're not deluded — so they can then pass the baby off as their own.'

Corry shook her head. 'The Pacheks aren't keen to talk. They're too upset by the whole thing. We followed up the Williams link to the baby group, but everything seemed normal there. Apparently Caroline only came to a few sessions, then left. And we can't find any connection between them and the Pacheks.'

'What about the staff interviews?' Guy asked. 'Paula's theory was the woman maybe worked at the hospital.'

Gerard confirmed this. 'Part of the reason the father never looked at her right was she must have seemed like a real nurse.'

Paula said, 'In these cases you also often get a dry run, preparing for it very carefully. If she doesn't work there she'll perhaps have been hanging round the hospital beforehand. Some-one will have seen her, I'm sure of it. We just need to jog their memories.'

Corry examined the nails on her left hand. 'Well, we're talking to all the staff who were there that day and so far nothing suspicious has come up, no unexplained newborns in the family. We'll move on next to those who weren't in, or shouldn't have been — sick leave and that.'

There was a short silence as they all considered how few leads they had in either case. Guy said forcefully, 'This Melissa Dunne woman is our best link for now. We should discuss divisions of labour, DCI Corry.'

'It's a murder case now, so we'll handle the interviews. I'm happy for you to look into the Williams case.' She made it sound magnanimous.

Guy smiled tightly, but didn't disagree in front of his team. 'I think we have considerable expertise here that would help the Bates case — access to all Southern databases, and, of course, one of the few forensic psychologists in the country with the right experience.'

'Of course.' Corry smiled back, equally fake. 'It's very kind of you to offer. I'll use what I need.'

'That's not quite — '

'Thanks, Inspector.' She pulled on her green leather gloves. 'Best be off. The most important thing, and I'm saying this to all my team as well, is to keep the press out of it. We say only that we've found Dr Bates dead. No word on how or where or any possible link to the missing baby. Is that clear? They'll have a field day on this one if we let them. Especially after what happened on the last big case we had.' Paula looked down, taking this as a dig at her. She'd gone to Aidan for help on their last unsolvable case, getting herself in trouble in the process. And now where was he? Nowhere to be found. Corry turned to Paula. 'Could you see me out, Dr Maguire? I'd like a quick word about those interview techniques you mentioned.'

They walked to the front glass doors, where an icy wind was blowing in from the car park. At the front gate, outside their high fences, several journalists were still toughing it out in the evening dark, shivering, wanting news of Darcy Williams and Dr Bates. Aidan was again conspicuously not among them, and that was strange. Usually he'd be in the centre of every scrum, with his difficult questions and his mocking smile. Perhaps he was off working on another exposé to discredit the unit.

Paula crossed her arms against the cold. 'I was thinking of a technique for improving the accuracy of eyewitness testimony — you could reinterview everyone on the maternity ward that day, and see if anyone noticed something which maybe didn't quite register at the time. I could train the officers, if you like.'

'That sounds useful.' Corry was digging in her bag (Mulberry) for an umbrella, looking at the heavy sky. 'We'll have more snow soon, I'd say. Listen, Paula — is it OK to call you Paula? Would you have a drink with me sometime? I've something I'd like to discuss with you.'

'A drink?'

'Yes. Just a chat outside work. Glass of wine.'

'Well, OK. Sure.'

'Give me a ring.' She slotted a card into Paula's folded arms and trotted off to her car. As Corry drove past the journalists in her Merc, sloshing melting snow at them and ignoring their shouts, Paula shivered and went back into the warmth.

Back in the conference room, she saw everyone standing about the phone, their faces set and drawn. 'What is it?'

'That was Heather Campbell's husband,' said Guy, carefully. 'Apparently Heather didn't make it home from the mortuary earlier.'

15

The news about Heather Campbell was worrying, but when they got Corry on the phone in her car she was reluctant to start another investigation. 'It's only been a few hours. She likely went to see a friend or something, needed some space. She'd just come from seeing her mother dead.'

Guy sat on his desk, talking into speakerphone so they could all hear. 'But with this snow, her husband is very worried. It's getting dark now.'

'We'd have heard if there'd been an accident. Let's leave it till morning. Not a word to the press, remember! I have to go, I'm about to get penalty points for being on my mobile.' Corry hung up.

Guy held the phone, as if trying to decide. 'I suppose she's right. It will have to wait till morning. I'll send someone round to the husband if she hasn't turned up.'

Paula was packing up some notes to take home with her. 'You think it's worrying?' Guy had made no motions to leave, though it was gone seven p.m. and the others had departed for the night. Paula wondered if Tess was waiting for him at home, dinner perhaps ready on the table. A cosy family scene.

He stretched, weary. 'I hope she did just go to a friend. She was very upset — in fact she collapsed in the mortuary when she saw the body.'

'How pregnant is she? Eight months or something?'

'Yes, I'd say she's quite far along.' They were both silent for a moment, not wanting to say or even think of the possibility taking horrible form in their minds. 'I've asked the husband to call us first thing if she's not back. It's not unusual for someone to take off, after such a shock.'

Paula looked uneasily out the window, where snow gave the street a rosy glow under the street lights. Where would a heavily pregnant woman go all night, in that? She could imagine all too easily how it was for Heather Campbell, the sheet drawn back on the familiar face, a little older, set in new, stiff angles by the force of death. Your belly swollen in front of you, kicking with new life. She realised she was holding her own stomach and quickly took her hands away. 'If I can do anything . . . '

'Go home, Paula.' He gave her a tired smile. 'Get some rest. We need to get started on all Corry's extra work tomorrow. I'd like you to go and see this Melissa Dunne too, when Fiacra does. If we get a jump on it Corry can hardly protest.'

'OK.' She lingered for just a moment. 'Shouldn't you be at home too?'

Guy didn't answer, just turning back to his desk. He looked so worn out, dark circles under his eyes, hair greying over his ears. She had an urge to touch the back of his neck as he sat there. Say — *Guy, guess what, I'm pregnant.*

140

You remember, that night when we . . .

'Was there anything else?' he asked.

'No,' she said, sighing internally at her own cowardice. 'Night, then.'

★ ★ ★

'You're late, pet. Your dinner's long cold.'

PJ was sitting with his leg up on what he called the 'pouffe', applying Deep Heat to the wasted muscles. After so long in plaster the leg looked weak and goose-bumped, like a scrawny chicken. She'd hardly seen him for days, Paula realised. 'Work's just gone crazy. Where were you today, did you go out?'

'I'd a funeral to go to.'

'Who was that?' She sat on the stairs to take off her boots, dog-tired and cold right through.

'Old colleague of mine. You wouldn't know him. Kevin Conway was the name — he was a young constable when your mo — hmph.'

When your mother went, he'd been about to say. This close brush was enough to still her heart. They didn't talk about her mother. It was a rule as binding as it was unspoken. 'What did he die of?' She moved them onto firmer ground.

He put the cap back on the tube. 'Cancer. Liver. Drank himself to death, God love him. Last time I saw him he was in so much pain he'd a mind to take all his pills at once and finish it.'

'Sad.' Ex-RUC officers battled booze and depression like the twin dogs of hell. She eyed her father, his craggy bent frame, his greying hair, thankful yet again he had Pat calling in, taking him out of himself. She'd likely driven him to the funeral, seeing as she knew every man, woman, child and dog in the town. 'Listen, Dad, I've a bit of work to do, so I'll be upstairs.'

'OK, pet. Let me know if you need a hot water bottle.' He picked up a notebook from beside the sofa — another of his small black ones from his policing days.

Upstairs, she took off her jeans, wet through with melting snow, and pulled on her pyjama bottoms, washed to a comforting softness. Then she opened the bottom drawer of her desk, where once she'd kept secret notes from Saoirse and old diaries. Now it held just one thing.

It was only an envelope. Dun-coloured, slim, dog-eared. It was exactly the same as all the others they handled at the unit every day. Except those were just names. This was blood and bone and the wrenching loss that woke you deep in the bowels of the night, grasping for something you couldn't name. This was her mother's file.

Guy had given it to her a month ago, when word came that a jailed terrorist had information on various missing persons cases. Sean Conlon, an IRA leader, had gone to prison shortly after the Good Friday Agreement for his role in dissident terrorist acts. He was also likely one of the men who'd shot Aidan's father, Pat's husband, in the newspaper office where he was editor and seven-year-old Aidan was playing under the desk. 1986. A bad year, among so many other bad ones. He had been interviewed in prison by the Commission for the Disappeared. This was an organisation with the sole

142

purpose of finding the remains of the missing IRA dead, and returning them to their families. The Commission ran on a strict amnesty basis — no one could face criminal charges, no matter what they told. So Sean Conlon had decided to talk, if they could promise him early release. During his interview, he'd mentioned the name of Paula's mother. That he might have information about her.

Paula took the envelope out. *Margaret Catherine Maguire*, said the scribble on the front. Whose hand had written it? In those days, in 1993, her father had worked in the old RUC station where the MPRU were now based. The slogan painted on walls then had been **RUC: 98% Protestant, 100% Unionist.** PJ Maguire was no Unionist, but he'd been one of the two per cent, a Catholic officer. Some people said that was why her mother had gone. Taken, as punishment. As a debt to be repaid.

She took out the file and her mother stared out at her. Paula remembered this photo well. She'd taken it, in fact, as the blurring and red eye attested. It was at a harbour somewhere in the west of Ireland. Galway, maybe. Paula would have been ten or so.

She noted, and set aside, her own detachment. It was just a picture. The dead and missing always looked that way. You'd see the photos after, examine them for some sign of the fateful unravelling, but really there'd be nothing. The truth is, everyone smiles for photos, even if they're dying inside.

On the back of the photo was a sticker saying

where it had been developed — their local chemist, where PJ still went to get his painkillers. Below was a series of handwritten notes. Her mother's background — the five children, the father dead at fifty-four, keeling over in the hay field. Education — local primary, then the nearest convent grammar. So that was Margaret Maguire, née Sheeran, the facts and figures of her life, but telling you nothing about who she really was, what might have made her go out on a blustery October afternoon in 1993 and leave the front door banging in the wind, never to come back to her silent husband and bewildered daughter.

Paula quickly put away a typed manuscript she recognised as her own confused teenage ramblings. She remembered in a flash the constable they'd got to interview her, a large woman with a farmer's build and thick-as-mud Armagh accent. *Have a wee think, pet. What did you see when you came in from school?*

Nothing. She wasn't there.

Did you not think that was a wee bit strange?

I dunno. Maybe she had to work or something.

She'd have known even then this wasn't true. Her mother had only worked mornings, so as to be home for Paula, who until that day had never even had to make herself a cup of tea. A physical shudder went through her, and she set that aside too.

Next, leads they had followed. Interviews with sex offenders in the area, statements from the neighbours. Every single one said they'd seen

144

nothing. And that was strange in itself. The house was on a narrow street of cramped terraced houses, some with alleys between them. People saw everything — you couldn't even drive two cars abreast. If you'd left your front door open, as Margaret had that day, they'd be onto you like a shot to see what was the matter.

There was nothing else to know. Trains, buses, and planes all drew a blank, ferries too. Margaret's passport had still been in its holder along with PJ and Paula's, in the special travel folder they'd got for their one overseas holiday to the Isle of Man. Her purse was gone, but her handbag was there on the peg as always. Neither had been able to say what clothes were missing, if any.

As Paula had told Guy when he'd given her the file, there was nothing in it, no new leads. Interviews and public appeals had all drawn a blank, and the two women's bodies discovered over the years had turned out not to be her. Nothing, nothing, nothing. As if her mother had opened that front door and vanished before she even had time to shut it.

Except for the man.

Of course, the man. He'd been so debated and discussed that at times Paula almost wondered herself if she had just imagined him. The memory had the fake, sweaty quality of a dream.

It was the day before her mother had gone. A normal day. *I came home from school and Mummy was at the back door* (had she really said Mummy? At thirteen?). There was a sketch of the house, the kitchen door giving out onto a

145

small back yard and lawn with a whirligig washing line. *She was talking to someone. She shut the door and then I saw a man going past the window down the passageway* (sketch of how the narrow alley led down the side of the house and into the main street). *I didn't see his face, he had a hat on.*

What type of hat?

I don't know. I don't know.

A memory popped up, as if things moved and breathed beneath the surface — her mother had been in her dressing gown that day. She remembered it now, her mother shutting the door, a flash of leg as she turned, Paula already opening the fridge, warning *don't make toast, you'll spoil your dinner.* She'd have asked, surely. Wouldn't she have asked why her mum was in her dressing gown at four in the afternoon?

Paula remembered nothing about that evening, the last one she and PJ would ever have had with her mother. What had been on TV on Thursdays? *X-files, ER?* She'd lived her thirteen-year-old life around school and TV, and now she remembered nothing, as if those years had pressed on her as blank and suffocating as a pillow.

Below the case notes was the list Paula had begun when Guy had given her this file a month before. Just names, meaningless on their own.

The first name: *Colin McCready.* Her mother's boss at the solicitor's office where she'd worked part-time. Paula remembered him, a soft-hearted man who'd once given her a packet

146

of Minstrels when she went to the office after school.

The next name was this: *Auntie Phil*. Her mother's family were dimly recalled from Christenings and Confirmations, all ties severed after Margaret went, during those weeks when her father was suddenly at home, and then his own colleagues came round one day to arrest him. Yes, those memories were all still there, under a barely healed scab.

She'd also written: *Pat*. Her mother hadn't had other friends, and even with Pat it had been a couple's friendship, forged in PJ and John O'Hara's shared pursuit of what they called justice, while their wives stayed at home and worried about phone calls, balaclavas, shots ringing out.

Another familiar name below: *Bob Hamilton*. She'd copied that from the front of the file, *Lead Officer, Detective Sergeant Robert Hamilton*. Sideshow Bob had led the hunt for Margaret, wife of his own former partner, even coming round in person to arrest PJ.

So far, that was all she had for her list of people who might know something about her mother. Her boss, her sister, her friend, and the investigating officer.

Slipped into the file was an extract from a longer interview transcript, with several lines highlighted in yellow. Paula made herself read it.

Commission for the Disappeared (CD): *And those missing people we showed you, did any of the names ring a bell? There's a*

147

lot of families looking for some answers, Sean.

Sean Conlon (SC): *I need assurances before I talk. I'll not answer for legitimate wartime acts.*

CD: *As we've made clear, Sean, there will be no recriminations for pre-Good Friday Agreement actions. We just want answers, for the families.*

SC: [Pause] *This name. Margaret Maguire. I remember her*

CD: *Yes? She's the only woman on the list, you'll see.*

SC: *Husband was a peeler, I mind. A Taig and a peeler.*

CD: *And was she targeted because of that?*

SC: *I'm not saying that. But I heard other things about her. Like she used to help out the Brits. Worked in some solicitor's, so she did. She'd have had access to things. Information, on Republican soldiers.*

CD: *Can you tell me more, Sean?*

SC: *Not till I get my assurances. I want protection, if I talk to you. I won't say any more.*

And he still hadn't spoken, but the hint was there, the sly half-moon promise of the truth after so many years.

Paula set down the paper, the edges sharp as a knife, and with an old chewed biro added the man's name to her list, though it felt like a malediction. *Sean Conlon.* That's who she had to speak to.

148

Getting into bed, shivering with cold, she realised again there was only one person who could help her draw this into order, tell her what to do. One person who'd understand what it would mean for her to speak to Sean Conlon, knowing he might be behind her mother's loss. No matter what was between them and whatever he'd done, she had to speak to Aidan. The simple fact was she couldn't do this without him.

16

'Are you sure this is her?' Paula looked askance at the large detached house they'd drawn up to.

Fiacra obligingly checked the map, where Gerard would have just told her he knew how to read a bloody GPS, thanks very much. Fiacra was very restful to be around, in fact, like the happy-go-lucky younger brother she'd never have. 'It is, so.'

'I suppose nutcases can live anywhere.' She shouldn't be using words like that. It was rubbing off on her, being around the police so much, and there was something about these pro-lifers that really put her back up. Melissa Dunne lived right over the border, in one of the oversized mansions that littered the no-man's-land there, farm vehicles parked up in their back gardens beside BMWs. It was technically in the South, hence Fiacra instead of moody Gerard. When Fiacra rang the doorbell they heard a rough chorus of dogs start up. Paula backed away slightly.

The door was opened by a small child of about seven or eight, unsuitably dressed for the cold in leggings, bare feet, and a pink scalloped T-shirt with what looked like ketchup down the front. Paula hoped it was ketchup, anyway.

'Is your mammy in, pet?' Fiacra bent down to the child, who he seemed to think was a girl. She had limp fair hair, unbrushed and hanging down her back.

'She's busy.'

'It's very important. Tell her the police are here and we need a wee word.'

The child called out, 'Mammy!' and the dogs started up again from deep in the house. Paula looked about her as they followed the child in, drawing her coat tighter. The house was very cold, and quite dirty, though the family clearly had money — there'd been a Mercedes and a Range Rover parked in the drive, and they glimpsed a huge TV set in the front room, playing *Finding Nemo*, with a collection of different-sized children and dogs watching it. Christmas cards were displayed haphazardly along the mantelpiece of the unlit fire. Paula tried to remember if it was the school holidays. 'Shouldn't at least some of the kids be in school?' she said to Fiacra as they went down the hall, wood floor stained with paw prints. There was a greasy smell in the air, mingled with what seemed to be dirty nappy.

'Mrs Dunne?' Fiacra tapped on the ajar door of the dining room. The carpet was napped in dog hair, and the room was dominated by a huge scuffed table which looked antique. Underneath it lay three dogs, a Jack Russell, a large black Lab, and an indeterminate terrier-type thing with beady eyes. Fiacra was polite. 'Can we have a word, Mrs Dunne?'

The woman at the table was large, a size eighteen or twenty at least. She had thick seventies glasses and mousy hair held back with a hairband, drooping over the shoulders of her jumper, on which was knitted a flock of woolly

151

sheep. 'Can you not see I'm busy?' She could barely be made out behind stacks of envelopes and pamphlets, the latter of which she was stuffing into the former. Paula moved closer to look at one and flinched. Anti-abortion leaflets. They'd spared no detail in their rendering of the mangled foetus. The red ink had been most liberally used. Paula had done some research after the briefing with Corry and it was true — Dunne's group and others had grown increasingly active in Ireland. There was money coming in from somewhere; as well as the leaflets there were billboards, even TV ads.

Fiacra said, 'Mrs Dunne, I'm Garda Quinn and this is my associate Dr Maguire. We're after looking into a case, and we'd like your help. You're the secretary of a pro-life group. Life4All, is that right?'

Melissa stopped stuffing and pushed aside her little netbook, which was cherry-red, and reminded Paula they still hadn't found Dr Bates's missing computer. 'I am. What's it to you? We've no government funding — too scared to stand up to the lefties and save our children, they are.'

'Well, do you know the name Alison Bates? Dr Bates?'

Melissa spat. 'That murdering bitch. Don't you say her name in my house.'

'We have it on file that you phoned the doctor up a few times. Threatening sort of calls. Maybe sent her a few letters too. Is that so?' Fiacra made it sound as if they'd been pen pals.

'I don't know what you're talking about. I'm a

152

busy woman, I don't have the time to be writing letters.'

'On your website, you mentioned the doctor, and you said, I think I have this right, 'She's headed straight for the fires of hell'? Is that so?'

Melissa was unmoved. 'That's nothing but the Gospel truth.'

'Well, thing is, the doctor's been killed, Mrs Dunne. And seeing as you may have threatened to do her some harm, we'd a notion you'd be a good person to ask about it.'

The woman was on her feet in an instant, despite her bulk. 'I most certainly did not threaten her. If I explain the consequences of her actions, it's a warning, surely. I was trying to help her.'

'You said she would 'burn in hell', did you?' Fiacra soldiered on.

'As she will, for the souls of all those babies she murdered.'

'Someone murdered *her*, Mrs Dunne. That's the thing.'

The woman paused; Paula saw with a lurch that she was smiling. 'I can't say I'll mourn her too much. That woman has the blood of innocents on her soul, and she'll be answering for it now.'

Paula broke in. 'Do you remember where you were last Thursday, Mrs Dunne? That's when Dr Bates went missing.'

'How would I remember something like that? I'm a busy woman, like I said.' Melissa Dunne met Paula's eyes, bullish.

Fiacra cut the tension. 'Ah . . . OK. We'd also

153

like the names of your fellow group members, Mrs Dunne — we need to know who might have targeted Dr Bates.'

She rolled her eyes. 'Nearly anyone, Garda. She didn't exactly make friends. And if you think I'm giving you anything without a warrant you're sadly mistaken. It's not right to be persecuting God-fearing Christians. We're only trying to warn people, help them turn away from sin.' With one chapped hand, Melissa took off her glasses and cleaned them on her jumper, exposing her saggy stomach. Paula looked away and the woman caught her aversion, addressing the next remark to her. 'You know what they do to the babies during an abortion, Miss?'

Paula struggled. 'I — eh. Yes.'

'Do you? They rip their wee heads off and they suck them out with a vacuum. Now you tell me that's right to do to a woman when she's vulnerable, tear the innocent life right out of her.' Paula stared at the dirty carpet, willing the woman to stop talking. She didn't. 'You look at this. Take some away with you. Tell your friends.' She was shoving some pamphlets at Paula, who backed away. 'Look at what it is they do.' Paula found one in her hand. The hollow eyes of the foetus seemed to stare at her, accusing.

'Mrs Du — Oh.' Fiacra stopped as a vile smell filled the room. The Jack Russell had squatted and left a fresh steaming turd on the carpet.

'Darragh!' Melissa turned and shouted. When the small child appeared again she picked the poo up in her bare hands and carried it out.

Paula realised she couldn't stay here another

second. 'Garda Quinn?' Her voice was unnaturally high. 'Let's go.'

'You better get a warrant for those names. I'm not breaking Data Protection.' Melissa was shouting after them as they beat a hasty retreat to the door and back to Fiacra's Fiat Punto. 'You'll be hearing from my solicitor!'

'God, what a tip,' Fiacra said, starting the engine. 'She's mad as a box of frogs, that one. Our Aisling went to the Bates woman when she first found out she was expecting — she wasn't going to have the abortion, but you know how it is, she was scared — anyway, that crowd were there picketing the place. Put her off going in.'

'How is Aisling?' Paula asked, thinking of the girl. She'd also had an unexpected pregnancy, but now she was full of joy and excitement. So it was possible.

'Ah, she's grand. Frightened, like, but she'll be OK. She'll do a better job than your one in there, I'm sure. Poor kids freezing to death, and on a day like this. Aisling might not be with the da but she'll love that wean, and she's her family around to help.'

Paula's numb hands crept under her coat to sit atop her thick jumper. So would she, if it came down to it. She'd do a better job too, and she had people to help her. But still the idea made cold dread percolate through her veins. She looked down and realised something was crumpled in her hand — that picture of the foetus, eyes black holes, head curved like a fragile little alien.

155

'Is this really all we've got?'

Guy was pacing in front of the whiteboard in the small conference room. Bob, his suit ironed into the same lines as his old RUC uniform, watched him anxiously, as if trying to learn the walk and the talk. Glances went between the kids — if Guy and Bob were the adults — Avril widening her eyes significantly at Fiacra, Gerard catching Paula's gaze before shrugging and biting his nails. No one wanted to go first. Despite Corry's warning, the press had discovered the location of Dr Bates's body, and the news had run all day with speculation about why she'd been found on an old pagan site.

'Come on, everyone, you must have something.' Guy was irritated.

Fiacra coughed. 'Sir. We looked into possible pro-life extremists in the area, like you said.'

'Yes?' Guy snatched at the information.

'And, and — we've a few hits on cross-referencing with hospital staff. Similar names or addresses. Might lead to nothing, but you never know. The Dunne woman says we have to speak to her solicitor if we want the names of her group.'

'Let's do that. Paula, what about your cognitive interviews?'

'I'm supposed to go in tomorrow and do some. What about the faith healer, are we any closer to finding out her real name? Magdalena must be an alias, surely.'

'Yes.' Avril pushed forward a newly printed

156

sheet of paper. 'I got this off the Guards this morning — she asked for a driving licence under her real name years ago.'

'Which was?'

Avril read out, 'Mary Conaghan. Born in 1960, near Tallaghmar.' She struggled with the Irish name. 'Where's that?'

'Donegal, I think,' said Paula. She'd been there on holiday once, with PJ and Margaret. A desolate place, with the same kind of beauty as bones stripped of flesh. 'It's remote. Very poor in the sixties. She probably moved to Dublin to find work. Where does the Croft bit come from?'

'She was married.' Fiacra took up the story. 'She married a man called David Croft in the late seventies. We lose her for a while, and then she resurfaces as Magdalena in this breakaway church in Dublin. Her real name was still Mary Conaghan — Avril found it on a tax return, of all things.' He gave the analyst an admiring sideways glance. 'Then she started up with this priest, Father Brendan, and she pops up here and there on the news archives. Healings, miracles, spiritual retreats, all that. Somebody gave her a load of cash and she opened her own centre for a time, in Dublin's north side. Sort of a church crossed with a hospice, by the sounds of it. People would go to her and get cures.'

Guy was listening intently. 'Can we tie her to anything, any crime at all?'

'Well, there's lots of rumours in the press, sir,' said Fiacra. 'Extortion and that, getting people to give her money for this church she wants to build. I suppose it sort of . . . well, if you believe

157

she sees the Virgin, you'd think she was a saint. But if not . . . '

'She's a manipulative charlatan,' Guy finished. 'I know what I think. I think I'd like to interview this Magdalena for myself, see what it is she does. Paula, will you come with me?'

Paula nodded, eyes lowered. She had no desire to see Magdalena Croft again. The woman's scrutiny had felt like plunging a hand into a muddy pond. All manner of things were now swirling in the eddies, after years buried in silence.

Gerard chewed on his cuticle. 'Are we saying there's officially a link between the cases, sir? The baby and the doctor?'

'I don't know.' Guy's eyes landed briefly on Paula. 'Paula thought there could be. We know Magdalena Croft spoke out against the abortion clinic, but then so did pretty much everyone else in town. What else?' Guy stopped, and pressed his fingers to his temples. 'As you know, Dr Bates's daughter didn't come home last night after identifying the body. Officers spoke to her husband and he says it's very out of character. She rang him before she set off, he says. She was upset, but she'd planned to drive straight home. She's eight months' pregnant at the moment, so we're going to launch an investigation right away. Let's get out the usual alerts — TV and radio, posters, and we're talking to anyone she might have known or turned to for help.' He stopped again. 'Anyone else feeling a bit overwhelmed by all this?'

There were noises of agreement. Guy said,

'We've had the results of Dr Bates's autopsy through. As you know, she was found with a scalpel in her hand. This was covered in her own prints, but no one else's. The pathologist thinks she made the cuts herself — but there were ligature marks on her wrists, and also traces of barbiturate in her system.'

'She was drugged?' Gerard squinted at the papers in front of them, a list of long chemical names from the toxicology report.

'It looks that way. She must have been kept somewhere for several days — why, we don't know. Then we believe she was driven to the standing stones and forced to commit suicide.' Guy's voice was toneless, but around the table everyone blanched. Avril bit her lip, pushing back the autopsy papers. Paula tried not to think of it — stumbling in the heavy snow, the sound of your breath in your ears, hands bound behind you, and then — cold ice beneath, cold steel at your belly. She shuddered. Guy caught her expression. 'Any thoughts, Paula?'

'This kneeling — it's a classic execution pose. The paramilitaries used it. Of course, they usually shot the person in the head. Not cutting like this.'

'What does it mean?'

'I — ' She shook her head helplessly. 'Honestly, I have no idea. We could look into similar old cases, but I can't see what the link would be.'

Guy took this in for a moment. 'I think we need to prioritise Heather Campbell and Darcy Williams's cases for now. We can also continue the background work and analysis on Dr Bates and Alek Pachek, but finding the missing needs to be our focus. Paula, you'll carry on working across all cases, as DCI Corry requests.'

'OK.' She thought of the business card tucked into her notebook and remembered she needed to phone the DCI. What was that about?

'Everyone else, go on with your tasks as discussed. As there's no solid lead on Heather Campbell we'll carry on with the usual, CCTV, traffic records, friends and family. Hopefully she'll turn up safe. Thanks, everyone.' Guy seemed to be rushing through things today, and as soon as they had finished he looked at his watch and went into his office, shutting the door. What was he up to?

Hopefully she'll turn up safe, he'd said. It was strange, Paula thought, as she got wearily to her feet. Research showed most people who went missing were fine and well somewhere — there was some kind of crossing on their line, an unravelling of the knots that kept them from drifting, but they were alive, and safe, and breathing. Yet somehow all the ones referred to their small run-down station ended up in the murkier waters of the unknown.

17

'OK, Chris.' Paula looked at the six foot seven man across from her, trying to put him at his ease. She didn't imagine he found himself in too many situations he couldn't control; the guy was huge. He was very nervous. 'This should be straightforward.'

'You're not going to like, hypnotise me?'

'No, it's not hypnotism. I don't suggest anything to you. I just help your mind relax and possibly remember things you've seen but forgotten.'

Chris Jones was a nurse on the maternity ward at Ballyterrin General Hospital, shaven-headed, tattooed. Ballyterrin not being the most progressive town, Paula wondered how the Mummy Mafia felt about having him weigh their precious newborns and check their episiotomy scars.

'Only I saw this show once on telly, and this fella hypnotised people to take off their clothes and that.'

Paula didn't think she could cope if that happened. 'I'm not Derren Brown. I'm just going to relax you, and maybe then you'll remember if you saw something that day.'

He was buzzing with nervous energy. 'I mean, I want to help catch the person, of course I do. We've never had this happen here before. It's a nice unit, we look after the wee ones well. Can't believe someone's taking babies. This town used to be safe. Now this murder too — it's hard to take in.'

'Well, if you can help us work out who took Alek, it may be we could find Darcy too. Can you close your eyes for me?' Paula nodded to Gerard, who dimmed the lights in the on-call room they were using, clattering out to guard the door. He was sceptical about the idea, but had agreed to help her out. He hadn't much choice.

She made her voice low and soft. 'How do you feel, Chris?'

'OK. Worried.'

'What can you hear?'

'Eh — I can hear noise outside, footsteps, phones — the nurses' station.'

'And further away?'

'Cars. The road outside.'

'Good. Focus on those sounds for a while, Chris, and just breathe slowly for me. In, out, in, out. That's it.' She waited as the awareness exercise went on, his large shoulders sagging as he breathed.

'Now. Can you feel the chair under you?'

'Yes.'

'Can you hear my voice?'

'Yes.'

'OK. I want you to think only about those things. If you get distracted, focus on the sounds outside again. I'm going to bring you back to the day Alek was taken. It was a Tuesday. Do you remember coming to work?'

'Um . . . I normally bike in but it snowed so I drove. I can't remember much about the day.'

'That's OK. Whatever you can. Remember

162

coming into the lobby? The sound of the doors. The lift?'

'I walked up,' he said. 'The lift was bunged, so I walked up. I knew there'd be chaos.'

Paula made a note. 'Good. When you came onto the ward, who did you see?'

'Um . . . the obstetrician, Dr Rasmus. He was pissed off because one of the nurses misread his chart. He's got awful writing. So I sorted that out. I'm head nurse, see.'

'Right. Then what? Did you have a coat?'

'Normally I'm in my bike leathers, and I get changed, put my helmet in the locker and stuff, but that day . . . ' He fell silent. Paula waited, listening to the muffled sounds from outside. 'It was all wrecked,' he said finally. 'Loads of people couldn't get in with the snow. The phone kept ringing and one of the receptionists, Sandra, she was bringing me lists of who wouldn't be coming. So I said phone round and see who's off; if they live in town they can make it. If you're out on some farm, you see, you can't get your car going when it's bad.'

'Sure. So who was in that day?'

'Not many people. Sandra, me, the doctor, Louise, Betty, Matt the porter, er . . . the ultrasound tech got in, I think . . . I don't know.'

'Then what?'

'We split the patients up between us and did what we could. Dr Rasmus wasn't a bit happy, so I was sort of trying to take the brunt of it off the girls, you know? I reckon I saw two patients, and then I was on my way to the Pacheks. She'd have been out that day, Kasia. She was doing grand,

163

stitches healing well.'

'What did you see?' Paula leaned closer, her voice soft.

'I went out of another room. It was a Mrs, Mrs — ' He snapped his fingers, trying to remember. 'Mrs Markey. Wee boy. I checked her C-section and went out. I passed — oh.'

'Do you remember something, Chris?'

'Yeah, I — ' He blinked his eyes, blue and striking. 'One of the midwives had come in to help. I suppose Sandra rang her. She lives in town, I think.'

'Who was that?' She braced herself for him to say Tess Brooking. Guy's wife.

He shook his head. 'I don't know her name. She's got dark hair. It's hard to know them all.'

Dark hair. That could have been Tess, all right. 'Was it unusual for a midwife to be there?'

'Not really. It was all hands on deck. Sandra must have got her in, I'd say. Maybe she'd know.'

'Did anyone else come in?'

'Yes, throughout the day. It's why we were so messed up — I'd have to check all the timesheets to say who definitely was in that day. Accounts would have them.'

'OK.' Paula made a note to get that done. 'Chris — can you tell me anything else? Anything around those moments when Alek was taken?'

His eyes were fully open now, full of the same helpless annoyance she recognised. The team had been living with it ever since this case came up. 'No. I've been racking my brains. I can't even remember where I was when it happened. You know, the father waited about twenty minutes before he came to the nurses' station — he thought it was a real test she'd taken the baby for. Then he came up — I remember this bit — he's all tired, God love him, doesn't want to bother us, and he just asks politely when the nurse might be back with the child, since his wife's ready to breastfeed, and . . . God.' Chris ran his hands over his face. 'Thank God the baby turned up safe. But I worry, you know, Dr Maguire? I worry every day someone's going to come back and do it again.'

Paula could have lied to him, soothed, said they were on top of it and the babies would be fine. She didn't. She leaned over the table to him, switching off the tape recorder. 'So do I, Chris, to be honest. You keep watching them.'

★   ★   ★

On her way out, waiting for Gerard to finish chatting up the nurses at the station, she stopped by the glass of the main ward. A woman dozed in bed, her baby tight against her body. Both of them red and exhausted, locked into each other. Paula watched for a moment, staring at them.

Oh God. She wasn't ready yet.

She looked down the corridor, trying to catch Gerard's eyes and tap her watch. Or rather her bare wrist, since she didn't have a watch. *Hurry up*, she mouthed.

'You're ready then?' Gerard strutted down the corridor.

'I've been ready for ages. Can we go? DI

165

Brooking and myself are supposed to go to Croft's again today.'

'All right, all right, no need to be so narky. I'll bring the car round.'

She almost ran out, but couldn't resist a final look back to the Maternity Ward. Where she was headed, if she didn't do something soon.

18

'What the hell's going on here?' As soon as Guy turned his car into Magdalena Croft's lane, the car was mired in traffic. The quiet country road was nose to nose in vehicles, people already getting out and walking so that it was impossible to drive any further. The air vibrated with the distant squeal of a loudspeaker.

'I don't know. We better just park up.'

The crowd seemed to be flooding to the mansion where the faith healer laid her head. The atmosphere would have been that of a rock concert, except instead of pierced teens clutching carry-outs, the attendees were virtually all middle-aged or older. Some led children by the hand, and among the crowd wheelchairs were being pushed, spokes sticking in the muddy banks of the road, where snow had hardened to icy patches. No one spoke or met each other's eyes. The only sound was feet trudging through the melting snow and mud.

Paula and Guy ducked in among them. 'There's definitely something up,' he said. 'I haven't seen a crowd like this since Glastonbury.'

She couldn't picture him at a festival, but ignored this. 'I think they're here for her. It's like the videos on her site.'

They followed the crowds round behind the house, where the gate to the field had been left open. Beside them, a boy on crutches was being helped over the cattle grid, his legs cruelly twisted. Paula suddenly realised what it reminded her of — a film they'd watched in school, the pilgrims in Lourdes flocking up the grotto, bathing in the scummy water and casting their sticks aside.

'It's some kind of prayer rally,' she started to say to Guy, but she was drowned out by the crackle of a handheld loudspeaker.

Up ahead they saw Father Brendan, who had it slung over his shoulder like a tour guide. 'Yous'll all get the chance to see Mrs Croft — just wait your turn. Anybody what can't stand for long can come up first.' Behind him, serene as an idol in a flowered picnic chair, sat Magdalena Croft. Or Mary Conaghan, as she'd been when she got married in 1978, if their research was right. Behind her, the half-built church took up one corner of her field, wooden beams and bags of cement stacked with a covering of fallen snow. They looked to have been untouched for some time.

Paula and Guy fought their way to the front, unsticking boots from mud. The crowd appeared to be passive, but when you tried to get through them, they had a tenacious elasticity. No one was going to push in, but equally no one was going to yield their place on the frozen ground. Magdalena Croft had a young woman in front of her, no more than thirty. The woman's heavy jumper was lifted so the healer's hands rested on the white skin of her belly. It was barely above freezing, and her flesh dimpled with cold, but she didn't move, staring straight ahead.

Paula put out her own hand and grasped Guy's arm to hold him back. 'No.' She could feel the muscles tense, but he waited. Croft's lips moved, her eyes half-shut. After a while she snapped them open and resettled her large glasses on her nose. 'There you go, pet. God will bless you with a child within the year.'

'Oh thank you, thank you.' The woman was crying, stumbling off to the side, fumbling a twenty-pound note into the old ice cream tub Father Brendan was holding. On the side, over the faded picture of Raspberry Ripple, the word OFFRINGS had been inked.

'Must be making a tidy profit,' said Guy. He had his warrant card in his hand as they approached, the line of people regarding them blankly. 'Father Brendan?'

An irritable look. 'Youse'll have to wait your turn.'

'Well, we won't, actually. We need to see Mrs Croft now.'

'These people have come for miles — '

'It's OK, Brendan.' Her voice was a surprise again. Deep and almost musical, the accent shifting like the wind. She was dressed in wellies, a tweed skirt, and Arran jumper, her hair twisted and plaited round her head. Half nun, half druid priestess. 'I'm always happy to help the police. Sure aren't they looking for poor lost souls, same as me?'

A murmur went up from the crowd as she stood. Father Brendan, who was wearing a ski jacket over his cassock, took to his loudspeaker. 'Mrs Croft will take a wee break, she'll be back

169

with yis soon. God bless yis.'

Inside the house was warm and dry after the damp field. 'Would you mind waiting here a moment?' Magdalena slipped off her wellies to reveal holey American Tan tights, and indicated to them to follow suit. Guy struggled with the laces on his good brogues. Underfoot, the cream carpet was thick and luxurious. 'I'll be with you soon. I need to refocus.' She shut the door into the living room and they waited in the hallway. The walls were lined with pictures of saints, wooden crosses, a huge Sacred Heart painting above the door, Jesus with his chest open and beating. Paula shuddered, remembering that her grandmother had had one exactly the same.

'Weird place,' said Guy, in a low voice. 'I can see all that money was well spent.'

'Mm.' She looked at him. 'Can I ask you something? You know the day Alek went missing?'

'I'm familiar with it, yes.'

'Was Tess working at the hospital that day?' The question burst from her. 'Only one of the nurses said there was a midwife in that day, and I just thought . . . '

'Just what are you asking, Paula?'

'I don't know. I — '

'I think we should leave my family out of this, don't you?'

'I — '

'Look, I know I made a mistake with you that night, but how long am I going to go on paying for it? Tess is my wife. I have to look after her. We have a child together.'

Paula stared very hard at the Sacred Heart picture, biting her lip and willing herself not to say anything. She heard Guy mutter, '*For fuck's sake.*' Then there was a shuffling and Father Brendan was coming to summon them.

'What can I help you with this time?' Magdalena Croft had settled herself in the living room, smoothing her skirt. 'Tea, Brendan, if you would.'

Guy sat down on the overstuffed armchair. 'Mrs Croft, I'm Detective Inspector Guy Brooking. I run the missing persons' unit. As you know, we're very stretched. We were delighted you helped us find Alek safe, but Darcy Williams is still missing.'

'I haven't been able to see anything for her. Sometimes I don't, sadly.'

'We've also had a murder. You've heard about that?'

She nodded. 'The death doctor. Unfortunately God is just. She's paid her debts now. I'll pray for her soul.'

Guy glanced at Paula. 'We understand you condemned Dr Bates.'

'I wouldn't say that. I spoke out against her at one of my rallies. Someone had to.'

'Is there a chance some of your followers might have interpreted it as a call to do her harm? They seem to do whatever you tell them.'

Her face was placid. 'I can't be held responsible if people are drawn to me. It's my gift, and my cross to bear.'

'Why Dr Bates?' Paula burst in. 'She was

171

trying to help people too.'

The woman's eyes rested on her, leaving a chill like touching a frosty window. 'Doctor. I get women coming to me five, ten at a time. Desperate for a child. None to adopt any more. Meanwhile, girls go round whipping their knickers off for any fella, and when they can't take the consequences it's the unborn babies who pay for it. I don't think a woman who'd help with that belongs in a God-fearing town like Ballyterrin.'

'Mrs Croft.' Paula tried again. 'So far we have no leads in this case, and I'm sorry to say Dr Bates's daughter has also gone missing. You may see it in the papers today. She's heavily pregnant and it's going to snow again tonight. We need to find her.'

There was some reaction to that, an odd flicker that ran across the face like a ripple on a calm lake. 'I didn't know there was a daughter. Was the Bates doctor not mocking God by living with another woman, flaunting her sin?'

'She'd been married before. As you were.' Paula couldn't resist the shot but it didn't seem to register. Guy shook his head at her slightly: *back off.*

Magdalena Croft had recovered and was once again calm as a statue. 'I'm sure she isn't far. Were you wanting to use my vision to find the daughter, is that it?'

Guy ploughed on. 'Mrs Croft, you're the only lead we have. We'd like to find out how you knew Alek would be in the church that day.'

The big dark eyes blinked behind the glasses.

'I saw him, Inspector. The Virgin came and showed me.'

'I'm sorry, Mrs Croft, but you must understand, he was lost, and you knew exactly where to find him. We can't explain it.'

'You see that board of pictures?' They looked where she pointed — a frame on the wall with spaces for maybe twenty pictures. Intended for grandparents with large Catholic broods, perhaps. Each one was filled with a photo of a newborn baby. 'Those are all children born to women I've helped. Women who were told by conventional medicine that they'd never conceive. How do you explain that?'

It set Paula's teeth on edge when people talked about 'conventional medicine', as if it were dangerous heresy. 'How do *you* explain it?'

Magdalena Croft looked at her. 'You've heard of women conceiving once they've adopted, after countless years of trying?'

Reluctantly, she conceded. 'Yes.'

'There are more things in the world than we understand.'

'You're saying they get pregnant just because you give them hope?'

She presented once again her inscrutable face. 'I'm not required to understand how it works, Dr Maguire. I've been blessed with the gift to help people. It's all I've ever known. Brendan!' The priest came scurrying, as if he'd been waiting outside the door, a tray wobbling in his hands laden with flowered mugs and a packet of Jammy Dodgers. 'I won't be needing any tea. Give some to these young folk if they want it. I must get back to my followers.' She stumped to the door on her horny stockinged feet, pausing as she turned. 'If you want my help with that poor missing girl, you'll need to bring me something she touched. Clothes are best. God willing she'll be found, and her wee baby too. If it's something else you want, then arrest me and I'll answer any charges. I've nothing to hide.' Something about the last statement was jarring, but Paula couldn't think what it was.

'Mrs Croft — '

She cut Guy off. 'I must get back. I have duties.' She was going.

'Mary!' Paula called after her as she went out. 'Why won't you tell us the truth?'

Magdalena turned, unblinking. She moved slowly back into the room, in front of Paula, looking intently between her and Guy. She smiled. 'So he's the one, is he? Isn't it about time you told him the truth, Dr Maguire? He'll find out soon enough.'

Paula gaped. Guy was frowning. 'What — ?'

'You have to stop putting things off, Paula. You have less time than you think. You should start now. What you're looking for might be saved, if you can only find the courage.'

And she was gone.

Guy looked at Paula, mouth open, about to speak. She shook her head, shaking. 'No. I can't. Just — don't ask me.'

They got back into Guy's car in awkward silence, the boom of the loudspeaker coming over from the field. They didn't mention what Magdalena had said, or their row before. As they

174

drove off Paula was sure she saw a new silver Mondeo parked up a side road — a car she recognised. Slumped at the wheel was a short, dark-haired woman, head bowed into her coat as if hiding. Saoirse. It didn't take a huge leap to work out what her friend, desperate for a baby, was doing out here visiting Magdalena Croft. Oh, God. And Paula had gone to her for advice on her own unwanted pregnancy, the product of carelessness and alcohol and despair. She was so stupid. She was careful not to look back, sliding down in the seat so she too could hide from the truth.

Guy pulled out onto the main road. 'Shall I take you to the office? I might go home. I mean, I'll work there.' He was stiffly polite. After their conversation, the word 'home' stung in the air. It was almost four, the chill of new snow hanging in the darkening sky.

Paula answered with the same distant tone. 'If you could drop me at my car, that'd do. There's someone I need to see.'

19

The woman in the stained armchair looked ancient, as craggy and indeterminate as stones in a field. Paula knew it would have been her eightieth birthday earlier in the year — summer. She remembered another party, a cake topped with hundreds and thousands, chasing her cousins in and out of fly curtains on a rare warm Irish day, Robinsons Fruit and Barley from a plastic cup that smelled of old sunshine. Sixty, that must have been. By the time her grandmother had turned seventy, Paula and PJ were no longer speaking to any of the Sheeran family.

'She doesn't always know you're here,' confided the young nursing assistant, who was busting out of her pink uniform in all the wrong places. 'Mrs Sheeran! It's your wee granddaughter to see you, isn't that nice?' They'd made an effort to create a festive air in the home, with a plastic tree in the corner, but it just looked sad among the walking frames and oxygen canisters. Paula realised she and her father hadn't bothered doing anything for Christmas — no cards sent, no decorations up, no mention of it. You didn't want to remind yourself there was someone who'd not be home for the occasion.

Wondering how old she'd have to be to stop getting called a 'wee girl', Paula sat down nervously on a low chair, which left her level with her grandmother's ageing knees, like a supplicant to a queen. Her bag puddled on the floor. 'Hello, Granny. Do you remember me?'

Kathleen Sheeran showed no sign of realising anyone was there. The face was sunk beneath waves of wrinkles like a sand castle on a beach, but the expression was the same — unyielding. She tried again. 'It's Paula. Margaret's girl.'

The eyes fluttered, irises pale and washed out. They had been blue, Paula knew, the same striking blue as her own were, as her mother's had been. *Were?* Tenses were a fraught issue with missing persons.

Kathleen croaked out some words. 'And who would you be?'

'I'm Paula. Your granddaughter.'

'Oh?' The tone between surprise and disbelief. 'Are you Cassie?'

'Paula. You haven't seen me for a long time.'

For a long moment she just processed this, arthritic fingers pleating the edge of her wool skirt. Then something seemed to shift and the eyes focussed. 'Margaret,' she said.

Paula swallowed. She was always being told how like her mother she was, wasn't she? 'I've been away.'

'Why did you not come to see me, Margaret? You sister's awful cross about it. You were on the news and everything. And your PJ's been shouting and giving out to us. We didn't know where you went.'

'I — I'm sorry.' She didn't even know how to phrase it. 'Granny,' she said, leaning in to the smell of talc and decay. 'It's Paula. Margaret's

177

girl. I haven't seen you in years and I'm sorry. But I'm here now. I need to know if you remember anything about her, about Mum. Because I need her, Granny. I need her because I'm having a baby and I don't know what to do.' She was shaking.

Her grandmother's eyes had wandered off. Paula reached for her hand, the skin cold and dry despite the clammy heat in the room. The school dinner smell of things boiled and kept under metal. 'Granny, do you recognise me?'

Again the snap, as if the brain was resetting itself. In the lined face, the woman's eyes settled again on Paula. 'Margaret. Where did you go?'

★ ★ ★

Paula drove home with extreme care, twitching at every turn of the wheels on ice. Outside the snow had started again, delicate wisps on the breeze, beautiful and soft. But if it went on long enough, deadly.

What did it mean, then? She'd said the words out loud, telling her unknowing grandmother, maybe because it was somehow the nearest she could get to her mother. It was pathetic really. She'd done without a mother all these years, through the blood and heartbreak of adolescence, the unformed anxiety of her twenties. She shouldn't need one now just because she'd accidentally got herself pregnant.

She'd left her grandmother after a short while of smiling and nodding, patting the old papery hand. It was clear Kathleen Sheeran existed somewhere fluid in time, where it could be simultaneously present and distant past. Paula was driving back to town against the flow of evening traffic, brake lights like jewels in the falling snow and dark. She realised she didn't want to go home, despite the weather. Not yet. She couldn't face her father's scrutiny and that file sitting on her desk, so many horrors behind its dun-coloured cover. She needed someone to talk to, someone to help make sense of this case. She couldn't go to Guy — he'd be at home with Tess and their daughter Katie, curtains drawn warm against the night. The thought of it knifed her in the guts. There was only one other person she could possibly go to. Almost before she'd realised it, Paula had turned her car towards the office of the Ballyterrin Gazette. Magdalena Croft's voice was in her head. *You've less time than you think.*

She pulled up in the side street. The lights were off. No one home — most days Aidan was the only member of staff in the once-bustling building. So where else would he be, at seven p.m. on a week night? She was almost afraid to find out the answer.

From the paper offices it was only a short drive to Flanagan's, the old-man's pub Aidan had started drinking in at sixteen, and now frequented when he was on his periodic bouts of whiskey and self-destruction. As she feared, there was his red Clio parked up in one of the pub's three spaces. She gripped the steering wheel. So he was drinking again. Well, she'd had enough of hauling him back from the bottom of a bottle.

179

Let him crawl out by himself this time.

She was about to drive off when the pub door opened, spilling out noise and warmth into the frozen night. Paula caught a glimpse of the dark-lit interior, a TV screen showing some kind of sport, a green background, and there was Aidan lighting a cigarette, wearing just a T-shirt on the icy night.

She was tempted to leave anyway, though he'd seen her, but she opened the door instead and they approached each other warily across the car park. She crossed her arms against the cold. 'Thought I'd find you here.'

Aidan dragged on his cigarette. 'You know me too well, Maguire. Haven't seen you much of late.'

'Been working. A missing baby and a pregnant woman, and a murder too; we're busy. Haven't seen you about either — too busy trying to undermine us?'

He ignored her. His cigarette glowed in the dark, and the smell took her back, to the summer they'd been teenagers and in love.

'I wanted to talk to you,' she said. 'These cases. I'm stumped.'

'You want my help?'

'Yeah. Don't tell me you've not done some digging.'

'I might have a few ideas.' He ground the butt under his Adidas trainers. 'Will we go back to the office?'

The office, dusty and empty, had been the scene of their ill-advised encounter two months before, which had quite likely led to Paula's

180

current predicament. She looked down, hands in the pocket of her coat. 'Not now. I have to tell you something as well.'

'Oh yes?' He was wary.

'Guy — DI Brooking — he gave me my mother's file last month. There might be new information about her.'

'Really? I thought they never found anything.'

'They didn't. But there's a prisoner, ex-IRA — he said he might tell something, if he got let out early. He hasn't talked yet but I might — I might go and see him. He said maybe he knew her name. Mum's.'

'Who is it?'

She said nothing.

'Who is it, Maguire? Someone local?' She didn't want to tell him. He knew anyway. 'It's Conlon, isn't it? Jesus Christ. You're going to talk to the man who shot my da right in front of my eyes?'

'We don't know that for sure,' she said weakly.

'Course we fucking know. I was there, Paula.'

He never called her Paula. 'It's my mother, Aidan! He might know something. I have to at least try.'

'And why are you telling me?' She hesitated. 'Fuck off. You want me to *help* you?'

She nodded slowly. That was what she wanted, wasn't it? 'I need you. I can't do this without you.'

Aidan put his head in his hands, making an odd sound. It took her a few moments to realise he was laughing. 'You're something else. You sleep with me, then you ignore me for weeks

181

while you prance about with fucking Brooking, and now you want me to help you free the terrorist who murdered my dad?'

'I didn't — '

'Save it. You and me go back a long way.' His eyes were very dark. 'There's a lot I'd do for you. But you ask too much sometimes. You ask too much, Paula.'

He turned and went back into the pub, and not knowing what else to do, Paula left.

★ ★ ★

When she turned her key in the lock at home she realised someone was there. The good teapot was out on the table and a plate with biscuits arranged on it — bourbons, custard creams. From the living room came voices, her father's deep rumble, and someone else. A woman, her face turned away. Paula pushed the door. The woman had once been a redhead, you could tell — the exact shade of the plait coiling over Paula's own shoulder. 'Dad?' Her voice stuck in her throat.

Light was falling from the lamp, pale and indistinct, and for a moment she couldn't see the woman's face. She wasn't tall, around five-five, her body compact under a North Face raincoat, hair short and greying. 'There you are, Paula. I knew you'd look exactly like that. Do you remember me?'

She did. She did. Her hands steadied on the wooden lintel of the door. *Not her*, no, not her, but close. 'Auntie Phil?'

'That's me. Philomena.' Her mother's sister moved towards Paula, assessing critically. 'I knew it had to be you. At the home they said one of Mammy's granddaughters visited. Well, I knew it couldn't be our Cassie because she's in court weekdays — she's a lawyer — and it can't be Mairead since she's off travelling in Australia. There's only one other granddaughter, you know; it was all boys otherwise. And I knew you were back. I saw Pat O'Hara in town when I was doing my Christmas shopping.'

Paula stood speechless during this stream of information. Her father shifted to his feet. 'You went to see your granny then?'

'Yeah. It's been too long.'

'I'd have brought you, if you wanted to go.' He manoeuvred past Paula, gently holding her elbow. 'Will you take more tea, Philomena?'

'No thanks, PJ. I'll be on my way, with all this snow.'

'Shocking, isn't it? You'd think they'd get the gritters out.'

'Well, what I heard was, PJ, the council have let all the stocks run down and now there's no more to get, so we'll have to sit it out. They've to order some in from China or someplace like that.'

'Awful. I can hardly step out the door, with this leg.'

'I'm sure, God love you.'

There was no indication that the two hadn't spoken for nearly twenty years. Did they know? Had someone passed on that Paula had openly declared her pregnancy, and her intention to start looking for her mother again? There was no sign they were interested in anything other than biscuits, and the perfidy of the local council.

When Philomena went, making a big show of thanks, and goodbye, and come out to the house sometime, sure Cassie would love to see you, Paula stared at her father. 'What was all that about?'

'She called by. She must have been in town to get her shopping.' He began putting the biscuits back into an old Quality Street tin.

'Called by? Dad, she hasn't been here in, like, seventeen years.'

He shrugged. 'Aye, well, we both said some things. 'Twas a bad old time. But it's water under the bridge.'

'Did they — ' She paused. 'You know when they — because you were suspended from work, did Mum's family think it was you who maybe — that you had something to do with it?'

He said nothing for a moment. 'It's what you do. If a woman can't be found, you always have to look at the husband.'

'But you'd an alibi. You were working on a case that day. Weren't you?' She hoped it wasn't obvious she'd been rereading the file very recently.

He closed the biscuit tin. 'I was. But they'd only you to say she was here in the morning, pet. You see? And you were just a wean.'

'Oh.' That silenced her. How much of a lynchpin she'd been in the case, the last person to see her mother alive and well in her proper place. 'What did she want, Auntie Phil?'

'I think she wanted to bury the hatchet. I'm glad, to be honest. It was wrong of me to cut you off from them. You need your family. I won't be around forever.'

'Dad!'

'It's true, isn't it?' He moved towards the living room, gathering his tea and paper. 'Maybe if you were married or something, pet. But I worry about you. You can't be alone in this ould world. You need people round you.' He stumped past her again, the limp making him seem older than his sixty years. She wondered if he was right. In London being alone had seemed like a luxury, an escape, something to be hoarded. It was only in Ballyterrin that it seemed like a disease.

20

'Paula? You busy?'

Paula looked up, confused. She was at her desk, the cursor blinking on a blank Word document, and she had the sliding sense that time had rushed past her. 'Um, no, just researching, why?'

It was Fiacra who'd spoken to her, coming in with a sprinkle of snow on the shoulders of his trendy reflective jacket. 'Boss wants you to go to the station, he's up there.'

'What's it about?' Paula rubbed her face, trying to hide her confusion; she was just so tired, day and night.

'Computer techs found something, he said. He wants you.' Fiacra was settling down at his desk with a jam doughnut, flipping his tie aside and turning up his iPod.

Avril gave a little tut from her own neat desk. 'Not Kanye again, *please*.'

'Who'd you want? Jay-Z?' Fiacra thumbed through the display.

'I don't mind him so much, I suppose. If Beyoncé likes him he must be OK.'

Paula left them to it and went out to her car, huddling into her coat for the short walk across the parking area, riven with icy winds.

She'd spent the morning updating her profile of the abductor, though it was difficult. You had to imagine that shadowy figure they'd seen

186

taking Alek Pachek, tall and dark in the nurse's uniform, doing all these other crimes too. Leaving the baby in the church and slipping out again unnoticed, onto a busy rush-hour street in town. Abducting Dr Bates, a strong and determined woman, keeping her for days, then forcing her to march in the snow and cut her own stomach open with a scalpel. Lurking on the path behind the Williams house, unseen by any neighbour or passer-by, waiting for the mother's back to turn for a moment, then seizing the child and making off with her.

It was hard to believe the same person could have done all those things, have the patience to wait, the strength to overpower. Sighing, Paula had discovered herself clicking through the archives to check which cases Magdalena Croft had worked on in the South. All children, all missing. Little faces and little lost bodies. All found, though some sadly when it was already too late. But could she possibly know, when all the police and experts hadn't a clue? How could she trace a four-year-old to a windswept beach where his body lay hidden in a cave by the sea? She remembered the woman's words. *I'm not required to understand.* When things were so far beyond what you could take in, it wasn't so surprising people made their own answers. Miracles. Visions. Psychic powers.

She pulled into the PSNI car park showing the pass she'd been grudgingly allowed, now she was working on the Bates murder case too. Guy must have found something important to call her up there.

187

Trevor the computer tech had to all appearances just recently finished primary school. He had pink cheeks and wore a suit his mum must have bought for him. Paula remembered the heady days when she'd always been the youngest on every team, fresh from her post-doc at Greenwich University. Not any more.

'So he's accessed Dr Bates's files?'

'They were stored online, apparently, and he's managed to access them finally.'

Guy and Paula were outside the interview room where Trevor had been working on Dr Bates's system with Erin, the doctor's unhelpful receptionist. She was a lot more helpful now, letting out bursts of laughter that could be heard down the corridor. Through the room's window they could be seen looking at something on Trevor's laptop — what appeared to be a video of a dog on a surfboard.

'Kids,' muttered Guy. When he went into the room Trevor quickly minimised the window on his computer.

'Inspector Brooking. Hello.'

'Hello.' Guy shut the door. 'Hard at work, are we?'

'Yeah. Erin's been very useful. She's the only other one who ever went on the system, see, so we had to get her in.'

Erin smiled to herself, playing with the ends of her long black hair.

'How are you, Erin?' asked Paula. She hoped the girl wouldn't reveal exactly why Paula had been at the clinic that day. Her lie about checking out a lead was flimsy in the extreme.

Erin looked martyred. 'I'm all right. We had her funeral the other day, Dr Bates. Humanist, but it was really nice. Sad. Poor Missus Cole.'

'What have we got?' asked Guy, impatient.

'Well!' Trevor beamed. 'It's a tough system, sir. Designed so not many could crack it. I mean, I could, but it took me a while.'

'So you have her patient records?' Guy asked.

'I'm getting there. Lots of names. But guess what, if you look at when the data was last accessed, it was the second of December.'

Guy took this in. 'You mean *after* she went missing? Erin, did you access them on that date?'

'No.' She shook her head. 'I've not been near the thing. I got signed off work with shock after Dr Bates died.'

She didn't look very shocked, Paula thought, but whatever. Guy was frowning. 'So what happened, Trevor? Did they know the password or was it hacked?'

'They must have known it, I'd say. There's no evidence of hacking.'

'But she'd never tell it to anyone, surely — oh.' Paula was realising one situation in which Dr Bates might have been forced to yield up this information.

She looked at Guy quickly; he got it. 'Erin,' he said pleasantly. 'Could you give us a minute, please? Thank you.'

She went, with a fair amount of hair flicking and a backwards smile at Trevor. 'You'll email me about that thing?'

'I will, of course.' But he had the grace not to stare after her.

'That's why,' Paula said, when the girl had safely gone. It was all very clear. 'That's why they took her. They wanted the password to her files, she wouldn't give it to them — that's why they kept her for three days. That was as long as she could hold out.' She remembered the autopsy report. 'Those cuts and injuries, the drug in her system. They were *torturing* her.'

'This is very troubling,' Guy was twisting his mouth. 'Are you saying someone out there now has access to all Dr Bates's records, Trevor? All the women in Ballyterrin who might have wanted an abortion?'

'Pretty much. They could get all the addresses, even. I already ran a search through, and guess what, Heather Campbell's in there.'

Guy's eyebrows went up. 'But she wants her baby. She told us she'd been trying for years.'

But Paula understood. 'That's not it. Do you remember, Heather told us her mother had added her onto the system like a patient appointment, when she went to see her? It seemed to especially hurt her. So her name would be in there for that reason.'

Guy asked, 'What about Caroline Williams or Kasia Pachek?'

'Not that I can see,' said Trevor. 'I'll take another gander.'

'Do. And see if you can find out what appointments Dr Bates had on the day of her disappearance. Maybe one of them was our killer. Anything else for us?'

'Yes!' He almost bounced in his seat. 'This is good, boss. Caroline Williams, the mother of that other baby who got taken — she was involved in some baby-breeding group, yeah? Little Monkeys?'

'I wouldn't put it that way, but essentially, yes.'

'Well, turns out they've a discussion forum online. Nappy rash and crayons and all that. Guess who else went on there for chats?'

'Who?' Guy sounded wary.

'Heather Campbell! We took her laptop in when she went missing and it's all on there, under her own name. Amazing how many people do that. Anyway, it turns out her and Caroline Williams got involved in a sort of online spat on there, and that's what made them both leave the group. So guess who that was with?'

'Just tell us, Trevor.'

'Sorry, sir. It was our friend Melissa Dunne. AKA Life4All. They have to give their real names on sign-up. I printed it all out for you, here. Melissa and Heather had some kind of row about hospital births. Heather it seems was all for them — babies died at home, she said, and it wasn't safe. Her dad's some bigwig doctor. Melissa of course was all in favour of dropping one in your kitchen. 'Get that, darling!'' He sniggered at his own joke. 'So, it got a bit heated, and Heather deleted her profile.'

'And Caroline?'

'She chipped in about choice and 'breastfeeding Nazis' and then deleted her account too in a huff. You know, it's more and more common these days, online rows spilling out into real life.'

Guy looked thoughtful. 'It's not implausible, I must say. Did Melissa Dunne seem the type to start online feuds, Paula?'

'Yes, frankly. Obsessive, petty, lives her life on the internet. Exactly the type.' Her mind was racing, fitting this information against the outline in her head, the shape of things. Caroline Williams and Heather Campbell knew each other. At least, online.

Guy was saying, 'Trevor, is there any way we could find out if Melissa was the one who accessed Dr Bates's files?'

'Oh yeah, if we had her computer. Even if she wiped it I can find the records. Very hard to wipe things entirely.'

'God,' said Guy. 'There must be hundreds of names in those files. What if that's it — the killer's targeting women whom she feels didn't want their child? If you find any more links between our cases and the files, Trevor, I think we should contact all the patients on there. Warn them, in case they went ahead with the pregnancy. They could be in terrible danger if the killer has access to these records.'

It was then Paula remembered that her own name and address would be in those files, for all to see. *Bollocks*. She tried to keep her face neutral.

'If you arrest your woman Melissa, I can requisition her computer,' Trevor was saying. 'I don't think we can do much without it.'

'OK. Thank you, Trevor.' Guy was still looking troubled. 'Let me see those forum print-outs.'

They made depressing reading, misspelt and

192

littered with smiley faces. Melissa Dunne, or Life4All, had used a picture of a foetus as her avatar. It appeared she had barged into a thread on hospital births and accused Heather Campbell, who'd started it, of trying to kill her baby.

Mrs H Campbell: I've spoken to my father about this and he says hospital birth is much the safest and home births aren't safe at all, what does anyone think about this? I'd like to have a water birth but maybe in the hospital. ☺
Life4All: that is rubbish and the usual lies from the mainstream media. Having the baby at home is the BEST for the baby and the BEST for mum. You only have to look at the MRSA and all those other nasty bugs they have.

Then Caroline Williams had also become involved.

SnazzyCaz: Life is right, I'm sick of being told by the nurses what I have to do with the baby, forcing you to breastfeed even if you've no milk and the baby's hungry, their like Nazis ☹
Life4All: that is very dangerous, u must not give Baby ANY other food or else u will kill it
SnazzyCaz: Er what r u on about? I COULDN'T feed my baby so I had to use formula
Life4All: Laziness is all. U don't see

animals not able to feed now do you. People just cant be bothered nowadays is all

Mrs H Campbell: I'm sorry but who are you to comment Life? My father is a famous doctor and he says babies die at home all the time. What medical qualifications do you have? But I agree we should all be breastfeeding for at least six months.

Life4All: I have five healthy children at home all home births all breastfed. More than any of u stupid girls I bet

SnazzyCaz: Mental cow

Paula lowered the paper. Guy was staring at her, worried. Trevor was fiddling with his computer again. So. Melissa Dunne had fought online with two women; now one of them was missing and the other one's baby had been taken. 'We have to, don't we?' said Guy. Sometimes they could do this, talk without words. At first it had thrilled her; now it was just a reminder of everything that was gone. She nodded. They had no choice.

★ ★ ★

'That was quick. They've arrested her already?' Paula had been at the station for barely an hour when she saw Dunne's round face through the glass at the custody desk. The sound of raised voices reached into the main station. She left her desk and caught up with Guy, who was walking quickly down the corridor to the interview suites. Tiled in squares of grey carpet, it

194

effectively muffled you from the world.

He kept walking. 'Corry leapt at it when I went to her. She was desperate to make an arrest, especially with a second child missing. The feedback from up above is Not Good.' He seemed to almost relish this for a moment, then his face turned sober again. 'Let's hope we get something from her.'

'Will she cooperate?'

Guy moved with long, purposeful strides. 'I doubt it. She's saying we need a warrant to access her computer files.'

'And you really think it's her?'

Guy slowed as they approached the incident room, lowering his voice. 'You know what I think. I agree we should talk to Mrs Dunne, but it's madness not to check up on Magdalena Croft. Corry's got a blind spot there.'

'Maybe she just trusts her. The Gardai did have success using Croft.'

'I don't see it. I feel like we're ignoring basic policing here — if someone knows exactly where to find a kidnap victim, chances are they must have helped put them there, not that they have psychic visions.'

Paula shrugged; she'd largely given up trying to translate it for him. 'It's Ireland. I'm sure Corry has her reasons. She doesn't believe for sure the cases are linked, so it makes sense to bring in the person who threatened Dr Bates.'

'But if she's wrong — '

'We don't exactly have anyone else. Come on, we'll be late for the briefing.'

21

'Yes. DC McGivern. What have you got for me?'

The middle-aged detective quailed under Corry's stare. 'Uh — we're still working through all the hospital staff — nearly a thousand of them. I'll reckon we'll know soon enough who was there that day on the ward.'

'Good. Liaise with Dr Maguire to set up more cognitive interviews if you need them, and check all the alibis for when Dr Bates and Darcy Williams were taken.'

The long conference table, four times the size of that in the MPRU's pokey unit, was surrounded by detectives and uniformed officers — rumour had it even the Chief Constable might be coming down to meet with Corry. The case, like Paula's 'situation', was spiralling. Two missing kids. A dead woman, and another gone too.

Corry was in her element addressing the room. She prowled back and forth near the large whiteboard, the leather of her expensive brown boots making a creaking sound. 'Melissa's not saying a word, but we'll soon have a list of all her Life4All group members, and then we can cross-check with the DVLNI to see if any of them drive Jeeps or similar vehicles. Melissa herself has a Land Rover. Unregistered — she claims it's off the road, but it hasn't been logged as such. It's impounded and being tested for DNA.'

'Has she an alibi?' asked Gerard, who was leaning on the table with his sleeves rolled up as usual.

'She claims she was at home with her husband the morning Dr Bates was taken. I've got him in another room, if you'd like a crack? I'll send Sergeant Hamilton in with you.'

'Me? Yes, ma'am.' Gerard's ears were going pink at the unexpected honour.

'And if the alibi holds?' Guy was against the wall, his arms folded.

Corry flashed him a look. 'We'll let her go.'

'Really?'

'What else would we do?'

'It just seems we're directing a lot of energy on this one lead.'

'On the woman who sent death threats to one victim and fought online with two others? I'd say that was wise, Inspector.'

Everyone was following the exchange, eyes flicking like children watching their parents fight.

'All right,' said Guy after a short pause. 'Have we made any other progress?'

'Nothing. So if you don't mind, Inspector Brooking, this is really our best lead for now. I mean, who else is there?'

'I have one suggestion,' said Guy quietly. 'This so-called faith healer, Magdalena Croft. She was able to tell us exactly where we'd find Alek Pachek. You don't think that's suspicious?'

Corry said, 'The Gardai have used Mrs Croft on a number of occasions, and she's often been very accurate.'

197

'You believe she sees visions?'

'I believe she helps find lost people. That's really all I care about.'

'I think it wouldn't hurt to check out her alibi for the other cases.'

Corry's mouth hardened. 'It's not common practice to question police experts on where they get their insights. Is that how you do it in London?'

'Experts? The woman's a fraud! You must see that.'

Corry's face was impassive. 'I mustn't do anything, Inspector. We can certainly check her alibis. But I think Mrs Croft's help has been invaluable. Alek's back with his family now, safe and well. If there's a chance to find Darcy Williams too, I'm not going to pass it up. Are you?'

'I wonder — ' Paula began, then stopped. All eyes were on her.

'Dr Maguire?' Corry, frosty and unreadable. 'Did you have something to say?'

'I just wondered if maybe we'd made too much of an assumption. That it's the same person, I mean, for all these cases. Alek, and Dr Bates, and Darcy Williams.'

'I believe that was your hypothesis in the first place. I've never been sure it was, but I agreed to make use of your profile.' Corry folded her arms.

'Well, I did think so, because of the cutting, and the womb symbolism — and because of sheer probability too. I don't believe there could be two isolated incidents of child abduction in a small town like this. But even if they're

198

connected it might not be the same person.'

A heavy silence. Corry staring. Guy said, 'Go on.'

'Well — you said it yourself, Chief Inspector, you've got Melissa Dunne's husband in for questioning to check her alibi. And we're ruling out people because they have alibis for Alek, or Dr Bates — but if there were two people, or more even, we could be making a mistake. Do you see?'

'And what do you suggest?' Again Corry was unreadable. Paula felt sweat on her forehead.

'Well — I'd say we keep following up all those leads — the hospital staff, the pro-life group, and the rest, traffic cams, CCTV. Whoever did this wasn't invisible. But maybe we can make the link in a more creative way.' Where was Avril? She found the analyst near the back of the room, hiding behind a computer. 'A while back Avril, er, Miss Wright, was talking about this software you can get, you see, and it sort of maps people based on acquaintance. Like, if they've ever phoned each other, or been on an electoral roll together, that sort of thing. You can see all the data laid out like a web of connections. It might throw up something we haven't thought of.'

'And do we have this software?' Corry fixed Avril with a glare. She cringed.

'Er — no, ma'am. I put in a requisition, but it's expensive.'

'Send it to me. Will it work?'

The girl blanched as heads swivelled towards her. 'Y-yes. I mean, it should.'

'Do it, then. Now can we get on and question

199

our witnesses, please?' She looked round the room at the mostly male faces staring back. 'Who here has a kid?' There was a surprised silence, then a few hands went up. Corry pointed to them. 'Right, one of you can come in with me. I'm not having some ham-fisted batterer interview Dunne. You'd be lynched.' She sighed at the blank looks. 'Remind me to hire some women next time. That's all.' Corry looked at her watch as she dismissed them. 'Dr Maguire, can you stay behind?'

Oh no, what now? Paula tried to catch Avril's eye to apologise for putting her on the spot, but she was gone in the sea of hulking policemen.

When she was alone with Corry she started babbling, 'I didn't mean to interrupt; it was just I wondered if maybe I'd sent everyone down the wrong road, and — '

'Paula, none of us have a bloody clue what's going on in this case.' Corry reset the clip that was holding back her blond hair. 'We're stumbling in the dark, and that's the honest truth. So whatever insights you have, for God's sake, share them, OK? That's your job. There's no point in having you if you don't add anything.'

'Um, OK. Sorry.'

'Now come and observe this interview. I've no idea if she's our woman or not, but at least we know she most likely sent those threatening letters, and that's something we can charge her with. Right now that's as good as we're going to get, I think.' She barrelled out, Paula tripping in her wake, always wrong-footed.

Today Melissa Dunne had dressed herself in what looked like a pyjama top covered in teddies, and a voluminous skirt over mud-encrusted wellies. The hairband and the Rose West glasses were still in place. Her hands were folded primly on the table. On the way down Paula had seen Michael Dunne, the husband, in another interview room, more smartly turned out in an old tweed suit. His lips were moving and he seemed to be praying as he waited for Gerard to interview him. He was an accountant, Paula knew, hence the big house and cars. A short, bald man, he was half the size of his wife. One of Corry's DCs, a nervous-looking lad with a pronounced Adam's apple, stood watch over Melissa.

'What do you reckon?' Corry asked Paula, as they looked through the glass. 'You've spoken to her. What will she do?'

'She's smart,' Paula said. 'She'll seem very stupid, though. I think it's her thing, to make you so frustrated you can't put up with her any more. And she knows the law. Has she asked for a lawyer?'

'She declined, I believe.'

'Right. She'll probably try to twist that round somehow. The main thing about her is she's absolutely convinced she's right and acting in God's stead. So she isn't a bit sad that Dr Bates is dead, even if she had nothing to do with it. She sees it as no different from the torments of Hell, where in her opinion the doctor most likely is now. You see? She feels no compassion.'

'You're saying she's a sociopath?'

'Possibly.' Paula thought about the neglect of those kids she'd seen, shivering, noses crusty. 'She's an obsessive, for sure.'

'OK. What's your gut feeling, Paula? I mean off the record. Forget all your research and your personality types. Could she have done this?'

Paula looked at the plump, blank-faced woman on the other side of the glass. Who'd rather save unborn groups of cells than care for her own living children. Who'd threatened to burn Dr Bates alive. 'No,' she said, finally. 'She's too controlled. That thing with Dr Bates — it was done from rage, not self-righteousness. Someone hated her. And Melissa has children, lots of them, so I can't see her stealing one, I really can't.'

Corry said nothing for a moment, then placed her hand on the interview room door. 'Thank you, Doctor. Do observe, please.'

22

'We're getting nothing from her,' said Corry, several hours later. Tight-lipped, she was expressing her dissatisfaction by very deliberately poking holes with her polished nails in the sides of the polystyrene coffee cup she held. They were gathered in her office — Paula, Guy, Corry. An air of inescapable weariness lay over them all. Guy had his shirtsleeves rolled up as the overhead grilles pumped out stale, burnt air. The reinforced window gave out on the car park, dark already at three-thirty p.m., snow pale and scurrying beneath orange security lights.

'It's not her,' he said, but the fight was all gone out of him.

'We can hold her another ten hours,' said Corry stubbornly. 'I'm not letting her go.'

'Was there anything on her computer?' Paula asked. It had been sent up to Trevor for analysis.

Corry shook her head slowly. 'No. No, there's nothing. No evidence she accessed Dr Bates's files. There's never anything in this damn case. But she knows something.'

'How can you tell?' asked Guy, rubbing his hands over his face.

'You can see the look on her smug wee face.' *Poke poke poke* went the nails. The sound made Paula feel sick. She was so tired the orange lights cast shadows on her eyes. She wanted to say something, but had no words.

The phone on Corry's desk shrilled, making them all jump. Corry answered. 'What? Oh for the love of God. Who arranged that? Jesus.' She slammed the phone down and moved over to the TV that sat on top of her filing cabinet, beside a dying plant. 'They've been on the bloody afternoon news.' She started stabbing through the channels.

'Who?' asked Guy.

'Jim Campbell. Caroline Williams. I'd like to know who put them up to this. I knew we should have let them have a bloody press conference.'

She'd found the right channel. Jim Campbell was speaking outside a country bungalow, a people carrier parked in the drive. Beside him, thin and pale in a parka coat, was Caroline Williams, her bleached hair lank. She didn't speak.

Jim was surrounded by reporters and talking to the cameras. In his early thirties, he was a tall, good-looking man with sandy hair, dressed only in a T-shirt and tracksuit bottoms despite the snow. His eyes were red-rimmed and his voice shook in and out of clarity. 'My wife has now been missing for three days. She is eight months pregnant with our first child. I'm begging anyone that might know something, please, please call the police. Please help me find Heather.' His voice cracked. 'I just want her back safe. It's nearly Christmas. Please give her back if you know something, anything.'

A reporter from the local news shoved a microphone in his face. 'Mr Campbell, what's your view on the police response to Heather's disappearance?'

He paused. 'I'll just say this. If you're going to come to my house and suggest to me my wife might have gone off willingly and not told me, and her hardly able to move with the baby, well, you don't have the first idea what she's like. I wouldn't trust them to find a lost dog, to be frank with you.'

'Do you feel the establishment of a specialist missing persons' unit in the town has helped at all?'

'It hasn't helped Heather,' he said bitterly. 'I honestly don't know what they're doing down there. My wife is missing and so is Caroline here's baby.'

The cameras trained on Caroline. Jim nodded to her, as if telling her to speak. On the screen came the caption: *Families of missing unite to challenge police.*

Caroline's voice shook. 'My baby is gone.'

'Mrs Williams, do you think the police have done everything they can to find your daughter?'

She seemed to freeze. 'I — ' She recovered a little. 'Please. I need to go inside now. Please help find her. Thank you.'

The piece ended and went back to the reporter in the studio, heavily made-up. Corry switched it off with a vicious swipe. Suddenly she was looking at Paula. 'Tell me. How do I break her?'

'Um — Melissa?'

'No, the Queen of England. Of course Melissa.'

205

'Well . . . let me . . . Emmm. I think she gets off on feeling superior, like I said. Like she pretends to be stupid, laughing at us the whole time. So . . . maybe we pretend to be stupider. See if she draws herself out.'

'I tried that.'

'Well — no offence, ma'am, but maybe you're not the best at pretending to be . . . slow. You know?' She waited to see how Corry took this. Could go either way.

But Corry was nodding. 'OK. So you're saying we need some big, thick, country constable who can soft-soap her, oh Melissa you're so smart, tell us how you got away with it, blah blah.'

'Essentially, yes.'

'So, who?' The nails drummed on the desk.

Paula and Guy looked at each other and she felt that surge, the joy of knowing someone was thinking exactly the same thing. 'Can we do it?' she asked him.

Guy said, 'I don't know. I'd say so, since he's officially on secondment.'

'Who in God's name are you talking about?' Corry was irritated. 'I don't speak code.'

Paula answered. 'Um — we were thinking of Garda Quinn.' We. The loveliest word in the English language. She didn't trust herself to look at Guy.

'You want me to let an Irish Guard interview my witness?'

'Mrs Dunne does live over the border,' Guy pointed out.

'And can Garda Quinn put on a convincing bogtrotter act?' Corry thought about it. 'Never mind, I've answered my own question. OK. Get him in.' She went to the door and shouted out. 'Monaghan?'

Gerard must have been hovering; he poked his head in. 'Yes, ma'am.'

'Tell Dunne we're taking a short break. We need a different approach to this.'

'Em . . . her solicitor's arrived.'

'What? I thought she didn't want one.'

'Aye, she's changed her mind, looks like. Will you let her see him?'

'Who is it?'

'Eh . . . Colin McCready.'

'For feck's *sake*.' Corry swore and clacked out, her heels echoing. Paula and Guy exchanged a quick look, which for a second made her entire body ache.

'That was a good idea about Fiacra,' he said politely. He'd thought it too, she knew. He was just being kind, letting her have the credit. He was always so kind.

'We should go,' she said. 'We're running out of time.' And she recognised the name of Dunne's solicitor. She'd been reading it in her mother's file just the other night.

★ ★ ★

There'd been a time, after it had happened, when Paula had realised her father couldn't look at her any more. One morning, struggling to get ready for school with no clean uniform or ironed shirts, she'd gone into the kitchen, where he sat in his dressing gown drinking tea. This was

207

before the police came to dig up the garden, before he'd lost his job and hurt his leg and everything had changed forever. When the hope they had was still full, not waned to a sliver like it was now after seventeen years.

Paula's hair had always been long, and her mother had liked to wash it for her over the bath, brushing it out into a fiery shine. Without this help, it was tangled in knots by the end of the first week gone. 'Daddy, will you help me?' She'd handed him the brush, and for a moment he'd raised it, one hand on her head like a blessing. He'd stood there like that, the brush in his other hand. Then he trembled and the brush fell on the ground, and her father had quietly left the room.

That look, the one she'd seen on her father's face, was the same one her mother's former boss gave her when Paula opened the door of the station tea-room to find him there, leafing through a file of notes. A small man, red-faced and balding.

He started. 'Is it — ?'

'It's Paula Maguire,' she said hurriedly. 'I'm Margaret's girl. Paula. Do you remember me? I work here now.'

He stumbled up with the air of a sleepwalker, holding out his hand. 'Of course, wee Paula. God, you're awful like her.'

She tried to smile, shaking. 'Everyone says that. Mr McCready — '

'Oh, call me Colin, love.' He was still staring. 'Is there a problem with Mrs Dunne's case? I haven't been let in to see her yet.'

'No, it's not about the case. I just wanted to

208

say hello. I remembered your name.' She paused. 'To be honest, I'd been thinking of coming to see you anyway.'

'Oh?' He looked puzzled.

'Let me explain.' She wasn't sure she could. 'I've been away for a long time, and now I'm back working here, it's made me think about things. About my mother. I sort of feel I need to understand what happened to her.'

'Closure, isn't that what they call it?' He fiddled with his papers. 'You want some kind of closure?'

'Something like that. I'm sorry — is there anything you could tell me? Maybe you don't remember.'

He made an odd grimace. 'Sure I remember everything about it. She wasn't in work that day, you know. She'd been off sick.' He scratched the top of his head. A balding man even in 1993, he now looked old, and tired, and portly. No wedding ring on his stubby finger, she noticed. There was a sad little model Santa Claus on the filing cabinet behind him, the whole room dingy and tea-stained.

'Did she seem strange before she went — did you notice anything weird?'

He shook his head, and the small hiccup of hope she'd felt quickly subsided again. *Stupid*. He didn't know anything either. 'Nothing, pet. She was grand, just like always.'

'Colin . . . ' She leaned forward. 'In the file, there was some suggestion that her disappearance might have been to do with the work you did.'

'The Republican POWs, you mean?' POWs, he called them. Terrorists, others would say. In Northern Ireland, words had real and fatal consequences.

'Yes. Were you involved with any cases like that?'

He rearranged his tie, which was red and had dogs on it. 'I was the solicitor for a few local boys accused of paramilitary involvement, yes.'

'And she worked on those cases?'

He frowned. 'The police back in the day — they tried to say maybe she took some documents, some statements relating to the clients, confidential things like that — and she showed them to people.'

'What people?'

He spoke reluctantly, lowering his voice in that way you learned to do when you'd lived in Northern Ireland through the worst of the Troubles. 'Special Branch. You remember the Army barracks outside town — they'd intelligence officers based there, who'd have given their right arms to see some of the documents we had. But I knew she'd never have done that. She was a professional woman. I trusted her.'

More than trusted, Paula thought, seeing how he was lost in memories. 'You think about her?'

He hesitated. 'Every day. When you walked in, I thought for a wee minute — well, you're the spit of her.'

She didn't know what to say to that. 'I don't remember, most of the time. I can't picture her — what she looked like. I can't remember at all.'

He didn't move for a moment. Then he made

210

a small noise in his throat, and pointed behind her. She turned and her own face looked out from the fly-blown mirror on the wall, pale with cold, puffier than usual in the cheeks. He said, 'Like that. She looked like you.'

She swallowed. 'Thank you. I'm sorry to land in on you. And if you think of anything — I mean, I'm sure you told the police everything at the time — but if there's anything at all you think of or remember, I'd really like to know it.'

'All right.' Reluctantly. 'They had some cheek, though, with their questions. Trying to say she'd done something wrong. Of course she'd have been looking through the files, it was her job! She's very neat, likes everything sorted. She was probably tidying them up was all.'

'OK. I better go. I'll get someone to update you on Mrs Dunne. Thank you, Mr McCready.' She couldn't seem to manage 'Colin' again, as if thirteen-year-old Paula were still making all the decisions.

'I wish you'd keep in touch, love. I still miss her.'

Paula tried to remember what she knew of her mother, those up-close childhood years when you might as well have asked what the entire world was like. A smell of Sudocrem and Anaïs Anaïs, red hair loose about her face. Just . . . Mum.

'Bye now. You take care.' He clasped her cold hand in both his clammy ones, and she felt a terrible lurch under her ribs, nausea and bottled-up sadness and awkwardness. When she shut the door again, out into the bustle and stress of the station, she realised what it was that had made her so uncomfortable. The present tense. It was just the once, but he'd used the present tense when speaking of her mother, which she hadn't heard anyone do in seventeen years. It made her realise that all this time she'd always thought of her mother as dead. But what if, what if? The what if, that was the thing that brought you to your knees.

★ ★ ★

Fiacra in a suit looked like he was about to make his First Communion. He'd shaved extra close for the occasion and a bit of blood had dried under his ear. 'Thank you for the opportunity, sir, ma'am,' he said for the hundredth time. 'I've never ran my own interview before.'

'Don't cock it up,' said Corry tersely.

Guy was more soothing. 'I'm sure you'll be fine.' Any minute now he'd be straightening Fiacra's tie, Paula thought. She was watching from a desk in the incident room, which Gerard was sitting on top of, shirt pulled out in his usual dishevelled style.

'How come a Guard gets to interview a PSNI witness?' *It's not fair*, he may as well say.

'He's on secondment, DC Monaghan. He's either one of ours or he isn't, no inbetweens.' Corry's tone was crushing. 'We want her to see someone from the South. Anyway, you had your go with the husband. Didn't find anything, did you?'

Gerard glowered. 'His alibi checks out for the

212

doctor's disappearance. He was at home, making phone calls to clients. Course, we've only his word the wife was there with him.'

Paula hoped the real reason for choosing Fiacra to do the interview never came out. Corry was clearly at the end of her legendarily short tether. 'Come on. We've got a few hours left to shut this down. I don't want any balls-ups.' Corry looked at her watch. 'Let's go, Garda Quinn.'

Fiacra's face was a mixture of excitement and terror. 'So I just be matey with her, like?'

'Yes. Make friends with her. Chummy chummy against the Northern police and all that. Get some answers from the woman. OK? Go.'

★　★　★

'Tenner says she'll make him cry,' said Gerard, as they all watched through the two-way window.

'No betting in my station, Monaghan,' said Corry. 'Anyway, you'd better give good odds. She won't.'

Guy said nothing, face drawn with tension. They were running out of road on this case, and fast.

Melissa hadn't taken too kindly to Fiacra's shuffling entrance, two cups of tea in his hands. 'Whoops!' He spilled a little as he kicked the door shut. It was impossible to tell if the messiness was real or not — Fiacra's desk at the unit was a public health hazard, which Avril often cleaned with wet-wipes when she could no longer stand being next to it.

'Where's the woman?' asked Melissa suspiciously, as Fiacra ambled in.

'DCI Corry? Oh, she had to go home to her kids. Career women, you know.' Paula looked at Corry — an eyebrow twitched. 'You'll have me instead, Mrs Dunne.' He stuck out a hand. 'Remember me? Fiacra Quinn. Detective Garda.'

She didn't shake. 'And where is it you're from?'

'Near Dundalk, out your way. Nice big place you have there. Do you farm much?'

'Michael does. My husband.'

'It's hard times in farming these days. My uncle John, he near had to give his up last year. The taxes, you know. They've their hand in your pocket at every turn.'

Melissa said nothing, but she did pick up her paper cup and sip the tea.

'Hope that's all right for you,' said Fiacra pleasantly. 'Just shout if you want anything else. I know you've been here a long time.'

'Hours,' she said huffily. 'I need to get back to my own children some time, you know.'

The children were with social services, as it happened, and possibly not likely to be delivered back to their parents without some serious questions being asked about their welfare, but Fiacra didn't say that. 'Of course, of course. We just need your help on a few things.'

'I've answered all your questions. It's against my human rights to keep me here.'

'Oh, of course, of course. Just run over it again for me, would you? I've a hard time getting my head round this case.'

Corry made a small noise in her throat — of triumph, or maybe amusement. Fiacra's bogtrotter act was flawless.

Fiacra was saying, 'Now. I have to ask you a few wee questions about Caroline Williams. Her baby Darcy went missing recently, as you probably saw.'

'What would I know? I've never met the woman.'

'Ah, but you have spoken to her online, haven't you? And you also spoke to Heather Campbell, who's gone missing too. That's a big coincidence, isn't it?'

'I've no idea what you mean.'

Silence while Fiacra put the print-outs of the discussion forum row on the table and Melissa read them. 'But you can't — '

'We know that's you, Mrs Dunne. You gave your real name when you signed up, and anyway, it will all be cached on your computer. They're looking at it right now. So there's no point denying it, you see that?'

Corry shifted on her feet. *Cached*. Was that too big a word for Fiacra's country-bumpkin persona to use? Paula watched intently.

Melissa pushed the paper away. 'I've no intention of denying it. Like I said, I never met either of those women. I speak to a lot of people online. Look, these are from months ago anyway.'

Fiacra went on. 'You sent those threatening letters to Dr Bates, who is Mrs Campbell's mother. That's a fact, isn't it? All this seems kind

215

of connected, would you agree?'

'I never — '

'Now, Mrs Dunne, we found your prints all over them. Tell me, to send those, you must have felt strongly that she was a bad person?'

'She was a murderer,' said Melissa, in her prim little voice. 'I know she killed babies, over in England. She should have been in jail. Now she's paid her debts.'

Fiacra leaned on the table with his elbows, lowering his voice as if speaking to a friend. 'My sister's after getting pregnant,' he said confidentially. 'I can see you won't judge, Mrs Dunne, so I'll tell you. The daddy did a flit on her. And I'll be honest with you, for a while she wasn't sure she'd keep it. She's not got much money, you know, and she's only twenty-two. But she's having it now, and sure we're all delighted.'

Melissa sat up as if electrified. 'That's just the thing, Garda — there's *always* joy when a baby comes. Even if you can't raise the child yourself, sure aren't there thousands of couples who'd be dying to take it and love it. Why should a wee innocent baby suffer because you're too selfish to pay for what you did? When I see all these couples here going to Vietnam or where have you and getting black babies, while Irish ones are being murdered, it just makes my blood boil.'

If Fiacra was startled by this eruption, he didn't show it. He blinked once. 'So when she came into town, the doctor, you didn't like it?'

'Garda Quinn, it's no skin off my nose what other people do. I'm living right, bringing my children up in a loving Catholic household.'

216

Yeah, right, Paula thought.

'But who else is going to fight for the unborn? The babies have no voice. Imagine it, their silent screams, and their wee fists clinging on to life, and they're being ripped out — shredded up — how can that be right?'

Her voice thickened, and Paula saw the woman was crying. What appeared to be genuine tears. To her horror, she felt her own nose start to ache in response. *Do not cry, Maguire, you sap.* It was bullshit, bullshit self-righteousness. She put up a hand to wipe her eyes, hoping no one would notice.

In the room, Fiacra was reaching over to pat Melissa's hand. 'So you were doing it for the babies. Sending the letters?'

'I just wanted her to see what she was doing,' Melissa sniffed. 'She was going to hell and she needed to know that.'

A confession. Bingo. You could almost hear the words ahead, the rest of it, perhaps the solution to this case suddenly rounding into view, like the moment you crest the top of a mountain. The air between Corry and Guy thickened. Paula held her breath.

Fiacra was soothing Melissa Dunne. 'Of course. And then did you think maybe you'd take it further, scare her a wee bit, or you know, warn her off? Show her the pain she was causing? So maybe you took her somewhere, waited outside her work for her that day . . . '

Melissa dabbed her eyes on her sleeve. Corry's knuckles whitened.

'Mrs Dunne?' Fiacra's face was open,

understanding. 'If you hurt her, you can tell us. It's OK.'

The voice went hard again. 'I didn't hurt her. She's the one who killed people. Hundreds of children she murdered. But no one's at her door dragging her out of her house in front of her weans, are they? No one's arresting her.'

'Because she's dead, Melissa. She got killed. She paid her debts.'

The same phrase Melissa had used. Paula wondered if the others had spotted it; it seemed familiar for some reason.

Melissa said, 'Yes, she's paid. She'll be burning in the flames now, and no one deserves it more. But I don't know anything about it. I was at home with my children on the day she went missing. I sent out an email newsletter from my computer — no doubt your clever fellas can check that. You've had my laptop long enough. And I went to Supervalu for my messages about eleven — they've a security camera, I'm sure. It's not a crime to warn someone when they're headed for the fires of hell, but that's all I did. Anyone can see I could never have made it to Ballyterrin to go anywhere near that woman.'

'But — Mrs Dunne, you never mentioned anything about this before. You wouldn't give us an alibi when we asked you.'

'Why should I tell you anything? You're all as godless as she was.'

Fiacra took a deep breath. 'And the brick through the window of Dr Bates's house?'

'I know nothing about this brick. Maybe someone else thought she was a murderer too.

218

You can hardly blame them. I did not touch the woman. I never even met her face to face.'

'You have a Jeep. We know the killer also drove a vehicle like that.'

'Yes, and mine's off the road. Surely your people checked that.'

'And — you're the right age for our suspect. You fit our profile — and you delivered your own babies at home, so you have some experience with medicine.' Fiacra must be desperate. You never told them they fit the profile. Paula sighed. It was over.

Melissa leaned in to Fiacra. She knew it was over too; you could see it in her smug expression. 'I know what all your questions are about, Garda. I'm not stupid. I had my weans at home with a midwife — healthy, normal weans. I'd have no more idea than you how to cut a woman open. It's the Bates woman who specialised in that. Now, I suggest you let me go home. I haven't called my lawyer in here with me because this is so stupid I wouldn't waste his time, but I'm sure we can find something you haven't done right in this interview, and then I could make things very nasty for you.'

And there she was, the real Melissa, sharp as a snake and twice as quick. Fiacra tried again, hopelessly. 'Dr Bates is dead, Mrs Dunne. Who could have done it? Was it one of your supporters? If you know you need to tell us.'

'I would doubt good Christian people could find it in them to slice a woman open. If you want to know who'd be able to kill in cold blood, well, she most likely did it herself.'

219

Outside the room, Corry let out all her breath. 'It's over. Let her go.'

Guy blinked. 'I'm sorry?'

'I mean it. You were right. She's not our woman.' And she turned on her heel and walked off, footsteps echoing. Guy looked at Paula, stunned. He spoke into the earpiece. 'Come out, Fiacra. It's over.'

For a moment, it seemed he couldn't let it go. He opened his mouth. Melissa stared at him, swollen with self-righteousness. Then he slumped. 'Interview terminated.'

He came out, shutting the door, and then he was talking very fast. 'Boss, I'm so sorry, I nearly had her, she was really crying, I think, let me try again, I — '

Guy clapped a hand on the younger man's shoulder. 'You did your best. She's not the killer. At least we know that now.'

Fiacra looked incredulous. 'But, boss — who else have we got?'

'No one. We've got no one.'

Fiacra's shoulders dropped. 'Shite.'

Guy didn't pull him up on the swearing. 'Come on, we'll — '

They heard feet running, and Corry was back, her normally impassive face stretched tight with anxiety. Her ID bounced around her neck. 'Brooking. You need to come and see this.'

* * *

'How many are there?'

'At least a hundred. They're blocking the

whole bloody road.'

They were looking out the window of Corry's office, where on the pavement in front of the station, behind the reinforced walls, the crowd of protestors were singing. What was it? Paula strained to hear through the strong glass. *Suffer Little Children to Come unto Me.*

'Fuck.' Corry balled her fists. 'There's going to be an accident if they don't move.' There were so many protestors the traffic had begun to back up on the road, horns sounding and brakes squealing. The desk officers had already started trying to herd them onto the pavement off the road. Some waved placards, many of which displayed the now familiar dead foetus, alien eyes, delicate tracing-paper skin, fragile as hope.

'What can we do?' Gerard's shoulders were rigid. 'Should we call the Tactical Support boys?'

Corry said nothing.

'Ma-am — '

'All right, Constable, I heard you. Let me think.' For a long minute she stared at the crowd, lips pursed. Gerard looked at Paula, who shrugged helplessly. This night just got stranger and stranger. The crowd had lighters, and the noise of their singing reached through the bombproof glass. *Protect the Unborn. The Silent Screams. Let Me Live, Mummy.* Each placard like a direct message to Paula. Choice, they said. What choice was it when everything you did felt like wringing your heart in your own two hands?

'Right,' said Corry finally. 'Like I said before, let her go. Dunne. Let her go.'

221

Guy started. 'Is that wise?'

'We've finished with her. We've followed due process. I won't be bullied into a decision. Monaghan — go.'

Gerard went like a greyhound from a trap. Corry rubbed her temples. 'Fuck. Fuck this bloody case. Sorry, Inspector, Dr Maguire. But I'm done with this. She fitted your profile. She fitted it and she looked guilty as sin.'

Paula quailed. 'Yes, yes she did — but — '

'But what? I need answers. This is a safe town. That's what we always say. It's post-conflict. You can walk down the street without some maniac in a balaclava shooting you or mowing down your children in their buggies. And now this. I've a pregnant woman missing, another woman dead, and a wee baby out there on her own, no mother to care for her — ' For a horrible moment Paula thought Corry was going to cry. Instead a familiar steely look came over the DCI's face. 'Have we any other leads at all?

Guy waited a moment. 'You know my thoughts. The psychic — Magdalena Croft, I mean — she also fits the age profile.'

Corry stared out the window. 'I'd have to arrest her. Think of the publicity — I didn't want to move until we had more. Especially after this. Dunne was the only real suspect we had and we're letting her go. There's nothing on Croft — she was cleared for police work, for God's sake.'

'Well . . . ' Guy caught Paula's eyes; she nodded slightly. Corry had to know sometime. 'She used to go under another name. She was

222

Mary Conaghan when she first started out.'

Corry said, 'And you know that how?'

Paula and Guy said nothing.

'I see. You investigated without my say-so. You thought my judgement was off.'

Guy answered stiffly. 'I'm afraid I thought Croft was our best lead, yes. Under normal circumstances she'd have been the first one interviewed.'

'Normal circumstances meaning what?'

'Not Northern Ireland.'

Corry didn't speak for a while, and Paula held her breath. Then a slow nod. 'Well. Maybe my judgement *is* off. The truth is, this case is breaking me. You have children, don't you, Inspector?'

'A daughter.' That question again.

'I've a daughter too, and a boy. It kills me thinking of little Darcy out there. If she's even alive. Maybe I need to hand it over to some young fella who's never been near a child in his life.' She put her hands on her own stomach for a moment. 'It gets me right here. It makes me feel I've no strength at all.'

Paula said nothing. She knew exactly what Corry meant.

'Can you bring me something more on Croft? I can't afford another bungled arrest.'

'We'll check again,' said Guy. 'I really feel that's the best option.'

'Look,' said Paula, pointing out the window. 'She's coming out.'

The security gates were opening in front of the police station. Melissa Dunne walked out in her long skirt and Puffa jacket. She moved with a shuffling gait, and she carried her belongings in a plastic Sainsbury's bag, but when the crowd caught sight of her the roar was so loud it shook the glass of the office window. Paula took an involuntary step back.

'They love her,' sighed Corry. 'Unbelievable. The woman's wired to the moon, and they worship her.'

When Melissa raised her hands and smiled at the crowd, Paula thought worship was exactly the right word. In that moment there was no one she resembled so much as Magdalena Croft. And suddenly Paula knew exactly where she'd heard the phrase *pay her debts*.

23

Helen Corry lived in a fancy-dan house on the outskirts of Ballyterrin, on a road that quickly gave way to green fields, cut through by the motorway to Belfast. Paula was standing on the doorstep realising she should have brought something — wine, or chocolates, or a collection envelope for St Vincent de Paul. Her mother had drummed it into her from an early age, catching the child's arm as they walked to someone's doorstep — *never go empty-handed, Paula.* They'd arranged to have a drink after the end of a long, exhausting, and ultimately futile day. Melissa Dunne was free, and they had no other suspects.

She rang the doorbell, which gave out a tinkly bing-bong sort of noise. Nothing happened, so she put her ear to the door, which was thudding slightly. Was that Metallica? The door flew open, almost hitting Paula in the head, and there stood the Chief Inspector, in a luxury black cashmere tracksuit, a large glass of wine dangling from one red-taloned hand. 'There you are, Paula, I can't hear myself think over this racket.' She shouted, 'Shut that bloody music off! It's not even music, it's noise!' It was exactly how she spoke to her officers at the station.

There was a vibration from upstairs, and the din went down a fraction. 'Teenagers,' Corry said, by way of explanation. 'They've my heart scalded. Come on in, Paula.'

The house was very tidy, showroom-shiny with large vases holding bits of twig, abstract oils in splashy colours, slippery marble floors underfoot. Christmas lights had been strung over the pictures and cards lined the mantelpiece in the sitting room, glimpsed in passing. A huge TV blared in the same room, unwatched, and the place was as hot as a hammam. Paula took off her heavy coat and held it over her arm awkwardly, as the DCI led her into the (also marble-topped) kitchen. 'Have a wee seat.' Paula hopped onto a chrome stool at the kitchen island. It had been her mother's dream to get a kitchen island one day, not that there was room in the pokey terraced house they still lived in. 'You'll have a drink?' Corry was already filling a huge balloon glass.

'Well, I'm driving, so maybe just water — '

'Have a bit.'

A vast lake of wine was set in front of Paula, who regarded it helplessly. 'You wanted to see me?'

'It's about time we had a chat, I thought. Woman to woman, if you buy into all that bollocks.'

'Er — '

'You like working at the unit?'

'Eh — yes, of course. It's fascinating. I don't think there's another job like it in the country.'

'He's a good boss, Brooking?'

'Yes. Very good.'

'And good-looking.' Helen took a sip of her wine. 'Don't you think? Very English, but easy on the eye.'

'Eh — ' Paula tried to give nothing away. 'He's a very good boss, everyone says so.'

'I'm sure.' Corry set her hands on the marbled counter-top. 'I'm a good boss too, Paula. Ask Gerard Monaghan. I like to put the fear of God in the young fellas, but it's the only way to get their respect, you see, if you happen to have a pair of breasts. Breasts and terror together — they can't get their wee heads round it. But we need more women up there. Sexual assault, domestic abuse — sometimes people just want to see another female face, you know.'

'Mmm.' Where was this going?

'I want to create a job for you on my team,' said the DCI directly. 'A staff job. Permanent.'

Paula had been lifting the glass to her mouth, almost reflexively, and now set it down. 'Sorry?'

'You'd work for me. You'd stay in town permanently — there's only funding for one more year down there, isn't that right?'

'But they'll probably renew it, and — '

'I wouldn't be too sure. You know as well as I do Guy Brooking was never going to stick around here in Hicksville for long. Then you'll be working for Bob Hamilton. Don't tell me that doesn't put the fear on you.'

'Um — ' She thought of red-faced Bob, fat fingers helplessly pressing buttons on his newly issued Blackberry. 'I'm sure he'd do a good — '

'It's a vanity posting and you know it. That unit was just a sop — use up a bit of spare budget one year, look like you're working cross-border, put some old past-it Sergeant in charge. But then doesn't your man Brooking

227

come over and start getting up everyone's noses.'

'But the old cases — '

'Well, maybe they'll solve a few, maybe not. They had to do something. It was getting embarrassing, especially in the South.' She changed tack suddenly. 'I could use you on all kinds of cases. Murder, violent crime. You could do whatever you wanted.'

'It's missing persons that interests me. That's my research background.'

'Because of your mother?'

Did everyone know? 'I didn't think you were from Ballyterrin.'

'No, I'm a Belfast girl, but sure they told me all about you when you came to the station. The wee Maguire girl, they call you. Everyone knows what happened.'

Paula swilled her untouched wine. 'Maybe it is because of her. I don't know. It's just — if we can find them, we can fix it. If they're not already dead, or broken — sometimes it's not too late to bring them back.'

'You were twelve when it happened?'

Corry's directness made Paula swallow hard. 'Thirteen. Just.'

'Same as my Rosie. Doesn't bear thinking about. But as for missing persons, sure don't we do most of the work anyway?'

'Er — ' She'd nothing to say to that. 'I don't know, Chief Inspector.'

'Please, it's Helen. Are you not drinking that wine?'

'Oh! Yes.' She took a small mouthful, finding it sour and scorching on her tongue. One mouthful wouldn't make a difference, would it? 'The thing is, Helen, I'd always planned to go back to London myself. I came over for one case, and then there were some loose ends to tie up, and I said I'd do a year — '

'What have you to go back to? Boyfriend?'

The frankness was caustic. 'No, but — '

'And in Ballyterrin, have you nothing to stay for?'

She thought of her dad, of Pat, of Saoirse and Dave, of Avril and Gerard and Fiacra. Of Aidan. Of Guy. 'I don't know.'

'Well, think about it. I'm impressed with your work and I'd like to use you. You'd have a proper role, with the chance to change how we do things in future. All those cases you're looking at now — they're already gone, Paula. They're dead, ninety-nine per cent of the time. But we can help the people who haven't gone yet. Find them before they even get lost.' She was leaning across the counter now, elbows out, her voice earnest. Paula could see the smooth foundation on her cheeks. Who wore full make-up round the house at nine o'clock at night?

'It's a great offer. Thank you, Helen. I just need to think about it.'

'Fair enough.' She sprang back up. 'Paula, can I offer you anything else, a wee biscuit maybe, some crisps?'

'No, no, I'm fine, thanks.' She took another small sip of wine. 'I shouldn't stay, the snow is so bad.'

'I know, it's awful. They'll have the gritters out again tonight, if they've any sense in their heads.

229

Bloody council. The station car park's like an ice rink.' Helen was uncorking another bottle of wine. 'I have to say I'm really worried about Heather Campbell. You know as well as I do a pregnant woman couldn't get very far in this.'

'What else can we do?' Paula could feel the wine lying on her stomach like a layer of oil on water.

'I just don't know. We're doing everything we can. I mean, she's an adult, she could have just gone away for a bit, the shock of losing her mother — but the husband is adamant she wouldn't. And this snow . . . no, I don't like it. We've so far managed to keep it under wraps that she's Dr Bates's daughter, but it'll get out at some point. Bloody press are all over me as it is.'

'Yeah.' She missed this, talking over the cases with someone who shared her obsession. Thanks to her own inability not to sleep with any man she got close to, things with both Guy and Aidan were far too weird at the moment.

'Mum?' A girl had come into the room, pre-pubescent breasts poking out the front of her High School Musical T-shirt. This must be Rosie Corry.

'What is it, love?' Helen Corry stroked the girl's hair with careless affection. 'You're like a whin bush there, have you no hairbrush?'

The girl pulled away. 'Will you tell Connor to turn his music down, I can't hear *Glee*.'

'Can you not tell him yourself?'

'He doesn't *listen*.'

'And you think he'll listen to me? OK, pet. God forbid you should miss *Glee*.'

The girl lifted a packet of crisps from a large bowl on the counter. 'I Sky-Plussed it for you for later.'

'Thanks, pet. That's my Rosie,' she said to Paula as the girl went out. 'Connor is the noisy one upstairs, he's fourteen. A deadly age. Take my advice, Paula, leave it as long as possible. Have your youth. Don't get married yet.'

'Mm.' She rearranged her jumper, suddenly very conscious of her stomach. 'Not much chance of that.'

'I was a few years younger than you when Connor popped out. Probably never have married his dad except for that, but there you go. My mammy would have killed me otherwise. Anyway he's gone now, and good riddance.'

She'd heard as much from Gerard. 'You're divorced? I'm sorry.'

'Don't be. He used to be in sales, Johnny, but then he got made redundant and I got promoted. Somehow he didn't feel that being at home all day was compatible with looking after his own children.'

'Oh.'

'That's how it happens, Paula.' She waved her wine glass. 'They think they're so liberated, just because they change a nappy now and again, but when it comes down to it, it's you that has to sacrifice your body, your career, everything. So put it off as long as you can.'

'Why did you join? The police, I mean?'

Corry set down her glass and mimed. 'An ex-boyfriend punched me in the face.'

Paula looked startled. Corry smiled. 'I was a

231

bit more pliable in those days, let's say. Anyway I went straight to the police, dumped him, and all they could do was try to blame me. I provoked him, apparently. What was I wearing at the time? What had I said? Only one other woman in that whole station, and she was the tea lady. Even the bloody sniffer dogs were male. So I thought — Helen, be the change you want to see in the world. I know people say I got promoted on the back of being female, but I don't care. I'm better than most of those ould fellas that still have their heads stuck at the Battle of the Boyne as if it was last week.' She poured more wine into her glass. 'And you, why the psychology?'

Paula thought about it. 'I wanted to understand. Why they do it. What they're thinking. And most of all where they go.'

'Where who go?'

'The ones who don't come back.'

Corry nodded slowly. 'I see.'

Paula took a deep breath. 'I better be going, Helen. Thanks for the wine, and well, for the offer. I'll get back to you.'

'Safe home.' Helen examined Paula's glass. 'And here was me thinking you'd be a good girl to get plastered with.'

'It's just I've the car, you know, and the snow . . . another time.'

As Paula drove home, fresh flurries landing on the windscreen, she was thinking of the hand Helen had laid on her daughter's blond head. Watching TV together, eating crisps. That was a mother, a constant and unquestioned presence. Rosie Corry would not have considered anything different, and neither had Paula, until her mother was gone and nothing was ever the same again.

At home, she switched on her laptop and plugged in the internet dongle, surfing easyJet and Ryanair fares to London. Was it possible? Could she say she needed a weekend away, business to attend to in London, a friend's birthday? Go and get it sorted, then restart her life, drink wine and walk without fear over ice, eat cheese and prawns and go on rollercoasters, sleep around, never look back? She sighed and logged out, powering down the computer without a decision made, just as paralysed as ever.

24

When Paula was little — very little, before John
O'Hara had been shot and the place became
heavy with sadness — she'd loved going to Pat's
house. Hand in hand with her mother, shopping
in bags, breaking the walk back from town with a
cup of tea at Pat's. Paula would have Um Bongo
or Robinson's Barley Water, and choose a biscuit
from the large Tupperware box where Pat kept
treats.

Pat had always just been there. Paula
remembered that endless night, dark by four
p.m., when her father had come in and she'd
realised the thing she'd been ignoring for hours
was no longer standing behind her tapping her
on the shoulder. It was right in front of her eyes
— *her mother wasn't there.* That was when she'd
let go of the fears she'd been holding down, and
like a bunch of balloons they'd gone soaring and
never come back. Pat had come that night and
sat on Paula's bed until she slept some. She
remembered all this now as she sat, many years
older but feeling no wiser, at Pat's kitchen table
listening to the kettle boil. She'd called in on her
lunch break, needing to keep things moving
somehow now she'd spoken to her mother's
boss. And maybe, though she wouldn't have
admitted it to herself, hoping she might run into
Aidan and get past their most recent falling-out.

'Now!' Pat came in, having changed out of her

aerobics clothes into slacks and a long pink cardigan. She settled her glasses on her nose. 'Sorry about that, pet. If I'd known you were dropping in I'd have baked.'

'It's OK.' Pat was rooting in her larder, amid the same warm spicy smell Paula remembered. Safety and comfort and sugar all wrapped up. Christmas lights and holly over every window. 'I just thought I'd call in, see how you were. How's Aidan?' she said brightly, patting the elephant in the room.

Pat had found some flapjacks and was arranging them on a little plate along with several Kit Kats. She always did this, even if it was just two of them, even though Pat herself never ate anything, always on a diet. 'He's grand. Awful busy, I've hardly seen hide nor hair of him. Have you?'

'Eh — no. I've been busy too. Work's crazy.'

'Of course, you'll be working on those cases.' Pat always spoke of Paula's job in deferential code. 'God, it's awful, isn't it? That poor girl who's missing, and the wee baby out there somewhere. I'm glad you and my fella are all grown up, Paula. When you were wee, your mammy and me, we'd leave you both in the garden in your prams, no bother. We always felt safe, even with the bombs and what have you.'

Paula leaned on her elbows. 'That was what I wanted to talk to you about.'

'Mm?' Pat was stirring, tinkling teaspoons, pouring milk.

'Mum. About her.'

'Oh.' Pat spilled the tea on the table as she set

235

it down. 'Wait, now, I'll get a cloth.'

Paula wrapped her hands round the warm mug as Pat fussed. 'I just think it's time. I need to know what happened.'

Pat sat down, fiddling with the cloth and running her hands over it distractedly. 'Pet, you know what happened. As much as any of us does, that is.'

'Do I? Dad won't tell me anything. He won't talk about her.'

'He can't, love.'

'I know. But I can't not. I was only thirteen, Pat, I can hardly remember. I can't even picture her most of the time.'

'But what good does it do to talk about it, pet? There's nothing more to know.'

'I know — I just want to talk about her. I — I miss her.' The words fell into the kitchen, warm and safe and smelling of biscuits, the tick of the clock Paula had given Pat for Christmas when she was seven. It was in the shape of a cat, its tail the pendulum.

'I know you miss her.' Pat was looking upset, even more so than Paula had expected. 'Did your daddy say something, is that where this comes from?'

'No! He won't talk about it at all. Why?'

'Oh, nothing. I just wondered why now.'

'I suppose being back, being older — I might want my own kids someday. What'll I tell them about her?' The lie passed over her lips, glib and sweet as sugar.

'All right.' Pat's hands shook as she split a Kit Kat, running a nail down the silver foil. Paula

236

wondered if she even knew she was eating it. 'Well, it was my John and your daddy were friends, you know. From as soon as your daddy got posted to the town. And when he met your mum, he brought her here for her dinner.'

'Did you like her?'

'Of course I liked her, pet — '

'I mean really. Did you know her?'

Pat had flecks of chocolate on her lips. 'I don't know if I did, pet. We got to be friends — they married fast, your daddy and her, and John was your daddy's best man, so we saw her a lot. Then I'd Aidan, and you arrived, so we'd push our prams together, and I'd lend her baby things and that.'

'Pat — ' Paula hesitated. 'I spoke to Mum's boss. Do you remember him? The lawyer?'

'Oh yes, what was his name again?'

'Colin. Colin McCready.'

'And did he know anything?' Pat looked at Paula, glasses on a string, eyes tired and anxious.

'No,' Paula admitted. 'Well. He said there'd been talk about Mum, about the Army barracks in town. She'd stolen some papers out of work, given them to the security forces, that sort of thing. I don't believe it. I mean, how would she even have met someone like that? She never went anywhere except work and home.'

Pat swilled the last dregs of tea round her cup. 'There were rumours at the time, but you're not to believe it, love. It's just bad stories, because of your daddy's job. Your mammy wasn't political. She said the whole shower were as bad as each other.'

'So she wasn't unhappy or anything like that?' Paula was aware of what she was really asking, behind these simple words. *Was she killed? Did someone come and take her?*

'Well.' A slight hesitation.

Paula seized on it. 'What?'

'You don't know about the soldier, do you?'

'No.' Paula sat up straight. 'What was this?'

'It was a few years before we lost her.' That was how Pat said it — simply, we lost her, as if she were a purse dropped out of a handbag. 'Your mammy was driving home from work, and there was a checkpoint — you might not remember, but things were bad again round those times. Anyway, your mammy's stopped, and when it's her turn the soldier's checking her licence and doesn't someone take a shot at him. A sniper. Got him right — well, God love him, he had no chance. I don't like them over here with their guns and their helicopters, but he was only a young lad. She said she could see he'd cut himself shaving that morning.'

'He died?'

'He died in her arms. She tried to help him — she'd this nice silk scarf she used to wear, and she used it to bandage him, but there was so much blood, and the wee lad screaming and dying in her lap. There was nothing she could do.'

'Why did no one tell me this?' She'd been what age, eight or nine? Was it possible it had gone over her head?

Pat jumped up and started piling the cups into the sink, running water on them. 'They didn't

238

want to scare you. You used to have a lot of nightmares — you'd wake up crying about guns and bombs. It was a few years after John, you know. You were hit awful hard by that, wee tiny thing that you were.'

Paula shivered. If her mother had been known to help soldiers, people would have heard about it. And then there was the terrorist Sean Conlon, sitting in jail, claiming to know things. But no, she couldn't talk to Pat about the man who'd most likely killed her husband. 'Thank you. I just needed to talk about her. No one ever lets me.'

'I know, pet.' Pat was washing up the cups with a little plastic brush, whisking imaginary crumbs from the table. 'Will you tell your daddy I said hello?'

Paula put on her coat, flipping her hair out over collar. 'Of course, but will you not be calling up to see him?' Usually Pat was at the house every day.

'Ah, love, I'll leave him in peace.' She focussed on the cups. 'I'll tell Aidan you were looking for him.'

Though she hadn't been, Paula thought, going out to her car. And she wouldn't, no matter how desperate she was to know where he was.

⋆   ⋆   ⋆

The snow was coming down soft and relentless as Paula pulled into the office car park around three p.m. She sat for a moment with the engine off and watched it, before getting out and crossing the icy ground like an old woman. She

239

stood outside the door watching the lights through the window, trying to draw her thoughts into some kind of order, but they were swirling like the snow, Pat and her mother and Aidan and Guy, and all the missing and the lost she would never be able to find.

She drew in a breath of frozen air and was about to go in, when movement in the dark end of the car park made her start, slip. She reached for the breezeblock wall, heart thudding. 'You scared me!'

'Sorry.' Aidan had materialised out of the gloom, as if her thoughts had conjured him up. He wore only a thin leather jacket against the snow. His nose was red, eyes black in his pale face.

'Where've you been?'

'In the station.'

'I can see that. Why in the station?'

'I was talking to Sergeant Hamilton, if you must know. I had some things to ask him.'

'Oh.' For a moment she was flooded with such terrible disappointment she was sure it showed in her face. He hadn't come to see her. It was only to get a story. The silence of the past months was no accident. He'd slept with her and then moved on, and she hadn't, indeed she was probably carrying the weight of the consequences in her belly right now. She pulled herself together. 'What about?'

Snowflakes melted on his face; he brushed them off his mouth. 'Did you honestly think you could just tell me about Conlon and I'd do nothing? Orangeman that he is, I can at least

240

trust Hamilton to tell me the truth about what's going on.'

'I didn't mean to hurt you. You know that. I just have to know. You can't expect me not to try, Aidan.'

'And you can't expect me to help, *Paula*.'

He almost never said her first name, and it knocked the legs from under her, as always. 'Why would I even trust you to help?' Her anger startled them both. 'It's not like you've talked to me all month.'

Aidan's face hardened. 'I've been busy.'

'You've been in Flanagan's every night God sends.' He looked away. She went on. 'It's just, Christ, could you not have come to see me, or rung, or — after we — Oh God, Aidan. I don't know what to say.' Anger was making her inarticulate.

He still said nothing. 'Why?' she asked. 'Why would you do that to me? Twelve years I waited for it, for us to be together, and now this?'

'This is why.' His voice was very low. 'You're angry. We're fighting again. You're expecting me to explain myself to you.'

'Are you drinking again?' she demanded.

He stepped away. 'You're not my mother, Maguire. And you're not my girlfriend any more. Not since we were eighteen.'

'I — '

'Well, you're not. You've made it very clear you'll do what you want without thinking of me, so I'm going to do the same.'

She was so enraged she couldn't speak for a moment. 'Some things don't change, do they?

Fuck me, forget me. Nice work, Aidan.'

He looked up, and she saw his face, and she felt cold tears prick the corners of her eyes. She might have said something then, anything to fill the chasm opening up between them, but then the door opened, spilling light and voices.

'Paula?' Guy had a plastic cup in his hand. 'I saw your car turn in, but then you didn't appear — I was worried.' He glanced at Aidan. 'Should I leave you to it?'

Aidan was still looking at Paula. 'I was going.' He nodded. 'Good to see you, Inspector.'

'And you.' As much warmth between them as two icebergs. Aidan turned away into the dark, shoulders hunched against the cold, hands in pockets.

Guy blinked away snow. 'It's really coming down. You shouldn't be out in it.'

'No. OK.' She made herself go in, though not looking back at Aidan was as difficult as not breathing. Inside was warm and noisy. 'What's happening?' She unbuttoned her coat.

'Avril's had a bit of good news — she got engaged last night.'

'Oh yes?' They were in the corridor by Guy's office.

'Yes, I think her boyfriend's a church pastor. Alan, is that it?'

'Think so. What's that?' She indicated the cup.

'I got us some fizz. It's nice to celebrate good news, I think. Everything's been so difficult of late.'

'Sure.' She looked up at him and he paused at the corner before the main office, awkward.

'Are we all right?' he asked.

She shrugged. 'I wish you'd told me about Tess being back.'

'I wanted to. I'm sorry. It's — well, I can't really talk about it. It's harder than you know. I'm very, very sorry.'

Could she really be angry, with all she wasn't telling him? 'All right. I'll try to get over it.' There was more to say and they both knew it, but it seemed impossible to broach. 'Is it — is it going OK?'

Guy clammed up. 'I don't know. I don't know anything right now.'

'No. OK. Well, let's go in.' She turned into the light, smile pasted on ready to congratulate Avril, and left behind the stricken look on his face.

★ ★ ★

Avril's face was flushed as she took tiny sips from her plastic cup. She wasn't much of a drinker, Paula knew. She wore wide grey trousers and a pink cardigan, her fair hair plaited like an angel's halo. One finger rather self-consciously bore a medium-sized solitaire diamond. Pretty. Unimaginative. Paula, feeling frumpy in her jeans and thick grey jumper, did what was expected of her as a slightly older woman who wasn't engaged or married herself: she gushed. 'Oh, it's beautiful! Congratulations.'

'Generous,' commented Helen Corry, who was there for some reason, power-dressed in a purple suit and boots. 'He must be fond of you, your fella.'

Avril blushed, turning the ring, which was too big for her finger. 'It was last night, after church group. I didn't see it coming.'

Corry swigged her champagne, or whatever it was that Guy had bought in the corner shop. 'We have to say that round the fellas, but I think we always have an idea.'

'I didn't,' Avril said, somewhat anxious. 'Really, I didn't.'

Corry smiled. 'I'd have been a shite detective if I didn't figure out mine was up to something. He had the ring in his sock drawer. Dozy bastard.'

Paula, who'd never been proposed to, said nothing, regarding the fizzy gold liquid in her cup. Why was everyone suddenly pressing booze on her? 'Have you set a date?' She was racking her brain for girl-talk clichés. Overhead, the office Christmas decorations, put up by Avril, swung in the current of warm air trickling from the ceiling vent. Tinsel and glitter, sad and cheap in the fluorescent lights, reminding you the year was nearly wrung out and everything you'd meant to do was now too late.

All the men in the room, unit staff plus a few of the PSNI officers she knew by sight, had clustered around Gerard's desk in the corner, and were loudly discussing football. Gerard was deep in chat with one of the other DCs, his tie over one shoulder and a cup gripped in his large first, while Fiacra was perching on his own desk, swilling his drink round in an absent-minded way. Paula wondered about what his sister had said. If Fiacra had a wee notion of

244

Avril, this would be hard for him. Bob, who was of course Avril's uncle, had been hovering near the edge of the men, but now detached himself and went over to Guy. He didn't drink at all — ran the local abstinence group, in fact — and had no fizzy wine in his hand. Guy met Paula's eyes with a sad, twisting smile. She wished so much she could down the contents of her plastic cup, try to forget all the thoughts crowding in on her.

A while later, things were winding down. Corry, who had sunk a fair bit of the first bottle and produced another, more expensive one from her Mulberry handbag, had engaged Avril in a long discussion about marriage and what concessions she must and must not make. 'Do not wash his socks. Do not pick his socks up off the floor . . . ' Avril listened, nodding like a sort of dejected dog and taking larger gulps of her drink.

Feeling uninvolved, and trying to hide her own sudden teetotalism, Paula drifted over to Fiacra. 'All right?'

He blinked. 'Me? Oh aye.'

'How's your sister?'

'Ah, she's grand. She was pleased to meet you the other day. They're always on at me to talk about work.'

'You've a big family, have you?'

'Mammy and four sisters. Da's dead.' Fiacra took a swallow of drink, simply stating a fact of life. 'He was a Guard too, you know.'

'Oh, I didn't know that. Was he — did something happen at work?'

'No. Well, kinda. Heart attack, years back.'

It was a common ailment, carrying off many of those who'd survived the Troubles and their onslaught of bombs, bullets, and fire, only to keel over from delayed stress and fear. 'I wonder did he know my dad,' Paula said, putting down her untouched cup. 'PJ Maguire. He was RUC.'

'Mick Quinn, that was mine. Border areas. They'd likely have worked together, so.'

'I'll ask him.'

'Mick Quinn?' Corry had overheard, and paused her rant at Avril, who took the opportunity to slip from the room, muttering about going to the Ladies. 'Mick Quinn was your father, Fiacra?'

'Yeah.'

'I worked with him. My first case with the RUC. I was at his funeral. Terrible thing, he was very young.'

'Aye, a lot of people came.'

Corry was squinting at him. 'You've a look of him, now that I think of it.'

Paula looked round, restless and sober. She saw Gerard was gone from the room too, and Bob had sidled off to his office, leaving Guy to jolly along the PSNI officers. They looked grim, huge country guys most of them, who could birth a lamb or dig a septic tank just as easy as subdue a suspect. To them, Guy was yet another Brit cop come to poke his nose in. Unwilling to watch his struggle, Paula decided she'd also slip out, and while she was at it, pour away her drink. She didn't trust Corry's gimlet gaze. 'Excuse me.'

★ ★ ★

Paula had been at the unit for over two months now, and she'd yet to spend any time alone with Sergeant Bob Hamilton, who presumably would be her boss when Guy went back to whatever life he had left in London. This wasn't an accident. She was aware of it, the nasty nugget in the core of herself, the same raw ore of sectarianism she loathed in others. What made her any different? Wasn't she uncomfortable around Hamilton because she knew he marched in Orange parades, donned that sash and beat those drums? It was in everyone, however much you liked your Protestant neighbours and colleagues, however tolerant you liked to think yourself in this post-conflict society, shopping in House of Fraser and eating sushi. When it came down to it, down to bombs and shootings and blood running in the road, you had to pick a side. Yours, or ours. And Bob Hamilton made her want to draw up battle-lines. He was the man who'd been promoted over her father — unfairly, she was sure. Bob was at best semi-competent, and PJ, a brilliant officer according to everyone she'd spoken to, had been let go in 1998 after the Good Friday Agreement. But somehow Bob was also the person who might know what had happened to her mother. So here she was.

She tugged on her baggy jumper and knocked on the door of his office — a sort of converted supply cupboard linking to Guy's larger one. There were no ornaments or decorations, just a scuffed desk and old computer, and hunched

247

over it one even older-looking man. He'd been bald for years, ragged tufts round his ears as if someone had torn off a piece of paper. His eyes were pale and watery. 'Miss Maguire?'

'Sergeant, can I have a word?'

He looked baffled, as well he might. She'd never done anything but avoid having a 'word' with him. 'Oh aye. Take a seat.'

The seat was a warped plastic one with wobbly legs, a cast-off like everything in here, including the occupant. 'Busy?'

He made a gesture of weary resignation at the computer. 'Trying to get the hang of this database yoke. Our Avril gave us a lesson, but sure I can't take it in.'

She resisted the urge to show him. 'Sergeant — you worked with my father, I think, way back.'

'PJ? Oh aye. I worked with PJ on a lot of cases, until he retired. We were partners, for a time.'

'He didn't really retire though, did he?'

'I don't know — '

'Bob.' She sat forward, drawing her knees to herself. 'I'm going to call you Bob, is that OK? And you call me Paula. We work together. Call me Paula, OK?'

He nodded suspiciously, scratching at the scurf in his eyebrows.

'You were speaking to Aidan O'Hara earlier, from the *Ballyterrin Gazette*.'

Bob started to frown. 'That's confidential — '

'I don't know what he asked you, but I'm guessing it was about Sean Conlon. He wants to know what Conlon said, and how likely it is that he'll be released. He went to you because you

248

wouldn't try to protect me. Because you've no loyalty to me.'

'Miss Maguire, I — '

'I'm here about my mother,' she said, deciding just to launch into it. 'I know you worked on her case. I know Conlon's been talking about her.'

'I — '

She talked over him. 'It's been a long time, and we never found anything, and now there's this unit that actually does that, actually tries to find the people we gave up on. I know what that feels like. It's terrifying. It's like someone's dead and buried and you wake up one day to find them ringing on your doorbell. Do you understand?'

'Miss — Paula — I'm sorry about your mammy but — '

'I want us to look at her case. I want to know if something was missed.'

He froze.

She went on. 'I know that may be hard for you, to admit you might have been wrong, but I have to not care about that. I have to know if you did everything you could.'

'There were no leads. We can't reopen if there's no new evidence — '

'Look.' She removed the file from her bag and set it down on his desk. 'That's what was done in 1993. And it was you who led it, you who said, that's it, we'll stop looking. You who came round and arrested my dad — your own partner — and you who said dig up the Maguires' garden, and search the house and make sure you take the wee girl's diary too, I mean, she's thirteen, she

249

probably knows something. Imagine that, if you can, Bob, you're a thirteen-year-old girl, and the police come round and root through your stuff, and they say your mother's likely dead and maybe your father did it . . . ' She stopped. 'Do you have any kids, Bob? I never knew.'

He looked down at his hands, which were shaking. 'We've one boy. He . . . he's not well.'

'I'm sorry. But you can imagine how that was. I'm asking you as someone's father, look at that file again and tell me you did everything you could.'

'I — I can't reopen a case with no evidence. You know as well as I do I can't use any evidence from Conlon if he talks to the Commission for the Disappeared. It's part of the Act. It's not admissible.'

'I'm not saying reopen. I'm just saying look at it. Please, for me, and for my dad. I don't know if you liked him, but he's a good man, and it broke him, what you did, and he's never been fixed.'

Bob stretched out one hand to the file, as if it might burn him. 'I'm sorry,' he said shakily. 'I'm sorry for what happened to you. A lot of things happened in those years, bad things. Bad things to a lot of people. We were just doing our best, you know.'

She stood, with some difficulty. 'I know. But we've got a chance to do something about it, maybe. Please take it.'

She went out, barrelling into the corridor with shaking legs towards the Ladies, where she planned to empty her plastic cup.

Avril was not in them. Instead she was pressed against the noticeboard, up close to the health and safety signs and the holiday rota. In front of her, his hand resting on the wall by her head, but not touching her at all, was Gerard Monaghan. Seeing Paula, Avril made a small noise, darting out from the circle of Gerard's arms and slamming the door to the Ladies.

Gerard ran his hands over his face. 'Bollocks.'

Paula stumbled back, spilling her drink over her wrist. 'God, sorry, I — '

Then they heard the noise — twin beeps starting up, a fraction of a second after each other. Guy came into the corridor holding his pager, coat over his arm, and just behind was Corry, the relaxed, amused look entirely gone from her face.

'What's up?' Gerard moved forward, straightening his tie, ignoring Paula.

Guy said, 'Who's sober enough to drive? We need to go out.'

Paula said, 'I should be. Why?'

'Heather Campbell. She's been found.' He was already walking, and drawn into his wake Paula followed, before turning back for her coat, pushing her cup into the bin. 'Do we know what's happened?' she called over her shoulder. 'Is she OK?'

Guy held the glass door open, so crystal-cold air poured in on their heat and light. 'No. She's not OK.'

251

25

It was full dark when they reached the place, high in the Mourne Mountains. The hills, normally green and wet and rolling, smothered in white. Snow falling thick and fast.

Paula parked the car at the edge of the forest path, stopping as the wheels began to spin in banked snow. The trees were so close they scratched the car window. 'I can't get any further. It's blocked.' Slightly further up, police vans were drawn across the narrow path that led into dark fir trees, illuminated in cold snow light. Paula had gone with Guy to the lonely spot, her driving his car, Gerard with the PSNI. Fiacra and a rather teary Avril had remained behind at the unit.

'You know this place?' He was unbuckling, zipping up his North Face coat and rubber boots.

'It's the old Mass rock.' He looked blank. 'When Catholicism was banned — Cromwell's time, yeah? — they had Mass in secret places, like this. Every year they do a service up there at Easter, I guess to commemorate it.' She had also zipped up her coat, tucked her hair away. 'We don't like to let go of stuff round here.'

Guy was ready but had not yet opened the door. Outside it was hard to see much in the whirling snow, the path lit blue with police strobes. There was an impression of activity further up, dark shapes moving. 'It's the same, isn't it? An out of the way place, a sacred place — like an offering.'

Paula didn't want to think about it. 'What will they do?'

'Get up there. We got a tip-off a car was seen going up — it matched the description of Heather's. That was about an hour back.'

'So the abductor could still be up there?'

The killer, was what she really should have said. After Alison Bates had been ripped open and left to die, this wasn't just a harmless baby-hungry nut.

'Yes. We're working on the assumption that Heather is still alive. Otherwise — well, we wouldn't be out in this.' He scrubbed a patch in the misted-up windows and looked at her. 'You have to stay here, Paula. You understand?'

'But I need to see it!'

'It's far too dangerous, you must realise that. Wait until the scene is secured.'

'But — '

'Paula. After last month . . . *please*.'

She nodded reluctantly. She'd almost got herself killed, and Aidan too, going to the wrong house on her own at Halloween. But the truth was, this time part of her didn't even want to leave the warm interior of the car. This time she was actually afraid. She who'd faced down sociopaths, killers, rapists. She was scared. 'I'll stay. But please, will you let me know what happens?'

'Of course. I won't even go myself. There's a Tactical Support Unit heading up. We have to treat the situation as potentially dangerous. Keep the doors locked.'

He got out, letting in a blast of ice that soaked the seat, and vanished into the gloom of the trees. Suddenly alone, all she could hear was the wind. High above the path the Mass rock loomed, a cairn of stones with a cross on top, casting shadows in the snow. Paula remembered it from a school trip. Underneath was an alcove where worshippers could hide if soldiers came. She imagined how the wind would sound up there, nudging and moaning at each small rock, worrying its way into every weak spot.

Inches from the car windows, the trees whipped to and fro, scratching at the glass with each ferocious burst of wind. With the engine off, she could see her breath. She kept scrubbing at the windows. Nothing but the trees and dark and deathly blue light over everything. She waited, powerless, for struggle, shots, fire in the dark. Nothing. They'd be at the cairn by now, surely.

Paula couldn't stand it a second longer. She wrenched open the door in the wind, the cold taking her breath away after the warm car. Pulling her hood tight against her face, she battled up the path in the wind. The nearest police van was perhaps five metres away.

It was so fast she didn't know if she'd seen it or not. A flash in the dark, something white and quick, an impression of eyes watching, the crack of branches. Paula found she was crashing through the trees. 'Hello? Is someone there?' The wind snatched her voice.

She stopped. She was several metres into the forest, her own breath sounding in her ears, snow crunching underfoot. A stony chill radiated up from the earth. Branches scratched her cheek. 'Hello?'

Paula had a moment of pure terror — just a few seconds, but enough to paralyse her — and then she sensed movement behind, on the path. A powerful light came on, filling the forest with dazzle. Paula shielded her eyes, and then felt her arm yanked. She almost screamed. Behind her was a breathless Gerard, ears sticking out under a woolly hat. 'What the hell are you doing here? The car was lying open!'

She couldn't speak. The wind howled round them.

Gerard shouted, 'He says you've to come now.'

★ ★ ★

'Hurry up, Maguire!'

'It's icy!' The path was blanketed in new snow, white and perfect, dissolving to slush under her boots. She slipped and slid.

'Don't be daft, it's not even frozen yet. Come on.' Gerard took her arm in exasperation. He was radiating heat beneath his plastic jacket.

'They found her?' They were shouting over the gale.

'Aye. She's alive, barely. If they can get her to hospital she might have a chance, but — ' His face twisted. 'He wants you to see it.'

She took deep breaths. 'Was it — like before?'

'Aye.'

255

'She was cut?'

'Yeah. The stomach.'

Paula was shaking. Snow stung her lips, her eyelids. 'Gerard — what happened to the baby? Please tell me.' Because she didn't think she could handle it, not now, a baby cold and dead in the snow.

Gerard pulled her on over branches and tree roots. 'The baby's gone, Maguire.'

'You mean — '

'Someone cut it out of Heather, then left her up there. Half her blood's probably soaked into their car, whoever it was. But the baby's gone.'

At the top end of the path, through the snow, she could see an ambulance, the source of the blinding light. Being loaded into it, strapped to a stretcher, the white face and dark hair of Heather Campbell. Alison Bates's daughter, sliced apart in the same way. The paramedics were trying to shield her face from falling snow, so she must be still alive. Paula looked at her stomach but it was covered with blankets. Her eyelids fluttered and her blue lips moved, as if she had something to say, something important, but the words were lost in the wind. Then they were shutting the doors and reversing out.

'Did someone call her husband?' Paula's voice sounded strange inside the hood of her raincoat, louder and reverberating.

'He'll be at the hospital.' Gerard signalled to Guy, who was conferring with Corry near an open police Land Rover. 'I got her, boss.'

'Thanks. You saw that?' he asked Paula, cupping his mouth against the wind. 'She was

256

under the Mass Rock, they said, unconscious, laid out. It's horrific.' Snow was drifting onto his notebook; he brushed it off impatiently. 'The baby's been taken out and Heather was left to bleed to death. Same cuts as her mother — small, but deep, slashing across her stomach.'

'The baby's not up there?' Paula's hair whipped in her eyes.

'We don't think so.'

'But they'll look? Will they look?'

'Of course they'll — '

'Please!' She was shouting over the rising wind. 'Please look hard — it won't survive, not in this snow!'

'*Dr Maguire*. Calm down. We'll look for the baby,' said Corry, looking at her, and Paula realised someone had guessed her secret.

★ ★ ★

Snow melts. Seasons change. But some things are forever — the stilling of a beating heart, the snuffing of a human life. That was forever. And that moment came too soon for Heather Campbell. The ambulance carrying her raced into town on treacherous roads, lights striping blue across the drifts as snow fell silently over the town, over the grey streets and huddled houses and the lives inside.

As they unloaded her into A & E, and doctors rushed forward to lay hands on her body, Heather's heart stopped, leached almost entirely dry of the blood that had kept it squeezing in and gasping out for the twenty-eight years since her own mother had birthed her into the world. Scrabbling around on her bloodied stretcher, doctors tried defibrillation, then CPR, and then a desperate open heart massage, until one stilled the other's pumping arms with a shake of the head, and on the blood- and slush-covered floor of the hospital, they felt Heather's pulse stutter and calm, until the smallest thing of all, the beat of her heart, was gone entirely.

26

She was dead.

Dry-eyed, Paula took the news like a blow, lowering her head into her hands as they sat in the waiting room of the hospital. If she were honest, she hadn't liked Heather Campbell that much on their brief meeting, but that made it harder. No one deserved this. To be lost, and then found, but in this way. And besides, Heather had been pregnant, scared and pregnant, with no mother to help her. They were the same under the skin, all blood and veins and terror. Except now Heather was dead.

'We did everything we could.' Saoirse was the one who'd come to tell them. She looked exhausted. There was blood on her white coat and her face was pale as bone.

Corry was leaning against the wall in her long cream coat, turned beige by the sickly yellow lighting. 'If they'd got her here sooner?'

Saoirse shook her head. 'Even if the ambulance had made it to the hospital sooner, she was already gone. The helicopter couldn't take off in that weather. It was so cold, and she'd lost so much blood. Nothing could be done.'

Paula looked round at them, Fiacra and Avril pale as frightened children, with their near-identical blond heads. Bob accepting it, yet another death on his shoulders. So many he'd seen. So many taken. The whole team was there,

259

gathered in the hospital to see if they'd managed to find one of the lost. And they had, but too late.

Gerard swore softly, then pushed back his chair and went out, banging the door. Guy let him go, shaking his head briefly as Bob stirred. 'Leave him.'

Saoirse rubbed her face. 'Anyway, I thought you'd want to know. My colleague is in telling the husband. Can someone sign the paperwork?' Corry straightened herself and went to the door. Saoirse followed her out with a sideways glance at Paula, who still hadn't moved. The news seemed to have paralysed her.

Guy let the door shut after Saoirse and looked round at them. 'We've lost Heather. But her baby is still missing — she may be alive.'

'She?' Paula's throat was dry.

'Yes. They knew it was a girl. They were going to call her Lucy. So we can still find her, bring her home to her father.'

No one else seemed to believe it. 'Could she really be alive, sir?' said Fiacra wearily. 'The depth of the snow out there . . . '

'The doctors think she could be. We don't know if Heather was even killed at the cairn — there was a lot of blood, but perhaps not enough. If it was done indoors, if the baby were kept warm and fed, and they knew to clamp off her umbilical cord and so on, she could be OK.'

'It's true,' said Paula, wearily. 'I've read about cases like this.'

'It's happened before?' Guy looked horrified.

'It's called foetal abduction. They kill the

260

mother, cut the child out. The baby was quite often alive after birth. They found them too, a lot of the time. These women often aren't careful. They want everyone to think it's their own child, so they'll take it out, display it. These aren't hardened criminals, just desperate people.'

'Women?' said Avril, very pale.

'Yes. It's nearly always women.'

'Right. So it's very possible we will find Lucy.' Guy was doing his best to sound efficient. 'Now we need to look at the traffic data again. Heather's car was found halfway up the track to the Mass rock. Here's the odd thing — there is no blood in the car, though she was quite probably injured before being taken there. It's almost like they wanted us to find the car, and know she was there, but she can't have been transported in it.'

'How did they get her up there then?'

Guy acknowledged Fiacra's bewildered question. 'That's what we need to find out. We're working on the assumption that it's the same person who killed Heather's mother. The MO is exactly the same. So they must have access to some kind of off-road vehicle, a Jeep or a van or something — though in this case we don't know why Heather's car was also left there, or how they got her up there and escaped. Heather hadn't been there long when we found her. She'd have been dead otherwise.'

She was dead anyway. Worse, sometimes, to think you might have saved them, if only you'd been faster, a minute here, a second there, however long it took to keep their heart beating.

261

Timing. It could break you in two. Paula tried to think. 'So maybe there were two of them — a husband, perhaps, helping?'

'Maybe.' Guy ran his hands over his face. 'We must have barely missed them, too. She'd only just been dumped there.'

'The killer could have still been there?' Paula recalled the dark of the trees, the breathless silence of the snow.

'Yes,' said Guy briefly. 'They may well have been. So that's possibly three linked cases now — Darcy Williams, the doctor, and Heather, plus her child, who's still missing. We're leading on that case, while Corry's team launch the murder inquiry.'

'What can we do, sir?' Fiacra's voice was wavering. He was watching Avril, who was fighting back tears.

Guy said, 'It looks as if someone has a grudge against the family. I want to talk to Heather's father, and her husband if he's up to it, and I want TV and radio appeals to find the baby. Posters, ads, the lot. I want you on screen, Paula, interviewed on the psychology of this person. Explain what signs to look for, what people should report.'

She nodded, trying to see it as work, not a pregnant woman ripped apart, dumped like meat.

Guy went on. 'I want rock-solid alibis for all those prolife nuts of Dunne's. I want to know do any of them have Jeeps. I want everyone in this town looking for Lucy and Darcy. And I want an explanation from that bloody psychic woman.'

Bob stiffened at the curse. 'Will DCI Corry authorise an arrest?'

'I don't know. But I think she knows something, and I'd bet it's not through visions of the Virgin Mary, either.' He swept his eyes round the team. 'This case — it's getting out of hand. Let's bring it back. Let's find that child and bring her home safe.'

Paula had been thinking and thinking about what Magdalena Croft had said when they'd gone to see her, and what it was she'd found jarring, and now eventually she got it — *God willing she'll be found*, the woman had said. *And her wee baby too.*

Separately. As if she'd already known Heather and her child would be so violently torn apart. She got to her feet. 'I'll meet you back at the unit.'

★ ★ ★

Paula found Saoirse in her office, the door shut but not locked. She was sitting at her desk with her head in her hands. Paula closed the door behind her. 'Hey.'

Saoirse didn't turn. 'The baby.'

Paula moved closer. 'We'll find her.'

'She won't survive it. It's . . . look.' Saoirse gestured painfully to the window, where outside the blinds the snow continued to fall.

'It might be OK.' Paula hovered, looking at her friend's bowed back, her dark hair pulled smooth.

'No.' Saoirse looked up, blinking. 'Have you

263

done anything about it yet?'

'What?'

'Your baby, Paula.'

She recoiled. 'I — no.' It was true. She hadn't done anything, not been to the counsellor as suggested, not booked the flights to London. She was closing her eyes and battling through as if in a blizzard.

Saoirse spun her chair. 'You know what happens if you have a late abortion?'

'I . . . think so.' She thought of Melissa Dunne's leaflet, the mangled mess, the eyes.

'Do me a favour and don't let it get that far. It isn't going to go away, if that's what you're hoping.'

'I don't know what I'm hoping.'

Her friend got up, and took off her bloodied coat. She pushed this into a hazard bin and stood in just her scrubs before her mirror, smoothing hair behind her ears and wiping her glasses. 'I wish you'd think, Paula. You just never think.'

'Seersh, I — '

'I'm sorry. I have to work.' And she went. Not knowing what else to do, Paula let her go. She wondered if her friend was right. Was her problem that she didn't think, or that she thought too much? She looked at herself in Saoirse's mirror. Face clammy with fear and exhaustion. Hair in rat's tails. Her heavy coat stained in snow and mud. Anyone looking at her could see she was a mess.

27

'OK?'

Paula nodded at Helen Corry, pale-faced. The mike was clipped onto the lapel of the black suit she'd bought for the occasion. Marks and Spencer's. Boring. She'd had to get size twelve trousers to go over her stomach, and when the waistband of the ten had failed to button, she'd had a brief, angry cry in the changing rooms at the Meadows, Ballyterrin's soulless shopping centre, while 'Santa Baby' on pan pipes blasted over the tannoy. She'd pressed powder all round her red eyes to hide them, and changed in the toilets of the main police station while a crew from the Northern Ireland news set up lights and cameras. Paula was to be interviewed by famed local reporter Alvin Laurence, with Corry hovering in the background, eagle-eyed. Paula was terrified. A low-grade nausea brewed in her stomach.

'You're awful pale,' tutted the researcher with the clipboard. 'Have you a wee taste of make-up you could put on?'

'I've got some on already.'

'A bit more?'

Paula shook her head, sitting rigid, sure that someone would see any softness in her abdomen. She was nearly two months pregnant now. On Paula's laptop there was a permanent minimised window of easy Jet flights to London. Weekends

265

were ticking by. The price was going up, in more ways than one.

'Paula, how are you!' Alvin Laurence. Face of her childhood, fading TV star looks, caring expression a speciality. Years ago he'd done the nice news, the bits they showed before the bombs and shooting and failed peace talks, the Irish dancing stars and kids in wheelchairs learning to walk and that, but since the supposed end of the Troubles they'd shunted aside the more hard-bitten hacks and Alvin was doing the lot.

Today he'd left off his trademark check jumper in favour of a maroon sports jacket and lurid tie. Paula forced on a smile as he took her cold hands in both of his; she winced at the grip. Why did some men feel they hadn't greeted you properly unless they pulverised your metacarpals? 'Pleased to meet you, Mr Laurence. We were big fans of yours in our house.'

That was a lie. PJ called him 'that gobshite in the golfing jumper', but her mother had been fond of him, insisting on watching the early evening news when Paula had wanted *Neighbours* on, so that she could talk about it in school the next day.

'Ah now, you're very young.' He wasn't listening anyway. 'Amazing to think a wee girl like you has a big important job with the police. We'll do a wee quick interview. Now don't be nervous. Any mistakes can be done again, aye?' He had a tissue tucked under his jowly chins, a rash of powder caught in it, and Paula nodded again, clutching her hands in her lap.

266

'Er — could I have some water, please?'

Alvin nodded to the girl with the clipboard, who grudgingly brought over a plastic cup. Paula spilled a drop down her top. 'Shit!'

Alvin tutted. 'You'll watch the language on air, Miss Maguire, won't you?'

'Sorry.' Paula saw Corry sigh, and look at the clock. The watchful stare said *I'm counting on you*.

Finally they were ready, and all the faffing with cameras and lights seemed to be done. A boy of about fourteen held up a large white hoop behind Paula's head. 'She's awful washed out,' muttered Clipboard Girl. Paula took deep breaths.

'Don't be nervous, pet.' Alvin leaned forward and put an avuncular hand on Paula's leg.

She jumped, dislodging it. 'I'm not. Are we starting soon?'

'Yes, yes.' He looked cross. She could see the join where his hair weave met the grey underneath. Then it was all smiles and they began. It went like this:

Sombre Alvin: 'The province is living under fear tonight as a third infant is abducted by a suspected murderer. This time it's even more horrific — ripped out of her mother's womb before she was even born, Lucy Campbell is now missing. I'm here with Dr Paula Maguire, a top psychiatrist specialising in such cases. Dr — '

'I'm a psychologist,' Paula said, blinking into the vast light. She had black spots in front of her eyes.

Annoyed Alvin: 'I'm sorry?'

'Psychiatrists are medically qualified. I'm not. I'm a chartered forensic psychologist.'

He paused. 'We'll do that bit over.'

Sombre Alvin again: 'Dr Maguire. You're a '*psychologist*' (he applied almost imperceptible quote marks round the word) specialising in this kind of case, is that right?'

'Not really, I — ' She caught Corry's eye. 'I specialise in missing persons, yes, and I work with the MPRU, which is based in town here. But this is a very unusual case. I don't think there's ever been one in the UK before.' Paula had been researching the topic.

Interested Alvin: 'Indeed?'

'No. However there have been several in the United States, and in fact there's quite a large body of work that helps us profile the kind of person who might have done it.'

Relieved Alvin: 'Now you've hit on a question that I'm sure our viewers will be asking themselves. Who would do such a thing? Steal a wee baby, and cut up its poor mother to get it out? Does this really happen?'

'It's rare, but it does happen. I've examined around twenty instances, all in the USA. In most cases the mother is left to die, like Heather Campbell sadly was, and the baby is removed. If the baby's looked after properly, they often survive. In fact quite a few have been found safe and well again. The abductors usually get caught — these aren't criminals, you see, and they aren't usually suffering from mental illness. They're ordinary people who just . . . snap.

268

Sadly, I believe Heather encountered someone who was desperate for a child.'

Sad Alvin: 'Indeed. Our thoughts and prayers are with the family tonight, and of course with Heather's husband and her father, renowned cardiologist Dr Roy Bates. Dr Maguire — can our viewers help in any way? Is Lucy out there somewhere?'

Paula shifted in her seat; she was sweating under the lights. 'The person who did this, they want a baby of their own. And they want it so badly they have to pretend it's theirs, to loved ones and even to themselves. It's common for such women to actually think they're pregnant, a condition called pseudocyesis ... em, it's basically a type of false pregnancy. They may even have symptoms — putting on weight, and so on. But then there's no baby in the end. So they take the youngest child they can find, one that hasn't bonded with its mother, because it isn't even born yet. The act can be savage — it's very difficult to cut in the right place — but the impulse comes from love. They want the child for themselves.'

Nervous Alvin: 'That's very graphic, Doctor. We wouldn't want to alarm anyone.'

'I'm afraid they should be alarmed. We believe this person has already taken a child at least twice before, and it's likely we'll find other abductions or attempted abductions in their past. If for any reason Lucy doesn't survive, they will want to try again.'

'You're saying it was the same person who took the little baby Darcy Williams?'

269

'We believe so. We think they may also have taken Alek Pachek, who was abducted and then found safe.'

'Is there any chance they will return Darcy too, now that Mrs Campbell's child has sadly been stolen?'

'It's possible. We think they returned Alek because they failed to bond with him — this could also explain why they've moved to actually taking an unborn child, who didn't have the chance to know their mother before she was murdered. Darcy of course is a little older, so it's very possible. But we must carry on looking for her, because this person is capable of cold-blooded murder, as we've seen.'

He quailed. 'And — what type of person could it be?'

'A woman. It's nearly always a woman. She may befriend a family, perhaps at antenatal groups, or those, what do you call them — childbirth classes. She might even pretend to be pregnant as well. So I'd say look out for anyone who suddenly produces a newborn, or if you're pregnant, anyone who seems strangely friendly to you. Just be careful.' Under the suit, her fingers found the mound of her own stomach. 'Because this person really wants something. Like, more than most of us have ever wanted anything in our lives. And they won't stop until they get it and they feel the child is truly theirs.' She fell silent. Everyone was staring. 'Er . . . that's all.'

Alvin had rallied somewhat. 'And I gather the investigation has been looking at several avenues, including staff at the Ballyterrin General Hospital, and some pro-life groups in the area. Can you tell us why that is?'

Over his shoulder, Paula could see Corry giving a warning look. She wasn't supposed to discuss the rest of the investigation. 'Er . . . there was felt to be a link between this case and that of the missing family planning doctor, Dr Bates. The doctor had previously received death threats, so the PSNI have been following those up, I believe.'

'Dr Bates being the mother of Mrs Campbell, of course.'

Shit, so the press knew about that. She had a feeling Aidan might have something to do with it. 'That's correct.' She saw Corry frown.

'And the MPRU has been accused of harassment by a pro-life activist, is that right? A Mrs Melissa Dunne?'

'I don't know exactly what she said. But Alvin — we're talking about someone who thought it was OK to put a brick through the window of a doctor's house, just because she wanted to help people.'

He made a face. 'Dr Bates had a sad death, though many in Ballyterrin disagreed with her pro-abortion stance.'

'I doubt she was pro-abortion,' snapped Paula. 'I think she was pro helping people not being forced to have babies they didn't want. I mean, all those pro-lifers, do they ever stop to think a woman is involved too? Whose life is it exactly that we're talking about?'

The interview ended not long after this.

'Sorry. I did say I didn't want to do it.'

Corry didn't look up from her desk. Paula was seated on the other side, hands clamped between her shaking legs. 'He just riled me, you know? He's so condescending.'

'Mm.' Corry kept writing.

'What's going to happen now?'

'I imagine they're going to edit the piece down quite heavily. Then I'd imagine we might get a fair number of angry phone calls from pro-life groups, most of the churches in the area, and also any local baby groups, since you suggested their classes might be some kind of breeding ground for serial killers.'

Bollocks. 'I didn't mean to.'

'I know. It's an emotive subject and he shouldn't have brought it up.' She looked at Paula. 'And it's just as much my fault. I shouldn't have put someone who's pregnant on a case involving missing babies.'

Long silence. The faint hum of the overhead lights, and outside the noise of the station. Corry went on. 'You are pregnant, aren't you? I'm asking as a friend, you understand, not an employer.'

Paula nodded slowly. That was three people who knew now — Saoirse, and Tess Brooking, and Corry. Oh, and the midwife. It was spiralling. 'Yes. I am. I'm pregnant.' Saying the words aloud was like a release, a slow seep of air from the balloon of tension in her chest.

'And you don't know what to do?'

'No. I — that's how I got the Bates case so soon. I'd gone to see her that day.'

'I wondered. How far along are you?'

'Eight weeks. Ish.' Again, she tried to do the maths in her head, and failed utterly. She'd been good at maths at school, but apparently this very practical application of it was beyond her.

Corry said, 'You've time. If that's what you want.'

'I don't know what I want.'

'It's not so bad, if you decide you aren't up for going through with it.'

'Oh. You — ?'

'Yes. In the early nineties — I was at college, second year, and I didn't want to get married. My mammy'd have gone ballistic if I'd told her I was pregnant. So I took all my savings from my summer job and went to London for the weekend. It was the right thing. I've got two kids now and I don't regret it.'

'But do you ever — you don't think about it?'

Corry shrugged. 'Everyone's different. You can't tell how you'll react. What matters is you have to choose for yourself. No one else's experience will help.'

'I'm thirty,' Paula said, after a moment.

'Yes. I was younger.'

'This might be the only time. And what if I — I mean, I might not do all that. Wedding, husband, babies — I just might not.'

'It's not for everyone. I thought it was for me, and it wasn't. Not the babies, I mean, I love them to bits, but the marrying. You have family?'

'My dad.' And Pat. But no mother. The scrap

273

that was growing inside her, that was one more link to Margaret Maguire. Margaret, who'd untethered herself from all that, walked out the door, or been taken. 'How do you decide?' she burst out. 'In this kind of situation, when it's impossible? How do you choose?'

'I think you already know. It's just hard either way, so you stall, but you nearly always know inside you, if you're really honest. It was the same when I kicked my husband out. Took me months, but I knew what I should be doing all right.'

That wasn't what Paula wanted to hear. 'OK. So I just have to choose.' Like it was really that easy.

'If you need any cover for antenatal stuff, let me know. I presume you haven't told Brooking.'

Paula shook her head reluctantly, hoping Corry wouldn't guess the real reason she hadn't told Guy, and maybe never would.

'OK. Well, take care of yourself. You did look a bit pale on those monitors.'

'Oh, I'll put some blusher on or something.' She sighed. 'I'm sorry I ranted at Alvin Laurence about feminism.'

A brief smile tugged at the corners of Corry's mouth. 'It's about time someone did. Now we'd better get to this briefing — I'm meant to be running it.'

28

Paula went home early that night, afraid to stay in the office in case her TV appearance sparked off protests. You could never underestimate the capacity of a Northern Ireland audience to get outraged. She was so tired it was almost too much effort to switch off her computer, stand up, and go out to her car. Guy was still in his office when she left, tapping at his keyboard with vicious keystrokes. She knew why he found it hard to stop working. Looking out at the night, where the wind whirled breaths of ice through the dark, it was hard to think a child could survive that, ripped from the safest place there was, bloodily birthed into this world of snow and gloom.

Guy glanced up as she went past. 'Heading home to watch your big interview?'

She winced. 'Yeah. Car crash TV, isn't that what they call it?'

'I only hope it helps.' He looked at her. 'Is everything all right, Paula?'

No. 'It's fine. I'm just, you know — this is all overwhelming.' This wasn't the right time to tell him. Not when two children were missing. Not two weeks before Christmas, the first since his son had been killed. She forced on a smile. 'Goodnight.'

'Night, Paula. Take care driving.'

★ ★ ★

Her father was waiting for her when she turned her key in the lock. She hadn't been planning to watch the interview herself, but she could hear the strains of the early evening news in the next room. She hung her bag over a chair and leaned against the sink. Her father lingered, waiting for the kettle to boil. 'You look awful tired, pet.'

'I am. We're all working flat out on this case.'

'It's a bad one. The baby was cut right out of her, was that it?' He squeezed out the teabag and carefully added it to the new compost bin under the sink — Pat's influence.

'Yeah. Did you ever see anything like it before? The only cases I can find are in America.'

'Not exactly like it. Not trying to steal the baby. But I've seen something, aye, something a wee bit the same . . . well, never mind, pet. I saw some bad things in my time on the force. Nothing you need to know about.'

'We were having a party when the call came in about Heather Campbell. It was awful. We were all just standing about chatting, while she was dying.'

'You can't stop living. That's what your mother always used to tell me. They're dead, but you're still living.'

Paula blinked. He'd actually just mentioned her mother, as casually as anyone. She decided not to acknowledge it, make it weird. 'Dad, did you ever work with a Mick Quinn?'

PJ gave her an odd look, shutting the cupboard door again. 'I did. Mick was my opposite number in Dundalk. Any cross-border stuff came up,

276

he'd ring me. I knew him well. Why?'

'Oh, no reason. One of the guys in work is his son.'

'That's right, he'd a young fella and a whole clatter of girls too.'

'Yeah.' Paula thought of Aisling Quinn, so excited, her belly blossoming out in front of her, and how she'd patted it. It wasn't a good time to be a pregnant woman. Your stomach made you a walking target. Thank God she wasn't showing yet — *yet?* What did that mean?

'Are you coming?' PJ was headed to the living room. 'It'll be on in a minute. They've just finished a piece on this fella in Strabane who's been sent to prison for all the Christmas lights on his house. He tapped into the local grid, so they said. Eejit.'

'I can't watch,' she said, shaking her head. 'You tell me what it's like.'

Paula hid in the bathroom while it aired, but she couldn't escape a glance at the TV in the time it took to flee upstairs. There she was, pale and squeaky-voiced, her Ballyterrin accent pronounced, her hair carroty under the lights. She took refuge in the lime-green soap-scented bathroom, examining her puffy face in the mirror. She looked awful, pasty and exhausted. Maybe the TV people had been right about the extra make-up.

'You can come down, pet,' PJ shouted up when (in about five seconds) it was over.

As she came downstairs, Paula couldn't resist asking, 'Was it awful? Did they edit me all weird?'

'Not a bit of it, it was just you saying about this woman that might be on the loose. Then you were cut off awful sudden like.'

'I was cut? Oh good.' She was relieved. She didn't want to think about the consequences had she been captured on local TV giving a pro-choice rant, in a country where most of the population opposed abortion, and it was one of the few issues that hardliners on both sides might unite on. Get together, picket a clinic, that sort of thing. 'So it wasn't a complete disaster.'

'Well.' PJ hesitated. 'Could they not have put a taste of make-up on you? You were as white as the walls.'

★ ★ ★

'We've had a hit on Mary Conaghan.'

Avril's face glowed with purpose as she stood in front of the team the next day. 'As we saw, Mary was born in an isolated part of Donegal.' She called up a map on screen, the craggy coastline sparse and green. 'There are hardly any records — I'm not sure she even went to school most of the time. There's a birth certificate with her mother's name, but no father mentioned. When Mary was fifteen she was sent to Letterkenny to stay with her mother's cousin. She'd been there several months when the youngest child in the family went missing.' Avril pointed her clicker and the screen changed. 'The Gardai had this shot on file so I got them to fax it over.' A family gathered, the picture taken in the seventies by the look of the clothes. The

278

mother with stiff, bouffant hair, five children around her, a baby on her lap. Avril pointed. 'That's Mary, off to the side there.' A dark girl with coltish legs, a summer dress. 'The baby was called Michael. Michael Gillan. He was apparently abducted from the house in 1975 — Mary was supposed to be minding him.'

'Was he ever found?' Guy leaned in.

'Yes.' Avril consulted her notes. 'He was found safe in his crib the next day. Mary claimed she'd gone to the shop and left the door open, but it seems the Guard in charge suspected her of something. He did quite an in-depth interview with her. But they couldn't prove it, and anyway the baby was returned safe, so they let it drop. Very similar to Alek Pachek, in fact. It didn't come up in my child-abduction searches because it's outside the time frame.'

'I knew it.' Guy looked excited. 'I knew she had to be mixed up in it somehow. Any other links, Avril?'

'I'm still going through the files. If we can prove she was involved in another child disappearance, can we arrest her?'

'Maybe. It's almost identical to Alek Pachek. A baby taken then left back safe. That doesn't happen often, does it, Paula?' He looked at her.

'Not according to the case files, no. But sir — what about what DCI Corry said? Magdalena Croft is one of her accredited experts. We can't just arrest her unless we have a lot of evidence.'

'I know.' He thought about it. 'Let's dig a bit more before we move. Anything else that ties her to either case, Alek or Dr Bates. Let's also use

Paula's profile — Magdalena Croft is the right age and build. Is there any connection to the hospital? Would she know its layout well enough to walk in and abduct a child? Has she ever lost one herself?'

'Maybe we can send Paula round to shout at her,' said Fiacra innocently. Gerard and Avril immediately hid their faces, and Paula knew they'd all seen last night's news. She glared back at Fiacra.

Guy ignored the remark. 'I want to know as much as possible about her. Fiacra, see if you can find any retired Guards who might remember her as a healer — there might be something that's not in the files.'

'Sir?' Paula was tentative. She didn't usually call him sir — after they'd slept together that time it had just sounded odd, and not a little kinky. 'You seem very sure she's involved.' It was out of character. Usually she'd be the one jumping at hunches, and he'd be saying show me the evidence, don't get blinded.

Guy seemed to understand her concern. 'We should explore all the other avenues, of course, but I've got a strong feeling on this. I can't stand these charlatans. They prey on the weak, and pretend to help them, all the while taking all their cash.'

'There's plenty of rumours about her,' said Fiacra. 'She's never been prosecuted, but her Southern tax records showed up loads of donations. Thing is, she never actually built the church people gave money for. So where did it go?'

'Good, good.' Guy turned over a paper on the table. 'Follow up all of that. Now, there's a bit of good news — they may have got a usable print off Heather Campbell's body.'

'Really?' Paula was surprised. 'But the killer was so careful before — I mean, assuming it's the same person. There was no forensic evidence at all, was there?'

'No. Even if there were, the snow would have pretty much destroyed it. So this is a turn-up. It looks as if she was drugged, too — there's traces of the same barbiturate that was in her mother's system.'

'Where was it?' she asked. 'Where was the print?'

Guy checked his notes. 'On a piece of jewellery round her neck, apparently.'

Paula remembered. The crucifix Heather had been pulling at, as if it would save her. But nothing had, in the end. 'It couldn't have happened at the hospital?'

'Apparently the paramedics cut it off at the scene, and they were wearing gloves. It's promising, anyway.' Guy was finishing up. 'Anyone else have an idea?'

'Well — I did turn up something else.' Gerard was busting with pride. Good boy for teacher. 'I thought it'd be worth getting onto some of our regular PSNI, er, contacts, see if they might know anything.'

Informants, he meant. Many of them redundant now the Troubles were mostly over, but they still tended to have their ear to the ground in the town. Guy didn't like using them, with his

281

London by-the-book sensibilities. 'Oh yes?' he said, warily.

'Turns out Mrs Croft was involved in a case last year — but she was the accuser, not the suspect. She had an odd-job man at her house doing work, a bit of building and so on, and she said he was stealing from her. Got him fired from that and his other job at the council. He used to cut the grass in parks and things like that.'

'And?'

'Well, my contact, he says the guy — Duggan's his name, Patrick Duggan — hasn't a good word to say about Magdalena Croft. Which is unusual, you know, since everyone else seems to think the sun shines out of her . . . well.'

'Get him in. Soon as you can. That's very useful indeed.'

'Will do.' Gerard was red with smugness. Paula rolled her eyes at Fiacra, who shook his head. Avril was looking down at her laptop. Ever since the night of her engagement, when they'd found Heather Campbell's torn body, she'd been very careful not to get caught alone with Paula. Paula wasn't sure what she would ask anyway. *Is there something going on with you and Gerard? Did you know Fiacra's got a crush on you?* Who was she to be delving into other people's patchy love lives?

Guy was pleased with Gerard's information. 'This is exactly what I mean. Get me some dirt on her — any other case she was linked to involving a child, any convictions — a speeding ticket, even, I want to know about it. So you all know what you're doing, yes? Let's stay on top of this. We've had two deaths already. If we don't find Lucy or Darcy, it will be a tragedy, but it's also going to reflect on us very badly indeed.'

29

'What do you reckon?' asked Gerard.

It was later that day and Patrick Duggan was seated on the other side of the reflective glass in the interview room. He looked nervous. It was hard not to look nervous when you were in there, the door shut, only the blank walls to look at, the lino floor and chipboard table. Paula understood that.

Gerard was pumped to go in and crack him; she could practically see the muscles rippling under his thin blue shirt. His tie was cast over his shoulder again. 'He'll talk. My contact says he's been bad-mouthing Croft all round town ever since she fired him.'

'He looks scared.' Paula watched him. A ratty-faced man of around thirty-five, his light brown hair was patchy, as was his beard. He kept scratching at it, eyes darting about the room, and occasionally peering through the window, where they would disconcertingly seem to catch hers. He wore a farmer's uniform — combat trousers, paint-stained boots, a thick and oily green jumper. 'Should he not have a lawyer or someone in with him? An advocate, even? I mean, Corry gave us our assignments, and hauling him in definitely wasn't on the list.'

'Get a grip, Maguire, he's not been arrested. We only want to have a quick word.'

'Yeah, but — '

'He'll talk,' Gerard insisted. 'Anyway, the boss is coming.'

Guy strode towards them, his own expensive tie swinging with purpose. 'All right? Are you observing, Paula?'

'I think he's very frightened,' she said again. 'Maybe you should go easy on him.'

'He's a petty crook. Five convictions for theft in the past three years alone.' Guy adjusted his shirt cuffs. 'I'm sure he's more than used to the inside of a police station.'

Paula said, 'Are you sure this is a good idea?' The two men exchanged a quick glance, which wasn't lost on her. 'I just get the impression he maybe has learning difficulties. I mean it — go easy. If you get something from him it might not even be admissible.'

Guy was irritated. 'I'm not in the habit of intimidating witnesses, Dr Maguire, and I'm perfectly entitled to bring him in. We're just asking him for some information. Come along, DC Monaghan.' They went in and seated themselves, the door snicking shut. The red light illuminated to show sound was on. Tapping her feet anxiously, Paula looked in through the two-way window.

'Mr Duggan,' Guy began, after setting up his recording equipment and explaining who they were. 'I'd like to remind you that you aren't under arrest. Myself and DC Monaghan here are aware of your record, but we want to talk to you about something else today.'

'I never done nothing,' said Patrick, licking a

285

yellow tongue over cracked lips. 'Nothing, I swear to God.'

'We aren't accusing you of anything. But I believe you were previously convicted on several counts of robbery, is that right? When you worked for Magdalena Croft?'

He tensed. 'They said I took money from the collection pots. But I never! I'd never take money out of something holy, so I wouldn't.'

Patrick Duggan had been dismissed from Magdalena Croft's employ in 2009, and given a suspended sentence for the theft of £25.33 in collection plate money. At that time, Magdalena had been attracting hundreds of people each time to her rallies in the muddy field, all of them contributing money to her so-called church building fund. It seemed uniquely cruel and petty to pursue the man for such a small sum, if he had even stolen it, Paula thought.

'I don't want to talk about that, Patrick.' Guy was being gentle, as she'd urged. 'Tell us what you know about Magdalena Croft.'

The reaction was extreme. Patrick huddled his arms around himself and began to rock. 'Don't make me see her. Don't make me go back.'

'She isn't here,' said Gerard impatiently. 'She's far away.'

'I won't see her!'

'Patrick, she isn't here. We want to ask you questions about her.'

He lowered his arms. 'Is she in trouble?'

Gerard glanced at Guy. 'What makes you say that, Patrick? Are you a Paddy or a Patrick, by the way?'

286

His eyes flicked distrustfully. 'Paddy, sometimes.'

'OK, Paddy then. Why do you say that?'

'She's a bad one.' He whispered it. 'She says she talks to the Virgin, but the Virgin gives mercy, and her, she's no mercy in her body. She gave me the boot, and she'd never go near old Jack when he lay dying, for all he gave her his life savings.'

'Who's Jack?' asked Guy.

'Jack Magee. He gave her all the money for her church, to build it out the back of her big ould house, and she spent it on a car, so she did. You go and see — she's a big nice car, she has, so where'd she get the money for that? Then he was dying in the hospice and she never even went to see him.'

'Did this happen to anyone else?'

'Oh aye! All the time!' He raised his voice, then lowered it again to a whisper, looking fearfully round him. 'All the time people would come to the church, and she'd get them to give wee cheques — all their money, sometimes, then I'd hear her round the place ordering fancy big furniture or getting a new window in the house or something. She didn't spend it on the church. Sure it's hardly even built now, is it? She took it all for herself.'

'Why are you whispering, Patrick?' Guy leaned in.

'She listens.' His voice was barely audible.

'Listens how?'

Patrick pointed up at the ceiling, where a smoke alarm blinked red.

'The alarm?' Guy was being patient, but Gerard had his what-is-this-bollocks look on.

'Inside,' whispered Patrick. 'The wee listening things. When I done the electrics for her, like.'

'Why did she do that?' Guy was being very careful.

'So she could hear. She'd hear what all the staff said about her, and the people who come and seen her for the sickness, she'd listen so she hears them talking in the other rooms, and then she'd say, oh your mammy has liver cancer, isn't that right, and they'd think it was the Holy Mother telling it. You see?' He was becoming agitated.

'I see,' said Guy. 'So she could pretend she was having visions.'

'Aye. She's a bad one. She lies about God. That's the worst sort of lies.'

Gerard cleared his throat. 'Can you prove this, Patrick? If we went there, would we see these bugs, like you say?'

His eyes went wide. 'Bugs?'

'The listening things,' Guy explained, giving Gerard a warning look. 'DC Monaghan's asking would we see them for ourselves, if we went to Mrs Croft's house.'

'I'm not going back there!' The whites of his eyes were showing, like a horse in a lather of fear. 'I'm not, I'm not!' Patrick put his hands over his head, in the brace position, and despite coaxing from Gerard and Guy, they couldn't get him to say another word. Guy met Paula's eyes through the window — she'd been right. But something was making this man very afraid indeed.

288

'Aren't you going home?' Paula looked up from her desk, blinking. The office was empty, save for Guy standing over her. 'It's gone eight,' he said, checking his Rolex.

She rubbed her eyes. 'Will Croft be arrested, then?'

'Corry's still not sure. Says we still need more before she'll move.'

'What about the print from Heather's necklace, did it match anything in the database?'

'No. Nothing ever does in this case. And it was about the only usable mark from any of the scenes. Whoever's doing this knows to wipe.'

Paula shook her head. 'It just doesn't fit. The frenzied nature of the attacks, the impulsive snatching — and then this carefulness, covering their tracks quite literally . . . I don't know.'

She saw her own weariness reflected back in his eyes. 'I don't know either. I feel like we're at the end of the road.'

Paula thought about it for a moment. 'Would you let me go down to Dublin tomorrow? You know I have that contact there, Maeve Cooley. The journalist. She might be able to dig up something on Magdalena's first church.' Maeve was a friend of Aidan's, and Paula liked her very much, while at the same time being hugely jealous of their closeness. It balanced on a knife's edge most of the time. Maeve also knew everyone in Dublin and was almost Aidan's equal at digging up unsavoury facts on people.

Last time Paula had enlisted Maeve's help,

Guy had nearly fired her for going off on her own, but it was a measure of how much this case was foxing them that he was now nodding thoughtfully. 'I'd really like to find out more about what Magdalena — or rather, Mary — was doing before she started her ministry. Are you up to a trip south?'

'Of course. I'll call her now.' And there was also the chance that Maeve might know where Aidan had disappeared to. Not that that mattered.

Guy was looking preoccupied. She knew that look meant he'd spotted a potential exit from the labyrinth of this case and was heading straight for it. 'I think we've almost got her. Croft. Not just the abduction of her cousin, and the testimony of Patrick Duggan, but the fact she knew exactly where to find Alek. I want to really probe if she has alibis for Heather and Dr Bates. If she can't prove where she was, we can break her.'

'What about Corry?'

'I'll go over her head if I have to,' said Guy. 'This case has been mishandled from day one. Croft is the one thing linking them all. I think we need to find out if she's ever had any prints taken — if we match it to the one found on Heather, that's what we need. Can you look into that when you're down there?'

'Of course.'

'This is it,' he said, all the muscles in his neck tensed and ready. 'We just need a bit more evidence and we'll have her. I'm sure of it.'

'I hope so.'

He tapped the back of her chair. 'I'm off now. Drive home safely, OK? I'm worried about you.'

Her heart stuttered. 'I'm fine.'

'You just don't look well.'

For a moment she thought about telling him — *I'm pregnant, it's your baby*. Imagined how he would react, and how he'd take her in his arms, look after her, make it all OK. No more secrets. No more nights awake in her childhood single bed, staring sleepless at the cracked ceiling as car lights moved over the window. But it wouldn't be true, would it? She didn't even know if it was his baby. The lies were so much simpler than the truth. 'I'm fine,' she said again. 'See you.'

★ ★ ★

When she got home, something was off. She knew it right away. Pat was there — nothing strange in that. Except she hadn't actually seen Pat in the house for weeks. The little touches of her had gone, a tail wind of talc and biscuits, dishes rinsed and gleaming on a draining board, shirts taken from the basket and ironed, unasked for and unexpected.

Paula's stomach lurched as she set her keys down on the counter. Pat must know. That was it. She knew Paula was pregnant and that it could be Aidan's. Or worse, might not be. 'What's going on?' She could hear her voice was already high, defensive.

Pat and PJ were standing side by side in front of the window, the sink and washing machine behind them. Pat looked at PJ. She didn't meet Paula's eyes. 'Maybe I should head on, let you two have a wee chat.'

'No. You should be here.' Paula then saw her father had his arm around Pat, reaching across the sink and gripping her opposite elbow. She'd never seen him touch Pat before. Or anyone, in fact. Not since her mother went.

'Dad?' She had the sudden mad urge to start talking, make him not say whatever he was about to.

'Sit down, pet.'

There was something on the table. A piece of paper.

Pat babbled, 'Will I make a drink for us all? A nice drop of tea, maybe — '

'I don't want tea.' Paula made as if to go out again. 'I don't want this — I can't — '

'Paula.' Her father's voice was pleading. 'It's been long enough. You need to listen, and I need to say it.'

She was in the hall doorway, her back to them, when he said it.

'I've asked Patricia to marry me, Paula. We — I want us to live under the same roof, and she's a good Christian woman. I can't ask her to carry on like that without a wedding ring.'

Silence. Paula looked at the picture directly opposite in the hallway. Her parents' wedding. Those awful seventies suits, the flicky hair. It was stupid, what PJ had said. They had wedding rings already, both PJ and Pat. But Pat's husband was long dead and she was more than free to marry again. Whereas her father —

'Paula.' She turned, and instead of looking at them looked at the paper on the table. The words blurred into shape — DECLARATION OF DEATH.

'It's been long enough,' her father said, so awkward. His arm twitched away from Pat. 'Seven years, they need, and well — it's been seventeen. Love — '

She was moving. She heard Pat say, shaky — 'Ah look, PJ, she can't take it in. I'm sorry, pet! We won't do it. We were just being selfish. Paula!'

The stair carpet blurred under her feet. She was thundering up them. She was in the bathroom, retching into the sink, not caring that they saw. She retched and retched until she was an empty, shaking shell.

'There, there.' Hands were holding back her hair. 'Get it out. Get it all out.'

Paula started to cry. Her father sat heavily on the edge of the bath, bad leg splayed out, while she sank onto the toilet lid, leaning weakly over the sink.

'It was a bad idea,' he said quietly. 'I never thought you'd be so upset.'

'No — ' she coughed; her mouth was burning with bile. 'No. You have to. You'd be happy. I mean, it's Pat — of course you'd be. Of course you should get married.'

'But pet, look at the state of you.'

'It's just — we're giving up on her. We're saying she's dead.'

They hadn't spoken of this, the two of them, since she was thirteen and the night they'd sat at

293

the kitchen table, a week after her mother had gone, and talked through what they might do, the two of them. How they might possibly carry on. PJ said, 'It's the only way. I can't divorce your mother — Pat doesn't believe in it, and she wants to be married right. I wouldn't feel right either. It'd be like I was judging your mother somehow. But it doesn't mean — I still don't know if she is or not. I don't think we'll ever know, pet, and that's the God's honest truth.'

She was crying again, her shoulders shaking. The porcelain of the sink was cool under her cheek. 'It's just I need her, Daddy. I need her now. You see, I'm pregnant.'

For a moment he was very still, then he nodded. 'I knew something wasn't right with you. I've eyes in my head.' He passed a hand over his face. 'God almighty.'

'I'm sorry, Dad. I didn't mean it — it just happened. I'm so sorry.'

He raised his weary head. 'What would you be sorry for?'

'I know it's not what you wanted for me. I'm not married, I don't even know who . . . ' She gulped back the tears that were fizzing in her nose and throat.

'Ah, no now, no, no. Who'd be sad about a wean coming? It's the twenty-first century, love. It's just I don't know what I can do. She should be here, to help you. What can the likes of your ould da do?'

He seemed to have collapsed, sitting helpless on the side of the old lime-green bath. Paula wept over the sink for a few convulsing moments. Then she ran the tap, sluicing her face and eyes. She wiped a hand over her mouth. 'Look, Dad. The truth is, she isn't here. She won't come back just because you fill in a form. It won't change anything, will it? We still won't know anything about what happened.'

'No.'

She was very aware of the house round them, slowly collapsing under years of sadness, the hole in the middle where Margaret Maguire should have been. 'We'll manage, Daddy. Don't worry. We'll be grand.'

It was the same thing he'd said to her seventeen years ago, when they sat in this same house facing the fact that her mother wasn't coming back. And somehow, barely, scraping by, they had managed indeed.

She pushed her damp hair out of her face. PJ had gone silent. 'I never meant for this to happen, you know. I still might — I still don't know what I'm going to do.' She couldn't say the words to him, lifelong Catholic that he was, in Mass every week. She couldn't say she still might not have this baby. 'Dad? I mean, I . . . '

'Give us a hand.' He held out his arm and she helped him up. He squeezed her shoulders briefly. 'Let's not talk about it now, pet. You'll be OK. We'll help you.' He and Pat were a *we* now. It was a lovely word, when you thought what it meant. It meant you weren't alone.

Paula sniffed. 'I know. Pat will be good for you, I know it.'

'Ah.' PJ stopped. 'Tell me this, pet, before we go down. Is Aidan the father of the wean?'

295

She bit her lip. 'Dad — I don't know how to tell you this. I'm not sure. I — He might be. But he might not.'

He winced. 'Then don't tell Pat till you've told him, OK?'

'OK.' She took deep, shaky breaths. 'Dad?'

'Aye?'

'I — I hope you'll be happy, the two of you.' A weak smile flashed on PJ's face and was replaced by a look of weary sadness.

'We've as much a chance as anyone else in this ould world, for what it's worth. And so do you. Now come on downstairs.'

30

There was no answer the next day when Paula rang the door of Maeve's flat, in a converted warehouse close to the old meat district in Dublin. Smithfield, it was called, same as in London. She'd driven down that morning — thanks to the improved roads built with EU money, you could get to Dublin in less than two hours from Ballyterrin, though it might take you as long again to fight your way through the city's traffic-choked mediaeval streets. From behind the door of number five she could hear loud music: 'Sweet Child O' Mine'. Aidan had played that incessantly when he was eighteen, and they were driving about in his then-new Clio, drunk on freedom and youth and each other. 'Hello!' she shouted. 'Anyone in?'

The door flew open and there was Maeve Cooley, pulling blond hair into a messy ponytail. Despite the chill she wore shorts under a grey hoodie, her legs long and bare, chipped lime polish on her toes. 'Paula, howyeh. Sorry, I was working all night on deadline so I'm only up. Come in, will you.' Having been in Maeve's car, Paula was not surprised to find the flat was also a tip. A laptop sat on the hardwood floor surrounded by sheaves of paper and crumpled magazines, and every surface had collections of glasses, stained red with wine, or beer bottles, or plates used as ashtrays. The air smelled of smoke, and hangovers.

'Will you have tea or something?' Maeve threw back the curtains, wincing at the grey light which flooded in, and opened the fridge. A fluffy grey cat shot out from under the breakfast bar, giving Paula an evil stare and meowing loudly at his owner. 'Give over, Ernest. Bollocks, I've no milk.'

'I'm OK.' Paula moved inside, setting her bag down by the door under a framed poster of Oscar Wilde. *I have nothing to declare except my genius.* Maeve said something she couldn't hear over the music. 'Sorry?'

'That racket!' Maeve raised her voice. 'Shut that bloody din off, would you?'

'Oh, is someone — '

Too late. Paula heard a voice in the bedroom, an all too familiar voice, and then suddenly Aidan was in the room. 'It's Slash, you eejit — oh.' He stared at Paula. She took in the fact he wore only boxers and a T-shirt — one she'd bought him years ago, with Bob Dylan on it — and that he was coming out of the flat's only bedroom. His dark hair stuck up and he had several days' stubble on his face. 'What are you doing here?' he said.

'What are *you* doing here?' Paula must have backed away, because she felt the ridges of the door under her shoulders.

Maeve was swilling water in the sink. 'Aidan's down staying for a few days. Did you not tell her you were here, you eejit? I thought that's why you came, Paula.'

'No.' Paula's heart was thumping. 'No, I

298

wanted to speak to you about that faith healer, like I said.'

Maeve glanced between them. 'Aidan's on some story too. Won't say what, the dodgy bastard that he is.'

Aidan was still staring at Paula.

'I saw your mum,' she heard herself say. 'She said you were OK.'

'I am OK.'

'Oh, good. That's good.' Silence.

Maeve was either oblivious or choosing to barrel right through the acute tension in the room. 'Right. I've no milk and it's a mess in here, so I'm taking Paula out for a breakfast bap and a chat. Are you coming, William Randolph Hearst?'

'No,' said Aidan grumpily, rubbing hands through his tousled hair. 'I've work to do.'

Maeve rolled her eyes at Paula. 'Ah, the top-secret investigative work. Fair enough. You could load the dishwasher, if the mood takes you, before you win your Pulitzer.'

Aidan just turned and went back into the room. 'Grumpy arse,' sighed Maeve. 'Right, I'll put my jeans on and we'll go, will we?'

★   ★   ★

'Everything OK with you?' Maeve lifted the all-day breakfast bap to her mouth and took a huge bacon-filled bite.

'Fine,' lied Paula. She'd asked for a cup of tea, which came with sachets of creamer that floated unappetisingly to the surface. They were in a café

299

a few streets away, with metal tables and loud music playing, Christmas lights flashing like a warning sign. Directly across the street, in a pointed coincidence, was a large anti-abortion billboard showing a traumatised-looking woman. She ignored it. 'Aidan's OK then.' She itched to ask what he was doing in Maeve's bedroom, but she wouldn't let herself.

Maeve was chewing. 'Oh yeah. You know him. Narky as feck when he's not drinking.' He wasn't on the booze, then. That was one thing. 'You didn't know he was here, I take it.'

Paula shrugged. 'We haven't been talking much.'

Maeve clearly didn't want to get involved. 'Ah well, he's a difficult one.'

'Yeah.' Paula stirred the manky tea and forced herself to change the subject. 'Anyway, thanks for seeing me so quickly. I want to know about Magdalena Croft, the faith healer. She's been up with us for years but she started out here. We think she might be involved with these cases we're working on, but we can't get at her since we've actually been using her as an expert.'

Maeve licked her fingers and rummaged in her bag for a messy pile of papers. 'So. A gift of a story, that is. I spoke to my colleague at Religion and he'd a lot to say on the subject. Six whiskeys' worth, in fact, the tight fecker. So, this Magdalena first surfaces in Dublin in the early eighties. Claims to be having visions and offers healing out of some weird church on the Northside, run by this mental priest.'

'Father Brendan?'

300

'That's him. Joe, that's my colleague, he tried to do a piece on her once and she slapped an injunction on him. You didn't really get that out of mad religious women in the eighties, so shall we say he's followed her career with interest since. So she spends a few years here, collecting up money and followers. There's thousands of people will swear blind she cured their ingrown toenails or what have you.'

'That's what we came up with too.'

'Next there was the big mansion on the border, and she's raising money to build her own church in her back field, and the psychic visions she has, and the healing — people would take their disabled kids, I don't know, thinking she can rearrange DNA or something. Madness. But she'd nothing when Joe first knew her — she used to take the bus to the church and she hadn't 2d to her name. Then a few years later she's in a mansion in Ballyterrin and driving a Beemer. I think that's a bit dodgy, myself.'

'Dodgy, but hardly unusual, sadly.'

'You're telling me. So she made her money off her followers. People were giving cash for building the church — ten, thirty grand a go she'd ask for, her and Father Brendan. He got put out of his chaplaincy because of it, so now he just follows her round like a puppy dog. They take collections out of her house, too — people go to her when they're dying, and she's hovering over their relations saying what a shame, now get your chequebook out and make a donation for the Virgin Mary.'

'She has this board,' Paula said, tracing

patterns in the spilled creamer. 'All these babies she's supposedly helped people have.'

'Oh yeah. Cheaper than IVF, I guess.'

'But the thing is — I mean, there must be something in it. People believe she helps them. People do get pregnant. Even my DCI asked her to work on a missing persons case for us. So what is it she does?'

'Hope,' said Maeve succinctly. 'She gives them hope, and then sometimes people do get better or they do fall pregnant, and they think it's her. People trust her. She has a gift all right, but it's not being psychic. She can read people like a book, that woman.'

'You've met her?'

Maeve hesitated — which was so out of character it made Paula raise her eyebrows. 'Not exactly. I went to one of those rallies she does at her house. I thought it'd be a laugh, like that Derren Brown or something. Thought I could get a story out of it — why are the Guards using this fraud to help them, and so on.'

'I know. We're doing it now, too. But it wasn't a laugh?'

'No. She — well, she channels people. The dead, you know. It's one of her things. Load of bollocks, of course. But the thing was — she sort of channelled for me.'

'Who?'

'My dad,' said Maeve briefly. 'He died when I was ten. Cancer.'

'I didn't know that. I'm sorry.'

She shook her head. 'Don't be. That's why I was pals with Aidan, I guess — he understands.'

302

A stab of jealousy, quickly suppressed. 'What happened?'

'She — well, it was horrible to be honest. She said he'd been sick, and he'd died, and she knew all that and then she — ' Maeve frowned. 'She said, you and your daddy had the same birthday, didn't you? And we did, it's true. March the third. But it was so weird. I still can't figure out how she could have known that. She has something, you see. I don't believe in being psychic, it's bollocks, so she's working it out some other way, but she has it. She looked right into me somehow and I felt — I felt violated.'

Paula remembered the woman's quick, strong hand on her stomach. 'She's a very powerful presence. People seem drawn to that.'

'That's what Joe said. He's drawn himself, though he hates her. He was the one found out she was helping the Gardai. The thing is, she does really seem to help. Have you looked into it?'

'A bit. There were six cases or so, was that it?'

'I think so. She helped them find four missing children, and the bodies of two others who'd had accidents and the bodies not found.'

'What had happened to the other four?'

'Same as usual. Their dads had snatched them in custody cases. Gone overseas, a few times. I think one of them had just wandered off into woodland in Wexford. Croft said she'd be there, and she was, three days later, alive. Joe has a real bee in his bonnet. It drives him mad that she actually seems to get results.'

That was good. No one so useful as the person with the bee in their bonnet. 'Did he find out anything about her life before all this?'

'There was the husband no one ever saw — Joe dug up that they were living apart, while she pretended to be in a *good Christian marriage.*' Maeve did air quotes. 'David Croft died a few years back, I think. Natural causes, but she never had much use for him except his cash. He was one of her first devotees. Joe showed me photos — she was gorgeous back in the day, was Magdalena.'

'That's not her real name, is it? We traced a Mary Conaghan, like I said on the phone, and we think it could be her.'

'It sounds made up, doesn't it? No one's called Magdalena; I mean, it's not first-century Judea. Anyway, I did a search under the name you gave me and I actually did find a Mary Conaghan living in Dublin at that time.'

'Oh yes?' Paula set down her tea.

Maeve smiled. 'Guess what she did before? She was only a fecking nurse.'

'No! Really?'

'Yup.' Maeve dug around in her bag for a pen and clicked it, then scribbled on Paula's napkin. 'That's the details of the hospital where she started as a student nurse: 1982, St John of God's.'

'Wow, thank you.' Magdalena Croft had a nursing background. She could just imagine Guy's reaction when she told him that. 'I'll check it out while I'm here.'

'What else do you know?' asked Maeve, clearly

as hungry for the story as Paula was, if for different reasons.

'Well.' Paula looked round at the dingy little café before she spoke. Silly — who would be listening or even care? 'We traced a Mary Conaghan to Donegal and we think she was involved in a child abduction case as a young girl. Her cousin went missing as a baby, then was found again — similar to our Alek Pachek case. I think she came to Dublin not long after that.'

'I'll ask Joe, but he never mentioned anything. He said she was an orphan, no family at all.'

'I think she was hiding,' Paula said, turning it over in her mind. 'I think she was running away, when she came here.'

'From what?'

'From who, maybe. I don't know. It's just a feeling I have.'

Maeve scribbled something else. 'OK. Leave it with me. Tell me this, Paula — is Aidan on this story too?'

'I don't know. We haven't talked at all.' Another stab. He'd have helped so much, if only they were actually speaking. 'I don't know what he's up to.'

Maeve did a small eye-roll; it was uncannily similar to the one Saoirse always did when Paula tried to talk to her about Aidan. *You two again.* 'OK. You don't want to come back to the flat then?'

'I won't, thanks.' She wasn't going to ask how long he was staying. 'Thank you for your help.'

'No bother. I love all this.' Maeve stood up, all ripped jeans and tangled hair, and Paula thought

305

— wouldn't he? Wouldn't Aidan want to be with Maeve, so cool and gorgeous and uncomplicated, rather than someone who shouted at him and kept secrets from him and knew all his own painful ones, all of the dark inside of him? If only she could get over the raging anger that flooded her veins, she might not even blame him at all.

★ ★ ★

The hospital where Mary Conaghan had her first nursing job was grim, diseased green paintwork on the outside and the chill of old stone emanating out. At four p.m. on a winter Thursday, it was as far from warmth and comfort as you could imagine. Paula had an appointment to see Donald O'Driscoll, who rejoiced in the role of Personnel Director, and had worked in the same small office since 1982, when he'd hired Mary Conaghan for a trainee nursing post in the maternity unit.

Paula took the lift, feet clattering along cold stone corridors with depressing brown doors and metal signs, until she found the right one. Mr O'Driscoll was a corpulent man in his late fifties, wearing a pinstripe suit that looked as if he'd bought it back in 1982. He even had red braces. On his desk sat a picture of an equally fat woman and two plump children, plus a dog that was also in need of a few good walks.

She shook his hand. 'Mr O'Driscoll, thanks for seeing me. I said on the phone I work with the police in the North. You might have heard about our missing baby cases, and what's happened since. Well, we think we've turned up something you might be able to help us with.'

He looked wary. 'If it's a legal matter, I'll have to contact our lawyers before I say anything.'

'No, no, it's not like that. May I?' She sat on the hard plastic chair by his desk. It was a cheerless office, enlivened only by a stale coffee fug and a row of leather-bound legal books. All the objects on his desk had pharmaceutical branding. 'Let me explain. I'm looking for any records of one of your nurses — could you tell me anything more about her? She was from Donegal, I believe. Her name came up in connection with our investigation.'

'Oh yes?' He was looking more worried still.

'Could you just look at this for me and see if you recognise her?' She laid out the photo from Magdalena Croft's first newspaper article. She'd been twenty-five then, so it was just a few years after she'd got the nursing job, when she'd first started her healing work in Dublin.

'No,' said Donald, shaking his head and looking relieved. 'I don't recognise her at all.'

Oh. Paula tried again. 'You're sure? Mary Conaghan was her name before that. She changed it later, when she got married.'

'Oh, but this isn't Mary!'

'What?' Paula stared at the man.

'I remember Mary well. I interviewed her for the post. And that isn't her. She wasn't so dark, for a start.'

'But — ' Paula struggled to understand. 'We have a trail that shows Mary Conaghan changed her name to Magdalena, then married a man

307

named Croft — we found the marriage certificate. Her name is still legally Mary, in fact.'

Donald O'Driscoll pursed his plump mouth. 'Well, I don't know what to say. I've never seen that woman in my life.'

'You're positive?'

He peered again at the picture. 'I suppose there is some superficial resemblance, but it's not her. I'm sure of it.'

'Oh . . . Do you have a photo on file of your Mary?'

'We will do, I imagine, for ID badges. But that file will be buried in a basement somewhere, if she hasn't worked for us in years.'

'Can you find it?'

He gave an administrator's sigh. 'There would be significant Data Protection hoops to jump through, Dr Maguire, but I'll try. Leave your fax number and other details.'

Paula wasn't even sure they had a fax machine at the unit. 'I will. So — this Mary Conaghan who worked here. We're very interested in talking to her in connection with our missing baby case. I understand she worked on Neonatal while she was here — is there anything you could tell me about that? No complaints, no problems with the children, anything like that?' She saw his expression. 'I understand you might need to check the files, and that some of this might be confidential, but you'd really be helping us out. As you may have seen, another child went missing this week. That makes three in total, and two still not found. Someone is taking babies, and we have to pursue every lead we can.'

308

He gave her a searching look. 'Do you have police ID, Dr Maguire?' He said the 'Doctor' as if she were a little girl playing dress-up. She found a card in her bag and slid it over; he made a big point of scrutinising it. 'Well. We're always keen to assist the police, of course. I assume this is in connection with the Roberts baby case?'

Paula arranged her face carefully; she knew nothing about that. 'Can you tell me anything about it? What was the year again — 1983?' A wild guess.

''Eighty-four.' He pursed his lips again. 'Very bad publicity. But you see in those days, Dr Maguire, we'd no idea people would do such a thing. Not in Ireland. So we had no security on the wards. The hospital wasn't found to be negligent in any way, if that's what you — '

'No, I'm sure you did everything you could. The child went missing from the Maternity Unit, is that right?' She was guessing, free-wheeling off his reactions. Was that the same as what Magdalena Croft did, casting the runes of people's faces?

'Yes. We'd never had anything like that before. I must admit it brought it all back, when I heard about your case on the news. Ours was also taken from the Maternity Ward, right out of its crib.'

'Right. Alek Pachek disappeared from hospital too, but then was returned a few days later, safe. That's the oddest aspect of the case.'

He frowned. 'But the Roberts child was returned too, of course. Left on the doorstep here two days later, in a shoebox.'

She gave up pretending to know. 'And was it — ?'

'Dead.'

Paula flinched. 'Oh. Do you know how?'

'Exposure. Whoever left her back, they hadn't wrapped her up enough for November, and she died before anyone found her. The family were devastated.'

'It was a girl? What was her name?' There was no real need for Paula to know this, except that she had to. She wondered if the man would remember.

He hesitated just for a second, as if trying to recall. 'Orla, I believe. Orla Roberts.'

Paula rallied herself. 'And was there any connection to Mary Conaghan?'

'She worked on the ward at the time. But you know, a lot of other people did too. We all knew Mary could never have done such a thing — but there was some nonsense about a child going missing when she was younger. Anyway they let her go, thank God. No evidence.'

Paula thought fast. 'Mr O'Driscoll . . . I don't suppose they took any fingerprints at the time, did they?'

'I believe so, yes. I remember we all thought it was a disgrace. Of course Mary's prints would have been there; she worked in the place!'

Paula tried to stay calm. 'The fingerprints — if you have those on file it would be very helpful to us.'

'The Gardai may still have them, I suppose. You'd have to ask them.'

'Just one more thing. This might seem like a

slightly odd question. Did you like Mary? You thought she was a nice person? Did the patients like her, that sort of thing?'

He answered right away. 'That's why I remember her so well. Mary was the loveliest person you could imagine. We got more praise for her than any other nurse I've hired. We all backed her a hundred per cent — she'd never have hurt a child. And that's definitely not her in your picture.'

'OK,' said Paula, dissatisfied but not sure where she could go with this. 'Thank you for your help.'

★ ★ ★

'So how do you explain that? He was adamant.'

Guy was on the other end of the phone as Paula went back to her car, parked in a multi-storey on Lower Baggot Street. 'I can't. Either your contact was lying, or we've missed a step and it was the wrong Mary Conaghan after all. It's not that unusual a name, is it?' He sounded worried.

'No.' Paula fumbled her keys in the car lock, glittering with rime in the cold. 'And why didn't this case come up on Avril's searches, if it was in 1984?'

'I don't know. Maybe they kept it quiet, if it reflected badly on the hospital.'

'It just doesn't make any sense. I need to see the picture they've got on file, but I wouldn't count on him dragging it up any time soon. The good news is there may be prints.'

'That's fantastic. I'm afraid Croft appears to have concrete alibis for the disappearances of Darcy Williams and also Heather Campbell. She's a bit more vague on Dr Bates and Alek Pachek. If we got prints maybe it would help crack her.'

'Maybe.' Paula wasn't sure anything could. 'Any other progress?'

'No.' His voice was heavy. 'Not a single thing. No sign of Lucy or Darcy.'

'So what do we do?'

'Keep pushing. Follow up every lead there is.'

Paula was silent, thinking of two babies out there in the snow, Lucy ripped from her dying mother and Darcy vanishing from her garden in the seconds it took to answer a phone. 'Guy?' She hardly ever called him this, a symbol of their fraught work and personal entanglements. He sounded tired. 'Yes?'

'Are we wrong? What if it's nothing to do with Magdalena Croft? If she really had alibis . . . '

'So she claims.' Guy didn't budge. 'She's scammed us somehow, I'm sure of it. We'll find out how when we finally arrest her. Maybe the Williams case isn't even connected. You said it didn't fit the pattern.'

'It seemed odd, but two baby abductions in the same town?' She was doubtful. 'That just doesn't happen.'

'Copycat? Is that possible?'

'Um . . . in theory.' She wondered again at Guy's determination to pin it on Croft. 'Have you ever thought . . . ? Is it possible we're looking in entirely the wrong place?'

312

Guy said nothing for a while. 'I wish I knew, Paula.'

★ ★ ★

Paula went home, ate dinner with PJ. Potatoes, chops, peas. Tasted none of it. Straight up for a bath in the old tub, the trickle of limescale down the tap, the hot water running out in the middle. Into bed in her thickest pyjamas and jumper, clutching a hot water bottle between her calves, shivering for ten solid minutes before falling into a thick sleep. Which was shattered at seven a.m., when her phone began ringing close to her ear. 'Hello?' The room was filled with cold white light. She could almost see her breath.

Guy. 'Are you awake?'

'I am now.' *Duh.* 'It's Saturday, you know.'

'I know. Can you come in? They've gone to arrest Croft. We got the prints. They matched.'

Suddenly she was awake. 'The prints on file? They matched the one found on Heather?'

'Yes. Come on. Now.'

'But — Mr O'Driscoll didn't know her in the photo. He said it wasn't her.'

She heard the impatience in his voice. 'Paula, every other bit of evidence points to her. Maybe the man was mistaken, or trying to protect her, who knows. Just please get in as soon as you can.' He hung up.

313

31

The incident room in the main station was crammed with officers as Paula unwound her long green scarf. 'She's really here then?'

Gerard was on hold with someone, the phone receiver tucked under his chin as he bashed two-fingered at his computer keyboard. He looked up as Paula took off her coat. She'd dressed in two jumpers again. Everyone probably thought she'd put on huge amounts of weight. 'Yup,' he said succinctly. 'TSU brought her in an hour back.'

'They sent Tactical Support, for one woman?'

'Corry didn't want a fuck-up. She has all those followers, doesn't she? You'd never know who'd be there. And there's a lot of press interest so she's trying to keep a lid on it. Anyway, Corry's having a crack at her now.'

Paula was strangely nervous, knowing the woman was on the premises. Those eyes, they saw right through you. She was absurdly afraid that Magdalena would tell everyone her secret. She reminded herself they were looking for someone who could gut a pregnant woman like a carcass. Could the faith healer really do that, after all the couples she'd supposedly helped have babies, the sick she'd tried to cure? 'What should I do? Where's Gu — where's Inspector Brooking?'

Gerard gave her a sardonic look. '*Guy's* in

314

with Corry. Team effort.'

'That's unusual.'

'Aye, season of goodwill and all that. Look, they must be ready.'

Guy had just walked into the incident room, spotting Paula. 'There you are. We need you.'

'She came in OK?'

'Yes, she's been a model of good behaviour. Bewildered, polite, knows nothing. And she's only engaged Danny McShane as her lawyer.'

Even Paula knew that wasn't good. The top criminal solicitor in town, Danny was as slippery as they came. The station tea-room had a picture of him pinned to the noticeboard, ripped from some glossy magazine. His eyes had been blacked out and devil's horns drawn on in pen. 'So she denies everything.'

'Of course. But we've got the prints, she can't keep it up forever.'

Paula was uneasy with this confidence. 'What do you want me to do?'

Guy was rounding the corner. 'She's asking to talk to you.'

'Croft? Me? But — I don't do interviews! Corry'll never let me.'

'At this point she'll try anything. Come on.'

* * *

'You're sure about this?'

Guy and Corry were directing Paula towards the interview room like pushy parents on the first day of school. She was quivering, smoothing down the front of her jumper.

315

'We're sure,' said Corry, who was today attired in her grey suit, hair swinging in a ponytail. 'She's telling us nothing, and if we say it's a psychological assessment we can get that bloody shyster lawyer out of the room.'

'But — what will I ask her?'

'Dr Maguire, is this or isn't it your job?'

'It is, but I don't . . . '

'Dr Maguire doesn't usually interview in a criminal setting,' Guy chipped in. Corry and Paula both glared at him. She could fight her own battles.

She took a deep breath. 'What's my main focus?'

Corry said, 'If she knows anything about the murders. If she's ever lost a child. If she fits your own profile. Anything that will break her.'

'I'll try.'

'Don't try. Do it.' The door loomed. 'In you go.'

★ ★ ★

It was lonely on that side of the glass. Usually the interviewing officer would have a partner with them, and the suspect a lawyer hovering on every word. But now it was just Paula, pale, shivering with nerves, and Magdalena Croft, composed, attentive, dressed warmly in a tweed skirt, flat boots, and a plain green jumper. With her glasses and grey hair, she looked like a kindly aunt.

Paula cleared her throat. 'How are you, Mrs Croft? This must be very distressing for you.'

316

'Distressing, no. I only want to help. I've always done my best to help the police. Finding that little Polish boy meant the world to me. If only I could have traced the others.'

Paula looked back at the two-way glass, knowing Guy would be on the other side of it. 'I think it's been explained, Mrs Croft, that the police have discovered quite a few things. They know about Michael, for example.'

No reaction.

'Michael Gillan? Back when you were Mary Conaghan? Your cousin went missing from his crib while you were minding him. Can you tell me about that?' Nothing. Paula tried again. 'Mary?'

She slowly blinked. 'My name is not Mary.'

'But it was.'

'A lot of things were. A life is long and twisty, Dr Maguire. People change hugely. You should know that, of anyone.'

Paula ignored this, though her heart began to race under all the jumpers. 'Mary was your name though?' No reaction. Sweat was seeping into her armpits. 'They blamed you, didn't they?'

'I was a child. They asked too much of me. I was just an unpaid skivvy to my aunt. But I didn't hurt him. I'd never hurt a baby.'

Paula relaxed a fraction. Croft had as good as admitted she was Mary Conaghan; that was progress. 'Were you close to him? You looked after him.'

'I had little choice. In anything that happened to me as a child.'

'But you did take Michael?'

317

She seemed to think about it for a long time. 'I did. I hid him for a night only. He was never harmed. You see, I had no other way to escape.'

'Escape?'

'I needed out of that house. I needed to get home.'

'Can you tell me why, Mary? Why did they send you there in the first place?'

She gave a small, tight smile. Impossible to read. 'These things are in the past, Doctor. The past is a different country and we're all foreigners. I'm not what I was. None of us are.'

'I'm not sure I follow, Mrs Croft.'

'I think you do. This girl Mary you're speaking of. That isn't me. I left her behind.'

Paula made a small mark on her pad. *Dissociation*. She saw Magdalena looking and had the urge to cover it with her arm. 'Tell me about the hospital, then. St John of God's in Dublin. You were arrested again then, weren't you?'

Another blink. 'I'm not sure what you mean.'

'A baby went missing. Out of the labour ward, just like Alek Pachek. Her name was Orla Roberts. Only it didn't end as well for Orla. She was found two days later on the hospital steps. She'd died. Exposure.'

The woman locked eyes with Paula. 'That's very sad. Luckily I was able to help find little Alek before it came to that.'

'Are you saying you don't recall this, Mrs Croft? We have a record of arrest for a Mary Conaghan, who was working as a student nurse there.'

She shook her head. 'These things, they happened to a different person.'

'I see. Well, the thing is, Mrs Croft, that Mary Conaghan had her fingerprints taken as part of the investigation. It was the second time she'd been arrested over the disappearance of a child. Nothing could be proved — she worked there, so of course her prints would be on the scene — but as it happens they were kept on file. So that was useful for the police on this case.' Paula couldn't meet Croft's eyes, so she pretended to be making notes on her pad, staring at the lines. 'You may have heard, but Forensics did find one print on Heather Campbell's body. There wasn't much else. The person who's taking these children is very careful. But we did get that.' She looked up to find Magdalena staring at her. A trickle of fear ran down Paula's throat. *Focus, focus.* She'd interviewed worse people. 'The thing is, Mrs Croft, it matches the one on file for Mary Conaghan.'

The woman was very still for a moment, like a statue in a church. Then she blinked again, her eyes cold behind the glasses. 'Is that the reason I'm here? The fingerprint matches the one you found in Dublin?'

'Yes. You also knew exactly where to find Alek.' Paula tried to keep her voice steady.

'I see. The police doubt that I have visions. Well, not all are blessed with the gift of faith.' She raised her chin. 'I'm not that well versed in science, I'm afraid. Fingerprints remain the same all throughout life, is that right, Dr Maguire?'

319

'Yes. All through life, and no two are ever the same.'

'Not even twins, I once heard.'

'No. Not even identical twins.'

'So if mine didn't match the one you have, you'd have nothing against me?' She held out her hands, thin and pale, like ash branches in the snow.

'But they do match.'

'I mean my prints now. These ones in front of me.'

'Yes, but Mary — Mrs Croft — you must see they will match too. They never change, as we just said.'

She smiled. It was quite terrifying. 'Nevertheless, stranger things have happened. Why don't you take them again before we talk more? If they match, I will tell you everything.'

Paula looked helplessly at the window. 'I — you mean you want to wait until the results are back?'

'Yes. I'd like my lawyer back too, please.'

There seemed to be no choice. 'If that's what you want, Mrs Croft. We'll talk again later then.' Paula tried to leave the room confidently, but the trickle of worry had grown into a full flood, and as she looked back through the window Magdalena was staring through, as if she could see Paula, and still smiling serenely.

★ ★ ★

Getting fingerprints usually took at least several days, but Corry wasn't going to pass up this opportunity to prove their case, and had already rushed them through the lab. After Croft's request, she got on the phone and a young female constable was dispatched to take new prints of Magdalena's thin white fingers, and then, they waited. Could this really be the person who'd hacked into the bodies of two women, ripped out a child as it drew its first breath, drowning in blood? There was such a stillness about Croft. Paula realised with a sinking heart she just couldn't see it. But if it wasn't Croft and it wasn't Melissa Dunne, *who was it?*

The tension in the incident room was unbearable. Leaving Croft behind glass with her lawyer, perfectly calm, they sat about waiting. Occasionally a phone would buzz and everyone would jump, but it was clear no work was getting done. Corry paced back and forth in the doorway of her office, occasionally picking up her phone and barking into it. 'I don't care how much it bloody costs! Get it done! *Christ.*'

Guy was pretending to go through his emails at a desk, but he kept looking at the door of her office, and at 3.23 p.m. he walked over, shutting it behind him, which in no way stopped the whole office from overhearing their subsequent row. 'I said we should have got her in sooner. Look at all the time she's had now to cover her tracks.'

'Inspector, are you suggesting she's altered her fingerprints or something equally far-fetched?'

'No, but she's clever. She's known for weeks that we suspect her.'

'And whose fault is that? You've been acting

from day one as if she's guilty. It's highly unprofessional!'

After this there was a drop in sound, and after some more muffled exchanges, Guy emerged, closing the door with more force than was needed and going back to his desk without looking at anyone. They waited. At 4.03 p.m., Gerard pushed back his chair, balling up the paper he'd been working on. 'What's taking them so bloody long? We'll have to let her go soon if they don't get their arses in gear.'

Paula looked at the phone again. She had a bad feeling about this. Just then, a trill. Corry darted in, and it seemed she paused for a moment before lifting the receiver. Every eye in the room followed her. 'Hello, DCI Corry speaking.' A pause. 'I see. You're sure? Thank you.' She replaced the receiver. She stood at her desk for a moment, then passed a hand over her face before coming out into the main room. 'Everyone,' she said. They hung on her words. 'I'm afraid she was right. The print isn't hers. We have to let her go.'

Paula realised she was on her feet. 'But the name was the same! Mary Conaghan, that's her name, she even told me it was!'

Guy was at her side, gripping her elbow. 'Leave it.' He spoke low in her ear.

'But — she told me! How can it not be her?' Paula felt tears sting her eyes. People were turning, looking at her.

'*Paula*. Control yourself.' His face was set. 'I was afraid this might happen. I think there's more to this case than we've suspected. You said

322

so yourself — it doesn't fit, does it? The planning and carefulness, and then that savagery?'

'So what can we do? What else is there?' They spoke in hisses, as around them the team sagged into disappointment, low voices murmuring, computers switched back into life, but for what purpose? Their two main leads had petered into nothing, vanished overnight like the melting snow.

Guy whispered, 'I have an idea.'

'What do you mean?'

'Just something I want to look into. I think you and I need to take a short trip. Are you in?'

Paula passed a hand over her damp face, aching for Heather and her lost baby, and Darcy Williams, and all these other children being chosen by some dark logic, unstoppable. 'I'm in.'

32

Tallaghmar, Donegal.

In Irish it meant *the dead ground*, or *the barren ground*, and it was a very literal name — it was amazing to think of anything growing in those bare, rocky fields. The snow had melted in patches, though a bitter wind still blew in off the sea, navy and sullen. Even from up on the headland they could see breakers in the bay, and further out, at the westernmost tip of Europe, the islands, dark and unknowable. Tory. Inisbofin. Names like breaths of harsh wind.

'Is this the place?'

'It must be. We're practically off the map.'

Donegal in the deep mid-winter. This was Guy's trip idea, their last resort, so to speak. The birthplace of Mary Conaghan, whoever she'd really been. Time to go back to the start. He'd fudged it with Corry and he and Paula had left that morning, driving as far west as you could go before you dropped into the Atlantic, wide and deep and endless. Paula didn't know what he'd told his wife, and didn't ask.

They'd long since abandoned Guy's Sat Nav, were close to abandoning maps too. The address they had was no more than *Ceol na Mara*, Tallaghmar. Music of the Sea, the name of the house meant. Though it wasn't music she could hear as they rounded the coast, but a restless chomping, a gnawing at the land like some caged animal gradually eating itself free. The only house near the beach looked abandoned, a turf-roofed farm cottage with stone walls and tiny windows like narrowed eyes. There was no driveway, just a dirt track leading to a collection of outhouses.

Guy seemed to sense her reluctance to leave the car. 'Come on. It's all right.'

She followed, walking carefully on the cold ground, wishing she could grasp his arm. 'What if no one's there?' The place had no phone, so they hadn't been able to call ahead even if they'd wanted to.

'Then we'll ask around. Go to the local Gardai station, visit the pub.'

She imagined Guy's cut-glass English vowels amid the turf smoke and suspicious gazes of a Donegal pub. 'I think maybe we should leave.'

He looked at her in surprise. 'It's not like you to get spooked.'

'No. I just — ' She was afraid, she wanted to say. She'd been afraid from the moment that pregnancy test had turned pink. Despite her best efforts, and wherever she turned now, she had something to lose. 'Knock, then.'

The door was low and latched. Nobody seemed to have been there for decades. Paula fidgeted nervously from foot to foot, willing the silence to remain unbroken. One second. Two seconds. Three — footsteps, and the door creaked open. A stooped old woman stood before them, in a tweed skirt and heavy coat, a piece of twine wound round it to keep it shut. Her legs were bare and exposed, raw sores marking the shins, and she wore little ankle socks with hiking boots. She stared at them.

From inside, the squawk of chickens. Guy cleared his throat. 'Good afternoon, madam. We're from the police — we were looking for any family of Mary Conaghan, who we think lived here once?'

She stared. There were several distinct whiskers on her chin. Paula had the fearful impression of a goblin barring the way.

Guy tried again. 'Do you know the family, madam?'

The woman looked at Paula and said, '*An Sassenach é?*'

Paula froze. '*Er — Tá sé. Is mise Éireannach.*'

'*An bhfuil Gaeilge agat?*'

'*Cúpla focail.*'

Guy was looking stunned.

'She's an Irish speaker,' Paula explained. 'There's a few older folk about who are still more comfortable in it.'

'You speak it?' He was watching her with awe and surprise.

'A bit. That's what I told her. She's surprised to see an Englishman here, I think.'

'*Sassenach,*' Guy repeated. 'Is that derogatory?'

'Um ... depends on the context. I don't remember that much, to be honest. But I was quite good at school.' She groped for the word 'police'. '*Tá muid . . .*' she failed. 'Mary. Mary Conaghan. *An bhfuil si anseo?*'

Asking if Mary was there was the best she could do, though clearly Mary wasn't. She was in Ballyterrin in her mansion built with other people's money, unless they were very wrong about everything. But the woman understood. 'Mary.' The name was rusty in her old throat.

Paula nodded.

'*Tagaigi isteach.*' The goblin woman vanished into the gloom, and Paula nudged Guy.

'She says go in.'

He peered into the interior. 'It smells like animals.'

'Yes, well, you wanted to come here. Go on.'

The house seemed entirely preserved from time. Whitewashed walls, a cracked wooden floor, and scant light from the high, dirty windows. The animal smell came from the chickens which roamed, clucking, and three large black Labs slumped around the open turf fire. Paula noticed a line of large muddy boots by the door — perhaps the woman lived with a son, who looked after her. It was hard to imagine her coping with a farm, she was so tiny and wizened.

She muttered something. 'What did she say?' There was only one wooden chair, so Guy stood, almost banging his head on the low ceiling.

'Tea. She's offering tea.'

'Of course she is. Can I say no?'

'Nope.' Paula pasted on a smile. 'She can almost certainly understand you, by the way. It's not the Amazon. She's just speaking Irish by preference. Go *raibh mhaith agat*,' she pronounced, on receiving the tar-like tea in a chipped flowered cup. A packet of Kimberley biscuits added a surreal modern touch. Guy smiled uncertainly, but failed to hide his grimace on tasting the tea.

Paula was struggling to dredge up the distant memories of GCSE Irish, taught by Mr Ó Briain, a rabid Republican with gingery sideburns and a tendency to go off on rants about the Black and Tans. The tea had a distinct farmyard tang, but she drank it anyway, removing a dog hair surreptitiously from her mouth.

'Is mise Paula,' she said. Lesson one in first year, how to say your name. 'Guy an t-ainm atá air.' She pointed at Guy, hoping she'd got the right gender on the preposition. 'Tá muid ag . . . ' Crap, what was the verb to 'look for'? No. 'Mary. Ba mhaith liom Mary.' I want Mary. That should cover it.

'Níl sí anseo.'

Well, yes, it was obvious she wasn't there. She decided to ask the woman's name. 'Cad e an t-ainm atá ort?'

'Eilish,' said the woman reluctantly. She rocked in her rocking chair, smacking her lips at the tea. A chicken wandered over and settled at her feet, puffing its feathers. 'Ba chairde mise agus Mary.' She began to speak rapidly in Irish. 'Bhí sí ina cónaí anseo. Ba chol ceathrair liom í a mháthair.'

Paula nodded, trying to keep up. 'I think she's saying she's a cousin of Mary's mother, and they were friends. This was where Mary grew up. Cá bhfuil a mháthair de Mary?' Where's Mary's mother?

'Marbh.' Dead, as she'd suspected.

'*Tá athair?*'

Eilish shook her head. '*Níl aon athair aici.*' She had no father. '*Bh sí ina cónái anseo, lena mháthair agus tá lena hathair mór.*'

'She lived with her mother and grandfather,' Paula explained to Guy. 'No dad. They must be dead now anyway. How old was Mary when she left, Eilish?' She hoped the English would be understood as she gave up trying to knit together her meagre *focal* of Irish.

Eilish held up both hands, then one hand again. Fifteen.

Paula nodded; that fitted with what they knew. Mary had been sent away to live with her cousins as a teenager, then somehow ended up in Dublin. '*An raibh sí anseo* . . . um . . . recently?'

A strange watchful look crept over the face of the old woman. She shrugged her shoulders vaguely.

'Eilish — *an bhfuil photograph agat?*'

Eilish got up, leaving the chair to swing back and forth on its own. Guy was looking blank. 'I asked if she had a photo of Mary, just to make sure we've got the right one this time.'

'Good idea. Should we follow her?'

But Eilish was back already, a faded album in her hands, falling apart at the seams. She plonked it on the table, making dust rise, and opened the dark green cover to the first page. Under the tacky plastic was one picture. It had been torn across the top, so the head of one of the figures was missing. Paula shivered. She turned the page, the plastic squeaking under her fingers. The head of the same person was cut off

329

in every one, jagged and rough. A man.

'*Sin é?*'

'*An t- athair mór.*' Mary's grandfather, with his head torn off. Paula wanted to ask why, but the words failed her.

The first picture also showed a young girl of about fifteen, dressed in a seventies short skirt. She had bobbed hair and glasses, and stood stiffly with the man's arm about her. The picture was old, but the likeness to present-day Magdalena was clear. She even wore the same type of glasses still. Mary Conaghan. Magdalena Croft. The same person and this proved it.

But Paula's attention was caught by a third person in the picture — a younger girl, maybe twelve or thirteen. She was very pretty in a dark way, a wide white headband holding back her long black hair. She wore shorts and a pink shirt. Paula pointed to the girl. '*Cad é sin?*'

Eilish snapped the album shut, the severed edges of the pictures hidden.

'Eilish?' said Paula. 'Please, who is that? We need to know. Please, Eilish. *Cad é sin? Le do thoil.*'

For a moment she thought the woman really wasn't going to tell her. But she paused in the doorway of the room, album clasped to herself. 'It's Bridget,' she said in her croaky voice.

'Bridget?' Paula looked at Guy. '*Cad é Bridget?*' Who the hell was Bridget?

Eilish turned to go. '*Deirfiúr léi. Deirfiúr le Mary.*'

'What?' said Guy impatiently. 'What does that mean?'

330

Deirfiúr, Deirfiúr. Paula knew this word. *Think, Maguire.* She tried to remember the Irish classroom, the teacher's nasal voice.

'Well?'

Paula watched the woman shuffle away. 'Her sister. Bridget was Mary's sister.'

'A sister?'

Paula was on her feet, following Eilish down the dark corridor of the cottage. The woman stood in the doorway of a small, low-ceilinged room. 'Eilish . . . '

The room was lit only by a small, high window, crossed with metal bars. The only furniture was two narrow twin beds, made up in plain sheets. The white-washed walls were hung with pictures, three on each. The glass of each picture had been smashed, a helix of fractures hiding the faces of the people in them, but it was clear to see they were of the same man and girls in the photo album. On the wall a huge cross looked down, Jesus's face twisted in agony.

Paula found herself backing away, into the solid warmth of Guy, thank God. 'I think we better go,' he said.

33

'I can't believe it. In all our research, no one turned up the rather vital fact that Mary Conaghan had a sister?' Guy was fuming.

'I think she must have hidden it,' said Paula. 'I'm sure Avril would have spotted it if anything was on the records.' They were back in the BMW, Guy driving. Night had closed in, that wall of darkness you get in the country. A freezing sea mist hung over the coast road, and Guy was driving very slowly, peering through the windscreen.

'I've no bloody mobile reception. It's like *Deliverance* out here. As soon as we get back let's get a search on Bridget Conaghan. How old would she be now?'

'In her late forties, I'd say. A few years younger than Mary.'

'So there were two girls, stuck out here with the mother and grandfather.'

'Yeah. Then the mother died.' Paula lapsed into thought. Bridget had presumably been left behind when her sister was sent away. She'd have been twelve or thirteen at most. What had happened to her?

'I wonder where she ended up,' Guy said, with his trick of echoing her thoughts. It was disconcerting.

'Me too. I — Christ, watch out!'

It was all happening. A face had appeared out

of the gloom, and Guy was yanking the wheel to the left, cursing as the wheels spun and the car skidded off the wet road. Paula had a brief image of mangled features coming out of the fog — bulbous nose, tiny pinhole eyes — and then it vanished. The car ran up the bank and jerked over the turf siding. Paula was flung forward, bracing her hands on the dashboard. She hit her head awkwardly off the side of the car, then they came to rest.

'Are you OK?' Guy had his seat belt off in a flash. 'Paula? You've gone white as a sheet. Are you hurt?' He was feeling her forehead and throat. His hands were cold. His face was very close to hers.

Paula drew off all her breath in a shriek. 'Christ! What was that? Did you see that face?'

'No idea. Some local walking in the road, I suppose. Are you all right?'

Her hands had gone straight to her stomach. He'd seen. 'Does something hurt?'

'N-no.' She was OK. She was fine. Her heart must be deafening the baby. 'I'm just shaken up a bit. It's OK.' It was fine. Everything was fine.

'OK.' He turned his head. 'We need to push the car out. Can you help, do you think?'

'I don't know. I'm — I feel weird.'

'You've had a shock. We need to get some sugar into you, once we're out of here. If you can turn the wheel and rev, I think I can push.'

Under other circumstances, Paula would have found it funny when Guy went up to the knees of his hand-made suit in the Irish bog. 'Shit! I think I've lost my shoe.' He was scrabbling

333

around in the marshy undergrowth, trying to find his Italian loafer by the light of the car. But she could only sit frozen. It had been so close. So close. And part of her still thought — one bang could have been it. Erase, rewind, go back to September, as if she'd never come home at all.

'Ready? Rev the engine, will you?'

She pressed the pedal, and with Guy pushing in his shirtsleeves, they got the car back on the road and limped the rest of the way to the hotel.

★　★　★

'Right, the room's ready.'

Paula looked up mutely. The hotel had an open fire and glowing Christmas lights, and she wanted nothing more than to crawl into a scalding bath and slough off that cottage, the clinging feel of the mist all over her. The sweet, smoky smell of burning turf filled her lungs. She'd always loved that smell — of long, compressed summers, and life left to bed down. Now it made her shudder.

'The room? Singular?'

He looked awkward. 'Yes. I don't think they understood me on the phone, to be honest. But I'm not sure that tyre will last to get anywhere else. I can sleep on the floor, of course.'

'OK.' She couldn't look at him. 'I'm too tired to go anywhere else anyway.'

'Fine. Now come and have some food. We need to get your blood sugar up.'

Guy was at the bar ordering them pie and chips, while Paula sat warming her hands at the fire. Had it really been some kind of monster she'd seen on the road, or did the fog distort things, play tricks on her? And what of Bridget, Mary's unexpected sister? She thought of the man with his head torn off and shuddered again.

Guy was coming back and she smiled at him, grateful for his presence. He'd put a soft blue jumper over his mud-stained shirt, and there was a speck of dirt on his face. She wanted to rub it off, but as he put down the drinks — Guinness for him, a glass of something amber for her — she saw his wedding ring glint in the firelight. 'What did you get me?'

'Whiskey.' He held it up to the light. 'He looked at me funny when I asked for brandy. But drink it, you'll feel better.'

She gazed at the small glass of liquid, glowing warm and golden. Imagined it trickling down her throat, into her body. She stood up. 'Actually, I really hate whiskey. Sorry. Why don't you drink it?'

'Shall I get you something else?'

'No, it's OK, I'm just . . . ' She gestured to the Ladies and then bolted. It was a small room, and smelled of soap. She locked the door then fumbled down her jeans, where she'd felt the sudden wetness. She was braced and ready to see the blood, but there was nothing. Nothing. Everything was fine. Paula leaned forward onto her bare thighs, and began to cry, as noiselessly as she could.

* * *

335

Guy made a big fuss about trying to arrange pillows on the floor, until she stopped him, intensely weary. 'Just lie on the bed, will you?' She was already in it, pyjamas on and jumper over them — paranoid about any possible bump showing.

'Are you sure?' He'd stripped down to a T-shirt and boxers and she was doing her best not to look at his legs.

'Yes. Come on, I'm so tired.'

'OK. Tomorrow we'll try to find the local Guard and see if we can turn up Mary's cousins that she was sent to live with. Hopefully they'll know where she went after the baby's disappearance.'

'Yeah.'

He switched off the light, and then she heard his padding footsteps, the creaking as he settled into the bed, as far from her as possible. They'd spent the night together before, of course, but she'd been so drunk and exhausted she barely remembered falling asleep. The memory made her blush in the dark.

Guy cleared his throat. 'You're really OK? You'll tell me if you have any whiplash, or delayed pain?'

'Delayed pain? Is that even a thing?'

'Of course. Sometimes after a shock, you can't feel what's been done to you until it's much later.'

Paula thought about that for a moment. 'I'm fine.'

'OK. Sleep well.'

They lay for a moment, then she turned over

awkwardly. 'Sorry. I'm not used to this. I mean, I sleep alone usually.'

He spoke very quietly. 'So do I, Paula. For a long time now.'

She opened her mouth to ask, but what was the point? It wasn't her business if he was in the spare room or whatever was going on between him and his wife. She was still his wife. That was the point. And Paula was . . . nobody.

'Why were you so convinced it was her?' she asked, in the dark. 'Magdalena Croft, I mean. Mary.'

He said nothing for a moment. 'When Jamie died, my wife — Tess, I mean, she went to a psychic. Who said Jamie was at peace now, and happy. Charged her five hundred pounds.'

'Oh.'

'It's not that I — I think she got something from it, but these people, they find you when you're at your worst. That's what we do too, but we're supposed to help. People like Croft just exploit you, and your pain.'

She could feel him lying awake beside her, so she pretended to be asleep for a long while until his breath came slow and regular, and then she sat up. He was sleeping with one arm thrown across his face. A gap in the curtains let in the security light from outside, lashed by wind. She got up to fix it, looking out for a moment at the stormy bay. Even behind glass she could hear the roar of the waves.

There in the car park, someone was watching. Could have been a punter from the pub. She couldn't see clearly. Someone in black clothes, face white as bone in the mist. Paula stood for a moment, looking out, while he looked back at her, illuminated as she was against the light. Then she pulled the curtain tight and went to the bed. She curled herself against Guy, laying her back all along him, tangling her legs in his. He moved and took her in his arms, as if they'd done this every night for years. As if she were his wife, falling asleep beside him in the long dark. 'Are you cold?' he murmured, feeling the jumper under his hands.

'I'm fine.' She moved his arms from her stomach, crossing them over her breasts. As they fell asleep she heard him mutter something against her hair. It sounded like *I miss you*. In the morning, she wasn't sure he'd even known it was her.

★ ★ ★

Garda Michael Hanlon was not to be found in the small rural station he policed. Getting no answer there, Paula and Guy had instead followed the hotel owner's directions to the Guard's house ('out the road, past the big tree'), though Guy kept fiddling hopefully with his phone until Paula had to ask him to stop. 'People did find things before Google Maps, you know. Look, I think we're here anyway.' They'd reached a well-kept bungalow with a red barn behind it, which was indeed out the road, halfway past the middle of nowhere.

Guy pulled up. 'He's the policeman and he farms too?'

338

'Most people do two jobs. Not much money round here.'

The house had Venetian blinds and pillars topped with large stone eagles. The walls were seventies pebble-dash. Guy was all set to turn away when there was no answer at the doorbell. 'He's not in.'

'Now hold on, he's probably out back.'

'We can't just go round there!'

'Of course we can.' She laughed at Guy's expression. 'We're not in Kansas now, you know.'

Round back smelled of animals, the stone yard slippery with mud and straw. A strong man of about fifty was manhandling a sheep between his legs, while it bleated pathetically. He wore a green plastic suit and goggles.

'Garda Hanlon?' Paula called, over the bleating.

The man dumped the sheep in a pen behind him, where it shook itself, and then he locked the gate, removing his goggles and dusting down his hands. 'Aye?'

'We're from the North — we work at the MPRU? I don't know if you got our message from yesterday, only we were in the area, and — '

'Oh aye.' He rinsed his hands under a nearby tap and stripped off the top half of the suit, revealing an Arran jumper. 'Bloody sheep have all got hoof rot in the snow, so I had to take them down from the fields.' He had a singsong local accent.

Paula introduced herself. 'And this is Inspector Brooking, our team leader. He was at the Met in London.'

'Indeed. Well, I hope you won't find us too backwards, Inspector. There's only me part-time out here, you see.'

'Of course.' The men shook hands, sizing each other up. Paula saw the Guard look her over too. She knew she was a curious addition to a police team, a young woman with wild red hair and muddy jeans. 'What was it you were wanting?' he asked.

'We're investigating a link to one of our cases. A family who lived out here — the Conaghans?' Paula spoke for them both, sensing Guy was uncomfortable.

He wiped his hands slowly on his jumper. 'Which Conaghans would that be now? Sure half the area's called that round here.'

'Mary Conaghan,' said Paula. 'And — Bridget. There was a sister, we think, Bridget Conaghan.' The name was like a whisper on the wind. Why hadn't they heard a word about her, if she'd existed?

The Guard had stopped his wiping, and he sighed. 'I'd a feeling you might mean them. Come in and get a drop of tea.'

★ ★ ★

Paula suspected all the tea-drinking was the worst part of the job in Ballyterrin for Guy, a metropolitan coffee drinker used to having ten different blends at his fingertips. Still, he did a sterling job of smacking his lips over it, sipping from the *Bord Gais* mug it came in. They were in the Guard's good front room, the sofa stiff and unused, cheap tinsel draped over school pictures and wedding shots lining the walls. Paula nodded to them. 'The family?'

'Aye. The wife does be up in Letterkenny during the week. She teaches and there's no work round here now.' He said it matter of factly. The locals were used to the fact that their homeland was dying around them. 'Now what can I do youse for?'

Paula explained how they'd visited the old farm in the hope of learning something about Mary Conaghan, who they suspected was linked to a case they were working on. He nodded. 'The missing babies, is it? A terrible shocking thing. God rest the poor women too.'

'Mary will have changed her name,' Paula said. 'We've traced her up to the seventies, when she was fifteen, and it seems she was sent to stay with cousins in Letterkenny. There was an incident during her stay when a child went missing, her cousin. We don't know exactly where Mary went after that, but she most likely ended up in Dublin, working as a nurse. And we didn't know until yesterday that she may have had a sister. Did you know them?'

He nodded slowly, steam rising from the tea to veil his craggy features. 'If I remember right, Mary was a few years behind me in school. Skinny wee dark girl, glasses?'

'That's right.'

'She lived on that big farm with her mother and grandfather — everyone knew him. Liam Conaghan, he was. A bit cracked. He left the local church because it wasn't hardline enough

341

for his tastes. Rumour had it he started acting like a priest, dressed all in black and that, preaching sermons to the family every day. Big tall rake of a man. We were all heart-scared of him. Mary came in to school every day in the same dress, and we said she smelled of cows — well, you know what weans are like. Nobody really knew her well.'

Paula thought of the black-clad figure in the photos, head lopped off. The grandfather, that was. 'What about the mother?'

He screwed up his eyes. 'Her name was — Sinead, was that it? Sinead Conaghan. But I don't recall this sister at all. Bridget?' He shook his head. 'No, she wasn't at the school with us. And Mary never went past her teens, I don't think. The kids get sent to town for secondary school, maybe that's why she was in Letterkenny?'

'We checked the records of schools there. No sign of her. You said they were all called Conaghan, as in it was the mother's own name? She never married?'

'Aye, that's right.'

'So who was the girls' father?' Paula asked the question baldly.

The Guard considered it. 'I suppose no one ever knew. There was talk, you know, like in all small towns. But Liam kept them all on a tight rein. No one ever saw them much, at least not while he was alive.'

'And Mary — did she come back at all after she was sent away? When the grandfather died, was she here for the funeral?'

342

He stroked his chin. 'I don't recall. I'll see what I can find out for you, Dr Maguire. I was at the funeral — everyone was. Mostly to check he was really dead, I'd say. But Mary wasn't there, I don't reckon. Now that I think on it there was some scandal around it, but I couldn't say what.'

'When was this?' Guy had stayed mostly silent, but was making copious notes. Paula suspected he was struggling with the accent.

'Let me see, I was about eighteen — 1975?'

Mary would have been fifteen then. Paula nodded, it made sense. She left her aunt's in disgrace over the child who'd gone missing on her watch, then she went — where? Ran away to Dublin? 'Do you know what happened to Sinead, their mother?'

'Oh aye. She was dead years before — wee mouse of a woman, hardly noticed her going, but my ma made me go to the funeral and all.'

'So it was just the girls and their grandfather?'

He shrugged at Paula's questions. 'Aye, from when Mary was about twelve. But like I say, I never knew about any sister. She wasn't at any of the funerals.'

'And the woman who's out there now — she says her name is Eilish.'

He screwed up his eyes, trying to remember. 'The wife would know better than me, to tell you the God's honest truth, but if I remember right, she's a distant cousin of the Conaghans.'

'And why is she living there now?'

'I couldn't tell you, Dr Maguire. I'm sorry. The family were so secretive, you know.'

'Right.' She exchanged the quick glance with

Guy that meant they were done. They rose, Guy's tea barely touched.

She shook the policeman's hand. 'Thank you very much, Garda Hanlon. Do let us know if you find out anything more.'

'I will, but sure I don't know if there's anything else to find.' He waited in the door to see them out, mug of tea in his hand, wellies on his feet.

* * *

Back at the hotel, Guy said he'd take the car into a local garage. 'I don't trust it to get us back without checking the brakes. I'll call the unit too. I want to get Avril looking for Bridget Conaghan as soon as possible. I can't believe no one's heard of her before.'

'Except Eilish.'

'Oh yes, Eilish. Hmm. I'd rather not have her as our sole witness. Anyway, I'll just be an hour or so, then I'll settle up with the hotel. OK to wait?'

'Sure. I might wander to the beach.' She felt restless from sitting for so long in the car.

'Good idea. You still look pale. Get some fresh air.' He swept into the hotel.

Paula was glad to be alone. It was stifling, all that time with Guy. She was pulling obsessively at her jumper every minute, in case he saw the curve of her — even though she knew it barely showed yet. She could feel the secret clacking hard against her teeth, so badly did she want to tell him. But then there was Aidan, interceding in every word she said to Guy, between them on the bed, slinking round the corners of her vision. She thought of him in Maeve's flat, in his underwear, hair rumpled with sleep, and gritted her teeth. If only she could have discussed this with him. She imagined his eyes going wide when she told him there was a sister.

The beach was so windy she could hardly see, hair whipped and stinging into her eyes. The sea twisted like a coiled snake, turquoise over navy, and further out the white breakers crashed. Paula remembered being very young, coming to Donegal with her parents, her mother writing the child's name in the sand in a big heart — PAULA. PJ building a sandcastle that withstood the sea's onslaught. She shivered deep in her bones. To be truly alone, for the first time in months, it was freeing. She began to walk along the shoreline, feet pounding on the sand. The wind sealed her off, hard against numb ears and face.

Weeks had gone by, she realised. She was still pregnant, and every gesture made her wonder if she'd ever really planned to take that flight to England. Was it already too late for her? By failing to decide, had she let the decision make itself, in effect?

Paula walked for some time before realising she'd reached the end of the beach, and that she was no longer alone.

She righted herself when she saw the man on the rocks. He was sitting in the mouth of a dark sea cave, the inside already lapping with water as the tide came in, his soft-soled trainers soaked through. He was dressed all wrong for the day, in old-fashioned straight jeans and a denim jacket with badges on it. She was several metres away on the shore. Her heart beat fast, but something kept her there. 'Hello,' she called, the wind snatching her words. 'Are you looking for me?'

Silence. She tried Irish. '*Dia dhuit.*' Hello. God be with you, it meant literally.

He moved and she saw the malformation of his features, the eyes bulging over a ruined face and the patchy ginger hair she recognised from when he'd emerged in the fog.

'You were at the hotel? And before that, at the car?' She wasn't scared. The beach was isolated and the light low on that grey December day, the tide already licking her shoes, but she wasn't scared at all. 'I'm Paula.'

He was shaking, from cold or from fear or maybe both. 'Are you going to tell me your name?' No answer, but she heard a strange low noise above the wind and sea. Almost like a keening. She moved closer. 'You can tell me, you know — '

He moved suddenly, and was almost on top of her. Paula stood her ground, arms crossed over her stomach, shaking. As he came close, sliding to and fro on the rocks, he fumbled for her cold hand — his was pale and clammy — and pushed something into it. Then she just heard footsteps running away across the hard sand, and he was gone. She looked down, pushing away the wet hair that blinded her. Crushed into her hand, sodden with rain, was a bundle of old papers. Letters.

34

Stream Street, Letterkenny. That was where Mary Conaghan's aunt had lived, according to the Gardai files on the abduction case. Not really her aunt but a second cousin of her mother's, a Mrs Ann Gillan. There Mary had cooked and cleaned and helped care for the six children, until of course the youngest, Michael, went missing out of his crib.

Paula and Guy had stopped off in Letterkenny, Donegal's main town — for what it was worth — on the way home, rain lashing the windscreen. Paula had the letters in her bag, wet and tied up with string. She hadn't mentioned them to Guy and her mind was still reeling. If he knew she'd approached a stranger on the beach, he'd have gone ballistic. She was supposed to be curbing her maverick tendencies, after the Halloween incident. She kept the bag on her knee so her fingers could brush the packet, reassuring herself it had really happened. What did it mean?

The house they were looking for was on a narrow backstreet in the town. It was pebble-dashed and squeezed, a blue front door opening right out onto the pavement.

Guy shut the door of the car and turned the key. 'Is there any chance they'll still be living here? I mean, it was years ago.'

'You'd be surprised. People tend to stay put, in

Ireland. Here goes.' Paula rang the bell — they took it in turns to do this, both of them afflicted with a sudden crippling shyness just before they had to make the first approach. That wariness, the fear in people's eyes when they realised who they were. It could put you off.

The woman who answered had a baby on her hip and short dark hair in a bob. 'Yes?'

Paula's turn. 'I'm so sorry to bother you, madam, but we're looking for any information on a Mrs Ann Gillan, who used to live here in the seventies, if you — '

The woman was frowning. 'Mammy? She passed away last year. What are you wanting with her?'

Guy took over. 'I'm sorry to intrude, ma'am. We're from the police in the North. Would we possibly be able to take up a few moments of your time?'

She was holding the door open already, though her face was still confused. 'What did you want with Mammy?'

'It's about your cousin,' said Paula, unbuttoning her coat before they got kicked out. 'Your cousin Mary.'

'Oh,' said the woman, hoisting her child against her knitted jumper. 'Her.'

* * *

Laura Maginn, née Gillan, was the second-youngest member of the family Mary had cared for, or not cared for, depending on your point of view. 'She was a bit scary,' Laura confessed,

348

proffering fruit bars and tea. 'Sorry, I don't keep biscuits in the house.' The place was tastefully decorated in shades of taupe, a small real Christmas tree wafting a fresh pine scent. Paula was a little transfixed by it — the pretty lights, the wrapped presents, the sheer niceness of it all. This was how life was supposed to be just before Christmas. Not racing round the country with your married boss.

'Scary how?' Guy had declined tea on this occasion, perhaps feeling it wasn't likely he'd be lynched by someone modern enough not to purchase industrial-sized packets of Fig Rolls for the sake of any occasional visitor.

Laura said, 'I don't think she liked children all that much. I was six or so when she was here with us. Mammy and her were always fighting, and she was supposed to serve us our dinner and not sit with us, and pray on her knees every night for an hour. I remember Mammy was always talking about sin. It was almost like we had a servant for a while, but she was our cousin, or sort of, anyway. I didn't understand it.'

'What was your mother like, Laura?' asked Paula. The tea was horrible, made with tasteless skimmed milk.

'Harsh,' said Laura, after a moment. 'I mean she looked after us, but it was always about Mass and sin and God and what had we been up to behind her back. My oldest sister, Donna, she had a baby before she was married, and she didn't speak to Mammy for five years because of it. Donna would know more, in fact. I can ring her if you want. She lives in Canada now. To get away from Mammy, mostly, I think.'

'Would you?' said Guy eagerly. 'That would be fantastic.'

Laura glanced at the clock on the wall. Her lips moved. 'I can never work out the time difference. She'll be up. She has kids. What was it you wanted to know?'

'We want to know where Mary went after she was here, and anything you can tell us about what happened to her before that, about her family in Tallaghmar. Your cousins.'

Laura was shaking her head. 'We never met them, I don't think. Mammy and her mother weren't really cousins, just distantly. Mary was very strange, though — I don't think she'd been in a bathroom before she came to us, or seen a toilet inside, you know? Mammy said she was no better than a beast. She slept in the kitchen, on a camp bed.'

'And why did she leave, Laura?' Guy asked the question carefully.

Laura looked surprised. 'I'm not sure I remember.'

'It wasn't to do with your brother?'

'Oh.' She thought about it for a moment. 'Michael. You mean what happened to our Michael.'

'Yes. Mary was arrested when he went missing, did you know that?'

'No.' She shook her head again, as if to clear it. 'I might have done. I was only wee, you know. But I suppose it makes sense. I don't really remember, but everyone talked about it after. He'd gone missing out of his cot, and the front door was lying open, and Mammy always said Mary had lost him. She'd gone to the shops or something and left him there on his own. Then he was brought back, I think. That was the really strange part. They had the police in and everything, and then the next day he was just there in his cot, right as rain. He's in his thirties now, you know. He lives over in London.'

A better ending than that of the baby in the Dublin hospital, Paula thought. 'So your mother sent Mary away after Michael went missing?'

'I suppose. Where would she go, though? I mean, she was only in her teens.'

'We were hoping you could tell us. Do you think she went back home to Tallaghmar?'

Laura hesitated. 'I don't know. Donna knew her best — they were the same age, more or less. Whenever Donna would talk about it I got the impression Mary hated her home. That she'd never go back there. Donna wouldn't ever tell me why, though.'

Paula and Guy exchanged looks. He said, 'Strange. Where else would she have gone then?'

'I don't know. Here, I'll go and ring Donna. Would that help?'

'That would be fantastic. Thank you.'

Laura looked at the clock, then hefted the baby suddenly over to Paula, who took him in utter shock. He looked up at her doubtfully as his mother left the room. Paula found herself locked in by his large brown eyes, his stillness, the faint smell of milk and biscuits. What were you supposed to do? Could they understand you at that age? Then there was the sound of low talking from the other room.

Guy looked at his watch. 'We'll have to shift it to get back to Ballyterrin before five. I'd really like to run through some of these leads we've found.'

Paula looked at the pretty decorations. 'We're running out of time, aren't we? Christmas is in five days.'

'I'm confident we're close to a breakthrough.'

She wasn't, but she said nothing, cradling the child, who sat placidly on her lap. Then there was the noise of a phone being put down, and Laura was back, wiping at her eyes with the sleeve of her jumper. 'Sorry about that. It's — we don't like talking about our childhood. You know how it is.'

Guy made understanding noises.

'Right. Our Donna said — well, look, I'm not sure I can tell you this really. It's my family. But you need my help, don't you?'

'I'm afraid we do. There are two babies missing, as you may have seen on the news, and we think it's possible your cousin is involved somehow.' Guy had probably calculated this angle would work on Laura, and it did.

'That's what I said to Donna. So. She reminded me about something that happened, something I'd sort of made myself not remember. I was very wee, you know. But she said did I not remember what happened after Michael came back.'

'And what was that?' Guy was gentle but probing.

'Uncle Liam came. Well, we were supposed to

352

call him uncle but he wasn't, not really. He was Mary's granddad. He came to get her back. We were all having our lunch and she was out in the kitchen, washing the dishes. Donna said . . . ' Laura's face clouded. 'I did remember, when she said it. He dragged Mary out by her hair. Like across the floor, pulling her hair. And she was shouting and saying the Virgin could see him, she knew about what he did to them, about the . . . the baby.' Her voice faltered. 'That's what she said. Then she was gone and we never saw them again. We just never talked about it. I didn't understand.'

'Goodness,' said Guy. 'Can you tell us anything else?'

'No. Like I said, I was very young. I don't know what she meant by it.'

'Laura?' asked Paula. 'Was there only Mary in the family? She didn't have any brothers and sisters that you knew of?'

Laura looked puzzled. 'I couldn't tell you. I never heard of any others.'

'Well, you've been extremely helpful. Thank you so much.'

She nodded doubtfully. 'Do you think you'll find those poor weans?'

'I very much hope so.' Guy's hearty tone seemed to convince no one. As they left, Laura's son watched them go, his eyes dark as raisins, little monkey hands clutching his mother's jumper, as if he somehow knew the fate of the other children they were discussing.

* * *

353

They were back in the car, Guy shaking his head in disbelief. 'It's all about babies, this case. It's amazing.'

Paula knew exactly what he was thinking without them having to say. 'It makes sense, doesn't it? Mary must have been pregnant. That was why they sent her away in the first place. Not to go to school, but to hide her pregnancy until it could be given up for adoption.'

'She was sent to her cousins, and left in charge of someone else's baby, when she was about to lose her own. Christ, that's cruel.' Guy whistled.

'Someone else's baby who then disappeared.'

They thought about this for a moment. 'It adds up,' Paula said. 'If Mary — Magdalena — lost a child at an early age — who knows what kind of damage that would do. It would explain the compulsion to take children now.'

'I wonder what happened to it, the baby?'

'Given up for adoption as planned, I guess. It would be about thirty-five now.'

She found herself thinking about the man on the beach, his malformed features, his shaking hands. The letters in her bag, which for some reason she wasn't telling Guy about. The man had been so frightened. She needed to read them before she showed anyone.

'What do you think?' Guy asked, as he pulled out onto the main road. 'We're getting close, aren't we? We just need to work out where Mary went after she left home, assuming Mrs Maginn was correct about her being taken back there again. Then if she actually did have a child, see if we can track him or her down.'

Paula adjusted her belt. 'It's the sister I'm wondering about, though. I presume she was left behind at the farm when Mary got sent away.'

They drove on for a while in silence, Guy gradually kicking up the speed of the car as they crossed the border. It was three hours back to Ballyterrin, and Paula had so much to think about she looked out the window at the wet, green land, her mind churning.

An hour outside Ballyterrin he pulled into a garage. 'I'll just get some petrol now, I think, it's cheaper here.'

She stretched herself. 'Any word from the office? Avril might have turned something up by now.'

'The phone's on silent still. I'll check the messages.'

Guy was fiddling with his phone. She said, 'I hope Corry isn't too angry about this. At least we have another lead for her, and . . . What's wrong?' All the colour had left his face as he listened to his voicemail. 'Guy, what's wrong?'

'We have to get back right away.' He pushed the car into gear. 'There's enough fuel to get us there, I think.'

'Why? What is it?'

'It's Fiacra's sister. She's been attacked. The killer attacked her, and tried to cut her baby out.'

35

Five days to Christmas. The ragged edge of cheer in a town with no money. Everywhere Christmas clubs; how will we pay for this plastic tat, where will we find the cash? Keep smiling for the kids. Red sale signs already in the shops and an air of thin despair, flimsy and bright as tinsel. In the middle of the afternoon, the Meadows shopping centre in Ballyterrin piped in Christmas carol muzak. The police cordon round Flaherty's department store had attracted a crowd of gawkers, the elderly in flat caps, the disabled on mobility scooters, mums pushing Wotsity babies in buggies. Paula hated the shopping centre. It reminded her of being a teenager, too young to drive and nowhere to go except trail round the shops dabbing on White Musk in the Body Shop. And now, with what had happened, she knew she'd always hate it even more.

She and Guy had approached the shop at a slow run, leaving his BMW in the crammed car park outside. 'Where's Fiacra?' she called, breathless. 'Is he here?'

Guy halted at the cordon which blocked off the door. One of the biggest in the Meadows, the shop was strangely empty, racks of cheap clothes hanging limp, metallic Christmas decorations swaying from the roof. 'They sent him to the hospital with her. He dropped her off to go shopping, apparently. Christmas presents. Then it happened.'

'And is she — '

'She's alive.' Guy was fumbling for his warrant card as they approached the shop. 'The baby wasn't taken — someone interrupted the attack before it went too far. But it doesn't look good. She — well, you'll see.'

Paula couldn't take it in. Smiling Aisling, with her trusting nature and blond curls. She'd be nearly eight months pregnant. Even if the baby had to be born now, it could be OK. Please. Please be OK. 'Let me go in,' she said.

He hesitated. 'It's really a mess, they said.'

'I want to see.'

He gestured to the uniformed officer at the door, some young lad with spots, and she ducked into the shop. Near the cash desk Corry was talking to an irate middle-aged man in a cheap suit, his face red. He was saying, 'This is our busiest week — I need to reopen within the hour! It's late-night shopping!'

'Sir, a woman's nearly been killed in your shop. We have to investigate.'

'I need to get cleaners in. I can't have the customers looking at that, they'd be sick to their stomachs.' He reached for the phone near the till and Corry practically batted his hand away.

'Mr O'Leary. You're not going near that area until we've finished, understand?'

'Will it be on the news? I bet it'll be on the news.' He wrung his hands.

'That's really not my concern right now. Let us do our work and maybe you can open up

357

tomorrow. Get me that CCTV footage like you promised, that'll speed things up.'

He went off fretting, a fat-man waddle in his stride. Round the tills a group of middle-aged women in cashiers' uniforms had gathered, anxious and fluttering. Some had been crying. Corry saw Paula and nodded briefly to her before addressing the women. 'Now, who was it witnessed the incident?'

'Michelle,' muttered one woman, scared to make eye contact. Distrust of the police ran deep in Ballyterrin.

'And Michelle is . . . ?'

They parted, revealing a teenage girl slumped on a plastic chair, sobbing with her head in her lap. She couldn't have been more than fourteen. They hadn't even given her a proper uniform. She wore black bobbly tights, a white shirt, cheap and thin. Corry spoke gently — the girl wasn't much older than her own daughter. 'Michelle. How are you, pet?'

The girl just shook her head, crying harder.

'I know it was scary, but I want you to remember you saved that woman's life. If you hadn't gone in when you did, she'd be dead by now, and her baby gone.'

There was a murmuring among the women. 'Was it her then — the one who's after taking all the weans?'

'We can't be sure,' said Corry shortly. 'We need to find out what Michelle saw. Can you give us some space, ladies?'

Reluctantly, the women retreated, shaking heads and clucking with curiosity.

'Now, Michelle.' The DCI detached a tissue from a packet in her bag — purple with little hearts on. Paula wondered if they belonged to Rosie Corry. 'Wipe your eyes. Your mum will be here soon to get you, and an officer's going to stay with you all night. You'll be home in twenty minutes. But first you need to tell me and Dr Maguire here what you saw. Can you do that?'

'I — I'll try.'

'Good girl. You're a temp, are you?'

Michelle took a big blubbering breath. 'Y-yeah. For Christmas.'

'Are you at school?' Paula asked. She didn't look old enough to be legally working, which was far from uncommon in Ballyterrin.

'It's exams now, but like, I don't have any today.'

'And was it busy?' Corry prompted.

'No, it was quiet — we'd not had many in. Mr O'Leary — that's the manager — he said I was to tidy up the fitting rooms. We're meant to look out for loose security tags and that, in case people shoplift. We did a course.' She dabbed her red face, breathing hard. 'Anyway, there's no one on fitting rooms during the day. People can just go in themselves. The — the pregnant lady — '

'Miss Quinn is her name,' Corry supplied.

'I sort of looked at her 'cos on the course they tell us people sometimes hide stuff up their jumpers, like they're not really pregnant at all. I was in Shoes that day. Then I saw someone else go in the changing rooms after her — Miss Quinn.'

359

'A woman?'

'I thought it was. Men's is on the other side. She'd no clothes in her hands, though, so I sort of go to see do they need any help, like, keep an eye out, and when I get there — ' Her voice hitched. 'I — the first lady, the pregnant one, she was on the ground, unconscious like, and her, her — ' Michelle indicated her stomach. 'She was all cut there and the blood — there was blood everywhere, Miss.' She sobbed. 'It wasn't like in the films. It was *awful*.'

'It sounds it,' murmured Paula. 'Did you see the other woman, Michelle?'

'I don't know.' She balled the tissue in her fist. 'She'd her back to me, and sort of like a scarf round her face. She ran out the back door — that goes into the stockroom, no one's meant to have the key except Mr O'Leary. But it was open. I never saw it open before.'

Paula looked at Corry, who nodded. 'The stockroom leads out to the street. It's usually locked but they were expecting a delivery, apparently, so someone left it open. She got out that way, we were too late. She must have had a car nearby. We'll check the CCTV.'

Michelle was staring dolefully at the floor. 'It was just so fast. She had a long coat on and flat shoes, and this like big black bag. Like for PE. But the blood was everywhere, so I went to help the poor lady; she was out cold and there was like a needle in her arm, sticking out of her, and she'd been trying on a red maternity dress — it's nice that, a good seller — and her hair was all round her and her eyes were rolling. So I pressed

360

the dress on her tummy and I shouted out. I mean, I had to help her, didn't I? I couldn't go after the other woman?'

'You did the right thing, pet,' Corry soothed. 'You've saved Miss Quinn's life.'

'Will her baby be OK?' Michelle was anxious. 'Only there was all the blood.'

Corry hesitated for less than a second but Paula caught it, and the life inside her seemed to burn in protest. 'They'll do what they can,' said Corry neutrally. 'Now is there anything else you can tell us about the other woman?'

Michelle shook her head. 'I don't remember her face. She was tall — like a man, almost — and that big long coat, and the bag, and scarf round her head. That's all.'

'Well done, Michelle. You've been a big help. Your mum's here, I think, if you want to go out to the door.'

Michelle hauled herself to her feet with a weariness beyond her years, and Paula saw that her white shirt was marked with a bloody handprint. Corry saw it too as the girl moved off. 'Poor wean. She'll not be the same after this. They need to keep telling her she saved Aisling Quinn's life.'

'Did she?'

Corry inclined her head. 'Too soon to say. The killer had already cut into the womb, they said — all that blood, it was the uterine artery being severed. Place is like a damn slaughterhouse. I'll show you.'

Paula didn't want to be shown, but also knew she couldn't not see it. They started to walk through the eerily empty shop, mannequins watching them through painted eyes. Over the tannoy, 'Frosty the Snowman' on pan pipes. 'You reckon it's her then? The same woman?'

'It must be. Christ, I hope it is. There can't be two.'

'Will there be any prints?' Paula thought of the blood on Michelle's shirt. Who'd left that — Aisling, clinging to life? The killer?

'Maybe. There's enough blood.' Corry stopped at the entrance to the changing rooms. Dust in the corners and racks of cheap, glitzy clothes. One grey curtain was pulled down, fallen like a shroud, and a security door at the far end of the cubicles stood open, leading into a darkened space that seemed to be the stockroom.

The changing rooms, the walls and ceiling, and the grey carpet and curtains were patterned all over in blood. Long sprays of it, bright red, still wet. A larger amount had soaked into the carpet in a spreading stain — where Aisling had fallen, Paula guessed. On the door, bloody handprints like those on Michelle's shirt. Paula tried to stay on her feet at the sight of it, flashing red before her eyes, and the smell of the place, rusty and rotting in the heat that blew out from a dusty overhead grille.

'Don't go in. We're still waiting for Forensics.' Corry held her back at the entrance.

She had no intention of going in. They stood in the door by the racks of security tags, numbered 1 to 6. She'd never seen a crime scene like this, not yet cleared up by professionals, only the victim moved out to safety. The slashes of rage still hanging in the air as if you could breathe it in. Evil. You could feel evil in this room, gone out on a blast of cold air. On the ground rolled a syringe, as Michelle had said.

'She drugs them. That must be how she stops them fighting back.'

'We thought as much from Dr Bates and Heather. Why here, do you think?' Corry had her hands in the pockets of her grey wool coat, trying not to touch anything.

Paula looked round them, the large shop, cameras in the corner of the fitting rooms, a long way out through the pan-piped be-tinselled shopping centre. 'I've no idea. It's the worst possible place, you would think. If all she wants is a baby, there'd be much easier ways to get one.'

'We found this.' Corry held up a small plastic bag with something inside. 'It's Fiacra Quinn's address, written on a Post-it. It was on the floor and the bloody manager picked it up before I got here. I've half a mind to arrest him for obstruction, windbag that he is.'

Paula looked at it. Blue biro. Handwriting. The person they were seeking, they'd written this, touched it. 'Aisling's been staying with Fiacra. She's been going to Ballyterrin Hospital for her antenatal care. So if someone knew that . . .'

Corry's face was grim. 'Exactly. They knew just where to find her. I'd guess she was waiting at the door of the flat when Aisling came out this morning, but then Fiacra was with her so she couldn't strike, and she had to follow her here. I think this isn't random at all, Paula. Heather Campbell, Caroline Williams, Aisling Quinn — she's targeting them somehow. She's choosing them.'

36

That night, before the shortest day of the year, as Aisling Quinn fought for her life in Ballyterrin General Hospital, needing three pints of blood on transfusion and crashing twice, and her widowed mother and her sisters and her brother Fiacra wept at her bedside; as the parents of Darcy Williams and the father of Lucy Campbell ended yet another day without their children being found; as the unit team faced up to their own utter failure to protect the town; the snow that had gripped Ballyterrin for weeks began to melt. Drains filled up, worn pipes swelled, and by dawn half the town was without water, a situation that would last weeks, leaving the population unwashed and thirsty, queuing in the cold like refugees, but strangely buoyant with the kind of crisis spirit which made the people of Ireland most happy.

Paula had eventually gone to bed at one a.m., stiff and cold. Guy had to send her home in the end, from where she'd been stooped over a desk in the incident room. Forensics and CSIs had taken apart the bloody scene in the shop, trudging all night between the icy car park and the burnt-out lights of the store, the mannequins unblinking in the face of such carnage. Early results had yielded no prints again, though they were still hopeful some hair might be recovered from the tangle of threads and dust that littered the changing-room floor.

Getting into bed swathed in layers, Paula had tried to read the letters from the beach, but they'd dried to a brittle fragility, and the rain had smudged the ink. She couldn't see it in the dim light and she couldn't stay awake. All she could make out was the opener to each one: *My dear sister*. No names on any of them. There were two different types of handwriting, she thought, though both very similar. Letters between Mary and her invisible sister? A quick scan showed no addresses or other details. Tomorrow, she would tell Guy and they'd go through them in depth. He'd be annoyed she hadn't told him right away, but she'd have to face it.

She wasn't in bed long. PJ woke her at six, stomping in black welly boots. 'Pipes are burst,' he said succinctly. Water dripped off his boots onto the worn lilac carpet of her room, a relic of a ten-year-old's taste.

'What?' She sat up, blinking. The room was Arctic. 'Is the heating broken?'

'Aye, it's all off. No water either.'

'I can't have a *shower?*' Jesus, that was all she needed. After the late night, she felt coated in the sweat and coffee fug of the station.

PJ seemed oddly elated by these happenings. 'No, you can't, love. They say it might be off all week! I'm filling up the bath so we can boil some.'

'I can't have a shower for a whole *week!*' Paula started to panic.

'Never worry, pet, I'll rig something up. We can still have our tea, anyway.'

She pushed back her greasy red hair. 'For God's sake. Why'd you wake me up, then, if I can't get showered? I may as well stay in bed.'

'Oh, did I not say? There's a phone call for you.'

* * *

'Paula!' Guy was on the other end.

'What is it?' She was in the hall by the phone, shivering in her pyjamas.

'Is your mobile off or something? I've been calling you.'

'Um . . . I switched it off.' She didn't want to think too closely about why she hadn't wanted to sleep with her phone turned on next to her. Sending out radiation, possibly. 'What's wrong, anyway?'

'The Williams house. They've found something on the path behind the garden. The snow's melted, and a dog walker turned it up.'

Oh God. She could guess. It was one of the times she didn't want to know; she'd like to retreat back, rewind, not hear what he was about to say. 'Paula?'

'I'm here. What was it?' *Don't be what I'm thinking, please.*

'A baby's body. You see? This could change everything. What if it wasn't linked at all?'

She couldn't catch his excitement. Not about a baby in the snow. She felt weak.

'Be honest,' Guy was saying. 'Tell me what you thought when we first saw Caroline Williams.'

'Post-natal depression. Post-natal psychosis,

even. The thing about answering the phone didn't stand up at all. But then when we found the link with the forum, I thought I must be wrong.'

'I don't think you were.' Guy was wired. 'Croft had an alibi for the abduction, but maybe it wasn't part of this anyway. If we can her get back in again I can break her, I know I can. That issue with the fingerprints, I'm sure she tricked us somehow. There must be an explanation.'

Paula thought nothing could break Croft. You couldn't break what was already long destroyed. 'You know what you're saying, Guy — sir? There's a baby dead in the snow.' The little dress. The ducks floating in her bath. 'She's dead, and you're saying maybe her own mother killed her? Think what that means.'

Guy paused. 'I don't know who killed her. I'm just desperate to find a way through this. The Williams case, it distorted everything. If we can find who did this — Heather and Dr Bates, and Aisling — if we can find Lucy safe, if she's still alive — '

'I know, but I can't be pleased Darcy is dead.' He said nothing. She closed her eyes. 'I'm just — this case, you know?'

'I know. It's killing us all. That's why we need a solve. Meet me there, anyway. At least we can try to find out what happened in the Williams house that day.'

* * *

The place was exactly as it had been the first day they'd come — police vans lining the streets,

368

yellow tape fluttering, officers outside the door. The parents were inside with Corry. There was a jumpy feeling in the air. Guy parked on the pavement. Paula had dressed in three jumpers and old, baggy jeans, and she'd plaited her dirty hair round her head as best she could, adding a grey knitted hat on top. She looked ridiculous, she knew, but didn't care. She said, 'You're really going to take her to the station?'

'Why, you think I should interview her here?'

'No, but — I mean, they've found her baby's body, and you're going to arrest her? Where is she? Where is Darcy?'

'At the mortuary. Gerard's going to take the father to identify her, while we bring the mother in for questioning.'

'So it might not be Darcy?'

'Paula. We're sure that it is. The clothes, you know.'

'How could they have missed her, if she was here all the time?'

'We were so stretched. You know that. They searched the lane, but the snow was so thick the search dogs would have missed it, and it was buried slightly. Only the thaw has exposed it.' He looked at her. 'I know you don't want to believe this. But look at the evidence. Remember what you're always telling me — the most likely people to hurt a child are its own parents.'

'Right.' She shut her eyes briefly. 'I suppose we have to eliminate this case, if we can.'

'We do.' He was gentle.

'I can't watch you arrest her.'

'All right.' He undid his belt, passed her the

keys from the ignition. 'Why don't you go back to the unit? Get the room ready. I want you to help me interview her.'

This fucking job. Sometimes Paula felt like it was scraping her out, so she'd one day have nothing left at all.

★　★　★

Caroline Williams sat very straight in her chair in the interview room at the MPRU. Her hands with their chewed nails were placed on the chipped table. She was dressed in the same pink velour tracksuit as the first day. 'Did she come willingly?' asked Paula, watching her from outside.

Guy said, 'She did. Though the husband tried to punch Gerard.'

'Did he?' Shane Williams was about a foot narrower than Gerard, as Paula recalled.

'Yeah. Rather unwise of him, poor man. We have him in with Bob, but I seriously doubt he knows anything.'

'Has she a lawyer?'

'She said no to one.'

That was often the way when people were inexperienced with police stations. They thought getting a lawyer made them look guilty. 'So that's your theory — she did it alone?'

'It happens, doesn't it?'

'Yes, but — ' But Paula couldn't get the idea to fit into her brain. A mother killing her child. Was that what she'd been like, when she looked up those flights to London?

No, for Christ's sake, it wasn't the same. She had to believe that. 'OK.' She shook herself. 'If Caroline is like most infanticidal mothers, she may actually be keen to confess. It was either an accident she's tried to cover up, or a genuine psychotic moment where she felt Darcy had to die for some reason. Though in those cases the mother almost always kills herself too. Plus any family pets, for some reason. Did they have a dog, a cat?'

'I don't think so. What about that thing, that proxy syndrome?'

'Munchausen's by proxy? We tend to call it Fabricated Illness in the UK. It's rarer than you'd think from watching films. In that case she'd have courted publicity, got herself on TV, no doubt, all that. They do it for attention.'

'She did that press conference,' Guy reminded her.

'That's true. OK, it's possible, but there's another option too.'

'Yes?'

'She didn't do it at all. Someone really did come and take Darcy. Someone else, I mean.'

Guy scoffed. 'A dingo ate my baby? In Ballyterrin?'

'Er, wasn't the dingo case recently proved to be true?'

He paused. 'You're right.'

'And they pilloried those parents. So let's be careful, OK? Let's not jump to conclusions. Jumping to conclusions is what's sent us wrong from the beginning.'

'You're right.' He turned to look her full in the

face. 'We're good, you know. Me and you.'

A flush moved up from her neck to swamp her face. We. The loveliest word in the English language. 'Sorry?'

'On cases. You keep me tempered. I couldn't do it without you, you know. This one — it would have broken me otherwise.' She stared at her feet. 'Paula. I'm aware that we still never did talk properly, after Katie went missing, and all of that.' She presumed 'all of that' meant that they'd slept together and then he'd cut her off, terrified of prejudicing the case, and then his daughter had gone and he'd fallen off a cliff of grief, and she'd slept with Aidan and ruined everything.

She said, 'Tess came back.'

'Yes. I — what could I do? Katie needed us. And Tess, she — she isn't coping very well at the moment. I can't say more. But it's not been easy.'

'She's your wife.' They were speaking quietly, both of them looking in the window where Caroline Williams sat, a pale, silent wreck of a woman.

'I know she is.'

'So why don't you go back? Why don't you go to London, all of you? I'm sure Tess would be happier, and Katie hates it here, and you — the rain, the ignorance. I know you'd be better off. There's nothing for you here.'

Paula knew he was looking at her. 'You know why I'm still here. At least, I hope you do. I'd have been long gone, if it weren't for you.'

She regarded the splintered frame of the

window until the prickling in her nose subsided. Timing. Bloody timing. It was timing that brought you to your knees, crushed your pathetic human plans under the wheels of minutes and weeks and years. A day either side, and she'd maybe not be in this situation. She could go away herself and Guy could stay. She could get off this island, where the rolling land would never yield you up again. And for Caroline Williams, maybe a second here, a second there, and her baby would still be alive and she wouldn't be sitting in a small room with peeling grey walls, initials scratched into the chipboard table, surveying the end of her life.

'You better go in,' said Paula. 'Don't keep her waiting. Whatever she did — she'll be in hell. Either way, don't make her wait.'

'Come in with me.'

'But Corry — '

'I don't know about you, but I've had about enough of Corry for one lifetime. I need you. Come on.'

★ ★ ★

Caroline started as they came in the door. She was rigid, ready to strike. Who knew what she was expecting.

Paula went towards her with an outstretched hand. 'Caroline. I know nothing can make it better, but please let me tell you I'm so sorry about Darcy.'

Hesitation. Caroline bit her lip. Her hand in

Paula's was limp and cold. Her nose was red, blond hair lank.

Guy followed Paula's lead. 'It's a terrible thing, to lose a child. In fact I lost my own son earlier this year. It's devastating.' He meant it, too. And that was why Paula couldn't tell him to leave, go back to London, take his wife away and forget her. Because he thought this woman had killed her baby, and lied to them, and derailed their investigation, but he could still bring himself to shake her hand with compassion.

Caroline looked at them with pale faltering eyes.

'You're probably wondering why you're here,' said Guy, sitting down.

Nothing. She knew why she was here.

'I'm afraid now we've found Darcy, we have to open a murder inquiry.'

The hands convulsed. Caroline put them under the table, very carefully.

'Now, it can't be linked to the other cases, I'm sure we can agree.' Guy was leafing through his notes. Paula remained standing, so Caroline had to swivel to see both of them. 'Do you agree with that, Caroline?'

'I — I don't know.'

Guy said, 'Well, those babies are alive. Alek was given back, Lucy we hope was taken alive, and the pattern showed our suspect was moving onto younger babies, unborn ones. We never understood why they'd take one who was three months old. I don't think it fits at all. So what happened to Darcy?'

'I — someone took her.'

'Who?'

'Someone else. I don't know.' Her voice was small and cold.

'Caroline. Do you know the odds of another random child abduction in Ballyterrin? It's minuscule.'

She dropped her eyes.

'You said the phone rang,' said Paula, more gently, going over and sitting down. 'You had Darcy outside. I don't think she had her coat on, like you said. We found the coat buried in the snow beside her. Why would you have her in the snow?'

'Well — it wasn't that cold. It's so stuffy in the house. She needed air.'

'OK. So you went outside. I think you're a tidy woman, Caroline. I think you had the phone back on its hook in the kitchen, and so when you went in to answer it, you could easily have seen Darcy out the window. I think you weren't outside at all. No one hangs out washing in the snow, do they? It'd freeze. Then takes it back in, after their child has gone missing?'

Nothing. Head down.

'The bath.'

Caroline's head snapped up.

Paula went on, her voice quiet but merciless. 'There was water in it, when I looked in the bathroom. It seemed odd, when your house is so clean. That's how it normally happens, you know. You leave the baby for a minute, answer the phone, and then you get talking — the mortgage people, you said. Money troubles? You needed to take that call?'

Nothing.

'Was she in the bath, Caroline?'

'She'd been sick on herself.' Caroline's voice was small. 'She was always sick. She'd boke up her lunch every day on her clean clothes.'

'So you put her in the bath.'

'Of course. She was disgusting.'

'And you were only away a minute — but when you went back, she'd slipped, is that right? Under the water?'

Caroline looked at Paula. Her eyes were leached of colour. 'You don't have a baby, do you?'

The worst possible question. 'I — no.'

'Then you don't know. When Darcy was born, I didn't sleep for a second. Not a second for months. If you breathed on her, she'd cry. The car, the stairs, the knives — everything could hurt her. I was so exhausted. And she was sick all the time, you know? We practically lived in Casualty. And every day he comes home from work, it's where's this bruise is from, why didn't you watch her, and he's in his office all day, where people don't puke on you or scream in your ear for hours. And he can't even do the one thing he's meant to, and pay the bloody bills.' All this was delivered in a flat monotone. Vicious in its quietness. 'I tell you, miss. When you have a baby, it's like someone turned you inside out, so all your skin's on the inside. You're raw. Totally raw. Like every single thing can hurt you, and you'll never be safe again.'

Paula reached over the table and took the woman's limp hand. She gripped it tight. 'It's

376

nearly over, Caroline. You just have to tell us. She drowned in the bath, was that it?'

The first nod.

'I need you to say it, Caroline.'

'Yes. She went under. It was — I don't know, less than a minute maybe. I took her out, and she was all wet, and I pressed on her . . . I blew. But it was too late.'

'And you panicked — you put different clothes on her, and you hid her in the snow?'

'I'd seen the news. There was someone going round taking babies. I don't know, I just thought if I could hide her for a while, say someone took her — he wouldn't blame me. I knew he would. I was useless as a mum. Useless.'

Paula looked at Guy. He cleared his throat. 'Interview terminated. Mrs Williams, I think you might like to get yourself a lawyer now.'

37

Paula didn't sleep that night. Thinking of Caroline Williams, her white hands like little fluttering birds, the accepting nod as they'd taken her down to the cells and gone to tell the husband his wife had let their baby drown. Thinking of Aisling in hospital, clinging desperately to life, her child faltering inside her. Of Heather Campbell's husband, both wife and child gone in a blizzard of blood. If it wasn't Magdalena Croft doing all this, and it wasn't Melissa Dunne, someone else was still out there, waiting for their next child. If they'd gone after Aisling's baby, did that mean Lucy was dead? As they'd failed to get Aisling's child, they'd be looking for another. That meant no pregnant woman was safe.

Including her. She was a pregnant woman. She had to face up to that. Sleepless, Paula got up and dressed warmly, ready for work. The cold seemed to have penetrated to her very bones, and she put on layer after layer. She'd misplaced her green scarf, absent-minded, so she rooted through the hall cupboard to find another, red and old and a little musty with perfume, winding it round her neck. 'I'm off, Dad.'

PJ was still in bed for once, the cold making his bad leg stiff and sore. 'It's very early for you, pet.'

It was seven o'clock. Barely light. 'I can't

sleep. I'm going to call at the hospital first.' She went a little way into the room, the one her parents had slept in. Her mother's perfume bottle still on the dressing table, with a thick coating of dust. She wondered why her father had never moved it.

'Are you OK, love?'

Paula sighed. She sat down on the edge of the bed for a moment, shoving her hands in her coat pocket, where they brushed something. The packet of letters, still unread. 'I'd be better if we could get this case solved.'

'Aye. And Christmas round the corner too.'

'Dad — if I told you I did something a bit stupid, would you help me?'

'What is it this time?'

'Um — it's these.' She drew out the packet of letters, explained how the man had approached her on the beach and she'd taken them, but still not told Guy.

PJ, to his credit, didn't tell her she was an eejit, though she was. 'And you think he wanted you to have them, this fella?'

'Yes. I think he followed me there, whoever he was, so he could give me these.'

'You've not read them?'

'I was going to, but then with Aisling, and now the Williams baby being found, there just wasn't time. They're hard to read.' She showed him the spindly writing, faded and washed with rain. 'I think it's to do with our case though. Would you look at them for me?'

'Aye, OK. What can I do, though?'

'Just tell me if they're important, or they'd

379

help us find this Bridget. If I'm going to get in trouble, it may as well be for something useful.' She stood up, weary.

PJ coughed, stretching his leg. 'Take care, pet. Drive safe on that ice. It'll freeze again tonight, I reckon.'

'You be careful too. See you later.'

Do you have a baby, Caroline Williams had asked. And Paula had said — no. But she did. She did have a baby. And it was time to start doing something about that.

* * *

Paula's first call was the hospital, sitting squat under its blanket of melting snow, grit scattered over the entrances and steps. She stopped at the gift shop, dithering over the tired selection of blooms, before picking a bunch of yellow roses, budding and beaded with dew. Yellow in the snow. Some kind of hope, maybe. After paying she made her way upstairs to Intensive Care, showing her ID to the officer on duty outside Aisling Quinn's room. Through the glass she could see the girl connected to tubes, her eyes shut, arms hanging limp on the hospital cover. Beside her were an older woman and three other blonde girls, one pacing, one with her arm round Mammy, who was crying, and one hanging over Aisling, gripping her lifeless hand.

'Paula!' She turned to see Fiacra, shuffling with two paper cups in his hand. He looked grey and exhausted, his fair curls hanging limp with grease. He was wearing a dirty grey hoodie and jeans.

'Fiacra. I'm so sorry. I didn't want to intrude, I just thought I should . . . ' She held out the flowers, awkwardly, and he took them under his arm. 'I wanted to call by.'

'Thanks. That was good of you.'

'Is she . . . have they said anything?'

He shook his head. 'They think she'll wake up soon. We don't want to leave, in case she does and no one's here. We're just trying to work out who'll tell her she's lost the wean.'

Shit. 'I didn't know. I'm so sorry.'

Fiacra scrunched up his face. 'He couldn't hold on, not after what she did to him.' He took a sip of his drink, seeming not to even taste it. His hand shook. 'They said all the blood from the artery — the oxygen, like, it couldn't get through to his brain for too long. Aisling didn't even know it was a boy.'

'I'm sorry.'

'I keep thinking — what if it was that Dunne woman? And I had her there in the interview room, and I fucked it up, and she got our Aisling?'

'No, no, Fiacra, it wasn't her. You did your best. It wasn't her. I never thought it was, you know that.'

He just nodded, staring through the window at his sister. 'At least we'll get her back. Our Aisling. But I don't think she'll be the same, Paula, not when I tell her. She wanted the wean so much. I mean she was scared at first, who wouldn't be, but she didn't deserve this!'

Paula realised he was crying, his shoulders heaving. She leaned forward to take the drinks and flowers, sitting them down on a chair bolted to the wall below the window. 'Of course she didn't. No one deserves this.'

'She wouldn't have had the abortion! She just wasn't sure, that was all!'

'I know. I know.' She wanted to put her arms about him, but just stood awkwardly as he heaved and gasped. 'Listen, she did what anyone would have done. I promise you.'

'Who is it, Pau — Dr Maguire? Who's doing this? Can we get her?'

'We'll get her,' Paula said, hearing the doubt in her own voice. 'We're doing everything we can, Fiacra.'

'I just don't want any other family going through this.'

'No. We'll find her.' But even as she said it she felt no hope. None at all.

She left Fiacra and made her way to the lifts. Sitting on a bank of chairs in the atrium was a familiar figure, unshaven, in a fraying grey T-shirt. She stopped in her tracks. He was staring at his feet. Maybe he hadn't seen her. For a moment she thought about bolting.

Without looking up, Aidan said quietly, 'Maguire.'

She walked towards him. 'What are you doing here? Waiting for Aisling to wake up, is it? Didn't think ambulance-chasing was your style.'

He ignored the cheap jibe. 'I've been looking for you all weekend. Off with Brooking, were you?'

382

'Yes.' And he'd been practically living with Maeve in Dublin, by the looks of it. She had no reason to feel guilty.

'How's his wife feel about that?'

She counted to ten, gave up at five. 'You shouldn't be here. Give them some privacy, for God's sake.'

'Maguire. I'm not here for them. Jesus. I was looking for you. PJ said you were here. I've got some information on your case.'

'Oh really. Shame you couldn't have helped out before two women got murdered. While you were playing about in Dublin.'

'You think I wasn't working on this?'

'How would I know what you're up to? Maeve might, but I certainly don't.'

He ignored this too. 'Your suspect. Mary Conaghan — you think it's Croft, right?'

Maeve had been talking. Paula felt oddly betrayed. 'We're fairly sure it is.'

'There's inconsistencies, right? The prints didn't match? Listen, I've found something out that might explain it. Mary Conaghan had a sister.'

'Aidan, we know all this. Why do you think we were in Donegal? Bridget, her name was.'

He was taken aback for a moment. 'Well, OK. Did you know a Mary Conaghan also got married in 1990? At a church outside Ballyterrin? I found it in the parish records.'

They hadn't known this. 'You think that was Croft?'

'Croft was in Dublin at the time, plus she was already married. I think it was the sister, but she was using Mary's name for some reason. Maybe because she never had a birth certificate, she wasn't registered — you found no trace of her, right? She married a man called Brian Rourke. You ever heard your da mention that name?'

'What's Dad got to do with it?' Paula was bewildered.

'Ask him. Brian Rourke was executed by the IRA in the nineties. Your da was lead officer. Bob Hamilton told me as much.'

'Again, what does any of this have to do with our case?'

'The date, Maguire. It was October 1993. The twenty-eighth of October.'

She said nothing.

'It's when your mother went. The same day.'

'You think I don't know — '

'You don't think that's a bit coincidental? Just ask your da, Paula. I think he knows something. He'll maybe be able to tell you who the sister is. I think we can work it out between us, or maybe he'd recognise a photo, or — '

'For fuck's sake, Aidan. What are you even doing? My mother is none of your business and neither is my case. Just leave, will you? No one needs you here. You've done nothing but obstruct this case, then fuck off when we needed you. Just like you always do.' For once it was easy to walk away from him. Because now, every time they talked, it was hard to tell who she was more ashamed of — him, or herself.

★ ★ ★

The office was quiet when Paula made it in, Fiacra's desk glaring in its emptiness. The sad Christmas decorations drooped, as outside melting snow dripped a constant tattoo down the window. Guy was in his office as she unwound her scarf and took off her many layers. 'I heard Aisling Quinn lost her baby,' she said, low-voiced.

Guy rubbed his face. 'Yes. Poor kid. There was no chance, really. Our killer nicked the uterine artery. It's really a wonder Aisling didn't bleed to death.'

'God, what a thing to wake up to. Where are we with everything?' She leaned in the doorway of his office, adjusting her posture so her stomach was tucked in as much as possible.

'Where are we? Nowhere, pretty much. We're back on the hospital staff, going through alibis, trying to break one, fingerprinting them all, checking all the timesheets for that day. It's going to take forever. And Avril's having no luck finding any Bridget Conaghan. It's possible her birth was never even registered.'

Just like bloody Aidan had said. 'And Mary Conaghan's child? If she had one, that is.'

'Nothing. No trace.'

'Was there anything useful from the last scene? Any prints? Anything?' Even as she asked she knew there wouldn't be.

'No. Even the CCTV was broken in the stockroom. Same as before — she just vanished.' He ran his hands through his hair, distracted.

Paula sighed. 'Well — the computer files?

Aisling went to visit Dr Bates at the clinic, didn't she?'

'Yes. Aisling's name was on the files, and Heather of course, but not Kasia Pachek. So it may be there's no link at all to the clinic. What else? Did you ever get anything more from your Dublin contact?'

'Maeve? Um . . . I'm not sure. She said she'd look into Croft further for me.' She'd forgotten about that, in the isolation of Donegal and then the horror of what happened to Aisling. 'Maybe she emailed. Let me check.'

Going to her desk, Paula fired up her old machine and waited for her messages to download. 'There's one from Maeve,' she called. Guy came over to her desk. Avril, tapping away at her computer in the corner, looked up briefly. She still seemed to be avoiding Paula. No sign of Gerard or Bob, who were most likely up at the PSNI station.

'Here we go,' Paula said, scrolling through Maeve's email. 'So she's tracked a Mary Conaghan to 1980, when she trained as a student nurse in Dublin. She's fairly sure that was our Mary, at least. She found their graduation shot. Then in 1982 a Mary Conaghan also got the job at St John of God's, where the Roberts baby went missing and was found dead.'

'And that wasn't our Mary.' Guy frowned at the screen. She was very aware of how close he was, the faint lemon smell of his aftershave.

'It can't have been, if the prints were different.'

'So who was it?'

386

'Oh, look. Maeve says she dug up a picture. She went back to the hospital and basically bribed someone to get it out of the archives. Fair play. Here, she's scanned it in.'

Paula clicked on the link, and slowly the picture downloaded. 'Come on,' muttered Guy, as they waited. She wondered if this would be a good moment to ask for a better computer.

'There!' A picture had formed, grainy, much enlarged. A girl with bobbed dark hair and a pleasant smile. But not the Mary Conaghan they knew. Someone else. Someone they'd seen recently.

'It's the sister,' said Guy, slowly. 'It's the sister, isn't it? Bridget.'

It was. Several years older, the young nurse in the picture was still clearly recognisable as the girl in Eilish's album. 'They must have swapped identities,' Paula said, dazed. 'Why the hell would they do that?'

'Christ, who knows? Bridget needed a job, or they needed to hide . . . could be anything.'

Paula was trying to piece it together. 'So she took her sister to Dublin with her when she went — after their grandfather died. Then, what — at some point she lets Bridget pretend to be her? God, the sister must not even be qualified as a nurse.' And Aidan had been right. She almost told Guy, but couldn't bring herself to say Aidan's name.

'That doesn't matter. We just have to find her now.' Guy was already moving away. 'Avril, this is urgent, please — we need to double our efforts to find any references to a Bridget Conaghan, or

387

a Mary Conaghan. Even if they don't fit our timelines, we need to work out where our sisters went after 1982.'

★ ★ ★

For the rest of the day, Paula worked in silence, barely exchanging two words with Avril. She was checking and rechecking everything, all the possible leads, the avenues that seemed to loop back on themselves. Bridget. Mary. Mary and Bridget. Which was which and who was who? She stared at the picture of 'Mary', who was really Bridget. She'd have been about twenty when it was taken. Could Paula have seen her in the present day, under their noses somewhere? The killer, whoever she was, seemed to be able to vanish, pass through locked doors, escape from snowbound hillsides, leave no trace. Like a hungry ghost, leaving nothing behind but blood and loss.

She looked up the name Aidan had mentioned, and found that a Brian Rourke had indeed turned up dead in 1993 — she tried to blot out the date, which was hard seeing as it had been the worst day of her life — and that he'd most likely been made to kneel before being shot in the head. The kneeling was the same as Dr Bates, but it could just be coincidence. A wife was mentioned very briefly in the news reports, but with no name given. Bridget Conaghan, using her sister's name, her birth not even registered, had also been like a ghost.

Eventually, when the long evening dark outside had settled, Avril got up to pull on her neat cream coat, settling her fair hair over the collar. 'It's coming down again out there.'

'Yeah.' Paula looked out the window, where flurries were once again whirling in the gloom. 'Have you water in the house?'

'We do, thankfully. It was off for a few hours but that was all. You?'

'We've nothing. Dad's busy rigging up something to harvest the rainwater. He loves it, I think. I've never seen him so happy.'

Avril looked as if she were going to say something else, opening her small mouth and shutting it again. Paula knew they were both thinking of the same thing, of the night Heather Campbell had been found, and Avril and Gerard were pressed up against the wall by the Ladies. 'Wedding plans going OK?' she said hurriedly. *I won't say anything. It's not my business.*

'Yes.' Avril played with her diamond ring. 'We'll set a date over Christmas sometime, I suppose. I — '

Paula looked down at her desk. She didn't want Avril's secrets. Secrets were like stones in your pockets. The more you carried, the harder it was to swim away. 'Night, Avril. Safe home.'

Avril paused. 'Goodnight.'

Then it was just Paula and Guy left in the office. She stretched, feeling all the exhaustion settle in her bones. 'Not going home?' Guy had come out, his coat in his hand.

'I will in a minute. Aren't you?'

He was the one with a wife to go to, but Guy didn't put the coat on. He looked at her. 'Is everything all right, Paula?'

389

She thought about that for a moment. Over the past few weeks they'd had two women die, horribly, bleeding into the snow. One child was still missing, one was dead, and one had just been killed in the womb. Her own father wanted to declare her mother dead, and there she was still searching for her. Nothing had been all right for a long time.

'Yeah.' What could she say? 'Aren't you going home?' she asked again.

Guy paused for a moment. 'Yes. Things are — our water's off. It's making Tess — well, she's very anxious about it. They're saying we might have to queue for supplies.'

'I know. You must be thinking this is all a bit Third World. Supposedly the Water Board didn't maintain any of the pipes, not for years. Did you hear?'

But Guy didn't rise to the usual this-place-is-so-back-ward bait. 'I'm locking up now. Let me see you to your car.'

She said goodbye as quickly as she could, not wanting to linger with him under the snowy pall of the car park. As she waited for her windscreen to clear she watched Guy's car pull out, the lights fade gently into the night, and disappear entirely. She started the Volvo, sighing, and made her way home, visibility so poor the world had shrunk to the square before her headlights, the other lights of cars blurred in the distance. She couldn't remember when she'd last felt so alone. She found herself thinking of Aidan, wondering where he was on this bleak night. Back in Dublin with Maeve? Warm in her double bed, in the only bedroom? She gripped the wheel tight and tried to forget it.

Paula parked in the street, trudging up the slippery pavement and gripping onto front walls of houses as she passed. Behind every window light and warmth, the flicker of TVs and the glow of lit-up trees. Days to Christmas. Nothing right with the world.

At her father's, she paused, searching her bag for keys, before finding them in her hand. Already, her brain was turning to mush. Was this why she couldn't solve this case, the baby leaching into all her corners, a sea-change at the very heart of her? She turned the key in the frosty lock. 'Dad?'

No answer, no sound of TV. A light burned in the hallway but nothing from the kitchen, which was in darkness. A cold blast blew and she saw the back door was open, banging in the wind. Where was he? 'Da — ?'

She reached for the light, and as she did she felt something sticking her boots to the kitchen lino. She looked down. There was her father, on his back below the kitchen table. One of the letters she'd given him was grasped in his hand. His eyes were shut, and what was sticking her boot to the floor was the blood that had spread out from the scalpel stuck in his arm.

She rushed over to him, but hadn't gone two steps before a shadow moved, and something hit her from the left side, a searing pain scratching her stomach. There was a flash of black in the corner of her eye and she felt breath on her face, cold as the air outside.

38

'Dad? Can you hear me? Christ, what's wrong with him?' Sometimes Paula thought all the worst moments of her life had taken place in Ballyterrin General Hospital, racing down those puke-green corridors, lights fuzzing overhead, trying to still the dread that wrapped around her heart like a snake.

The past twenty minutes were a blur. Whoever had been there had pushed past her and out the open front door. Paula had raced out after them, the pain in her side slowing her. There was no sign in the street. Vanished like a ghost again, except for the footsteps in the new-fallen snow leading away. They must have disappeared into one of the alleys along the street. She'd called an ambulance, giving the details in a strangely calm voice, then she'd gone back in to her father, tied a tea towel round his upper arm as a tourniquet, and held his head on her lap. 'It'll be OK,' she'd muttered to him over and over. His eyelids fluttered and a thin moaning seeped out of his mouth; he was awake, but only just. In the past she'd often wondered how she would react in an extreme situation, and this job had given her the answer — with eerie calm, almost not taking it in until it was over and she'd collapse, weeping. She'd hardly dared lift up her layers of jumper and coat, now ripped with the knife the assailant had tried to stick in her. It wasn't so bad. Blood stuck the wool to her skin, but the injury wasn't deep. Helping PJ was more important.

Now she put up her arms to crash through the doors of A & E, her father strapped to a trolley, his eyes closed. Nurses and doctors fussed round him, checking his pupils, feeling his wrists. Paula hung alongside, nervously wringing her hands. 'Please! Is he still awake?'

'You can't be in here, miss,' said one doctor officiously. 'Mr Maguire's to go for emergency surgery. We have to get him ready.'

PJ cut a forlorn figure, all six foot three of him dressed only in torn pyjamas, his face grey and drawn. The arm was bandaged roughly, blood blooming through above the elbow. As they wheeled him into a cubicle, his eyes fluttered and Paula saw his lips move. He was trying to talk. She fumbled past the nurse. 'I'm his daughter, I need to speak to him. Dad, what happened?'

PJ could barely move, but was beckoning her over. She grasped his hand; he smelled of blood and fear. 'Someone came . . . knife.'

'Who was it, Dad? Please tell me.'

'I've . . . to tell you something, pet. Remembered something, s'very important. Letters . . . letters you gave me.'

'Dad, don't sit up!' She gently pushed him down. 'Whisper to me.'

'Mr Maguire, you really mustn't move! Miss, I'm going to have to ask you to leave.' The doctor wasn't happy.

'I'm with the police,' Paula shot over her shoulder. 'Just give me a minute. What do you mean, Dad?' She bent down low.

'Remember . . . funeral I was at — Kevin . . . Kevin Conway.'

'Your old colleague? Yeah, I remember, but Dad, don't worry about that.' She gripped his rough hand. 'Try to tell me who did this to you.'

He coughed, crushing her hand with a surprising strength and finding his voice again. '*Listen*. Saw Kevin before he died, and he said . . . he'd seen someone. A woman. Woman we both knew. We worked on her case years back. Bad business.' He stopped to cough again, his body convulsing.

'Mr Maguire! You really mustn't talk!'

Paula shooed the doctor away, who started muttering about getting the consultant and pushed out of the cubicle. Her father resumed his fevered whispers. 'This woman . . . she was . . . married to some small-time crook, stole cars and ran guns for the Provos and that. They'd this farm way out near the border. Anyway we went out when her husband turned up dead in a bog. Place was all locked. She was in the kitchen.' He stopped, coughing hard. His speech speeded up, as if he were desperate to get the words out. 'Not a good story, pet. I'd not tell you for a million years, but you need to know. You need to know. She's in the kitchen and they'd handcuffed her there and taken the husband. The IRA. You know . . . came for the husband and left her there. Thing was, she's pregnant, and she's gone into labour the same day. They beat her. Her face. All ruined.'

Paula was almost dancing with frustration. 'But what's this got to do with — '

394

'*Listen*! There's no one to help her. No one. Miles from anywhere, they were, and the husband shot in the head in some bog and there was a sister but she lived in Dublin. And the baby came.'

'What happened?' Paula's voice was trapped in her throat.

'She cut the wean out of herself,' said PJ in his dying rasp. 'We were . . . too late. Wee thing was dead. Three days she'd been there. Thought she was dead too.'

'But she lived?'

'Aye. Kevin was . . . with me. First . . . month on the job, God love him. Bob Hamilton, he was the Sergeant. And when we went to hospital with her the doctor gave her . . . hysterectomy.'

Paula's heart was beating fast. 'Which doctor, Dad?'

'The Bates woman. The one who's dead, with her stomach all sliced.' He waved his hands weakly in the direction of his torso.

Fuck. 'Oh Dad. You mean . . . you think this is all connected?'

'I know. I know, pet. I was thinking all this time . . . cuts across the belly, exactly the same. Should've remembered. Then you said, had I ever worked with Mick Quinn. Should've remembered. It was him found the husband's body. Think the letters . . . the letters you had, think they were from her. To her sister.'

Her mind was whirring. Seizing. Stopped. *Come on, think!* 'And Kevin said he saw this woman again? Dad, was it Magdalena Croft? The faith healer?' His eyes had sagged shut

395

again. She squeezed his hand. 'Please Dad, just try to tell me. Was it her?'

His voice seeped out of his closed mouth. 'That was . . . the sister.'

'The *sister?*'

'Aye.'

Paula frowned. 'But how . . . The woman — Dad, was the husband called Brian Rourke?'

'Aye.'

'And the wife . . . fuck, Dad, was she called Bridget?'

He didn't even scold her for swearing. 'Mary Rourke. Called herself that. Letters from her to her sister. You see?'

'Where did he see her? Where did Kevin see the woman?'

'Here. Hospital. Went for a scan and she walked in to see . . . radiologist. She said hello Sergeant Conway. She *knew* him. And he couldn't place her, the way you do. But he remembered after. Her face looked different — that'd be right, it was all smashed up, you see. And she'd a new name on her badge. Wasn't Mary any more.'

'What was it?' Paula had to stop herself from crushing his hand. 'Dad, what was the name? Who is she?' Rourke, Rourke. Had she seen that somewhere recently?

'He couldn't remember, love. All those drugs. And then I never saw him again, he went that quickly. Never got . . . to ask him.'

'We can find out. We must be able to find out.'

He tried to sit up again, speaking rapidly. 'Love, I want you to be careful. That's the doctor

396

gone, and her daughter, and that poor wee Quinn girl lost her baby, you said? Mick Quinn was the one found the husband's body.'

'Yes, but we thought — shit. You think, what, the killer's targeting anyone involved in the case?'

'Not us,' he said, coughing. 'Our children. You see? We could have helped, all of us, but we didn't. We couldn't. She lost a baby that day. She wants us to know what that feels like. Now Kevin never had any weans, but Bob has one that I know of, and there's you, pet. Take care, will you?' His hand slipped from hers. 'Just take care. I think . . . maybe it was you . . . you see?'

'What do you . . . ?' Then, she got it. Whoever had done this to her father, they'd been looking for Paula. Paula and her baby. 'Dad! Oh God, what do I do?'

'Miss Maguire, we really have to take him down,' said the doctor more urgently, whisking the curtains aside as she came back in. 'He's lost a lot of blood. He's in danger. You've been injured too, we need to examine you.'

'OK. Christ, just wait a second. Dad, I have to go — I have to do something about this. Pat's on her way, she'll be with you. Will you try to remember more? I need to tell all this to Guy, and we have to warn Bob, and whoever else — *shit*.'

'Don't swear, pet,' said PJ, being wheeled away and closing his eyes against the pain. Left alone, Paula put a hand to her side, where pain still throbbed, and realised when she took it away it was covered in blood.

She raced up the stairs of the hospital, too impatient to wait for the lift. The doctors in A & E were preoccupied with her father. She needed to find someone and get them to check out the baby. The knife must have gone in deeper than she thought. She could feel blood seep out as she half-ran, half-staggered up.

Her mind was whirling. If Aidan was right, the Mary who'd married Brian Rourke, and who'd lost her child, was really Bridget Conaghan, using her sister's name. And she was somewhere in Ballyterrin. Paula barged out of the stairwell on floor three and ran down to Gynaecology. It was closed up for the day, the reception desk unstaffed and no one waiting in the seats. The water shortages meant the hospital was operating reduced hours. Please God someone would be there. She pushed open the door of the midwife's office and saw someone sitting there.

'Tess?'

Guy's wife was hunched over the desk in the darkened room. Paula stopped short. 'Are you OK?'

Tess raised her head to Paula, eyes red buttons in a drab white face. 'You told him, didn't you?'

Paula didn't even get it for a moment. 'Guy? No — I haven't.'

'But you were with him. This weekend.'

'I — for work, that was all.' Paula thought of their night in the hotel, when she'd fallen asleep in his arms and he'd whispered into her hair. Words she wasn't even sure were meant for her.

'I can see it on him.' Tess kneaded her temples with her long fingers. Her bun of black hair was coming down at the back. 'He comes home every day and I see it in his eyes. It's you he's thinking about. He barely even touches me, and I'm his wife.'

'Tess — no. There's nothing going on with us.'

'I want you to leave.'

'What?'

Tess pushed back her chair with a scrape and walked over to Paula, holding her elbows in each hand. She was a tall woman. Tall and dark. In nursing clothes.

A woman aged between thirty-five and fifty, tall, with dark hair, likely with medical training . . . How old was Tess? No matter, Paula knew it exactly. She was forty, the same as Guy. Tess was in front of her, and she reached out now and took Paula's reluctant hand, squeezing it in front of her.

'I'm begging you, Paula. I know there's something between you and him. And God, you're maybe having his baby. I tried so hard after Jamie. I thought a baby might bring us back — we were destroyed. We were falling apart. But I couldn't, it never happened. I'm too old, maybe. And you — you waltz in with your red hair and your Irish cheek and it's all Paula this, such a bright girl, such an asset to the team . . . '

A woman who has lost a child . . .

'Please Paula. Give him back to me. Don't have this baby. We have a child, me and him. We still have one child alive and that's all I have to bring him back to me. Don't have yours. I know

399

you don't want it anyway.'

Paula shook off Tess's touch, angry. 'You left him! You tried to divorce him, when he was at his lowest point!'

'I wasn't thinking right. I was mad with grief for my son. What would you know about it — you've never had a child. It kills you when you lose them. It makes you into someone else. But when I saw you were pregnant, I knew I'd made a mistake leaving. I love him. He's my husband.' Tess's eyes were dark and hooded. 'There's still time. You don't really want this child. You told me.' Her hand moved to Paula's stomach.

Paula grabbed it, pushed it off. 'Look, I'm sorry you lost Jamie. But there is no time, none. You don't understand. I need to get help. Let me go.'

For a moment Paula wasn't sure she would let her. Suspicions crowded — *a woman in her forties, who's lost a child, who can't get pregnant, who's tall, with medical training* . . . But no, it made no sense. It couldn't be. God, she was so confused.

She backed away to the door, then felt it open behind her. 'What's going on?' Bernice the midwife. Paula had never been so happy to see someone.

'I was looking for you — I need help.'

'Good Lord, I can see why! You're bleeding. We need to get you looked at.' She hustled Paula out the door, leaving Tess standing there hugging her elbows.

Paula's head reeled as Bernice practically

marched her down the dark, empty corridor, feet squeaking on the plastic floors. Jesus! She couldn't believe it, not Guy's wife. It didn't fit. She had to talk to him. Tell him everything, upturn it into his lap, and it would all make sense. The end of the corridor by the consulting room was deserted, a faulty light flickering on and off above.

Bernice opened the door to her office. 'Go in, pet. You're white as a sheet, are you OK?'

'Yeah, it's just a scratch I think, but I — '

'Sit down.' Bernice ushered her into the room and sat her down on the bed, which was shrouded in blue tissue paper. 'You look like you've had a shock.'

'I have, but — '

'Any nausea?'

'Um, a bit, but — ' She tried to get up but Bernice held her wrist, feeling for the pulse.

'Paula, your heart's racing. I think the baby might be in trouble. You need to lie down, let me have a look at you.'

'No, I need to call the station, I — can I phone from here? Do you have a phone?'

'Of course,' she soothed. 'But think of the baby first. She'll be getting an awful dose of anxiety right now. Whatever's in you is in her, you know. She won't be happy.'

'I — ' *She?* Had the woman said she? 'Please, I really need to phone someone.'

'It's OK, Paula.' Bernice turned around. She was strapping a surgical mask over her face. 'We're going to take care of the baby. Just a shot to calm you first.'

'I don't want a shot!'

'You need it. The baby's in distress. There.'

'Ow!' Quick as a snake, Bernice had jabbed a syringe in Paula's arm, into the crook of her elbow. Blood beaded.

'Press that down or it'll bruise.' Bernice passed over a cotton pad and stunned, Paula did what she was told.

'What did you give me?'

'Just something to relax you. You're always running round the place. Aren't you? I've watched you in the snow, at crime scenes, racketing round with that newspaper editor — he's a bad boy. He'd make a terrible father. Not to mention the married policeman. Really, Paula, you've made some very bad choices. That poor wean, with you as her mother. No, you're not really safe with a baby, are you?'

'Wh-what do you mean?' Paula's mouth felt stiff and dry. The lights overhead began to blur. 'What did you give me?'

'Lie down now.' Bernice was arranging her on the table, Paula's limbs flopping. She felt her legs opening, arms pushed behind her head. Bernice loomed overhead, her masked face terrifying. 'I think it'll be better for that wee girl if we get her out as soon as possible and away from you, before you decide to go to some abortion butcher and have her flushed down the toilet. You still haven't made up your mind, have you, and she's been growing inside you for months now!'

'Wh — aa?' Paula tried to speak but her tongue was frozen. She realised she couldn't move at all. It was like switching off a light inside her. Before she went off altogether the last thing she saw was Bernice's ID badge, wavering over her head on a lanyard. The name: BERNICE ROURKE.

39

The world came back as a slow lap of noise, like waves on a distant beach. There was a rattling, and a weakness in her bones, and the whoosh of what sounded like cars in the distance. Then her sight returned, under a grey film. She seemed to be on a stretcher in a large car — her hand, lolling useless, bumped on the dirty floor of it. The van, she remembered. She tried to blink, seeing red stains on the floor, like dusty rose petals.

Her thoughts were on a slow spin cycle. The van. The stains. She thought of Heather Campbell, bleeding out on the hillside, her mother dying too. She felt a dampness on her thighs and wondered dimly if she'd wet herself. She tried to speak but her voice was a gurgle that lived and died. The bumping seemed to go on and on, her body thrown round like a sack of spuds. She couldn't move her arms or legs; all she could do was shut her eyes and wait for it to end.

★   ★   ★

Light. Silence. The shaking stopped. Paula tasted bile. If she threw up, would she choke? The door opened, Bernice's face in a square of light from the car. An ordinary woman, kind-faced. Hands rough and efficient. The stretcher was wheeled out into the freezing air. They were in some kind of yard, a house with blank windows. Dark, the hush of snow in the air. The light of the car was dying. She wondered if she was, too.

She tried to speak; move her tongue. Nothing. She squeezed her lids shut. The trolley was moving. A door, then overhead an ornate ceiling, chandelier lighting. The smell of the place was familiar, polish and flowers, somehow unlived-in. A heavy tread and then another voice. 'What in the name of Our Lord have you done now?'

'I had to. She's ruining the child. I had to get it out before she kills it.'

'I told you it's too early! She's not even three months yet.'

'But I have to!'

A sigh. 'Bridget, I won't stand in your way. It's your right. But I'm telling you, that wean won't live if you do it now.'

'She'd have flushed it away. She didn't want it.'

'Maybe. But can you not just wait a while? Keep her, wait for it to grow. Then get it out.'

This was her they were discussing. This husk to be harvested, that was her body, which was currently lying useless on the trolley. She tried to turn over, but all that happened was her foot shook gently. She couldn't even move her head to see the speaker, but the voice was familiar, and something in the light was too, the smell of the place, dust and paint.

'Did you give her something?'

'A shot. She'd have kicked up a fuss.'

The other voice tutted. 'It's not safe, I keep

telling you. It hurts the babies.'

'I have to get her out soon. The wee girl. It's a girl.'

Paula felt damp seep from her eyes. A girl. All the guesses were right. A little girl.

'What are we going to do with *her*?'

'I want to do it now.' Bernice — Bridget, the voice had called her — sounded mutinous, almost tearful.

'If you do, they'll both die. Have some patience, pet.'

A choking sound. Bernice was crying. She was saying something like, 'I'm barren ground . . . I'm dead . . . barren . . . It's not fair.'

The other voice softened, and from the muffled sound Paula guessed the two were hugging. 'I know it's hard, love. I know you want it. Where's the other one?'

'She doesn't love me. She was too old, she doesn't need me.'

'Bridget! Where is she?'

'I — I left her down there.'

'You left that baby alone?'

'She doesn't love me. She knows I'm not her mother.'

'Go and get the child, Bridget. Don't make her suffer too. They're innocent, all of them, until they grow up. You know that. Never mind. We'll care for them both, and when we can we'll give her back, like the Polish boy. That's what we agreed, isn't it?'

'And I can have this one for myself?'

'When the time's right.'

'But they'll notice! They'll come for her.'

406

'Let them come. We'll be ready.' A shadow fell over her, and Paula found herself looking into the hard face of Magdalena Croft.

★ ★ ★

She'd passed out. At least, she must have. An orange bulb burned overhead. They were in a basement room and she was lying on a bed. Small windows set high in the walls. Paula tried to lift her head. One wrist was handcuffed to the bedhead; the metal of it rattled as she moved.

'Rest yourself, will you. She gave you a wild dose of sedative.' Magdalena, again. She was sitting across the room in a hard-backed chair, legs crossed. Paula could see the wrinkles where her tights pooled.

'H-hu . . . '

'Shush now. You won't be able to talk yet.' She got up and went to the bare table. There was a sound of water glugging, then she held a glass to Paula's mouth. 'Take this now, you'll be thirsty.'

She was, her mouth raw and dry. She gulped too fast, choking. The water ran over her face and Magdalena wiped it with a dry facecloth. Efficient, not ungentle, like the nurse she'd been, and her sister wasn't. Not really. She took a small key from the pocket of her cardigan and undid the handcuff. Paula's arm fell to the bed, lifeless.

Paula tried to look around the room, which was difficult when she couldn't move her neck. There seemed to be a machine in the corner, something with a lot of buttons, and a yellow bin

407

like they had at hospitals. Bernice had been stealing more than babies from her workplace. There was a table with a jug of water on it, and a large black laptop, closed up. Was this the doctor's missing computer? Some papers were taped to the concrete wall above it; Paula couldn't see what they were.

'Help me,' she croaked. The cold water made her gasp.

'I can't help you.' Magdalena tidied up the cloth. 'It's too late, Paula.'

'Stop her — '

'I won't stop her. She needs to do what she does. We both do. No one can ever understand that. She's my sister. But you know all that, don't you?'

'I . . . went there.' Her voice broke. 'Donegal . . . the farm.'

A slow nod. 'I'll never go back there again.'

'We found him. The man. Yours? Your baby.'

Magdalena laughed, short and cold. 'I've never had a child in my life, thank God. He was Bridget's. She was twelve years old when she had him.'

Paula's hands curled in the old blue blankets, feeling coming back in a storm of prickles. 'Grandfather . . . he?'

Magdalena sat down in her chair. 'You've got it all worked out, I see. We weren't to blame. Not Bridget or me. I'll tell you, since you'll be here a while. I know you like to have things sorted in your head, Dr Maguire.' She smoothed her skirt on her lap. 'Our grandfather tried to abuse us from when we were young, as you may have guessed. Well, he was afraid of me. That's why he sent me away. From when I was a wee girl I told him I could see the Virgin Mary. Put the fear of God in him and he'd stay away from me — unless he'd been drinking. I'd tell him I could see Her standing behind him, waiting to take him to Hell. When I got older, he sent me away to my aunt's. I had to leave my sister there with him. By the time I got back it was too late. Her baby was coming. And you know what he did, our grandfather, the so-called man of God? When the baby came he swung its head against the wall. Trying to cover up his sins. That was poor Jimmy. He was never the same again. That night we ran away, left him with our cousin.' She paused, rubbing down her skirt again. 'Our grandfather died that night. Heart attack. He was scared of me, I told you. I took Bridget away with me but she was never the same since. Well, you found out about the baby in Dublin. I let her be me for the nursing. That was my price for letting her down. Being around the babies, it helped her for a while, until she had to go and steal one, so I couldn't let her do that any more. Then she got married — I let her be me for that too — and she was pregnant again. She was so happy.' Magdalena looked at Paula. 'You know about that, yes? Your father, what he did?'

'He tried . . . he . . . '

'Aye, they all tried. Him and that doctor and the Garda too. Bridget still lost her husband and her baby died, and they never caught a single person for doing it. I couldn't help her any more after that. I moved up here to be with her, tried

409

to keep her away from children. I got her to change her name again in case anyone found us, and we were OK. I made sure we had money — if you'd been as poor as we were, you'd understand that. But she was bound to snap one day. Saw that Polish wean and took him. I did what I could, but she had to have something. It was her right. So I just directed her. I made her leave him back. Said we'd choose them together. Only the ones who deserved it. There's a list and everything. Do you want to see it?'

Her voice was almost friendly. Paula tried to struggle but her limbs were jelly.

Magdalena detached something from the concrete wall and brought it over. On it, in a girlish curly hand, were written several names, lines coming out of them and leading to others. Alison Bates linked to Heather Campbell. A note beside it: **eight months**. Then Mick Quinn, leading to five names. One was Fiacra's. One Aisling's. The others must be their sisters. Aisling's was underlined and again beside it: **seven months.** There was also Robert Hamilton, leading to Ian Hamilton. That must be the name of Bob's son. Kevin Conway. No children listed for him. The final name was PJ Maguire, and leading from him, Paula's own name: **two months.** It was underlined with vicious slashes, like the ones made across Heather and Aisling's stomachs.

Cold tears pooled in her eyes. 'Help . . . me . . . '

'You didn't want your baby, did you? We are helping you. You sinned, and that was the price,

410

but you wanted to be let off, didn't you? Well, that's not how it works. Now Bridget's owed a baby, and you don't want yours, so that's fair.'

Paula started to cry, a mewling sound in the base of her throat.

'Oh, you do want it now? Well, it's not yours to pick and choose, Paula. It's God's will. Bridget wanted her baby too, but she lost it and couldn't have any more, thanks to that butcher of a doctor and your useless father. Why should they live and be happy and have families, when Bridget had to watch her baby die in that kitchen? When her first got his head bashed in against a wall? No, it isn't fair.'

'Too soon . . . s'too soon . . . '

'Aye, I know it is. Your baby won't survive if she comes out now. Still, that's what you wanted, isn't it?'

'N-noo . . . '

'You should have thought of that. I'll try to make Bridget wait. She thinks if they're young, she can get them to love her. Didn't work with that one, mind. She wants rid of it now too.'

She nodded to the corner, and Paula managed to turn her head and see where the glow was coming from. The baby in the incubator was alien-like, tubes connecting it to life, its little arms and legs red as its chest rose and fell in rapid time. As if she were panting, desperate to suck in life.

'L-Lucy?'

Magdalena inclined her head. 'Bridget wouldn't have called her that. Anyway, she can't stay. Not what Bridget wants, she says. Ah well. She never would listen to me.' She was getting up, leaning on the door as if her bones hurt.

Paula tried one last time. 'The police . . . police will come. Find her . . . '

'Aye, they'll get to her name eventually, for all they are useless. Maybe they'll even work out it's her fingerprint they found, not mine. But they'll not break her. We learned to hide early on, us Conaghan girls. There's not much can hurt us. You sleep now, Paula. You'll need it.'

The light went off.

* * *

For a while Paula couldn't even move, the drug pumping her veins full of despair and lassitude. As soon as she could she pulled her shirt out of her trousers and felt her stomach, still smooth, still uncut. A soft but insistent swelling under her hands, like the bumping of the tide against a boat. There was only one incubator, and Lucy Campbell was in it, balling her pink fists. Magdalena had wheeled her out of the room, hopefully to somewhere more welcoming than this. Paula didn't like to think of the baby looking at these cold grey walls, concrete underfoot. They'd take care of her, surely. They were nurses. One nurse between them, anyway. Lucy was still alive. Maybe they would give her back safe to her father.

Time went by. It was dark — she knew her own father would be waking up in hospital, coming round, and her not there to see him. If he was even all right. At this more cold tears

412

leaked from her eyes. She had to stop crying. It was only a house, not a prison. There'd be a way to escape — she'd heard Magdalena turn a key in the lock as she went out. And they wouldn't hurt her, would they? Not while they wanted her baby.

Paula thought of Bernice in her surgical mask, the needle in her hand, and struggled up into a sitting position. It wasn't going to happen like this. She'd made mistakes, yes, and she hadn't been sure about the pregnancy, but she was having this baby. She realised she'd known that for a while. *Hold on, OK?* Inside she could feel the child, its vague flutterings of life. It was still safe within her, not like Lucy, ripped into a cold, bright world she wasn't ready for, her sparrow lungs swimming in toxic air.

She remembered the askew look in Bernice's eyes, and it pushed her to her feet, the room swaying. Nothing in the room but the table and chair, the laptop, a plastic jug of water and a cup, a bare light bulb, the metal camp bed. There were alarming marks on the wall, like splashes of some dark liquid. Paula pushed the thought away. She dropped to her knees, panting with the effort, head swimming. She could turn the table onto its side, maybe, climb up to the small windows. They looked thick. Could she punch one out, detach one of the table legs maybe?

Paula looked under the bed and felt around in the dust for anything worth having. Her fingers brushed a small object and she pulled it out. Cold metal, a clip in the shape of a butterfly, like you'd use to put up long hair. She couldn't place

413

it for a moment, then she did. This clip had been in Heather Campbell's dark hair — she'd taken it out when complaining of a headache that day in the station. Before she'd been butchered, her child cut out and her body tossed away.

Paula sat on the floor, winded by the realisation. They didn't feel anything for her, these two sisters. She was nothing but a husk. All she had was time.

40

Light. Silence.

When Paula woke again, the handcuff was back on, her arm twisted painfully over her head. Magdalena stood over her. In her hands was the soft red scarf Paula had snatched from the wardrobe the day before — was it the day before? She didn't know — thinking only to keep warm in the cold. Magdalena's eyes were closed as she muttered softly to herself. Without opening them she said, 'So you did bring me something of hers after all.'

'What?' Paula was barely awake and didn't understand. Then she remembered. That red scarf, just lying around the house for years, that had been her mother's.

'I can see her.' The woman's fingers gripped the wool and she opened her cold eyes. 'Paula. You know why you're here. You won't come through this. Your father — he deserves to lose all he has. Bridget did, so he has to as well. That's how it works.'

'He tried to help her.' She couldn't form the words and anyway she knew it was useless to plead.

Paula closed her eyes. She heard Magdalena lean down to her and whisper. 'Be at peace, now. There's nothing you can do. But I'll tell you this one thing I've seen from the scarf, if it helps you be easy.'

Her eyes flew open. Magdalena Croft was bending over her, the scarf held tight in both hands. When she looked at Paula, her eyes were kind. How terrible, in the midst of all this, to find kindness. She said, 'She's alive, Paula. Your mother. I've seen her alive.'

Paula opened her dry mouth. 'No. No.'

'Yes. I see her over water, getting on with her life. She's not alone. I can't see who — but there's people. A family. She's happy. She's let you go, Paula, so you should do the same.'

Something in Paula was convulsing as she lay immobilised. *It's lies, lies, all she does is lie.* But her heart was a city going up in flames, a land reduced to ash. The ugly toad of hope was hopping to its death because this was the worst, wasn't it? The worst thing she could have heard. Part of her had imagined her mother in a quiet grave, frozen under warm soil, gone, dead, and when Paula's time came, maybe she'd see her again. She'd imagined this despite her own atheism, a deep comfort. And now what — she wouldn't even be there, when the time ran out? Now that Paula couldn't escape?

There was a loud noise, and Magdalena froze, frowning. Paula tried to listen, shaking her head to clear the tears that filled her eyes. It came from upstairs. Someone was knocking at the door.

Magdalena turned and looked at her for a moment. Then she placed her hand over Paula's mouth. It was dry and cold, smelling faintly of antiseptic. 'Be sensible,' she said in a quiet voice. 'No one can help you now.'

416

They stayed very still. Paula had little choice, her arm chained, her heart racing, struggling to breathe through her nose and straining to hear. Upstairs was the slow tread of feet, and the knock on the door came again.

Magdalena removed her hand from Paula's mouth, with a warning look, and went to the window. Underneath it was a small box Paula had assumed was a light switch. Magdalena flipped it and noise filled the room.

Paula tried to say something, remembering Patrick Duggan — *she listens, the wee listening things*. Her voice came out as a low moan, and Magdalena immediately was at her side, gagging her again. 'Be quiet, girl.'

Voices. A high, nervous one she recognised as Bernice's. A deeper male one. It was crackly and difficult to hear. Magdalena was poised and rigid, her hand gently but firmly smothering Paula, who wasn't sure if she had the strength to scream anyway. Who was it? The police? One of Magdalena's followers? Or something innocuous, like a salesman? Imagine if you could have been saved by someone delivering pizza flyers.

The man's voice said, 'Good evening, madam. Is Mrs Croft here, please? I'm from the MPRU in town.' Gerard! It was Gerard. Paula's heart pounded at the sound of his nasal Ballyterrin tones, and Magdalena felt her tense and pushed down harder.

'No, she isn't here. I'm sorry, officer.' Bernice.

There was a pause. 'Would you know where she is? She's been helping us on some cases, but we've not been able to get hold of her. Thing is, one of our own staff went missing last night.'

I'm here I'm here look down.

Bernice sounded perfectly calm now. 'I'll tell her you were asking for her. She's out of town for a few days.'

'Do you know where?'

A pause. 'She didn't say.'

'And who would you be, madam, if you don't mind me asking?'

Again a slight pause. 'I'm her cleaner. I just come in once a, week.'

'Are you the owner of the van parked outside?'

'Yes, that's right. For my supplies.'

Paula was desperately trying to think if Gerard would ever have seen Bernice at the hospital. *She's lying she's lying, please Gerard, come into the house, find me . . .*

'All right, madam. Please do tell her we'd like to speak to her.'

'I will.'

Silence again. The sound of the door shutting. Magdalena relaxed a fraction. 'I told you, we know how to cover — ' They both jumped as a pair of legs appeared at the small, high windows. By the looks of it, Gerard was peering through the back windows of the house. Paula tried to wrench her face away but Magdalena held her fast. 'No,' she said quietly. 'Come on now.'

Paula had to lie there as the legs stretched up when Gerard craned to look at something. *Look down look down.* He didn't. The window must not be visible from up there. The legs moved away, and soon there was the sound of a car starting up.

418

Magdalena sighed and took her hand away. She laid the scarf on the bed, and gently she touched a finger to Paula's face. 'I'm sorry,' she said. 'That's it for you. But what I said is true. Your mother is alive. She doesn't know you'll die in this wee pokey room. But maybe now I've told you, you can go with a bit more peace.'

She went out, closing the door gently. Paula shut her eyes, feeling tears run down the sides of her face.

★ ★ ★

More time went by. Paula didn't know how much any more, her body held fast in the grip of the drug, her mind turning in slow, lazy circles. She knew there was no way out of this room. She would die here. But she lay there, and every time she opened her eyes she saw the same grey walls, and still nothing had happened.

She woke. There were voices outside the door of the room. Her heart began to race as she listened.

'Bridget, for God's sake, you'll kill them both. There'll be no baby then. You know I'm right.'

'But they might come back! You heard him. He didn't believe me.'

Magdalena sighed. 'I can hardly blame him. Could you not have told the truth?'

'They know me. They've spoken to me twice at the hospital. I told them I wasn't there that day the baby went, and I never claimed for working it, so they didn't have me on their interview lists. But they've seen me. It's too risky.'

'Well, you've certainly made them suspicious now.'

'That's why I have to do it!'

'Pet, could you not wait a few weeks? We can take her away somewhere. What about to your house?'

'Too small. The neighbours'll talk.'

There was a long pause. 'I won't stand in your way, if that's what you want. But you know what will happen.'

'I have to. I'm getting my things. It's time.'

Silence again. They'd moved away. Paula sat bolt upright, pulling herself up with both hands. This was it. She had to get out and now. The police might be coming, but it would be too late.

When she stood up her legs collapsed under her. She hauled herself up again, pulling on the table. The windows seemed impossibly high. She staggered up, putting one knee on the table and with a huge amount of effort dragging herself onto it, hands on the narrow windowsill. Then she just had to stand up. She felt around the edges of one tiny window, set in place with putty and shot through with wire. There must be a way to get it out. She looked around for something to use but there was nothing, unless she dismantled the furniture. Even the jug of water was plastic. Outside she heard a noise, and panicking, snatched up the laptop from where it lay on the table, and swung it as hard as she could against the window. There was a loud crack, and she almost blacked out with the effort. Once more

420

and the glass began to shatter, though it didn't budge from its frame. *Come on come on.* Another swing took all she had, but she felt the pane shift a little. She was gathering strength for another go when she heard the door open.

Bernice/Bridget was dressed all in blue surgical scrubs, a cap over her hair and a mask on her face, eyes unreadable above it. Without even looking at Paula she whisked in, carrying a tray she set down on the table. On it, surgical knives, glinting in the dull light. Panic took hold of Paula's throat and her voice forced its way up from the torpor. 'Let me out! Get away from me!'

Without looking up, the woman shook her head slowly. She moved to Paula and lifted her straight off the table, dumping her on the bed as if she weighed no more than a child. Paula trembled, all her panicked energy leaked away from the effort of standing.

'Please, Bridget.' No answer. Her arm was lifted and snapped into the handcuffs again, a piece of skin painfully trapped. Bernice turned back to the knives, laid out on surgical paper. Why bother to clean them, Paula wondered, when she'd be left to bleed anyway, blood rushing for the gaping lips of her skin? Habit, maybe. She remembered those autopsy pictures of Heather Campbell and talked faster, though her voice was weak and cloudy. 'It's your name, isn't it? When you lived at *Ceol na Mara?* Bridget.'

Nothing. She saw the muscles in Bernice's back, under the scrubs. Held taut.

'Bernice?' Paula's voice cracked. 'Bridget, sorry. I know you're still Bridget, aren't you? You were kind to me. I needed help when I came to you, and you were nice.'

Silence. The slow exhale of breath. Outside the heavy press of snow.

'I want her,' Paula said. Her voice seemed leached of all strength. 'The baby. The little girl.'

Nothing.

'I want the baby, Bridget. I'll look after her. I know I was confused, and I didn't realise before. I was stupid. I'm young — OK, I'm not that young, I know — but I was scared. Please, Ber — Bridget. Please don't hurt my baby.'

Nothing. The clink of the instruments as she examined each, the sound of her breathing against the surgical mask.

'OK,' Paula said, faster. 'Maybe you were right. I don't deserve her. You'd be better than me. I'm a mess. I sleep around, I drink — though not since I found out, I swear. I want her to be safe. So you can take her, if you need to. But Bridget — she isn't ready yet! It's too soon. You know that. She'll die.' Paula's voice broke. Surges of terror were running through her body, the handcuff chafing at her wrist. The bed creaked under her but nothing gave. She felt pain shoot through her skin. 'Bridget? Are you listening? You will kill the baby if you do this now. I know you gave back Alek, and Lucy is OK, she made it — but you know what will happen. You've worked in neonatal units. You know the babies don't live if they're too small. My baby's not even three months inside me. You will kill her. You will kill us both.'

Nothing. The woman didn't even turn. Paula began to cry again, harsh, dry sobs catching in her mouth. She felt so dried up there were no tears left. The only sound was her desperate, empty weeping. She'd lost. She knew it.

There was movement. Bernice/Bridget turned. Above the mask, her eyes were blank and expressionless. The grey showed in her roots, and Paula could see no trace of that girl in the picture, in a small cottage by the sea, where the wind blew hard and lonely. The girl with the quick smile, and the man's hand on her shoulder, his head ripped off. Up close, knowing what she did now, Paula could see the scars running down the sides of the woman's face. She must have worn make-up before. She'd had something done, surgery maybe, and that was why no one had recognised her as Bridget Conaghan.

'I'm sorry, Bridget.' Her voice was failing. 'I'm sorry he hurt you. Your grandfather. I know it was him.'

Bridget was turning towards her. In one hand another syringe. Rohypnol, Paula had worked out, or something like it. Keeping her quiet, pliable. Unmoving. Bridget lifted Paula's free arm, which was floppy as spaghetti. The syringe plunged in. Paula could barely feel it. She moaned. It flowed through her veins, dark and deep, putting her under. Then Bridget picked up the tissue she'd discarded and pushed it deep into Paula's mouth. The paper was dry; she retched against it.

423

'Breathe through your nose,' said Bridget flatly, turning back to the table of knives. Her voice and her tread had the impersonal grace of a nurse. When she turned again the scalpel was in her hand. It glinted under the orange light. She moved the three paces to Paula — not quick, not slow. In control. She pushed up Paula's jumper, exposing her to the dank air. One hand was placed on Paula's white abdomen, goose-pimpled with cold. The other brought down the knife, and Paula felt the steel touch her skin, then go into it. A bright rainbow of pain. That was all.

Epilogue

White.

Silence.

At first there was so much pain she thought she couldn't be dead. Wasn't there meant to be peace in death? She imagined people — her mother, standing in the corner of a hospital room, hair still red but her face older, smiling, and she failed to get to her, but someone was holding her down. Then her father, but sitting down for some reason, and Guy, and Aidan, and Saoirse — so many people she cried to be alone, burying her face in the pillow. The pain was a rack she twisted on, a ribbon of agony round her middle. The world coming back grey and noisy, bumping over ruts, and then.

White.

Silence.

Things were happening around her, or maybe she was remembering, or dreaming. How did you tell? There was a rush of noise, footsteps and doors banging, shouts, and then one sound she couldn't escape — the high scream of a woman, going on and on until it got into the marrow of your bones. Hands were lifting her, and the air seemed to hurt her skin, and she cried. There was a screeching of sirens, then more white light, impossibly bright.

Silence.

This must be how death was. It was what

she'd imagined when she tried to taste it as a teenager, the peace, just to lie down and forget your own name. For a while, she did. For a while she just floated, in the peace and the white and the stillness. For a while, Paula was quite happy to be dead.

Then she woke up.

★ ★ ★

It came back slowly, so blinding she couldn't open her eyes. Her mouth was sore, as if her teeth had been knocked out of place. Her limbs were heavy, molten, and when she could see there was a pressure cuff on one finger and a catheter going into her arm. Below the waist was foreign — she couldn't feel what was what going on down there, but it rustled when she stirred, and it felt like it wasn't even a part of her.

'Paula? Paula?' Her father was there, in fact. She hadn't dreamed that. And he was sitting down, or more strictly, in a wheelchair, one arm bandaged painfully in front.

She swallowed. There seemed to be sand in her throat. 'Are you OK?'

'Am I OK?' PJ was gripping her hand in his one good one.

'Yeah.'

He sighed. 'You'd me worried sick, and you're asking am I OK. I'm grand now you've opened your eyes.'

She blinked round the room. 'Daddy . . . What happened? I thought I was dead.' Flowers, cards, a blur of pastel.

'You nearly were.' He shifted so he could reach the bed, patting the arm with the pulse monitor on it. 'They found you. One of your colleagues went to the house.'

'Gerard came. I heard him. But he didn't see me. I tried to call.'

'He knew something was up when the sister answered the door. He'd seen her at the hospital — she'd even been interviewed a few times — and he didn't buy her excuse, so they came back with a Tactical Support team. They saw the van outside, you know. It must have been bought illegally because it never came up on any of their searches of hospital staff. Anyway, she was in the room with you and she was about to — well — do you remember what happened?'

'She cut me.' It was easy to say it, somehow. The certainty of a blade slicing flesh. That had happened.

'Yes. Well, she got the skin and muscle, and she'd nicked the — eh, your womb, pet — but not the artery. So they found you in time.'

'Oh.' She licked her dry lips and rustled again, tentatively. 'I didn't know . . . She was there all the time, and I never even realised. Is she — ?'

'You don't remember what happened?'

'No — it's all sort of like a dream. I remember someone screaming.' She shivered under the blankets.

'She cut herself. Bernice. When they came in for you. Tried to slash her wrists, but they got her. She's in a different hospital. The sister's in custody. She admitted the whole business. She thinks they were in the right, you know. Doesn't see a thing wrong with it. Anyway they found the wee Campbell baby safe. I thought you'd want to know that. She'll be grand.'

Paula moved, cautiously, trying to work out what was going on below her waist. 'Am I stitched?'

'You've staples in, but they'll be out in a week or so.'

'Dad, I . . . am I . . . '

He took her hand. 'Paula, you're still expecting. If you want to be. The baby's grand. She really is.'

She. Paula put her hand under the sheets, and felt the gauze dressing on her stomach, and underneath a line of staples holding her flesh together. Pain flared and she drew in her breath in a hiss.

'They said it'd be a challenge, since your skin'll stretch a fair bit more, but you've time, and they'll do their best.'

She was taking this in. 'I'm having a baby.'

'Looks that way, pet.'

A baby. That iron grip of life, the one she'd told to hold on no matter what. It had.

'I'll have to tell them,' she said, panicking suddenly and trying to sit up. 'Guy and Aidan. I'll have to tell them I don't know whose it is.'

'Never mind those eejits,' PJ said. His hand was rough and warm. 'They've both been in pestering me day and night.'

'Aidan too? Aidan came here?' For a moment she wasn't sure which was more painful. Assuming he wouldn't care if she was dying, or thinking that maybe he did care, but just not enough. Never enough.

'Of course he came. He's not bad through and through. Though God knows how he'd take to being a father. Pay no heed to them now. I'll mind you, and Pat too. We'll get you well and the baby will come and we'll sort it all out later.'

'Dad. Magdalena — Mary, I mean. She said something to me, just before her sister — before she cut me.'

'Don't think about that now. It's over. They've been caught, and they'll not be hurting anyone else again.'

'No — she said she saw Mum. She told me Mum's still alive.'

He stopped patting her hand. 'And how would she know a thing like that?'

'She sees things. Visions.'

'And you believe her?'

'No. I don't know. But, Dad, I've been looking. I've been looking at Mum's file. I've been talking to people.'

'I know you have. I've eyes in my head.'

'But I want you to be with Pat. You have to be with Pat.'

'Pet, you know that means I have to say your mother's dead. There's no other way.'

'I know. But I have to keep looking, too. Even so. You understand that?' She was pleading.

PJ sighed. 'It seems like a lot of heartbreak for no reason. But you do what you have to, and I'll do what I have to. I can't let Patricia down now. She's a good woman, the best. You'll have to tell her, you know. About the wean. That she might be Aidan's.'

429

She. There it was again. No longer an it, a situation, a problem, but an irrevocable person on her way to them. Paula looked at the screen of the monitor, which was attached by a cord to her stomach. Not her heart, she realised, but the baby's. Proof it was still there, and fighting, under those layers of skin and muscle so nearly laid bare. The pulse of it juddering, stuttering into life. It was the smallest thing. But it was everything, too.

Paula put out her hand. 'Dad. Help me sit up, will you? I've got things to do.'

Acknowledgements

I'd like to thank everyone at Headline, Hachette Ireland, and my overseas publishers for their support and belief in my books, especially Ali Hope.

Thanks to the staff at Johnson and Alcock, Blake Friedmann and AM Heath literary agencies, especially Oli Munson.

Thanks to my Twitter friends for help with many random research questions (eg What is the biggest town in Donegal? How quickly do you die from scalpel wounds?) especially Maitiú Ó Coimín who helped with the Irish (any remaining mistakes are down to me, or as I'm going to claim, 'regional differences').

Thanks to all my fantastic friends and family, who helped get me through this year. Especially thanks to Sarah Day and Angela Clarke for a riotous writing trip to Russia, in which not much actual writing got done. Thanks to Elizabeth Haynes for organising a great writing retreat in which quite a lot did.

Thanks to Oliver for reading early drafts of the book. Thanks to Jake Kerridge once again for support, helpful comments, and burgers, and to Stav Sherez for his invaluable help, without which the book would be much weaker.

Finally thanks to Iain, for coming along at exactly the right time.

To anyone who reviewed my previous books or

contacted me to say they liked them — thank you so much, it means the world that you take the time to do this.

If you've enjoyed this book, I'd love to hear from you. Visit my website at http://clairemcgowan.net, or find me wasting time on twitter, where I am @inkstainsclaire.